Cold AS ICE

BETH BOLDEN

Earl Gray Publishing LLC

www.bethbolden.com

beth@bethbolden.com

Publisher's Note: This is a work of fiction. Names, characters, places, and incidents are a product of the author's imagination. Locales and public names are sometimes used for atmospheric purposes. Any resemblance to actual people, living or dead, or to businesses, companies, events, institutions, or locales is completely coincidental.

Book Layout © 2024 Beth Bolden

Book Cover © 2023 Book Brander Boutique

The people in the images are models and should not be connected to the characters in the book. Any resemblance is incidental.

Ordering Information:

Quantity sales. Special discounts are available on quantity purchases by corporations, associations, and others. For details, contact Beth Bolden at the address above.

Cold as Ice/ Beth Bolden. -- 1st ed.

AUTHOR NOTE

Cold as Ice and the Portland Evergreens series take place in the wider Beth Bolden universe: a universe that is more inclusive and welcoming than our own.

In Beth-world, the first professional athlete to come out of the closet was Colin O'Connor (*The Rainbow Clause*), and after this happened, approximately ten years ago, there have been numerous players, coaches, and even owners who are living their best queer lives freely.

PORTLAND EVERGREENS

HOSSA ICE RINK

STEVENS TRACK

TILLAMOOK BLVD

FACULTY OFFICES

MULTNOMAH WAY

WASHINGTON AVE

CLACKAMAS ST

FRATERNITY ROW

1. The Quad
2. Lewis Dorm
3. Clark Dorm
4. Hazel Hall
5. Beard Dining Hall
6. Bachelor
7. Jefferson
8. Hood
9. Hoover House
10. Knight Athletic Complex
11. Harrington Field
12. Gym
13. Lovejoy Apartments
14. Jimmy's Joint
15. Darcelle's Bar
16. Star Signs Arcade
17. Sammy's Subs & Smoothies
18. Koffee Klatch

CHAPTER I

One year ago
August

It was him.

Elliott Jones stopped in his tracks, the party noise resonating around him, the music thumping and lights strobing, but the sight was undeniable.

Him. Malcolm McCoy. Living and existing in all his dark-haired, fucking-gorgeous-faced glory, leaning against the wall, an inscrutable expression on his face and an intense look in those unearthly blue eyes.

Elliott felt his heart stutter and stop, and his cock twitch in his jeans.

It had been this way the first—and the last—time he'd seen Malcolm too. He'd been visiting colleges, trying to decide where he was going to commit to playing hockey for, and Portland U had already been high on the list, but then he'd spotted Malcolm in the locker room after a game, pulling his helmet off, sweat-damp dark hair falling across his forehead, paired with a jawline that could—and *had*—changed lives.

One life in particular.

Elliott's own.

His sister Macey had teased him that he'd made one of the most important decisions of his life because his dick had been hard, and he'd flushed bright red because he hadn't been sure she was wrong.

Of course, it helped that the Evergreens had a great coach that Elliott would love to play for and a storied history of not just team greatness but of sending players to the NHL.

He wanted a piece—a *big* one—of that success for himself.

And he wanted Malcolm McCoy.

When he'd arrived on campus, he'd planned to tackle both goals at the same time.

When Ramsey, one of the upperclassmen on his team and a crack defenseman, had invited him to this party, he hadn't assumed he'd see Malcolm here.

But here he was.

Scowling, now.

Well, Elliott could do something about that.

He'd never failed to put a smile on someone's face. In high school he was the easy, charming life of every party, and even if he wasn't particularly interested in women, they loved him anyway. And guys? Well, even at the age of eighteen he'd been responsible for at least a few bisexual awakenings.

Elliott didn't feel an ounce of shame about it. He enjoyed men and he enjoyed sex, and as long as it was consensual, there wasn't any reason to regret it.

But Malcolm was a whole different story.

Elliott *craved* him. Just one look at him and he'd *known* they were meant to hook up.

Elliott sidled up to him, plastered one of his best smiles—the one that had almost never failed to seal the deal—onto his face and said, "Hey."

In his opinion, it was always better to settle for something simple. Simple couldn't backfire in your face the way over-complicated could.

Malcolm looked over at him, startled. Like he couldn't believe Elliott was talking to him.

Like he'd just died and gone to heaven.

Elliott puffed out his chest a little. This was going even better than he'd imagined.

"Hey," Malcolm said gruffly.

He had the kind of voice—rough and low—that Elliott could already imagine hearing as Malcolm murmured into his ear as he thrust deep inside him.

Elliott shivered and refocused, more determined than ever to make this happen.

"I'm Elliott, I'm—"

"You're the new freshman. Right winger."

"Yeah. That's me." Elliott nodded. Knowing that Malcolm played left wing. If he earned the spot, he might even end up on the same line as Malcolm. Working closely together. *Very* closely together if Elliott had anything to say about it.

Mal didn't say anything. In fact, he looked away, like he hoped Elliott might go back to wherever he came from.

Usually Elliott didn't have this much trouble getting someone—anyone, really—to talk to him. But it was like pulling teeth to get Malcolm to even engage.

Frustrating. But Elliott wasn't ready to give up. That easily, or at all, frankly.

"This party seems pretty great," Elliott said. His first college party. With his first college hookup.

"You like this sort of thing?"

If Elliott wasn't so focused on Malcolm he'd have given the party a once-over glance, but instead he kept his gaze on Malcolm.

"Yeah. But more like . . .I was wondering if this party would be like every college party they show on TVs and in movies, and you know what?"

Elliott paused. Waiting for him to answer.

"What?" Malcolm finally replied, the acknowledgment dragged out of him way more reluctantly than Elliott would've liked, especially when he was doing half-decent work here.

"It actually kind of is? You know, the sort of trashy hedonism of it all? I only had to wander in the kitchen for someone to hand me a bottle of tequila. And then there's all that out there . . ." Elliott gestured towards the makeshift dancefloor, where a dozen or so students were gyrating together to some old-school 90's R&B. "And don't forget the beer pong in the garage. I'm sure if I wandered out the back door, I'd see a couple inching their way towards hooking up."

Malcolm gave him a blank stare. "Why would you see that?"

"It's like every episode of bad teen TV ever. Like *The OC* or *One Tree Hill* or even *The Vampire Diaries*. I guess we can't really count *Gossip Girl*, because they weren't in college, yet, but they did get there, I guess? But they wouldn't know what to do with a trashy college party, honestly."

Malcolm was still staring at him, a tiny crease appearing between his eyebrows.

"What's *Gossip Girl*?" he asked.

Not what Elliott had expected, but that was okay. He wasn't telling Elliott to fuck off and for a second, he'd been afraid that might have been the next thing out of Malcolm's mouth.

"You've never seen *Gossip Girl?*" Oh, Elliott was already planning some watch parties in his head. A few nice long evenings, Netflix playing, and anything but chilling happening on the couch.

"No."

"It's a . . .uh . . .kind of trashy teen drama about a bunch of rich kids in NYC who go to this private school—"

"That sounds terrible."

"Well, yeah, terrible, but *also* great," Elliott said. "And this party is right out of that playbook, honestly, which is kind of cool when you think about it?"

"It is?"

"Well, *yeah*. It means they got something right? And if they got *all this* right, that means I'm going to end up making a very bad choice—maybe even more than one—with an inappropriate hookup, but they end up being so good, so fucking memorable, I won't be able to forget them." It was a lot to pile on, but *fuck it*, Elliott did it anyway, fluttering his eyelashes in Malcolm's direction.

Hoping he got the memo: that his possibly bad, but very memorable choice was going to be Malcolm.

"I don't understand," Malcolm said bluntly. "Is there something in your eye? Do you have a medical condition?"

"No," Elliott said. He sighed. Maybe his subtle approach was not working. Hadn't he just thought it earlier? Better to keep things simple. Straightforward. "Here's the thing. I'm hot. You're hot. We're at a party. We should go out there—"

"What?" Malcolm looked floored now. "*What?*"

"I said it—"

But Malcolm didn't even let him get the sentence out again. His eyebrows drew together—two dark slashes against his olive-toned skin, as he continued with, "I don't make the line assignments. That's Coach Nichols."

"Well, *yeah*." Elliott dredged up *that* smile again, hoping that he might see a repeat of that look on Malcolm's face. The one that said, *I just fucking won the lottery*. "That's not why I came over here."

"Are you sure?"

Why did Malcolm look so confused? Didn't men—*and* women—cross rooms to talk to him all the fucking time? Surely Elliott was not the only person on earth who looked at this guy and wanted him in their bed?

Elliott had expected to have to wade through a whole bunch of interested people. But no, Malcolm had been standing here, on his own. Alone.

"Like I said. You're super, crazy hot. Like . . .melting my clothes right off my body hot. And I'm not so bad myself so . . ."

Malcolm didn't say anything. Just stared.

Elliott realized, belatedly, that he'd seemed fine with his whole situation before Elliott had chosen to cross the room to talk to him. Comfortable, even. Eyes steady, not darting around, looking at who was looking at *him*.

He'd *liked* being alone.

Well.

Elliott could still change that.

"Like I said, I'm not so bad myself, and I'm feeling a little lonely. New school and all . . ."

He took a risk and sidled closer, angling his body towards Malcolm, heart rate accelerating at his nearness. He was maybe an inch or two taller, but his shoulders were broader and he was thick with muscle. Elliott's stomach clenched.

He'd won and bedded tons of hot guys. Hot wasn't necessarily the thing Elliott wanted.

It was Malcolm's brand of hot. The guy had buried himself inside Elliott until he felt like he was going to go crazy if he couldn't have him.

How many times during the last eight months had he touched his cock and Malcolm's face had sprung, uninvited, into his head?

Every single goddamn time.

"I'm sure you're gonna be just fine," Malcolm said dismissively.

"I'm . . ." Well, he was not fine. Not really at all. "I'm not fine, actually." Elliott laughed self-deprecatingly. "I don't usually have this problem."

"What problem?" Malcolm asked. *Demanded.*

"How about this, let's go grab a drink," Elliott said. "Start over. You need more of a warmup, I get that now. I'm alright with that. I like flirting and it's not so hard when you look like that."

"Like what?"

"Like . . ." Elliott rolled his eyes. "You know what you look like."

Those brows drew together. "No."

Jesus. Okay. Elliott sighed. "Let's go get that drink." He'd already had two shots of tequila and a lukewarm red Solo cup of beer, but he wasn't nearly drunk enough to be dealing with this.

"I don't drink."

Elliott supposed he shouldn't have been surprised. The guy didn't know he was hot, and didn't drink and was apparently perfectly content standing on the outskirts of the party, not actually participating in it.

"Uh, okay, so I'm sure they have something . . ." But Elliott stopped in his tracks, because he realized something else.

Malcolm looked surprised again.

Not like he'd died and gone to heaven.

More like he'd journeyed to hell.

Or even worse, like he didn't want to be having this conversation at all.

Like he couldn't wait for Elliott to move on.

"I'm actually impressed by the whole sober guy attitude," Elliott said, dredging up another one of his killer grins. Laying on the charm nice and thick. "We can just stand here and I can flirt with you and you can stare at me. That works too."

8

"Does it?" Malcolm seemed surprised by this.

"Is it so crazy I'd want to meet you? Hang out with you?"

"We met," Malcolm said dismissively. "And for the rest, I'm sure we'll see each other at practice next week."

Nobody had ever called Elliott a freaking quitter. He retrenched. "Actually, we met last year."

Met was probably an oversimplification but Elliott wasn't going to admit that to Malcolm, or even to himself. Technically, Coach Nichols had introduced Elliott to the whole group and Malcolm had given him a single solitary nod.

Some of the other guys—Brody and Ivan and Ramsey—had come over to greet him, chat him up a bit, probably with the hope of convincing him to ultimately attend Portland U.

But what none of them knew was that Malcolm's solitary nod had done more to recruit Elliott than any of their friendly overtures.

"Okay," Malcolm said. Still dismissively.

Elliott couldn't help his frustrated outburst. "Why are you at a party if you don't actually want to talk to anyone?"

Why are you at a party if you don't want to drink or dance or flirt?

Because his hands were empty and he was against the wall, like he'd chosen it, and he definitely didn't seem to want to flirt with Elliott—or Elliott to flirt with *him*—even as a way to pass the time.

Malcolm's mouth pressed firmly together. That kind of pissy look might turn Elliott off with anyone else. But his body—his *cock*—wasn't cooperating and hadn't gotten the memo.

9

"I didn't *want* to come. I have some reading for econ to do, but . . ." Malcolm looked up and there was Ramsey Andresen, their teammate, wandering over. "But Ramsey convinced me." He made a face. "Wouldn't take no for a goddamn answer. So here I am."

Malcolm didn't need to finish his thought for Elliott to know what it was. *So here I am, being bothered by you.*

Elliott didn't know what to say.

Never once in all his fantastical, X-rated imaginings had he thought that once he and Malcolm met that he'd fail to entice him.

That he'd fail to even convince the guy to have a basic conversation with him.

That he'd rather go back to his probably spartan apartment and read about *economics.*

Elliott was more than a little horrified, stuck in silence as Ramsey approached.

"Mal. Being the life of the party as usual?" Ramsey's mouth quirked up as he greeted the other guy. He was *also* attractive, in that blond gregarious way, but Elliott wasn't particularly attracted to him. His eldest sister Nina would have told him it was because it would be like fucking himself.

She was probably right.

Malcolm rolled his eyes. "I don't know why you bothered to make me come, Andresen. This is a waste of fucking time. Why would I want to drink watered-down booze that'll give me a bitch of a headache in the morning? As for the apparently 'great company' you promised, I'm not impressed."

"It's to be fucking social," Ramsey said, grinning. He turned to Elliott. "Good to see you, kid."

Elliott's spine straightened. He was not a kid, and he was *definitely* not a kid when it came to Malcolm. "Thanks for the invite. This seems like a cool party. *Seemed* like a cool party." He shot a glare he barely even meant in Malcolm's direction.

Ramsey laughed, pounded Malcolm on the shoulder. "This one just wouldn't know fun if it came up and bit him in the ass."

Elliott was close enough to Malcolm that he could practically feel him stiffen.

And not in the fun place, either.

Disappointing. Catastrophically fucking disappointing.

"Apparently," Elliott said, trying to match Ramsey's casual tone. Like he didn't give two shits at how un-fun Malcolm McCoy had turned out to be.

He'd hoped they'd have *some* common ground other than hockey and liking guys.

But, he reminded himself, *you don't need to have anything in common or even to have fun to fall into bed together.*

That was true. He wasn't looking for a relationship or love or that whole happily-ever-after thing, though he supposed he might *someday*. But for right now, he was having too much fun.

Or at least he was *trying* to have too much fun.

"Malcolm, you really need to get out more. Talk to people," Ramsey said.

"Sure, I guess so, but *this* guy?" Malcolm glanced over at Elliott. "You should have seen him peacocking right over. Reminded me of someone. Oh yeah, that's right. *You.*"

Ramsey just laughed again, like Elliott's ego puncturing like a sad balloon was the funniest shit he'd ever heard.

Well, at least *someone* was laughing.

"Hey, kid, it's alright," Ramsey said, patting him on the shoulder and giving him a commiserating smile. "That's just how our Malcolm is. I should've warned you before you came all the way over here to strike out."

"Strike out?" Malcolm looked confused again.

"It means we get you're not interested in us fun-loving plebeians," Ramsey teased. "We get you're focused and we're just a distraction. Right, kid?"

Elliott ground his teeth together. "Right."

"Well, good news is that I know a *lot* of guys who'd love to meet you," Ramsey cajoled. "You wanna meet some of them?"

"Yeah. Yeah, I would." He straightened his back and shot Malcolm one last hot glare before walking off with Ramsey.

So he couldn't have the brain-melting, sex-on-a-stick guy? That didn't mean he couldn't have plenty of fun.

After Ramsey lured the young idiot kid with promises of debauchery and drink, of people who actually *wanted* to party, Malcolm didn't see much reason to stick around.

He'd put in his time, attending even when he hadn't wanted to, all because Ramsey had batted those big baby blue eyes and convinced him it was 'good for the team' or some other such bullshit.

And it had been bullshit.

Sure, a handful of their teammates had been there, but the only one he'd talked to had been the kid.

Elliott, his uncooperative brain supplied as he walked home on the dark streets towards Clark, the dorm he was living in this year.

A lot of juniors moved off campus, but Mal had decided to stay. He didn't mind the slightly stricter rules because he didn't drink and he didn't party and he had no interest in finding a roommate to help offset the costs of living in an apartment.

Mal took the stairs instead of the elevator, running up the three flights to his floor, to compensate for the burger and fries he'd shared with Ramsey and Ivan at Jimmy's diner before the party.

Really, he reminded himself, it was so much better this way. This way he had his own single room, with no need to make small talk unless he felt the need.

And he rarely felt the need.

Of course, that was when he turned the corner and stopped dead in his tracks.

Jane. Sitting next to her door, knees tucked up under her, leaving an expanse of bare thigh visible that he knew she wouldn't be showing him if she didn't have that sheen of booze in her eyes.

He didn't know Jane well, but she'd made an impression in the half dozen times they'd talked—or when *she'd* talked at *him*.

She'd chattered much like Elliott had, but while he'd found that overconfident, cocky idiot not worth a breath or any of his brain molecules, he'd kind of liked the way that Jane chattered at him, never minding if he barely answered her.

Mal approached her carefully, telegraphing his intentions way in advance, settling down on the floor next to her.

He had at least a foot on her, and two years to boot. Nevermind a whole wealth of bitter experience.

She hadn't said that to him, of course, but he'd seen the innocence glowing in her light brown eyes, the excitement in them as she'd told him about the party she was going to tonight and the guy who'd invited her.

Mal wished he'd been paying more attention.

"Hey," he said gently, touching her briefly on the arm then withdrawing his hand. "You okay?"

She glanced up at him. "Malcolm," she murmured, slurring a little, "I think I'm drunk."

Shit.

"Yeah, honey, I think so," he said, and she sighed.

"I didn't mean to," she said.

"I warned you." He had. He'd paid *that* much attention, at least.

"I know. You were kind of right." Her voice went wry, and the humor there relieved him more than he wanted to admit. She wasn't bleeding. Violated. Or in some ways worse and some ways better, bitter like him. Over it, like him.

"Party not so great?"

"Alex kept trying to get me to drink more." She squeezed her eyes shut. "I didn't really want to. I just wanted to flirt with him a little, you know?"

"I do know," Mal said gravely.

She laughed. "Do you though?"

He almost told her that someone had flirted with him tonight—or had *tried* anyway. That young stupid peacock who seemed like a chip right off the Ramsey block. But Ramsey's antics hadn't been as much of an issue because he gave a shit about what they did on the ice. Never hit on him, either.

Ramsey had instinctually seemed to understand that Mal didn't want him to, so he didn't. For which Mal was *very* thankful.

"No, not really. You caught me." He laughed, a gravelly sound, which told him—and probably Jane—that he didn't laugh enough.

"There you go," she said, sounding very satisfied with her analysis of the situation.

"We should get you up, into your room. Drinking some water."

Jane giggled. "I know. I knew I should unlock the door but . . ." She pulled her keys out of her pocket and jangled them, trills of laughter still escaping from her pink-painted mouth. "I couldn't find the right key."

Malcolm plucked the ring from her fingers and shifted through the keys, easily finding the right one, because he'd seen her mark it a week ago with red glitter pen.

"You're so smart," Jane said, sighing with resignation.

"Thanks," he said dryly. "But I think it's more sober than smart."

Suddenly, she turned to him. Petite nose upturned. She looked like he imagined a little sister might look, if his mother had ever stuck around to make another "mistake" with his father. And if any of them had ever had blond hair.

"What's *your* key?" she demanded to know.

"What do you mean?" For a split second, he was terrified that *she* was hitting on him too. And that had been bad enough with Elliott, who at least possessed parts he was interested in. Jane did not.

"I mean," she said, patting him insistently on the chest. "You're so . . .so . . .so . . ."

"So?"

"So *alone*. So lonely."

"Those aren't the same thing," he said, to avoid the question. If there even *was* a question there.

"Where's the key that unlocks you? Makes *you* happy?" she demanded with all the delicacy of the drunk.

"I *am* happy. Dean's list. And Coach all but promised me first line, this year," Malcolm insisted. Not sure why he was going to the trouble with this girl. He should just change the subject.

The way he'd kept trying to do with Elliott.

Elliott had *also* blundered in with the finesse of an elephant, all outraged, oversized bruised ego when Mal hadn't been interested.

Well, that isn't necessarily true, is it?

But for a moment, Mal *had* looked at him and felt something. That same something that probably led to people making very stupid mistakes and then regretting them in the morning.

Before he shut it down, anyway.

He knew better than to go down that road, again. Especially with a guy like that.

"There's more to life than school and hockey," Jane protested.

"Come on," Mal said, lifting her to her feet easily. "Let's get you into your room and some water in you. You'll be glad in the morning."

"But—"

"No buts," Mal said firmly. He tugged her by the arm, gentle but insistent, pulling her into her single, next door to his, after he'd unlocked the door with the red glitter key.

He deposited her on the edge of her twin bed, decked out in delicate purple florals. In the future, he'd need to keep a better eye out for her. The Alexes of the world would take advantage, so easily, of all this kind, innocent sweetness, and there were enough crumbs of his own left in him that explained his concern.

He didn't want her to be another him by the end of her freshman year.

"I looked for you, at the party," she said, as he leaned over and rummaged through her mini-fridge, finally unearthing a bottle of orange Gatorade.

He passed it over to her, but instead of opening it, she toyed with the lid.

Mal realized she was waiting for an actual answer.

"I was at the Gamma Sigma party," he said. "Must've been a different party."

"Must've been. I don't remember which house it was." She looked painfully young like this, feet not even reaching the floor as they dangled over the edge of the bed. "Alex wanted to take shots at his place, first."

"Goddamn Alex," Mal growled. "You should've told him no. You don't *need* shots."

"I was nervous," she admitted with a sardonic smile. "I wanted him to like me. Don't you ever want anyone to like you?"

Just once.

"No. I don't need people's affection, I'm just fine on my own. Self-sufficiency is important," Mal said, painfully aware he sounded just like his father.

It had never hit him as hard as it did right now.

He forced himself to soften his tone. "But I get it. You like him."

"I *liked* him."

"What happened?"

"He was pushy. Weird. And then he disappeared. When I found him, he had his hand up another girl's skirt."

Mal's fists creaked as he clenched them. "I'm gonna kick his ass."

"No need," Jane said. "I kicked him real hard in the balls."

Mal laughed again, the sound escaping out of him rustily.

"I know just where to aim," she said. "My dad taught me."

"Good dad."

"The best," Jane agreed. She looked over at him. "And you're not so bad, yourself."

"Drink your Gatorade," he said gruffly. "It's late. And I need to read my econ chapters still."

"Alright, but don't be a stranger, okay?" she asked hopefully, gazing at him like she'd seen something in him that he'd missed.

"I won't," Malcolm said, promising himself that he'd be present the next time an Alex came around to take her to a frat party. Maybe her dad couldn't be here, but he could.

"Good." Jane took a long drink of Gatorade. "Next time you're coming with me. Or! Better yet, you can take me to one of *your* frat parties. I bet there's so many cute athletes there."

"No chance," Mal said.

But he already had a feeling she'd be the second reason, besides Ramsey's passive-aggressive entreaties, that he returned to the Gamma Sigma house.

CHAPTER 2

A year later
October
"Are you fucking kidding me? Where the fuck is he?"

Ivan glanced over at Mal, apparently unconcerned by Mal's anger as he stomped around the locker room. "It's still early, Mal. He'll be here."

"I told him to be here early. I even texted him to remind him." Mal's temper was usually firmly under control. Except, of course, when it came to Elliott Jones.

Elliott always seemed to make him lose control. Even when he was determined to keep himself locked down tight.

Last year had been difficult enough. The guy bent every rule, though never breaking them, never enough to get into serious trouble. And then there was the way he sauntered around campus, like he was every inch the hot shit hockey player Elliott believed he was. The worst of it was that everyone else seemed to agree, like he was the heir apparent to Ramsey's bullshit.

But Ramsey's bullshit had never bothered Malcolm. Not like Elliott's did.

But this year had been even worse—at least the first few months of the season had been.

Last year Elliott had been relegated to the second line.

But this year, Coach Blackburn, newly returned to Portland U, decided that Elliott had improved enough that he'd ended up on the first line with Mal.

It was intolerable. Made even worse by his deliberate flouting of even the most minor instruction by Mal.

Elliott wanted to play by feel. He didn't want to practice. He didn't want to come early or stay late or work on their play formations and liked to skate free and easy, coming up with shit on the fly.

And the *worst* was that it worked!

Mal had only tolerated it at first because he'd believed Coach would quickly figure out that it was a terrible idea to let Elliott do whatever the fuck he wanted.

Their goals would go way down, and the line—and the team—would suffer, and Coach would shift things around again, removing Elliott from the first line and reducing the thorn in Mal's side.

That had not happened.

Elliott had another speed during a game and an instinct for the puck that Mal hated but couldn't deny *could* be effective. Their line had scored lots of goals already and seemed to get better every week.

Of course he'd never actually admit that out loud.

"Hey, guys." A pause and Mal looked up and there he was. No trace of guilt or shame on his face. A hickey on his neck and what looked to be beard burn disappearing under the collar of his T-shirt. "Malcolm."

His voice was pointed. Insolent.

Like he was rubbing his face in the fact that he'd just had sex.

He doesn't know. He can't know. Nobody knows.

But Mal knew, and as much as he tried to pretend it didn't matter, it was eating him up from the inside out.

"Where have you been?" Mal demanded even though he really didn't want to know.

Elliott dumped his bag in front of his locker and pulled off his T-shirt.

"Here and there. Doing some stuff," Elliott said, shooting Mal a glance that, if he'd given it to anyone else, Mal would believe was flirtatious.

But it wasn't. It was a taunt. Not a flirtation.

There had been no overt flirtations, not after the first time he'd shut Elliott down, which only proved that he'd been right about him.

Mal forced himself to look at Elliott's face. Not the undeniable flush of beard burn leading all the way down his bare chest.

"Oh, yeah," Brody said, laughing behind Mal. "Doing some *stuff*, huh?"

It was possible Elliott's deliberate taunting was for *his* benefit, because this was *Elliott*, but why would he? Mal had just been one of dozens—maybe even hundreds at this point—of guys Elliott had hit on during his time at Portland.

He hardly seemed to be carrying a torch for him, and besides that would be ridiculous.

They'd had one almost-civil conversation and hundreds of non-civil ones.

Doesn't stop you from looking at him.

No, it did not. But that was just an unfortunate accident of genetics which made Elliott so goddamn attractive Malcolm found it almost impossible to ignore the heat burning inside him every time he saw the guy.

"The stuff was pretty hot stuff, actually," Elliott murmured.

He was looking at Mal again, like he was trying to get a rise out of him, and Mal looked away, feeling his temper spark inside him again.

"Next time," he said, slapping his hand against Elliott's bare chest. Ignoring, as much as he could, the firmness of it and the way his muscles tensed at his touch and the sparks that shot up his arm, "ignore the hot stuff and be on fucking time, okay?"

He stomped off towards the ice, pulling on his glove and wishing away the feel of Elliott's skin.

Behind him, he heard Elliott say, "Who shit on his cornflakes this time?"

A round of laughter.

"You, always," Brody said wryly.

Mal pushed himself hard, before practice even began, skating in hard lines back and forth on the ice, and by the time Elliott arrived with the team, his hair was damp and his face streaked with sweat.

"Trying to make the rest of us look bad?" Elliott commented between drills, wiping face down.

"No. Just trying to be a damn good hockey player." And he *was*. It bothered him more than he liked to admit that Elliott's free and easy play, all instinct and no preparation, made him doubt if that was true, sometimes.

His dad had always told him if he was going to play games for a living, he'd better be damn good at it.

"You'd be better if you'd stop worrying about doing it by the book every goddamn time and let your instincts guide you occasionally," Elliott muttered.

"So we can all be random and do whatever the fuck we feel like? I don't think so. This is an *organized sport,* Jones. Play like it."

Elliott flipped him off and Coach Blackburn sent them a warning look before calling out the next set of drills.

By the time practice ended, Malcolm was exhausted—too exhausted even to respond to Elliott's blatant stare as he stripped down for his shower.

He was just about finished, enjoying even the weak stream of lukewarm water, when Elliott stepped in front of him.

Mal worked hard to not look down. To never, ever let his gaze drift below Elliott's chest, even when he was pretty sure Elliott looked *his* fill of Mal's body.

"What do you want?" Mal demanded. "To insult me some more? To call me a stodgy old man?"

Elliott shrugged, the corner of his mouth tugging up into a smile. "If the label fits . . ."

Mal knew he could be too serious, though it wasn't like he had the bandwidth or even the ability to change. He was twenty-two and too set in his ways, though frankly that had happened long before this.

Maybe he'd never had a chance to be that carefree guy, even if he'd wanted to be.

Which he did *not*.

You're happy just the way you are.

Even if Elliott is an idiot and doesn't like you.

"You'd think after all this time you'd at least get creative with your insults," Malcolm retorted, flipping the water off and grabbing his towel.

"Creative," Elliott scoffed. "Like you'd ever know what *creative* is."

Malcolm's skin burned as Elliott's gaze drifted down his chest, like he was tracing the path of every single rivulet of water.

"Did you need something?"

Elliott's gaze didn't return to Mal's face quickly. He took his damn ass time.

Mal knew his body was fit. He'd always considered it a tool. To help him skate better and faster and longer than anyone else.

But in the last few years, he'd begun to wonder what *else* it could be used for.

And Elliott definitely didn't factor into that wondering.

Nope. Not even a little. Not even if Elliott had made it clear he'd know *all* the ways it could be used.

"Coach wants to see you. Wants to see both of us," Elliott added.

Mal felt a terrible foreboding. Yes, he and Elliott bickered. Loudly. At length. Their center, Ivan, spent a lot of his time refereeing them. But they were five and one this year. Coach Nichols, who'd left at the end of last season for a more prestigious job at an east coast school, had just let them fight it out, though the fighting *had* been more minimal last year. If only because they hadn't had a reason to interact as much.

But now with them on the same line, it was a different story entirely.

Was Coach Blackburn going to read them the riot act?

Shame crawled up Mal's spine.

"Fine," Mal snapped. The self-reproach echoing through him made his tone even harsher than normal.

"Bet you're so picture perfect, all tight corners and straight A's, you *never* get in trouble," Elliott sneered back.

And yes, that was true.

Before Elliott, he'd only snapped once before.

And well . . .he was not going to consider why it was that Elliott was now the second to add to the list.

What the two situations had in common.

"You say that like it's something to be ashamed of," Mal said as they headed towards the locker room to get dressed. "It's something to be *proud* of."

"Never unbending? Never having a bit of fun? Never flouting the rules, not once? Sounds fucking boring to me." Elliott's tone was flippant and Mal found himself glaring at his bare back as he pulled on boxer briefs and then sweatpants.

So what if he was "fucking boring."

He wasn't trying to appeal to Elliott Jones.

Not even a little.

Elliott was sweating, a trickle of it working its way down his back and making his T-shirt stick to his skin, even as he tried to pretend that everything was fine.

Mal looked pissed off, though that wasn't really anything new, but what *was* new was that he looked worried, probably because he didn't know why Coach wanted to see them.

But Elliott knew why—or at least he strongly suspected.

No doubt Malcolm believed it was over the near-constant battle of words they exchanged, but he'd heard Coach B tell Zach, the new assistant coach, that he didn't mind because, "they're pushing each other harder and faster."

At the time, that had pissed Elliott off because he sure fucking wasn't skating better than he ever had because of *Malcolm*, but right now he was grateful for it because that meant there was one less thing Coach B could be pissed at him about.

Leaving the one, very big thing.

Mal shot him a worried look, even though he was definitely trying not to get caught doing it, as they sat next to each other in chairs opposite Coach B's desk, waiting for him to walk in.

Zach was leaning against the back wall, arms crossed over his chest, his expression difficult to read.

But Elliott's subconscious screamed theories at him.

He was pissed off.

He was frustrated.

Even worse, he was *disappointed.*

Elliott liked Zach a lot. In the future, he'd like to *be* Zach, though maybe with a few more years in the NHL before he retired. But still, he was worth emulating, and now Elliott had fucked this all up.

Coach B walked in and next to him, Elliott felt Malcolm stiffen in his chair.

No doubt he was preparing himself for the hammer to come down on *him* for some imagined slight.

Elliott supposed he could have told Mal what he was almost certain the summons was about, but he hadn't been able to get the words out of his uncooperative throat.

He wasn't sure he could live through a Malcolm McCoy *I told you so.*

It had been hard enough to live through a Malcolm McCoy total rejection.

Today's hookup had had dark, wavy hair just like Mal's and for a second, when he'd been blowing Elliott on his knees, he'd been able to imagine that it was Mal's mouth around his cock, Mal's hands on him, Mal pleading with him to come.

His orgasm had been a notch better than lackluster for the first time in what felt like months.

Fifteen months specifically. Ever since Mal dismissed you like you were just another guy.

"Elliott, you know I didn't want to have this conversation," Coach B said, settling into his chair, steepling his fingers in front of him. "I hoped we wouldn't have to."

Elliott had hoped so, too.

But it turned out that grades weren't really *up* to him. Ironically, even when he tried, even when he tried to turn the backslide around, it hadn't helped.

Maybe statistics just wasn't his thing.

Okay. It *really* wasn't his thing.

"Me too, sir," Elliott said.

"What *is* this about?" Malcolm asked.

"Elliott didn't tell you?" Coach looked surprised, and of course, Mal's accusatory gaze swung in his direction. Those dark blue eyes were full of demanding questions.

"I'm failing statistics."

Turned out it was easier to say it than to sit back and listen to Coach B say it.

Malcolm frowned. "Don't you study? Did you blow off all your classes again? You can't fucking skip classes, Jones. You know that you can't do it and pass and when—"

"That's enough." Coach B's voice was mild but he raised a hand and cut Mal off mid-lecture.

Elliott would be relieved, but he had a feeling he was going to get it from Coach regardless. Just delivered in slightly nicer packaging.

"But—"

"Malcolm. I didn't call you for a lecture," Coach B said, still mild. "I called you in here because I thought you could actually help Elliott."

"Help?"

"What?"

They said it at almost the same time. Then their gazes met in the space between them. Mal looked horrified, and Elliott had a feeling his expression was similar.

"Malcolm has excellent grades. It's in his best interest to keep you on the team. On your line, to be specific."

"Are you sure that's true, sir?" Elliott asked skeptically.

Because he didn't think Malcolm McCoy would spare a second or a second glance if he got kicked off the team. He'd only be relieved that the pebble in his shoe was finally gone.

"I'm not *that* bad," Malcolm said dryly.

"You'd throw a parade if I got kicked off this team," Elliott retorted. Then added, "Oh wait, a parade would be *fun* so maybe not a parade. A funeral procession, maybe, with a nice sedate dirge accompanying it?"

Mal's eyes flashed hard. "If you know what *dirge* is, and you know how to use it in a sentence, correctly, why the fuck are you failing statistics?"

"Because I like to read but I fucking hate math, okay?"

"Zach," Coach said, his voice a plea. "Separate these two, please."

Zach chuckled under his breath, then pinned them both with a hard look. "Kids. Behave."

Mal opened his mouth but Zach was too quick. "I know you're too old to be behaving like this, McCoy."

It was true. Malcolm was a twenty-two-year-old senior. A man. *A grown ass man you'd like to fuck you into next year,* still, Elliott's uncooperative brain—or his dick—added.

Only Elliott made him into a whining petulant child.

A fact he was almost proud of.

"It's not my fault, Zach. He's . . ." Mal huffed out a frustrated breath. "He makes light of *everything*, even failing a class, which could lose him a spot on this team and his scholarship." *And,* Elliott noticed Mal did not add, *his shot at being drafted into the NHL in the spring.*

He didn't have to say it, because Elliott already knew it.

"Elliott, we need you to take this seriously."

"I *have* been trying," Elliott argued. It was true. Maybe he hadn't gotten anywhere, but he *had* tried. He'd gone to class. Done the reading. The homework. And it had still been fucking incomprehensible. At least that was the conclusion he came to when his tests and quizzes kept coming back to him with D's and F's.

"I've talked to Dr. Prosser. There's an end of unit test coming up, in two weeks. If Elliott can get a B plus or better on the test, it'll improve his grade enough that he should be safe, at least conditionally. He'll need to continue to do well for the rest of the semester to truly solidify his grade and his position on this team." Coach B turned to Malcolm. "And you'll be helping him do that. You got an A in this class. I checked."

Malcolm let out a gust of breath. "And if I say no?"

Elliott couldn't say he was all that surprised. Why would Mal ever want to help *him*? But Coach looked incensed.

"Mal, see fucking sense." Zach was the one who answered. "You don't want to doom this kid's future—his *bright* future, which I know you can see, even if you're trying to pretend it doesn't exist—just because you're pissed off."

Elliott wanted to argue *again* that he wasn't a kid. He was *nineteen*, but he kept his mouth shut, because he could tell, probably better than anyone, when Mal was about to blow.

"I'm not—" Mal huffed out a hard breath. "I'm worried we're going to kill each other. He doesn't take *anything* seriously."

"He does, actually." Coach B, shocking Elliott, chimed in to defend him. "Just because he takes things seriously differently than you—"

"Yeah, just because I don't act like a freaking monk," Elliott inserted, and Coach's stare swung his way. Pinning him to the chair. Coach pinched the bridge of his nose.

"Zach, please remind me again why I thought this was a good idea," he said mildly, but his frustration was clear.

"Because it *is* a good idea?" Zach was smirking now.

"Not if they kill each other. Not if *I* kill them first." Coach shot Elliott another stern look. "Elliott, I *am* trying to help you out here. Let me do it."

"Yes, sir," Elliott said.

Maybe he was failing statistics, but he wasn't stupid.

"And McCoy, stop fucking pulling his pigtails just because you can."

Mal looked confused. "What? What does that mean?"

Because he didn't even understand basic pop culture references. Elliott only didn't say so out loud, because as galling as it was, he did need help. *Mal's* help, specifically.

Coach rolled his eyes. "Nevermind. Just . . .try to get along. I know that's asking for a lot."

"A lot," Zach added emphatically.

"Hey, we get it," Elliott said.

"And that's the best I can do. Ask for you to put aside your many, *many* differences, because you both want this team to win, and this team is better equipped to do that if Elliott's on it."

Malcolm sighed, like this was the biggest imposition of his whole life. "Fine. I'll do it. I'll tutor him. But *only* because you're right, and this team is better with him on it than off it."

Coach nodded. "Now get out of here before you give me a worse headache than I already have."

Zach gave them both a look as they stood that said, *if you do give him that headache, I'll knock your heads together myself.*

Mal stopped just outside Coach's office, in the hallway. Just out of earshot of Coach and Zach. Elliott didn't miss that. Truthfully, he didn't miss much, despite Malcolm's constant accusations that he just floated through life, unconcerned and unobservant.

"This is how this is going to go," Mal said in an annoyingly officious tone.

But Elliott had behaved in Coach's office and while he *was* grateful Mal had agreed, he wasn't about to let Mal lecture him until he died from boredom.

"Did that hurt?" Elliott interrupted.

Mal frowned. "Did *what* hurt? That massive asshole shoving me into the boards in the last game? You checked me out earlier, didn't you? I'd have thought you'd have seen the bruise."

So he'd caught that. Well, Elliott had never pretended that Malcolm wasn't delicious, and he wasn't about to start now.

"Noticed that, did you—"

"Do not ask me if I liked it," Mal said between clenched teeth.

"Must've loved it, then," Elliott teased.

Mal rolled his eyes.

"I meant, did it hurt admitting that the team's better off with me on it?"

Mal froze. "No," he said stiffly, finally. "It's just the truth. You know how good you are. You don't need me to say it. What you *do* need is for me to push you to not just skate by on your natural skill. Skill improves when *you* improve it. Do you want to be just good? Or do you want to be *great?*"

"I want you to stop fucking lecturing me," Elliott muttered.

But he *did* want to be great, sure. Didn't everyone?

What he didn't know was if Mal's tactics were the magic key for *him* being great.

"Well, that's never going to stop happening now," Mal said, and was that a *smile?*

Of course, only Malcolm would smile at the thought of lecturing Elliott until he was blue in the face.

"I'm sure it won't."

"*Now,*" Mal repeated, "this is how this is going to go. I'll set the times. You won't just be on time, you will be *early.*"

"Sounds like a great time," Elliott retorted sarcastically.

"We want to make it through this unscathed? This is how we're gonna do it," Mal said. "This is how we *have* to do it."

"Fine."

"And we're gonna meet three times a week." Malcolm paused. "Starting tomorrow. The library. Eight PM. I'll reserve a private room."

Elliott wanted to argue, because Thursday night was poker night at the Gamma Sigma house and he had a standing invite, but he had a feeling that if he did, Malcolm would freak out. Claim he cared more about parties than his grades. Cared more about having fun than playing hockey.

It had never bothered him before that Malcolm might feel that way, but Elliott realized that he didn't *want* Mal to think any of those lies were actually true.

So he just nodded. "Sure, I can do that."

Mal squinted at him. "No bitching? Complaining? Whining?"

"I don't do those things," Elliott protested, wincing inside.

No wonder Mal hadn't wanted to hook up with him, ever, if this was what he felt about Elliott. A bitchy, whiny kid who couldn't stop complaining.

If he'd needed to get his ego in line enough to get him to accept Mal's help, that would probably do it.

Mal shot him a look. "Sure you don't," he retorted.

Ouch.

"Okay. So rule one. Gotta be on time."

"Early," Mal inserted.

Elliott rolled his eyes. "Early. Rule two, three times a week. Any other rules?"

"I'm sure I'll think of a few."

"Probably more than a few, knowing you and your love affair with rules," Elliott muttered.

"Cute," Mal drawled. Leaned back against the wall, crossing his arms over his chest. His T-shirt sleeves hugged his biceps, his pecs, outlining his abs in the thin cotton. Elliott pushed away the reminder of just how attractive he was.

"I guess . . ." Elliott swallowed hard. Really, *really* resenting how viscerally aware of Mal's body he was. Mal's very presence. All that icy sternness should've turned him off. Given him frostbite. But it didn't. It never had. It just made Elliott more determined than ever to burn it down.

You're never going to get that chance.

"I got homework to do," Malcolm said. "See you tomorrow."

"Eight PM. Library," Elliott parroted back at him.

Mal shot him one last hard look. "Early, Jones. *Early.*"

CHAPTER 3

"You look disgruntled, even for you," Jane said as she slid into the booth across from Malcolm. It was just after ten, and Jimmy's was still more than half full with students and staff eating a late breakfast. Just like him and Jane.

Last year, he and Jane had shared a hallway, living in singles next to each other.

This year, they were sharing an apartment on the other side of campus.

Jane was on the dance team, and her practices and Mal's practices often meant they rarely saw each other if they didn't make specific plans. And Jane *always* made sure they made plans.

Malcolm didn't know how this girl, two years younger than himself, sweet with a spine of steel, had ended up deciding he was worth her effort, but he considered her one of his best friends.

Okay.

His *only* best friend.

Your only friend. That voice wasn't his own, but apparently belonged to Elliott. He swatted it away. Annoyed the guy had not only invaded his quiet, ordered life, but his brain now, too.

BETH BOLDEN

"Coach called me into his office last night, after practice."

Jane arched a blonde eyebrow. "Is this why when I got home from my date you were barricaded in your room?"

"I was barricaded in my room because I was studying," Mal claimed, but it was annoying how right she was.

Jane knew how important his studies were to him—one of the many reasons they got along and he liked her so well—so if she came home and his headphones were on, she'd generally leave him be. He hadn't felt the need to close the door in ages.

But he had last night.

He still wasn't sure why Coach's request had upset him so much.

"Bullshit," Jane said succinctly, stirring sugar into the cup of coffee Mal had ordered her. "What's going on? Why is Coach B upset with you?"

"He's not upset with *me*. Jones is failing statistics and Coach wants me to tutor him into a miraculously non-failing grade."

Saying it out loud did not make it magically suck less.

Mal ground his teeth together.

"Well, that should be fun," Jane said brightly. "Should I expect to come home one day and see the apartment building reduced to rubble?"

"*No,*" Mal said emphatically.

"Just asking," she said in a light, casual tone.

Mal glowered and then felt guilty for glowering. It wasn't Jane's fault. "I can control myself. I don't want to physically attack him or anything."

"No? You sure about that?"

"Jane—"

"You know my theory."

He knew her theory. She'd imparted it last year, in the late spring, just before the semester ended, after she'd gotten drunk on coconut rum and confessed that she was pretty sure Mal's annoyance with Elliott Jones was mostly frustration that he wanted him so badly and had decided he couldn't have him.

Him. Wanting Elliott fucking Jones.

"That's ridiculous."

And okay, Elliott *was* good-looking. That was a factual thing, not an opinion, even. And not even *Mal's* opinion—more the opinion of the many, many guys desperately panting after the jerk.

Otherwise, he could barely stand to be in the same vicinity as Elliott.

"It's not ridiculous, it's clear as day," Jane said bluntly. She leaned in. "You're in major denial. He hit on you, and you froze—"

"He hit on me in the most ridiculous, smug, egotistical, over-the-top way. I was never even tempted to say yes. I did *not* freeze," Mal reminded her. Especially since after that night, more than a year ago, Elliott had had what felt like hundreds of guys looking at him and he'd hardly stopped himself from looking back.

Mal hadn't been special. Elliott hit on everything that moved and breathed and had a freaking dick.

"You should've said yes," Jane said sternly. "Maybe that would—"

"Don't say it!" Malcolm yelped. "God, don't say it out loud."

"You have a real problem, Mal, and he could *help*," Jane said with a sigh.

"It's not a problem," Mal insisted, though it kind of was, at this point. "It's a situation, and I'm not unhappy about it. I don't mind." Though, yes, he kind of *did* mind.

At twenty-two it would be kind of nice to have someone touch his dick besides his own right hand.

"You're lying to yourself. You're not a virgin out of choice. You're a virgin because one bad experience soured you and then you got caught up in the bullshit your dad told you was real and you didn't know how to untangle yourself."

"I wish you would stop saying that word," Malcolm said. Ignoring the rest of what she'd said about his dad.

He didn't know if it was true.

He didn't know if it was *not* true, either.

Jane leaned back in the booth. Crossed her arms over her chest. She was wearing a baby pink sweater today. It should have made her look like a delicate prima ballerina, priming to get on stage. Instead, she looked more like a drill sergeant, ready and willing to kick his ass.

"You wish I'd stop because it *bothers* you and you don't even know how to go about dealing with it. That's why. You know how to solve every problem in your life except this one. I'm begging, let the two of them solve each other."

"I'll tutor him and that's all," Malcolm said with finality, and he hated how much he sounded like his dad.

Jane had only met his father once, but she probably heard it too, in the inexorable, iron edge to his voice. She might've said it, too, but there was evidence of just how much Jane loved him, because she didn't.

"And you also reserve the right to change your mind," Jane said lightly even though they both knew how infrequently Mal changed his mind.

The waitress showed up, they ordered, and then Mal decided it was time to change the subject.

"How was your date?"

Jane rolled her eyes. "A complete waste of time. He spent the whole date staring at my boobs."

"I hate men," Mal said. "I told you he wasn't good enough."

"You *love* men."

"I'm sexually and romantically attracted to men," Mal said firmly. "That doesn't mean I love them. They kind of suck, most of the time."

"Oh, you'd like them to suck *more*," Jane teased.

Malcolm flushed, in spite of himself. Did not imagine Elliott on his knees in front of him, his never-ending bullshit finally silenced because his mouth was full . . .

He cleared his throat.

"Can we *not* talk about sex?"

Jane laughed. "That's what we do when we're not having any, Mal. Anyway, no, the guy was a waste. But there's plenty of fish in the sea. I'll find someone, someday. Until then?" She grinned at him. "There's always my dear, darling Malcolm."

He didn't know how she'd come by her relentless positivity, but he'd gone from finding it a waste of energy to a nice change of pace.

Anthony McCoy had told him after the single time he'd met Jane that he wished Mal had been interested in her as more than just a friend.

She's a good one, he'd said.

After that conversation, Mal had forced down another round of guilt that he hadn't been the son his father had wanted.

"I'm not going anywhere," Mal told her. Not just because he genuinely liked her, but because she was so sweet and re-lentlessly optimistic, he felt she needed protecting. People took advantage of people like that, and damned if they'd do that to Jane on his watch.

Jane shot him a warm smile as the waitress set their food down in front of him.

His dad wasn't homophobic necessarily—just very set in his ways. And he'd raised Malcolm to be unflinchingly honest, so he'd seen no problem voicing, at age twelve, just how he didn't feel a thing for girls, but liked guys instead.

Never taking the easy path. That's my Malcolm, his dad had said then, patting him on the shoulder.

It hadn't been reassuring, necessarily, but at least he hadn't done something terrible?

Jane would have said that was hardly anything to applaud Anthony McCoy for, but then her feelings on his father were hardly a secret.

"I think I'm going to get the lead in a new piece in the winter dance showcase," Jane said as they finished up their food.

"Really? That's great." Mal didn't understand anything about dance, but he'd learned—because she'd been forceful enough to insist, finally producing a twelve slide PowerPoint presentation, that dance was just as athletic as a regular sport was—that it wasn't easy.

There was an excellent dance program here at Portland University, and he was proud how Jane, still just a sophomore, seemed to be one of the brightest lights in it.

"Yeah," she said, "there's a new choreographer coming up from U of O, kind of an exchange, and Orla said that he really loved my audition. The one you filmed last week?"

Mal nodded. "It's a guy?"

"Don't worry, he's probably gay. Almost definitely gay," Jane said wryly. "Maybe I should introduce him to you."

Malcolm rolled his eyes. "I don't have any time for dates. Or meeting choreographers. Especially not now that I'm going to be tutoring Jones three times a week."

"Three times a week?" She raised an eyebrow.

Mal realized he'd made a tactical error by returning his friend's attention back to Elliott.

"He's failing statistics, Jane. He needs help. A *lot* of help."

She waggled her eyebrows. "Oh, I just bet he does."

"That's enough about Elliott. You're so caffeinated you're becoming delusional. No more coffee for you today," he said, with mock sternness as he grabbed the bill off the table, ignoring how Jane made a face at his highhandedness.

She laughed. "I'm not sure *I'm* the delusional one."

"We'll see tonight." Though Malcolm already knew he wasn't laboring under any illusions that this would be painful and ugly and if it ended without them wanting to strangle each other, it would be a miracle.

"We sure will," she said knowingly. She put an arm around his much bigger frame as they walked out of Jimmy's. "I can't wait to hear about it."

Outside the private room Mal had reserved, Elliott took a deep breath and then another.

He'd spent the whole day—since he'd gotten Mal's text with the room number—telling himself that he wouldn't poke or prod him. That he'd be appreciative and grateful that Mal was willing to do this.

He'd even focus—and *not* on the way Mal's curls fell over his forehead, or the dark intensity of those gorgeous blue eyes, or his broad shoulders and meaty biceps.

Pushing open the sliding door, Elliott met those blue eyes as they eyed him, top to bottom. Normally, Elliott might interpret that thorough examination as interest.

But he knew better.

Mal was cold as ice.

He glanced down at his watch. Elliott didn't need to look at his to understand the gesture.

"So, you *are* capable of being early," Malcolm said.

He seemed even colder than normal today.

I wanna be burned by all that ice.

Elliott pushed the thought away. He wasn't thinking about sex. He definitely wasn't thinking about sex in conjunction with Mal. He was *focusing*.

"Shocking, isn't it?" Elliott said, sitting down opposite Mal. He pulled his laptop out of his bag, and then his statistics book.

"You don't need either of those things," Mal said firmly. "We're starting more basic today."

"More basic? I don't need more basic. I need to pass this freaking test."

"And you will. But statistics builds on basic principles and if you don't get the basic principles, you'll never be able to understand anything more advanced." He glanced down at a paper in front of him. "If Dr. Prosser is following the same syllabus she was two years ago, then this test is about standard deviation."

Elliott nodded. "Sounds about right."

"Alright, we're going to start with the basic concepts and I'll work through up to that point. The idea's by that point, with the right, *focused* preparation, it shouldn't be an issue to understand standard deviation."

Elliott stared at Mal.

He should've guessed that Malcolm wouldn't approach this problem like anyone else. Anyone else might've just pulled up the textbook exercises on standard deviation and pounded them into Elliott's brain until he sort of understood. Until he got the concept well enough to pass the test.

But Mal wanted to actually *teach* him.

"Anyone ever tell you that you'd be a good teacher?"

Mal looked surprised. "No."

"You didn't have to go to all this work—"

"Yes, that's me. Malcolm *Workaholic* McCoy," Mal interrupted. "We've long established I like to do things by the book.

That I'm too serious. That I'm too committed. I get it, Elliott. Trust me."

Elliott opened his mouth and snapped it shut again. He'd actually meant it as a compliment, but naturally, Mal was so fucking prickly he'd thought Elliott was poking fun at him again.

"Actually, it's a good idea."

Normally, Elliott might've rather *died* than admit to Mal that any of his serious over-preparation was good.

Mal didn't need more encouragement in that direction.

But for someone he didn't want to help and a task he didn't want to do, he'd still put the time and effort and *thought* into this.

It was impressive. And interesting.

"Are you okay?" Mal asked, staring harder at him. "Are you really Elliott or are you a shapeshifter just pretending to be Elliott?"

"Elliott *can* take some stuff seriously. Like passing this class," Elliott said bluntly.

"Alright then." Mal nodded. Pulled out a notebook. "Let's start with the basic building blocks of statistics."

The next hour might've been the most boring of Elliott's life. At the end of it he still didn't like math, but he *did* understand it a little better.

Malcolm pushed the notebook away and leaned back in his chair. "Good job," he said. "If I'm being really honest. . .I didn't expect that to go so well."

"I'm not stupid," Elliott retorted. Telling himself that he wasn't upset, not in the least, by the surprise on Mal's face.

Maybe he *had* thought Elliott was stupid. That wasn't another fucking blow to his ego, or anything.

"No, you're not," Mal said dryly. "But I was more talking about your ability to be focused on one single topic that isn't hockey or a hot guy or a beer pong tournament or a party on frat row."

"Ouch." Elliott winced. "I'm not *that* bad."

Mal shot him a look.

Okay, maybe he could be, a little. But this was *college*. Shouldn't he be having some fun, too?

God knew Malcolm's general personality could be improved by some fun.

"Maybe I *was* focused on a hot guy," Elliott teased, leaning in a little, just to see how Malcolm would react.

Would he freeze him out? Or would he melt a little?

Mal stiffened and shifted away, looking down as he slid his notebook into his backpack. "Don't be ridiculous," he said firmly.

Elliott had actually gone out of his way *not* to check out Malcolm during their tutoring, but now that it was over, he let his gaze sweep over him. And his cock still loved the way he looked. His body still wanted to get as close as possible.

See what he looked like—what he *felt* like—when he lost some of that serious reserve and got desperate.

"I'm not being ridiculous. You are, factually, *hot*."

Malcolm glared. "You just behaved for a whole hour. Don't start that shit again."

"Jesus, you can't even take a fucking compliment," Elliott retorted. "With how much you hate me even telling you that you're attractive, I'd think I was some gay guy hitting on a straight bro who didn't even look at his *own* dick."

Mal's jaw dropped. "Are you kidding me? Just because I don't want *you* means I don't want any guy? I gotta go, because if I'm being honest, I'm not sure there's room in this room for me and you and your fucking ego."

He picked up his backpack and before Elliott could attempt to explain—though he wasn't going to fucking apologize for thinking the guy was hot, okay?—Mal was gone, storming through the door.

"Well, that went fucking wonderful," Elliott said to the empty space where Mal had been sitting only a moment before.

He pulled his phone out of his pocket. Typed a text to Ramsey. **Let's go grab a drink.**

Spoiler alert: you're not twenty-one, Ramsey texted back.

Then let's get a smoothie at Sammy's.

Ramsey sent a thumbs-up.

Ten minutes later, he was sucking down his favorite peanut butter banana smoothie—and wishing it had a nice shot of peanut butter whiskey added to it—when Ramsey slid into the booth opposite him.

"It go that badly?" Ramsey asked mildly. "I swung by the library. It was still standing, so it couldn't have been *that* terrible."

"Have we ever taken a swing at each other?" Elliott demanded.

No, they hadn't. Because if he touched Mal, it wasn't going to be with aggressive intent.

Ramsey considered this. "Maybe you should," he suggested.

"Are you crazy? I'm freaking trying to pass this goddamn class so I can *stay* on the team. If I took a swing at Mal, I'd be off it in point five seconds."

"Or, option number two, you could just tell him you want to fuck him, badly," Ramsey said bluntly.

"Or he could fuck *me*. I'm not picky. But you were *there* the first time I tried that. You saw how it went."

"Yeah, you pulling out the cheesy lines and trying to flirt with him. With *Mal*. AKA a block of ice. You don't *flirt* with a wall. You break it down. You *melt him down*."

They'd talked about Elliott's frenemy status with Malcolm more than once since Elliott had come to Portland U. Okay—a *bunch* of times. But Ramsey had never been this blunt before.

"I think I was plenty clear—"

Ramsey sighed, running a hand through his short blond hair. "I didn't say you weren't."

"Oh."

"I mean actually *seduce* the guy. You're cute. You know you've got moves. But every one of them that works on all these other poor suckers I see you move in on at the Gamma Sigma house every Saturday night—they're not going to work on Malcolm. You should know that by now."

"Aren't you worried that we're going to finally fuck and it's going to ruin the team?"

Ramsey shot him a frank look. "I'm worried that if you don't fuck, you'll kill each other instead and then nobody's going to be scoring any fucking goals."

Elliott stared at his smoothie. He understood what Ramsey was saying. Sometimes it felt like there was a rubber band stretched tight between them, and it kept straining harder, until one day it was just going to snap.

Would there be collateral damage if that happened? Elliott didn't want there to be, but he was beginning to think it might be inevitable.

Still, it didn't feel great to have Ramsey—practically his hero—lecturing him on how to pick up a guy. He knew how to pick up a guy.

"Well, don't hold back or anything," Elliott complained. "I'm not *trying—*"

"Lie to yourself if you want but don't lie to me. You still want him. You wanted him the moment you showed up at that first party. Your eyes lit up when you saw him there. I *saw* it. And I saw the fucking aftermath. I'd tell you that he doesn't want you, because past experience is generally an indicator of future success." Ramsey paused, and Elliott knew there was a *but* there.

Waited for it.

And not just because he wanted to finally get Malcolm McCoy naked, in his bed, scratching the itch that had been tormenting him for ages now.

"But..." Ramsey sighed profoundly, like he already knew he was going to fucking regret saying the rest. "*But,* I've been playing with the guy for four years and I've never seen him get pissed off. Not once. Not until you."

"So, you think I should seduce him." Elliott grinned around his straw.

"I'm sorry, haven't you been trying to do that this whole time? I mean, don't just spout some nonsense and lean in and then yank his string when he doesn't immediately fall to his knees in front of you."

Elliott winced. "Ouch."

Ramsey reached across the table. Patted him on the shoulder. "You have potential, Jones, but you're *not* me. Not yet."

Elliott rolled his eyes. "And people say *I* have an ego."

"Is it ego if it's true?" Ramsey laughed. "But seriously. It's in *everyone's* best interest if you two can figure your shit out. Besides, it's good for a guy to learn to work for it every once in awhile."

"I hate you," Elliott said. "You won't even tell me how?"

"How I'd crack Malcolm?" Ramsey laughed again and shook his head. "Hell no. You want him? You gotta figure out how to get him. And don't tell me you're not interested, because if you weren't, you wouldn't be constantly needling him for any kind of reaction."

"I *really* hate you."

Elliott sucked down the rest of his smoothie as Ramsey chuckled.

"Well, how 'bout this? What went wrong tonight?"

"It was fine. He'd totally pulled a Malcolm and done all this prep work to tutor me. It was actually . . ." Elliott took a deep breath. "It was actually really thoughtful, especially considering how much he didn't want to do it."

"So he was typical Malcolm—maybe even more than that. And you bit his head off."

"I did *not*. We studied together for a whole hour, and it was fine. Actually more like good. A whole hour with no bickering. And then he says something about how shocked he was, that I could pay attention for a whole hour to something that wasn't drinking or partying or hot guys."

"You did not," Ramsey said, before Elliott even had to admit how he hadn't been able to let the opening go.

"I . . .it's not like it was really even true! Though it wasn't a lie either. If I could take him, who is absolutely smoking hot, or another tutor who *wasn't*, you know what I'm picking. That doesn't mean that I . . .or that I didn't . . ." Elliott trailed off. Buried his face in his hands.

"Not that Malcolm isn't attractive, 'cause he is, but honey, I got to tell you, the only one who's obsessed with his business is *you*. But here's the thing—you hitting on him? It's not going to work."

"You said that already," Elliott said sullenly.

"What you said tonight, that pissed him off, didn't it?"

Elliott shrugged, not wanting to say it out loud—*he* had an ego too, thank you very much, Ramsey, and this was puncturing it more thoroughly than it had been in a long, long time.

Maybe since early last year, when he'd hit on Malcolm and he'd just brushed him off.

"You gotta stop telling him you want him, that you think he's hot, etcetera etcetera, and make him want *you*. Make *him* think *you're* hot."

Elliott opened his mouth but Ramsey just shook his head. "Please don't claim those two things are the same."

"I wasn't going to. I get the difference," Elliott retorted. "But you just said, I should ask him to fuck me."

"I did, but what I meant was ask him *after* you've gotten him. Now, for the love of God, please *use* some of this gold fucking star advice." Ramsey slid out of the booth. "See you at the game tomorrow night."

Elliott sat there for a long moment. Then another. And another still.

Long enough the guy at the register craned his neck to make sure he was still sitting there.

But the whole time Elliott was thinking of what Ramsey said.

If he could be right.

Not just that, even.

But if Elliott *wanted* him to be right. If Elliott was willing to figure this shit out, and even if he did, if it would make any difference whatsoever.

This was a lot of fucking work just to get a guy underneath him—when he could have nearly anyone else.

He could swing by the Gamma Sigma house tomorrow night after the game and pick up anyone else he wanted. Even guys who claimed they were straight—he could tempt them onto their knees.

Finally, he left Sammy's and on his way back to his dorm room, he decided once and for all that he was done with lusting after Malcolm McCoy.

He was too much work. Too difficult. Too prickly.

Elliott ignored the voice that said what he was really afraid of was trying and failing, *again*.

CHAPTER 4

ELLIOTT'S DECISION HELD FIRM all day.

He woke up and silenced the quiet voice that claimed he was just a fucking coward, and set out for his morning of classes with optimistic determination.

This was the right call.

He and Mal didn't need to fuck this out.

They could just . . .agree to disagree.

People did that all the time. Disagreements didn't always have to end in fucking or fighting.

He gave his number to the cute new barista at the Koffee Klatch when he stopped by to grab a cold brew just after lunch.

Told himself he'd go out with the guy when he inevitably texted.

But he already worried, that voice in the back of his head growing louder, that he wouldn't.

That he wouldn't *want* to. That he couldn't, not until he figured out this thing with Mal.

You did figure it out. You're going to let it go.

But had he?

Elliott was sure he had, at least that was what he kept insisting to himself, until he walked into the locker room and there was Malcolm, back to him, stripped down to the waist, and his body froze.

But instead of going up to him, instead of saying something that would inevitably make him turn around, make Malcolm *talk* to him, even if it wasn't positive, Elliott went quietly to his locker and began his game prep.

He didn't need to prod the beast. Not if he wasn't going to take advantage of it.

A few minutes later Ramsey wandered in, glanced over at Mal, and then much to Elliott's frustration, sauntered over to where he was stretching.

"I took you for a lot of things," Ramsey said under his breath, "but not someone who bows out before they even try."

"I'm allowed to decide it's not worth it," Elliott muttered.

Ramsey raised an eyebrow. "And since when has he not been worth it to you?"

"Since I realized it's just sex. He's just another guy." Elliott paused. "Thought you'd be happy to know it's not going to end in fucking *or* fighting."

"What? That it's just going to *end*? Peacefully? Amicably?" Ramsey rolled his eyes and smacked Elliott on the shoulder. "We both know it can't. It won't."

"It's going to end how I say it's going to end," Elliott said.

"What's going to end?"

He looked up, and Mal was standing there, that all-too-familiar arrogant blankness on his face. It made Elliott want to smack him. It made Elliott want to kiss it off him.

But he took a deep breath and didn't do either one.

He just said, "Nothing. Ramsey and I are having a pointless philosophic discussion that he's losing."

"Pointless but it still matters that I'm losing, huh?" Ramsey teased.

Elliott shrugged. "It's a waste of effort when I'm trying to get ready for this game."

Mal looked surprised. And for a second, like he might actually smile, but he didn't, and Elliott told himself firmly that he wasn't disappointed.

This wasn't a tactic. As far as Elliott was concerned, this was the new norm.

He watched as Mal and Ramsey exchanged confused glances.

Hesitantly, even though Malcolm McCoy had probably never hesitated to speak the truth in his whole goddamn life, he said, "You know Bend has that really aggressive defender. We need to make sure we're staying on-play. Don't let him bust it up."

"I saw the film," Elliott said steadily, not retorting wildly, the way he wanted to, that he wasn't stupid, that he'd been playing hockey for a hell of a long time too, and that he didn't need Malcolm's advice.

"Then you know—"

"That he's going to want to play one-on-one? Close? I know."

Mal exchanged another glance with Ramsey and nodded. "Okay, then. You know the game plan."

"We've got this," Elliott said firmly. Confidently. But not *over*-confidently, in the way that typically pissed Mal off.

"Uh, yeah. We do."

Mal slunk off to his side of the locker room without another word.

Ramsey turned to him again. "What the fuck was that?" he demanded.

"What?" Elliott asked even though he knew exactly why Ramsey was incredulous. That kind of exchange would've usually fueled a pre-game bickering session that might've even lasted all the way through warmups and sometimes even into the first period.

Elliott pissed off that Mal felt he needed to be reminded of basic facts and in response, picking and pecking at all the soft spots in Mal's usually tough armor.

Ramsey just shook his head. "I can't fucking believe after all this bullshit that you've put all us through you're just going to slink off with your tail between your legs and not even *try*."

"That's—"

"Enjoy fucking your way through the boys of Portland U. Save the men for me," Ramsey said, and after tossing that last bomb, strode off.

"Fuck him," Elliott muttered to himself.

But the thought remained with him through warmups.

Did he always go for the easiest hookups? The guys most like him who didn't really give a shit if he said yes or no? Who'd just move onto the next if he wasn't interested?

Was he afraid of a challenge?

No, he fucking was not.

He'd not be on this hockey team, playing on the first line as a sophomore if he was afraid of hard work. Of getting his hands dirty.

But even that anger at Ramsey seemed to fizzle out almost immediately after their first face-off.

Mal handled it, as the senior guy on the team, and flicked the puck his way, as the enormous giant who would probably be shadowing him the whole time he was on the goddamn ice practically blanketed him.

But Elliott was faster. Quicker. Much more agile.

He skated around the defender, shifting the puck with his stick, keeping it away from the giant.

The moment his body was angled right, the guy shoved a gloved fist into his side, away from the view of the ref. Elliott grunted but took the hit in stride because he'd known it was coming. He skated around the back of the goal, looking for his opening with the goalie. Didn't see anything he liked the look of, so did another one. Still with the giant hot on his ass. He was annoying, sure, but it was extra annoying how Mal kept moving into his field of view, frustration etched on his face.

Like he wanted Elliott to take the shot, even if it was a bad one.

There was a flurry of excitement just out of his periphery, and that was all the giant needed to steal the puck.

Elliott glanced over to the bench and Zach nodded to him, indicating a line change. He skated over, vaulting over the wall and settling down on the hard wooden bench, breath coming in short gasps as he wasn't quite warmed up fully yet.

"What the fuck was that?" Mal spit out as he dropped next to him. "You had a shot."

"Eh, it wasn't a shot," Elliott said, reaching for water. Shooting it into his mouth, between the metal bars of his face mask.

"When have you *ever* not been tempted to take a half-ass shot?" Mal demanded. "Usually I have to *stop* you from taking wild shit that's never going to go anywhere."

"It just wasn't right."

But Elliott could admit that he hadn't felt that intense urgency he sometimes did. Okay that he *always* did. He usually was desperate by the time they got onto the ice, needing to show Malcolm that he wasn't some idiot who couldn't score to save their fucking life.

He hadn't felt that way today. He hadn't . . . well, he'd been *trying* not to care. But now Malcolm was kind of pissing him off again.

"Next time, let me have the fucking puck," Mal muttered.

"Kids, it's fine," Ivan inserted. "Ell controlled that gigantic defender. He can do that the whole game. Distract him. While he slips one between his legs. What is he, six foot fucking ten?"

"Big enough," Mal bit off.

Normally, Elliott might say something else to piss him off. Something like, *I bet he's got a bigger dick than you, McCoy.*

Which would both annoy and disgust the guy.

But this time Elliott swallowed down the comment.

He was fine. Everything was fine.

But as the first period ticked down, it didn't appear that everything was fine.

Coach ducked down at three-quarters through the first period, reminding them that they missed one hundred percent of the shots they didn't take.

Elliott didn't have to look at the board to know their usual shots were way down, and it wasn't because of the giant who kept dogging his skates.

When the period ended and they tromped down towards the locker room, Mal caught his arm.

Pulled him into one of the nooks in the hallway. "What are you *doing*?" Mal hissed.

He'd taken off his helmet, and his dark hair was sweat-soaked, falling over his forehead. He shoved it back, eyes blazing.

Elliott felt that same thrum he always did—an inescapable awareness that he normally reveled in, but had lately begun to resent, because what was it for if they weren't ever going to act on it?

Or *Malcolm* wasn't ever going to let them act on it?

"What am I doing? What am *I* doing?" Elliott retorted in a hard voice. It was easy to let some of that frustration bleed into his voice because at this point he wasn't sure he could keep it out anymore.

He was *trying* to let this go. Let go of their stupid fighting. All the pigtail pulling. All the endless unsuccessful attempts to get into Mal's pants. And instead of just letting him, Mal was here, in his face.

"Yes, what are *you* doing? You fucked around with the puck for ages. You could've taken at least five shots and you just *didn't*. If you're trying to piss me off—"

Elliott's jaw dropped. "Trying to piss you off?" he interrupted. "Are you fucking kidding me? I would *never* do that. I would never fuck up a game just to get a rise out of you. No matter how satisfying it is."

Mal just stared at him.

Elliott poked him in the chest and hoped he felt it, even through his chest pad. "Is that really what you think of me? That I'd fuck up a game?"

Finally, Mal broke. Grabbed his arm. Elliott ignored the thrill that shook him at his touch, even through God knew how many layers of padding and cloth. "No. No. God. No." Mal shook his head, like he could barely believe he'd made the accusation. "I just . . .what is up with you? Why are you not taking the shot?"

"I . . .I don't know," Elliott confessed. He hadn't *felt* any different. Only calmer. Less like he was playing to piss Malcolm off. The first game they'd played together on the same line, late last year after an injury to the normal right winger, he'd scored two goals and played fearlessly, pushing hard as if he wanted to prove to the guy that he belonged. So he'd stop looking down his nose at him.

But of course that hadn't happened. Mal had kept doing it. Kept lecturing him. Kept being a patronizing ass. Now, Elliott could look back and see that this was just how Mal was. Of course even after that realization, it hadn't helped him *like* it.

Mal's attitude, even if he couldn't help it, still pissed Elliott off.

"Are you hurt? Is there a problem?" Mal demanded to know.

"I . . ." The only problem—the only *difference*—was that he'd made the decision pre-game not to be pissed off.

Not to let Malcolm get to him any longer.

He'd gone out there on the ice without that chip on his shoulder.

Had *that* made the difference?

"For fuck's sake," Malcolm muttered. He gripped his arm harder, making Elliott realize he'd never let go of it. They'd drifted closer together as they'd argued, Mal's body practically blanketing Elliott's, the heat of him inescapable.

Elliott's pulse accelerated.

"I was trying not to be angry at you. You know, like always. You piss me off practically by breathing," Elliott finally admitted.

Mal looked floored. "That's why you . . ." He took a short, deep breath. "Don't answer that question. Just . . ."

"Just *what*," Elliott retorted.

"Just . . .fucking get your head in the game. I don't care what it takes. You're making us look bad. Our whole fucking line. I hate it."

Elliott felt that familiar fire catch inside him. "You mean I'm making *you* look bad."

Mal paused, so briefly that Elliott almost missed it. But he was looking for it. Knew what Mal was doing now. "Yeah. Yeah, you are. Get it fucking together, Jones."

He had a choice. He could ignore it. Or he could let that admonition eat away at him the way he always did.

In the end, it was inevitable. They couldn't be *nothing*. They were *this*.

Elliott let the frustration he'd been holding back wash over him.

Didn't try to fight it. Embraced it, instead.

He shoved Mal back. "Fuck you," he said, "you could take the shot."

"Maybe I will," Malcolm countered. "Maybe I'll take the shots *you* won't."

"I dare you to fucking try," Elliott said, elbowing him back even farther. "I dare you to fucking *try*."

Satisfaction ghosted over Mal's features.

Elliott knew he'd been played but he let that annoyance fuel him even further.

Malcolm wanted to piss him off? Well, he'd be good and pissed off then.

It had been a calculated risk.

Mal still couldn't believe that Elliott's weird first period play had been because he'd been . . .well, *not* angry at him?

Trying to pretend like everything was fine?

Why would he even do that?

Coach had never gotten up their asses about fighting, or bickering, even, and it had never occurred to Malcolm that Elliott *wanted* to stop fighting.

If that was true, maybe he shouldn't have pushed him again.

But Elliott had clearly not minded, because he was currently tearing through the Bend's defense like it was butter and he was a hot knife. Carving them up, taking shot after shot, most of them good, some of them even brilliant.

He'd scored one goal since the first period and assisted Ivan on another.

But regardless of the score on the board, it was his attitude that was back.

That *fuck you* chip was back on his shoulder, and every time he took a shot, he'd look right over at Mal.

On the last one, he'd shot him a triumphant smile that was no doubt calculated precisely to piss Malcolm off.

And it *did*, but it had another unexpected effect, too.

It made him nearly stop in his tracks.

He *knew* Elliott was attractive, sure. He had been pretty fucking good at keeping that particular fact buried deep.

But the hallway had loosened it, and now that smile had unearthed it, big time.

Elliott feeling himself made Mal want to feel *himself*.

He skated to a halt, sending a shower of ice against the boards as the final horn of the game sounded.

The Evergreens had won four to one, and it felt damn good.

"Great play today, McCoy," Zach said to him as he walked through the doorway towards the locker room. "Aggressive. I like it."

"Better than the first period, for sure," Ivan retorted, pulling up next to them.

"Yeah, what the hell, guys?" Brody wondered. "But you turned it around."

"Wasn't me," Mal said, even though it kind of *had* been him.

"It sure fucking wasn't," Elliott retorted as he dropped down next to Ivan. "I wasn't waiting around for you old men to get your shit together."

Mal chuckled darkly. Hated, a little, how Elliott insulting him somehow felt better than Elliott saying nothing.

"I'll show you old," Ivan muttered.

"Nobody's old," Brody said, forever the peacemaker.

"I like to think of myself as well-seasoned," Ramsey added with a smirk. "In all the best kinds of ways."

Mal rolled his eyes as he began to strip his equipment off. "You *would* think that."

"Hey, I'm a real catch," Ramsey insisted.

Maybe he was.

But Mal had never been tempted by his looks. Same as he'd never been tempted by Brody or any of the other guys on their team.

Only one guy had ever caught his eye, despite him despising the fact that it was *him*, of all fucking people.

He was on the other side of Mal now, pulling off his gear, wiping down his damp chest with his shirt.

Malcolm averted his eyes. He told himself it was out of respect that he didn't look—and certainly he'd *never* been as blatant about it as Elliott himself—but he was beginning to wonder if it was actually something else.

He didn't know why Elliott snapped at him, other than the obvious. Or why he'd stopped.

But he was worried he was starting to understand why he sometimes started it.

Why he antagonized the guy, when everyone else's bullshit had always slid off his shoulders, effortlessly.

Jane hadn't been the only one to suggest it was because he secretly wanted Elliott and didn't believe he could have him.

But Jane's theories, no matter how wild, were more difficult to ignore when that throb of desire that had lit in his belly seemed to just pulse harder the more he was around the guy.

He'd just gotten back from the shower and pulled a T-shirt and his boxer briefs on when a hand fell onto his shoulder.

Mal looked over and was surprised to see Elliott there.

He pulled his hand back, almost immediately, and Malcolm was reminded why they didn't touch all that frequently, despite that this team was generally a pretty touchy-feely bunch.

He always felt every single bit of every single touch, deep down, in a place he wanted to pretend didn't exist.

But it existed, and he was feeling it, inevitably, now.

"What?" Mal barked, some of his edginess no doubt a result of that unfulfilled desire—not just his frustration with the guy in general.

"You fucking baited me," Elliott said under his breath.

The team was beginning to slowly filter out of the locker room. There were only a handful of guys left. Mal pulled on sweatpants, then his sneakers. Ignoring the insidious voice that said it was easier to deal with Elliott when he had more layers of armor on.

"You needed it," Mal reminded him. "You came out in the first period like you were out for a Sunday stroll, not a hockey game."

"I was biding my time," Elliott argued.

"I did what needed to be done." Mal hesitated. "About tutoring—"

"You gonna give me what I need there too?" Elliott interrupted with one of those sly grins that Mal told himself firmly that he did *not* like.

Oh, I wish you'd give me exactly what I need.

Mal pushed that thought away, hard.

"I'm going to help you pass statistics," he said coldly. "Keeping you on this team and on the fucking ice."

"God, you *are* an asshole," Elliott said. But his voice didn't sound particularly angry. More amused. Affectionate. Like he liked knowing exactly what the score was. And bickering with each other was the score.

"Being focused and serious about what we're doing here doesn't make me an asshole."

But he *could* be an asshole about it. Didn't know how else to *be*, based on the examples he'd been shown, but that didn't mean he couldn't see it, sometimes.

Jane told him sometimes that he was too unforgiving, that he had no *give*, and it wasn't like Malcolm didn't know that. He did. But he'd been created, more than raised, by a tough, no-nonsense father. His dad had never met a gray area he didn't hate, and if Malcolm was the same? Well. That happened.

"The way you bludgeon all of us with it does," Elliott muttered. But then, to Mal's shock he added, "When are we meeting next?"

Malcolm had certainly had no intention of quitting the tutoring. Not when Elliott's contributions to the Evergreens were annoyingly vital, but also because he'd given his word to Coach Blackburn.

Another thing his dad had always imparted was that your word was solid. Ironclad. And that was something Mal was never going to apologize for.

"We can do it tomorrow," Mal said. "Tomorrow night. After the game?"

Their game was slightly earlier, a five PM puck drop instead of seven, in deference to the weekend.

"Not the library this time. Sammy's."

Mal frowned. "If you're looking for a way to distract yourself . . ."

"I'm looking for *dinner*, you idiot," Elliott said and smacked him in the shoulder.

Even Elliott hitting him affected him.

Imagine if he touched you and it was purposeful and sweet and hot . . .

Mal jerked his attention back to the conversation. "Uh, okay. Yeah. We can do that. Sammy's makes a good sub."

"So you *are* human, after all," Elliott teased. "You even eat, like a real boy!"

Mal glowered. "Not everything has to be a joke."

"But it's fun when it is," Elliott said, nudging him again.

He still wasn't wearing a shirt and even though Malcolm was now, he still felt the imprint of Elliott's heat, even after he shrugged on a hoody and stepped out in the cold, rainy Oregon fall.

"Hey," Ramsey said, calling out to him as he headed towards his apartment. "Wait up."

"Are you going to guilt me into going to another party?" Yes, it was a Friday night, but Mal didn't feel like faking a smile and watching as Elliott Jones took home yet another unsuspecting, completely thrilled guy.

He'd seen plenty of that, over the last year and a half.

Ramsey grinned. Slung an arm around Mal's shoulders, and to Mal's annoyance, he could *still* feel that last touch of Elliott's.

"Would I do that?" Ramsey asked earnestly, the corner of his mouth turning up into a very Ramsey-like smirk.

Here was the thing: he could tell Ramsey the truth about his virginity. Ramsey wouldn't laugh, wouldn't even joke about it. Would probably, in a serious, Ramsey-like way, offer to alleviate that concern for him. Maybe Malcolm would even enjoy it—*oh, his dick cried, you'd enjoy it*—but it would fuck everything up, and while Mal might feel a little desperate, he was not that stupid.

At this point, maybe sex might not mean something, not like flowers and chocolates and Valentine's Day kisses, but he wanted it to be more than just scratching an itch.

"You absolutely fucking would," Mal said.

"Maybe I might've done it a few times, but you had a good time." Ramsey paused. "Okay, a *decent* time. If you'd get out of your comfort zone, have a beer, relax a little—"

"No," Malcolm said, with finality. "*No.*"

"Alright, alright. No beers, no relaxation. I get it. You're primed. And well . . ." Ramsey shrugged, wincing a little. "You're a little primed, buddy."

"What the hell does that mean?" Mal was afraid he understood, though, a little too well.

He was feeling a little edgier than normal. Yes, it was par for the course for Elliott to churn him up, but today's bullshit had done more than just churn up the normal kind of annoyances. He felt different…aching and desperate in a way he didn't want to examine too closely.

"You bit *my* head off a few times."

"That was just the frustration of the game. The first period—"

"Yeah," Ramsey said. "About that. Let's talk about the first period."

They turned down Washington Avenue, and Malcolm realized, belatedly, that Ramsey had actually walked way farther than he needed to—if his destination was the Gamma Sigma house—only to keep talking to him.

And here was the thing about Ramsey. He appeared congenial and friendly and non-threatening. But Ramsey was actually so much more than that. A master planner in innocent sheep's clothing. He worked everyone, effortlessly and easily, and barely anybody even realized.

But Malcolm knew. He just preferred it when Ramsey's superpowers were not turned on him—and he was afraid that right now, he was dead in Ramsey's sights.

"What about the first period?" Mal asked testily. Worried what Ramsey might say. Worried about what Ramsey *wasn't* saying.

"We all noticed that you and Ell were being weirder than normal," Ramsey pointed out.

"Elliott's the one being weird," Malcolm said and then wished he could snatch the words back. Because there was a telltale gleam in Ramsey's gaze that told him he'd betrayed too much.

"Don't like it when he ignores you, huh?" Ramsey said bluntly.

Mal rolled his eyes. "That isn't . . .*no.*"

"I think you hated it. 'Course, it's not like he enjoyed it either. When he's trying to show you up he's got a whole other level."

It was the exact same conclusion he'd come to, and the hypothesis he'd tested by poking Elliott in a spot he knew might be vulnerable. He wasn't proud that it had worked, but it *had* worked. Elliott had gotten pissed off and had played like a demon for the next two periods.

But just because they'd both been right didn't mean Mal wanted to admit it.

Especially to Ramsey.

"Come on," Ramsey continued, tone entreating. "You know I'm right."

"Ugh, yes, but don't . . .don't read something into it. Especially something that's not there," Mal said.

The Lovejoy Apartments came up on their right, emerging from the damp gloom.

Ramsey stopped in front of them, an expectant look on his face, like he knew Mal wouldn't just turn around and walk away.

"You sure there's nothing there?" Ramsey asked.

He heard her before he saw her.

"Oh, hey, Mal," Jane exclaimed as she walked up behind him. "And Ramsey."

"Honey," Ramsey said, smirking.

Mal shot him a glare. "Don't," he said.

"Oh, Ramsey's harmless," Jane said, tilting her head in the very-not-harmless Ramsey's direction.

"I'm gonna have to side with you on this one, Mal," Ramsey agreed. "Nowhere near harmless. But really, think about it, okay? 'Cause I think, and so would you, if you really considered it, you *actually* should be reading something into it." He shot Jane another wink and then turned and sauntered off.

"What was that about?" Jane asked as Mal unlocked the door to their first floor apartment.

"Don't ask," Mal muttered.

"I saw on my phone alerts you guys won." She gave him a look. "Started a bit slow, though."

"Don't ask about the first period," Mal muttered.

"Why? What happened?" Jane frowned, setting her book bag on the couch. "Are you alright?"

"I'm fine," Mal said, even though he wasn't sure that was actually true anymore.

He felt . . . discombobulated.

By what Ramsey had said? By what *he'd* said to Elliott working so well the guy had gone on a tear at the end of the game?

He didn't want to be tied to Elliott this way. It made him uncomfortable. And the more he looked at it, the more Ramsey and even Jane pushed him to look at it, the more uncomfortable he was with it.

"I'm not sure you are," Jane said, tucking her knees underneath her on the couch. "You want to talk about it?"

"Not yet," Mal said. He needed to understand it better himself, first.

CHAPTER 5

AFTER SUNDAY'S GAME—A FRUSTRATINGLY close one-zero loss—Elliott finished dressing in the locker room, then looked around for Mal. Assuming they'd walk over to Sammy's together.

But Mal, who Elliott swore he'd only seen a few minutes ago, was gone, the space in front of his spotless locker empty.

"He took off already," Brody said when he saw Elliott looking around in confusion. "Said he'd meet you there."

"Ugh," Elliott groaned. "Why can't he be normal?"

Brody grinned at him. "Who's even normal, anyway? Besides, normal is overrated, Ell. You know that."

"Yeah, but I didn't think he was so eager to avoid me he'd ditch me to walk there *alone*," Elliott grumbled.

"His dad called and I think he wanted to call him back," Finn offered from the other side of the locker room.

"Oh, alright," Elliott said. Of course Malcolm had a father. He hadn't sprung to life, fully formed, explicitly designed to torment Elliott.

He'd just never heard Malcolm say anything about his dad before, not the way all the rest of them offhandedly mentioned their families in the middle of practices and workouts and crammed together in booths at Jimmy's.

But then Mal was more serious, and a lot more focused than most of them, too, so maybe that made sense.

He pulled his phone out of his pocket and texted the sister chat on his way to the little tucked away sub and smoothie shop.

Going to my second tutoring appointment, he sent.

The sister chat was practically never quiet. The moment anyone popped up in it, it was like the freaking bat-signal for the rest of them to appear.

Like it was freaking magic.

Nina texted: **You're going to pass that test, Ell. I've got faith in you.**

Macey chimed in next, as always, true to her middle-child self. **God, Nina, you sound like a Tony Robbins seminar.**

But she did love Elliott, and clearly, despite her comment to Nina, agreed with her, because the next text she sent read: **But you DO have this, Ell.** Accompanied by that gif meme of the kid in the audience pointing and shouting, "You can do it!"

Elliott chuckled under his breath. He hearted Macey's gif work, then coming in last was his youngest sister, Constance.

You still being tutored by the super hot guy? You'd enjoy that.

He and Connie were the closest, and she'd told him more than once, swearing him to secrecy, that she sometimes felt closer to him than to their two older sisters.

Connie—don't encourage him. That was predictably from Nina, but to Elliott's surprise, Macey hearted that comment.

It wasn't often the two of them actually agreed on anything.

A second later Connie sent a text just to him. **Don't listen to them. He's super hot. You can get him, I know you can!**

Elliott laughed again. He loved his sisters so goddamn much. Even when they, in their collective, tried to mom him.

Aren't you supposed to be encouraging me to pass my stats test?

Ah, you got that, we both know you do. Especially with Malcolm on the case. But the real question is if you're ever going to get into his pants?

Ramsey thinks I should seduce him.

Well, by all means, listen to Ramsey.

I'm going to tell Nina you were being a bad influence again.

Ugh. You're the worst, baby bro.

You love me!

Constance sent him a whole string of different colored hearts, and he glanced up from his phone to pull the door to Sammy's open.

Immediately he spotted the back of Mal's head, curls damp from the shower, in the far corner.

He'd dump his bag off, then order, but as he approached, something in the way Mal spoke brought him up short.

"Yes, sir, of course sir," Mal said and in the season and a half they'd played together, Elliott had *never* heard that particular deferential tone from the guy. Not even to their coaches, and of all the guys on the team, he was probably the most respectful when it came down to it.

But this wasn't just respect. It was something more than that.

Something deeper.

Almost something...well, Elliott would've called it fearful, but he'd never seen Mal afraid of anything.

"Yes. I'm taking care of it."

Elliott watched as the back of Mal's neck tensed at the reply.

"I apologize. I . . .I *am* tired. It was a long game. We—" He hesitated. Had the person he was talking to interrupted him? Elliott didn't generally feel protective, and he'd never imagined that the person he'd begin with would be Malcolm, but he didn't like any of this.

"Yes, well, it was a tough game. Lots of shots on goal, but no luck."

Elliott knew he should make himself known. He should tap Mal on the shoulder and let him know he was here. Or drop off his bag, unobtrusively but obviously enough, and go order. Stop listening in to at least Mal's side of the conversation.

But he couldn't quite make his feet move.

Instead, he stayed put and listened to Mal continue to apologize without actually saying the words, *I'm sorry.*

"He always has a lot of shots." Mal paused. "I'm okay with the number I have. It's a good supportive line. A team. His style isn't always mine, but that's okay." He paused a second time. "No, it really is okay."

Elliott realized that Mal was talking about *him.* He knew out of everyone on their line, he had the most shots on goal this season, but then Malcolm wasn't that far behind. While he liked his approach—it worked for *him,* and that was all that mattered—there was something to be said for Mal's more deliberate, studied approach too.

Mal was a *great* hockey player, and it seemed like he was also apologizing for maybe not being great enough.

Maybe if they'd been friends, Elliott would've sidled up to the table, snatched the phone, and told the person on the other side of the line just how full of bullshit they were.

But he and Mal weren't friends.

On top of that, there was something in the way Mal spoke to this person—so fucking carefully—that made Elliott hesitate.

Made him not want to dig Mal further into this hole.

Even if it was a hole that Elliott didn't quite recognize.

Mal went so long without replying that for a minute, Elliott wondered if maybe he'd ended the conversation. But then Mal said, "No, sir. I know my grades are important. I'd never prioritize hockey over them. I know—"

His neck tensed again. "I know," he continued again, in a voice that sounded forcibly relaxed, "I understand that to you it's a game, but I know I can make it my career."

There was another short pause, and then Mal said, "Bye, Dad," and Elliott nearly fell right over.

Sure, Finn had said Malcolm's dad had called and that's why he'd ducked out early. But Elliott had never imagined that the person he'd been talking to—the person who'd undeniably been lecturing him, riding him, and ultimately giving *Malcolm* hell—was his *dad*.

They all knew Finn's father kind of sucked. Not specifically. Specifically, he was a kind, generous guy. Tough, but decent. Finn's struggles didn't originate with the way his dad treated him, but the way the world treated *him* because of who his dad was.

Malcolm's dad seemed like a whole different story.

Elliott shifted his weight, watching as Malcolm set his phone down on the tabletop and he reached behind, using his fingers to work out the tenseness in his neck.

He *knew* he should go over there. Stop staring. Stop theorizing. Stop wondering if that might be why Mal was the way he was—because he'd been *built* that way.

Battered into acquiescence against a set of inexorable expectations.

Elliott resolved to be nicer. Somehow. Without losing his edge. Without sacrificing anything.

He turned and walked back to the front counter, eyed the guy who was behind it.

"Hey," Elliott asked, "did the guy over that way order yet?"

The guy looked bored, but glanced over in the direction Elliott was pointing. He shook his head.

"Okay, good." Elliott proceeded to order a giant Italian sub and two smoothies. The peanut butter banana for him and the strawberry pineapple for Mal. He knew he liked sweet things and whenever they got shakes at Jimmy's, he *always* got strawberry.

This time when he approached the table, he didn't walk quietly, but advertised his entrance loudly. Grumbling under his breath and sliding into the other side of the booth in a pile of flailing limbs, tossing his backpack next to him on the bench seat.

Mal's eyes were shadowed, but a moment later, the pain was gone, smoothed over like he'd never felt it.

For a split second Elliott almost resented the knowledge he'd just inadvertently come by. He didn't really want to feel sorry for Malcolm. It felt uncomfortable.

It would've been so much easier to just keep lusting after and bickering with the guy.

But now, Elliott already knew nothing would be that simple or easy again.

"Hey," Elliott said. "I ordered for us. Italian sub. Strawberry pineapple smoothie for you."

If Mal asked, he was going to say, *did you think I wasn't paying attention?* And he was going to repeat it, if needed, and hopefully make it clear it wasn't just because Mal was really fucking great to look at.

Sure enough.

"How did you—" But then Mal stopped abruptly mid-sentence and took a deep breath. "Thanks," he said, finally, in a much softer tone.

"You took off pretty quick after the game," Elliott said.

He didn't think Mal would tell him anything. After all, he'd never heard Malcolm mention his dad, not once. He was good enough friends with Ivan, and even with Ramsey, that he had a feeling Mal might have confided in them—but nothing in the last year and a half had made Elliott think that they knew anything either.

This was a secret Malcolm held close to his chest, and he wasn't about to confess it to Elliott.

But that didn't mean he wasn't going to try, anyway.

"Yeah, I . . . uh . . . my dad called. I wanted to call him back."

Maybe it was a little wrong, but Elliott pretended ignorance. "Your dad didn't know when your games were? I swear to God, my family knows my schedule better than I do. My three sisters—"

"You have three sisters?" Malcolm interrupted.

"Yep," Elliott said wryly. "Three older sisters. And yes, it's like having four moms, but they're really active on the sister chat during the season. They share livestreams and stats and everything. It's great."

"Ah," Mal said noncommittally, and Elliott realized a second too late that maybe he shouldn't have shared too freely—he'd hoped that by sharing he might get Mal to reciprocate a bit, but instead Mal seemed to have shut down. Maybe because his dad was not nearly as invested in Evergreens hockey as his sisters were.

"Does your dad ever come to games?"

"No," Mal said, with no additional explanation. It was clear he didn't want to be asked any more questions about his father. Which, of course, only made Elliott want to ask them *more*. But before he continued to push, he remembered Ramsey's advice. *Get him to want you.* It also went along with . . .*make him want to tell you.* Elliott resolved to try that, instead. Not being pushy. But by being open.

"How did you know I wanted the strawberry pineapple smoothie?" Mal asked, and it was such a blatant attempt to change the subject Elliott almost wanted to call him on it, but that wouldn't serve his goal, so he let it go.

Let Mal take the win.

"Whenever we go to Jimmy's, you *always* get the strawberry milkshake. Even when Ramsey gives you shit."

"I don't care what Ramsey thinks of my preferences," Mal said stiffly.

"That's what you're going to focus on?" Elliott teased, leaning more across the table. Mal tensed, but didn't move back. "Not me memorizing your food orders like a creep?"

"You said it, not me," Mal said dryly. "Now that we've established that, pull out your book. There's a list of calculations in the back I want you to do while we wait for food. Page 357."

Elliott wrestled his statistics book out of his backpack, flipped to the page Mal noted, and then took the notebook he slid across the table.

A few minutes later, his name echoed through the little sub shop, and Elliott glanced up, ready to go grab their food, but Mal just shook his head. "I got it," he said, sliding out of the booth.

A few moments later, he was back, his big hands juggling two big smoothie cups and the gigantic sub, wrapped in Sammy's striped green and white paper.

"Peanut butter banana," Mal said, setting his cup in front of Elliott.

"Now who's the creeper?" Elliott joked.

Mal rolled his eyes. "I knew you got me the strawberry," he said, tilting his cup towards Elliott. "Now, how's it going?"

This time it was him who leaned forwards, his dark hair falling over his forehead as he frowned, squinting at what Elliott had scribbled down on the notebook page.

Elliott watched him as he gazed down at the page, that same pulse-fluttering, cock-twitching attraction unfolding inside him.

You could do it. You could make him want you.

"Pretty good, I think," Elliott said. "But this one, I wasn't sure I understood what they were asking for." He pointed to one of the questions in the textbook. It was the truth—but maybe a few days ago, he'd have pretended that everything was fine. Not wanting to look bad in front of Malcolm.

But Elliott could see now that had just pissed Malcolm off more.

"Here," Mal said, plucking Elliott's pencil from his hand, and leaned in, scratching out the problem a different way. "Does that make more sense?"

There was an apprehension in his blue eyes as he glanced up at Elliott. "Yeah, actually," Elliott said and then smiled. He made it slow and sure and pleased and sure enough, Mal not only looked flustered by it, but leaned back into the booth.

"Come on," he said gruffly. "Let's eat. Then you can do the rest of those."

They split the Italian sub, eating in silence.

Elliott took another risk. "Must kinda suck that your dad doesn't come to games."

"He's too far away." Mal paused. "And too busy."

"Work?"

"Yeah he's . . .well, he's in the military still. Up at Fort Lewis-McChord."

"That's not too far, really. Just outside Seattle, right?"

Mal nodded. Set the remainder of his sandwich down. "He . . .he thinks it's kind of a waste, playing hockey. So I guess even if he isn't too far away, he wouldn't want to come out and see me play."

"He thinks it's a *waste*? Mal, I gotta tell you—next year you'll be in the NHL and I don't think anyone thinks that's a waste."

"That's not a given," Mal said.

"Come on," Elliott said. "You're one of the highest-rated players in Toronto's system. Sure, nothing's a guarantee but you're going to be on their roster after you graduate. They'd be stupid not to move you up."

Mal nodded absently. "Hard to say it's important though, playing games for a living, when the alternative is devoting your life to your country."

Elliott supposed he shouldn't be shocked, not after listening to his half of Malcolm's conversation with his dad earlier. But he was, anyway. "Is that what your dad tells you?"

Mal wouldn't meet his eyes. Picked up his sandwich and finished the rest of it in four or five big bites. "It's fine," he said evasively. "Finish your food. I've got other homework to do tonight, not just help your sorry ass out."

Elliott got it. This was as much as Mal was willing to say—for *now*, anyway.

But he'd said more than he had a feeling anybody else knew.

"Well, that makes sense then."

Mal's brows drew together. "What makes sense?"

"That you want to be in the front office, ultimately. That you're taking all these classes, to make that happen," Elliott said.

You've been told the whole fucking time that just playing isn't good enough, not for a McCoy.

Mal shot him a look, hot around the edges. Elliott wanted to say it didn't singe him, that he didn't want to lean in and feel even more of that heat.

"Or maybe I really want to do that," Malcolm said.

"I think whatever you end up wanting to do, you should do it," Elliott said. "You're definitely fucking capable."

Mal's gaze softened. "What? No lectures about being serious and focusing? No snarky retorts about how fucking boring I am?"

"I mean, you *are.*" Elliott winced. Because it was true. Or sort of true. Elliott couldn't help but wonder what he'd be like, if he did let go, even for a minute. "You could use a little more—or a *lot* more—fun in your life, but as long as you're happy, that's the most important thing."

"Thanks," Mal said sarcastically. "I think there was actually a compliment in there, somewhere."

"Yeah," Elliott said.

"Buying me dinner *and* giving me compliments?" Mal shook his head. "Not sure I know what to do with this new Elliott."

"He's grateful you're bailing his anti-math ass out," Elliott said.

It was a little more than that—but it was that, too.

"Well, finish those problems and then we'll start the next part," Malcolm said.

Before, Elliott might've pushed him more. Might've shot him a bitchy remark. Just because. Or okay, not *just* because. Because he'd enjoyed the way Malcolm's blue eyes flashed, loved the way that for just that second Mal's attention was solely on him.

But it was also on him now. No snarky comments necessary. So now, he just bent down to his work.

Malcolm pulled his laptop out, and for the next few minutes, there was nothing but the scratch of Elliott's pencil against the paper and Mal's rhythmic typing.

But then Mal made a sound under his breath. Then another. When he grunted, Elliott looked up. "Everything okay?"

Mal made a face. "I'm taking this writing class. I thought it would be good to have, for. . .for, well, *later.*"

"For when you take over the NHL with your superior intellect and preparation?" Elliott asked with faux seriousness.

"Something like that," Mal muttered. "But we're working on this paper, and the professor keeps making comments on my first draft. Like . . .*Needs more detail. Needs more personal connection.* And this last one? *I'd like you to work on finding your voice.* I *have* a voice."

Elliott raised an eyebrow. Pleased, despite trying hard not to show it too obviously, that Mal had confided in him *again.* "Do you, though?"

"What do you mean?"

"I mean, what do you normally write? Business papers?"

"Yeah. For economics and math, sometimes. Not a lot of papers. But I *can* write."

"Of course you can. You're Malcolm McCoy. I told you, you can do anything. But writing something like this—what is it, exactly?"

"A narrative experience."

"Exactly. What your prof means is that you need more of *you* in it. The business professors probably told you to leave out everything personal, right?'"

Mal stared at him blankly. "She wants me to get personal?"

"Are you feeling uncomfortable yet?" Elliott teased gently.

Mal made a face. "I don't like this."

"Good writing means you're in sync with your own thoughts and feelings and beliefs. That they shine through every word you write."

"I think I'm fucked then," Mal said, giving a short bark of laughter.

Elliott didn't even think. Just put down his pencil, and before he could reconsider, he got up from his side, and slid onto Mal's side, nudging his hip with his own.

Ignoring the way the sensation raced along his skin.

"What are you doing?" Mal demanded. Putting a hand up so he couldn't see the screen.

"I'm helping you continue your Malcolm McCoy unbroken streak of never giving up, ever," Elliott said. When Mal still didn't move his hand, he nudged him again. "Come on, let me read it."

"What are you, some kind of writing expert now?"

Elliott shrugged. "No. Not an expert. But I *am* a lit major."

Malcolm looked astounded. "You're a lit major? How did I not know this?"

"Because you're not actually a creeper?" *Because you aren't paying close enough attention to me. Unlike how closely I'm studying you.*

"It's not very good. *Clearly.*"

"Well, I'm shit at statistics, so we're even, then."

"It's not the same thing. It doesn't feel . . .statistics aren't *personal.*"

"It felt pretty goddamn personal when Coach B called you and me into his office and asked you to tutor me so I wouldn't fail."

Mal just stared at him. Those blue eyes, so beautiful. So apprehensive.

Elliott wanted to wipe all that away.

"Why are you being so nice to me?"

"Don't you deserve me being nice to you?" Elliott retorted.

"I certainly don't think I deserved you giving me all the shit in the universe," Mal said wryly.

"There you go," Elliott said. He took another risk, reaching out and taking Mal's hand, gently moving it down. "Promise, this is a no-judgment zone."

He didn't usually touch him—Mal probably thought it was because they didn't like each other—but it was for much more complex reasons than that. But here they were, pressed together, hip to hip, shoulder to shoulder, and Mal's callouses were brushing against Elliott's.

Elliott let out a deep breath. Wondering how he could feel something so fucking acutely when it didn't seem to affect Mal at all.

"Fine," Mal said and shook his hand off, finally revealing his screen.

Reaching over him, Elliott hit the up arrow key, scrolling all the way to the top of the document.

Mal had a sparse, efficient style that probably worked great for the business papers he wrote, but was entirely wrong for the narrative style the professor was asking them to emulate.

There was no personality whatsoever in it, and very little detail. But then . . .Elliott wondered if he *knew* Malcolm's personality.

He was quiet, yes, and intensely focused, but once he thought about it, Mal did have a dry sense of humor. He didn't talk a *lot*, but what he said was always funny in that know-it-all, smart-ass kind of way.

It suddenly occurred to Elliott that was maybe why he kept trying to make the guy talk. Because whatever he said was always interesting, and usually funny, too.

"Well, am I hopeless?" Mal asked.

They were still pressed up together. There was potentially room on the other side of Mal that he could've used to give them a little more space, but he hadn't moved into it.

Elliott told his mind—and his cock—not to read too much into that particular situation. But his dick wasn't really paying attention. It was close to the super hot guy whom he'd been fantasizing about forever, and Elliott was grateful he'd changed into his loosest sweatpants after the game.

"No," Elliott said. He leaned back. Enjoying the way Mal's arm, draped over the back of the booth, seemed to frame him.

"Just no? That's really fucking reassuring," Mal retorted.

"*No*, you have a personality and you can show it, in the text here. You just haven't yet."

Elliott pointed to a spot in the narrative, where Mal talked about the first game they played this year. "You don't want to just say here, we won, two to one, and the opponent was the Ducks. That's not the point."

"Okay, what *is* the point?"

He could feel Malcolm tensing now.

"Hey, hey, you're fine," Elliott soothed and gave him a reassuring squeeze on his other arm.

"Maybe I'm annoyed that you're all up in my business," Mal retorted. But there was no heat in his words.

Elliott just chuckled. "Sure. Let me just finish this. So . . .it's the first game of the year. How do you feel?"

The look Malcolm gave him was full of disbelief. "How did I *feel*?"

Elliott nodded.

"Uh . . .I don't know. I guess I was ready to start the season. To get back on the ice."

"*Ready* isn't a feeling, Mal," Elliott reminded him.

"Okay, uh . . .I was excited. A little nervous." Mal shot him a glance. It felt as good as a caress. "I was worried, too. Anxious that maybe we wouldn't gel as a line. But mostly excited. It's a good feeling, like right before you step on the ice for the first game."

"Yeah," Elliott said. "Use *that*. Talk about *that*."

"I know this'll come as a huge surprise, but I don't spend much time focused on my feelings."

Elliott probably could've guessed that, but then, he'd always seemed pretty worked up emotionally about Elliott himself.

Maybe Mal wasn't as immune as he kept pretending.

After all, he preferred to pretend those pesky emotions didn't exist at all.

"Really? *No*," Elliott said, faking a shocked gasp.

Malcolm rolled his eyes, but he was smiling. It was only with the corner of his mouth, but that was enough. Elliott fucking loved it.

"And that," Elliott added, "is more like what you should be including."

"Sarcasm?"

"*Personality*. You have one. That's what your prof was talking about too, with your voice. Those little snarky asides about me? About our team? About how Ramsey doesn't know how to stop smirking at anything that moves? And how Ivan is way too stoic? All of that."

"Ah. Okay." Mal nodded. "I think I understand. That's . . ." He cleared his throat. "I don't normally focus on any of that. I always thought it was extraneous. Unimportant."

"It's the opposite, man," Elliott said, punching him lightly in the arm. "It's what makes life interesting and fascinating and every single day different."

"Oh. Huh. I never thought of it that way." Mal looked genuinely surprised. Maybe not pleased, but contemplative.

That alone—besides the love of reading—was why Elliott loved books. Loved experiencing different perspectives on things. Often they made him see the world differently than he had before.

"You're welcome," Elliott said, patting him one last time and sliding out of the booth. He hadn't wanted to leave, but he also hadn't wanted Mal to tell him to get out. To remove himself from his personal bubble.

Let's share it again, soon, okay?

Mal cleared his throat. "You finish those problems yet?"

"Just about done," Elliott said, flashing him a grin. "Give me five."

Six minutes later, by his watch, he'd passed the notebook across the table to Mal, and as he finished his smoothie, Mal's gaze skimmed over the page.

"These are all right," he said, with an approving nod.

Old Elliott would've taken offense to that. Would've seen that as patronizing approval that he didn't need or want.

But Elliott understood this guy a little better now. It helped to not constantly misunderstand him or interpret everything he said and did in the worst possible light.

"Awesome. You fix your essay yet?"

"Working on it," Malcolm said. Hesitated. "I'm only asking this because . . .well, I don't know why I'm asking it, really." Suddenly, he seemed more flustered than Elliott had ever seen him before. "Okay. No. That's not true. I know why I'm asking. Because I don't get B's, and this professor has made it clear this isn't A work. Would you . . .*could* you . . ."

Elliott grinned. "Yes, Malcolm, I'll look over your paper for you after you finish editing it."

"Thanks," Mal said. He was flushed now, and *God*, it was an attractive look on him.

"See, that wasn't so hard, was it?" But Elliott had known it was. Maybe not for anyone else, but for Malcolm.

No doubt his dad had instilled this idea that accepting help made you weak, or whatever bullshit they were cloaking toxic masculinity in these days.

Mal rolled his eyes, but before he ducked his head down, Elliott swore he got a flash of a smile.

They hadn't agreed to spend the rest of the evening studying together, but Sammy's was open until midnight, and it was warm and comfortable, and apparently neither of them wanted to move.

Okay, *Elliott* hadn't intended to leave, not until he got kicked out, but to his surprise, Malcolm made no move to pack up and go, even after he clearly moved on to the next item on his to do list, pulling out a thick workbook that proclaimed on the front it was about creating business plans.

Elliott wanted to tease him about it, but he didn't want to remind Mal that he was still *voluntarily* spending time with him, either.

Elliott did his new problems for statistics and felt like *yes*, it was getting slightly more comprehensible, then pulled a much smaller book out of his bag.

That was when Mal looked up. "*Wuthering Heights?*" he asked.

"Don't tell me you've not heard of Emily Brontë," Elliott said with faux seriousness.

"It does ring a bell," Mal said. He waved at Elliott's book. "Is that for a class? Or just because you like reading?"

"Can't it be both?" Elliott wondered.

"I . . .uh, I *guess* so." Mal rubbed his neck.

"In this case, for a class. Nineteenth century lit."

"That sounds . . ."

Elliott grinned. "Like you'd hate it?"

Malcolm actually laughed, and Elliott was reminded, sharply, of why he'd wanted him the first time he'd ever seen him.

Reminded of when he'd looked in Mal's face and felt something inside of him that he'd never felt, before or since.

"Yeah," Mal mumbled.

Elliott opened his book back up and used it to hide his own smile.

Forty-five minutes later, Elliott looked up from Cathy and Heathcliff's epic bullshit to see Malcolm packing up his stuff.

"I gotta take off," Mal said.

"Alright." Elliott stretched, and on a whim, decided to go too. Yes, it was almost definitely drizzling and cold and he *could* stay here for another few hours, but he realized he didn't want to. Especially not if it meant he could spend another minute or two in Malcolm's company.

He tucked his book into his bag and slid out of the booth, following Mal as he headed towards the door.

"You're coming too?" Mal looked surprised.

"Might as well. Can read in my bed just as well as I can read here. It's warmer there, too."

Mal pushed open the door. Muttered, under his breath, "Thought you'd have other things to do in bed."

Elliott could believe all of Mal's affronted outrage at the guys he slept with. What he *couldn't* believe was the undeniable thread of bitter envy in his tone.

He'd *tried*. Okay. Admittedly, only the once, seriously, but still.

"Believe me," Elliott said slowly, "the only thing that's sharing my bed tonight is *Wuthering Heights*."

"Not that I care," Mal said quickly.

But it was clear that he *might*.

Elliott didn't know what to do—but with Ramsey's advice echoing in his head, he knew the one thing he *couldn't* do.

Be an asshole. Rub Mal's face in it. Be a dick, generally or specifically.

"'Course not," Elliott said mildly. "Hey, thanks for the tutoring."

"When's your next class?" Malcolm said, shoving his hands into the pockets of his hoody.

"Tomorrow."

"Let me know at practice how it goes, okay?"

Elliott nodded. Took a chance. "Hey, I really appreciate it, again." And then before he could even brace himself for rejection, wrapped his arms around Mal, pulling him into a quick, tight hug.

He hugged his other teammates all the time. But not Malcolm.

Malcolm froze. And for a second—the longest second in eternity—Elliott just enjoyed the feel of Mal's big, warm, firm body pressed against his own.

Tried, but not very hard, not to think about how it would feel without any clothing between them.

Mal's arms didn't return the hug but he also didn't shove Elliott, which he would one hundred percent take as a win.

Take the win, Ramsey's voice echoed in his head, and Elliott let go.

"What was that for?"

Mal's face was full of shock—and astonishment too.

And Elliott knew he'd done the right thing.

"It was a thank you and hey, great hang out—" Elliott paused because Mal made a disgruntled face at *hang out.* "Okay, *study session.* Not a hang out, we *studied.* It was a good study session."

Mal nodded once, sharply.

"And also, 'cause that's how friends say goodbye," Elliott said gently, and before Malcolm could tell him they had never been friends and never would be, he turned and walked away.

Didn't look back even though he felt the pull of Mal's gaze on him every step of the way.

CHAPTER 6

"GOD, I NEED THIS coffee," Ivan groaned as he opened the door of the Koffee Klatch.

It was busy this morning, half a dozen students and staff in line.

"Why?" Elliott asked, not mentioning that this would be his third cup of the morning. Why? Because he'd stupidly lain awake in bed for hours, trying unsuccessfully to sleep. Trying unsuccessfully to not think about Malcolm.

The way he'd felt against him.

The way he'd smiled.

The shadows in his gorgeous blue eyes.

How he and Mal had only needed a slight shift to turn their endless bickering into something like flirtation.

Connie would tell him he was in deep.

Macey and Nina would tell him he was barking up the wrong tree.

What would Ivan say?

Elliott didn't know and he wasn't about to find out, because he wasn't going to be the one to tell him.

"Martina and I were up half the night working on this stupid joint project," Ivan said, rolling his eyes. Martina was Ivan's girlfriend of a few years, and it had only taken one meeting for Elliott to know, without question, that someday she'd govern a small country with an iron fist but so competently that the whole population would probably love her.

Kind of like Ivan did.

"Hey, you wanted to be a poli-sci major. That's practically declaring you *like* group projects," Elliott joked.

Ivan elbowed him in the side. "And what does being a lit major mean? That you enjoy being a lone wolf?"

Elliott grinned. "Oh, you know it."

"Explains why you and Mal can't get along for five seconds," Ivan muttered. "I'm surrounded by fucking lone wolves."

Elliott wanted to say they weren't that bad, but they could be—and he knew that Ivan also took the brunt of that.

"Aw, I'm sorry, sweetheart," Elliott crooned, slinging an arm around Ivan's shoulders, tugging him close. "We'll try to get along better."

Ivan shot him a skeptical glance. "Since when?"

"Since now?"

"I've got a better chance of not needing any more caffeine today," Ivan said bluntly.

"He *is* tutoring me, and we haven't destroyed a building yet."

"Did you finish *Anna Karenina*?" Ivan asked, changing the subject because clearly Ivan didn't feel the same about the subject as Elliott did. The way he and Mal interacted was all Elliott could think about. All he *wanted* to think about.

"I'm still working my way through it. It'll be a good contrast for this paper I'm working on," Elliott said. "I'm also reading *Wuthering Heights*."

"That's not Russian," Ivan said, brows drawing together, face disgruntled.

"A plus observation," Elliott teased.

Ivan elbowed him again.

"I'm working on a thesis they both take different angles to the romance, but ultimately they show it as doomed. We could even say they're warnings," Elliott said.

"I bet you'd agree," Ivan said. "Don't you think romance is shit?"

"Hey, just because I don't bother to stick to one guy—"

One of Ivan's eyebrows skated upwards. "*One guy.*"

"Okay, just because I don't stick to *any number of guys* doesn't mean I think love is automatically shit. I just . . .why should I bother with it right now? I'm having too much fun."

"Love can be fun, too," Ivan replied dryly.

"Yeah, you tell yourself that in twenty years when Martina is ruling you *and* a whole other country beneath her boot."

"That could be fun, actually," Ivan said thoughtfully.

Of course he'd think that.

"Anyway, I think it's a good subject and I'm impartial about it. It's not that I believe love is bullshit. Just . . .never needed it *not* to be, before." Elliott shrugged.

"Sure," Ivan said.

Finally, it was their turn at the register, and for a second, as Ivan ordered a triple shot latte, with an obscene number of flavors, Elliott couldn't place the guy taking his order, gaze skimming right around Ivan.

Then he remembered.

Less than a week ago, he'd flirted with the guy, given him his number, and promptly not texted him back when he'd reached out a few days ago.

Whoops.

He'd *meant* to. But then Mal . . .

Well.

Way back last year, he'd sworn to himself that he wouldn't let Malcolm McCoy and his complete disinterest in sharing his bed hamper his ability to share anyone else's and he wasn't about to start now.

Ivan paid, stepped to the side, and Elliott turned on his widest, highest watt grin.

"Hey," Elliott said.

"Hey," the guy said. His nametag read Austin. Which Elliott was forty-seven percent sure he'd remembered. The guy's name had been saved in his phone as "cute coffee guy."

"Imagine seeing you here, again. I must have the best luck in the world."

"Kinda what I thought," Austin said. He didn't need to add, *but then you didn't text me back.*

"Well, seeing you right here, just reminded me I met this really cute guy at Koffee Klatch a few days ago, and I meant to text him back, but I got busy. You know, all that hockey I've been playing." Elliott leaned against the counter and barely refrained from fluttering his eyelashes at the guy.

Austin's slight standoffishness melted right away.

If only Malcolm was this easy.

"Ell," Ivan complained, whacking him in the back. "Stop flirting and start ordering. We have to get to practice soon."

"Yeah, yeah, give me a second." He turned back to Austin. "Cold brew. Room for milk."

"Any sweetener?" Austin grinned. "Or are you sweet enough?"

"Oh, baby, I'm plenty sweet enough."

"Could've guessed that."

Next to him, Ivan made a very obvious vomit noise.

After he paid and Ivan practically dragged him away towards the other end of the front counter, he hissed, "What the fuck are you doing?"

"What does it look like I'm doing? I can draw you a diagram, if you'd like."

"You don't want this guy," Ivan said bluntly. "You didn't even remember his name."

"I . . ." But he couldn't really claim he had, and he didn't want to lie to Ivan. He'd only ever been a great friend and teammate.

"Exactly. You shouldn't lead him on. Not when you're . . ." Ivan cleared his throat.

"Not when I'm *what*." Elliott had a feeling he knew what Ivan was about to say—and why he'd stopped. And Elliott wanted him to fucking *say it*.

"Aw, Ell, you know what's going on with you two. You want Mal to want you, and he doesn't know how to want anybody."

It was exactly what Elliott had hoped—and dreaded—that Ivan would say.

"Maybe," Elliott said lightly, eying Austin over the espresso machine as he helped the next set of customers.

"Ramsey told me he suggested you seduce him—but then you just did *nothing*."

"Why are you listening to Ramsey?"

"As much as I try not to, the guy has a point *and* he has a history of actually knowing something about how to get someone into bed."

Normally, Ivan had a bluntness that Elliott liked. No worries about other shoes dropping, or finding out a secret, insidious truth. Not with Ivan. He didn't even know how to lie.

"And I don't know how to get a guy into bed?"

"These boys that pant after you 'cause you're a cute hockey player, sure. But *Mal*? I don't think you have a clue."

There was that trademark Ivan honesty. It cut, yes, but it also often provided clarity.

Today, it did the latter.

How good had it felt to just sit there and study with the guy? To hug him?

And Malcolm had liked it too. Elliott knew he had.

Don't just tell him you want him. Make him want you.

The other barista called Ivan's name and he picked up his gross marshmallow-salted caramel-pumpkin spice monstrosity.

"I don't know how you drink that," Elliott said, watching as Ivan guzzled it.

"It's nice and sweet," Ivan claimed.

"*Too* sweet, probably," Elliott said.

What *would* it look like if he tried to seduce Malcolm? If he really, *really* tried? If he touched him more and more like he had last night? If he kept gently invading Mal's personal bubble. Until he liked it.

Until he *admitted* to liking it?

If it happened, Elliott wouldn't even look twice at the Austins of the world.

"You're right," Elliott said, interrupting Ivan's long diatribe on sweet coffee drinks.

"You mean you're *finally* going to stop drinking that abominable stuff that'd strip the paint off my car?" Ivan asked. "Or—" He paused, looking closer at Elliott's face. "Oh, you mean, about Mal. Well, of course I'm right. Or maybe Ramsey's right, really."

"Well, definitely don't tell him that," Elliott said.

"So you're—"

"Don't say it," Elliott interrupted.

"Why the hell not?"

"Plausible deniability?" Elliott tapped his fingers on the counter. Then picked up his cold brew when the barista slid it over to him. He walked over to the condiments station, topped it off with some skim milk. Closed the lid and shook it, gently. "Also, 'cause I'm kind of terrified it's not gonna work out again and I . . ."

Ivan put a hand on his shoulder. "It's gonna be okay. Whatever happens. Nobody ever died because of blue balls."

Elliott laughed. "That's 'cause you don't get any."

"You don't think Martina busts my balls?"

"I *know* she does." Elliott pushed open the door and they stepped outside. "You just like it."

"True," Ivan admitted wryly.

They had about an hour before practice started, but they headed towards the athletic complex anyway. There was some thin sunshine attempting to break through the thick clouds covering campus, and Elliott tilted his head back towards the sky. Wanting to soak in what little of it there was.

"You're gonna text that guy, then, and tell him it's off?"

Elliott took a long sip of his coffee. "Yeah. I think so. I . . .you're right about that, too. It wouldn't be fair. Maybe I'll tell him it could happen later, I just have to see how this thing goes, first."

"Mal's not going to be an easy nut to crack," Ivan warned.

Like Elliott needed to be told that Malcolm McCoy would be difficult to seduce.

Ha.

There was a reason he'd considered this route before and to use Ramsey's terminology, *chickened out.* Why he was still considering calling it all off now.

But then as they turned towards the rink, there was Mal's distinctive head, ahead of them, his dark curls, a hair too long, blowing in the breeze, and his head was tilted back too, just as Elliott's had been, only a moment before.

Elliott swallowed hard.

He'd been chasing this high since last year. But only Mal made him feel it.

"No," Elliott agreed, "he won't be easy. But that doesn't mean he's not worth the effort."

Ivan made a satisfied noise, and Elliott looked over to see him smiling encouragingly. "There you are, that's the Elliott I know," he said, patting him on the back.

"Should you be so excited that I'm going for our liney's dick?"

"You've been going for his dick since the moment you showed up on campus. Now you're just finally going about it in a way that means it might actually happen. So yeah. I'm thinking it's for the best. This is good. A good day."

It *was* a good day, Elliott agreed as he finished his coffee.

They caught up to Mal as he headed towards the players' entrance.

Mal turned as he heard them, and their gazes met.

That heat he was too familiar with bloomed inside him. Normally he'd say something cutting. Or explicitly designed so Mal wouldn't dismiss him. Wouldn't look away.

But Mal wasn't looking away now.

"Ivan. Elliott. Good to see you." His voice was as serious as ever. But even as they walked into the facility he hadn't taken his eyes off Elliott.

"Malcolm," Elliott said, and if he stepped a little too close to him and felt Mal stiffen in response when they walked through the doorway, then that wasn't a bad thing, either.

Usually Mal ignored him until he didn't have a choice—at least until Elliott *made* him pay attention to him, typically by saying or doing something that would ensure all his attention was focused where it belonged: on him.

But today, he actually turned to Elliott and as they walked into the locker room, said, "Hey, how was your statistics class today?"

He was supposed to ask. But Elliott didn't bother to tamp down the thrill that all that serious intent was focused on him.

It turned out that was even better than having the bright, burning spotlight of Mal's frustration and annoyance blinding him.

"Good. I think I followed the lecture a bit better. There's a quiz next class."

Mal nodded gravely. "We'll make sure you're ready for it. I know the goal is the big test, but it doesn't hurt to ace these, too."

"Sounds like a very Mal thing to say," Elliott teased, but gently. Easily.

And for once, Mal didn't take offense.

He smiled.

He goddamned *smiled*.

"Hey, acing things isn't a bad thing," Mal said.

Elliott nodded. "If it's statistics, I'll take it. How's the paper coming?"

Frustration burned in his blue eyes. "I don't think it's very good. Or that I'm very good at this."

"Must feel weird to not be brilliant at something." Elliott stopped in front of his locker.

Mal's was two down.

Someone, probably someone very intelligent, had put Brody between them. Likely with the hope that they wouldn't destroy their easygoing teammate just to get at each other.

"Not weird, but . . .worrisome," Mal said, and to Elliott's continued astonishment, he didn't immediately head to his own locker.

"You'll get there," Elliott promised.

"Right." Mal shifted from one foot to the other, and Elliott realized this was one of a very limited list of times he'd ever seen the guy look uneasy. Unsure. "You wanna study tomorrow night?"

"We can do a tutoring session, yeah," Elliott said. Even if he had to rearrange his schedule, he'd make it happen.

"Ah yeah, yes," Malcolm said, nodding, as he turned away.

And Elliott wondered if that hadn't been what he'd actually meant at all.

Maybe he'd enjoyed last night, too.

Mal was sure that the pleasant after-effects of yesterday evening—how much he'd actually shockingly enjoyed just studying with someone, with *Elliott*—would fade, especially during practice.

Because practice was generally where the two of them sniped at each other the most.

Mal took practice seriously. Elliott did not. He didn't put his full effort into drills. Goofed off and spent more time laughing with Ramsey and Ivan and Finn than he did focusing on how they could make their line even better.

It drove Mal nuts, and now he was beginning to wonder if he'd done that on purpose.

Because it was similar today, Elliott a shade slower than he was during a game as they skated through the first set of back and forth drills, but it didn't feel insolent, like a slap in the face, like it always had.

It was still a little grating, and Mal didn't *like* it, because he'd never approached anything he didn't commit a full effort to, but he was beginning to understand that when it came down to it, when it *really* mattered, he could trust Elliott to bring it.

Or at least that was what he told himself.

He took a break, grabbing his Gatorade from the wall, squirting it into his mouth.

Ivan skated over, sending up a shower of ice as he came to a sharp stop next to him. "You seem marginally less pissed off than normal," he observed. "You finally getting used to the kid?"

"He's *nineteen*," Malcolm said, even though just a few weeks ago, he'd probably have made a similar comment—and in a far more disparaging way.

"You tryin' to convince yourself he's all grown up, now?" Ivan joked.

Mal rolled his eyes. "No."

But Ivan was observant and unflinchingly honest, and probably more than a little right.

Because, yeah, Mal couldn't forget how he'd felt against him in the booth yesterday. He'd certainly felt like a man. Firm and confident and reassuring. And that was just his attitude.

There was his body . . .

No. You are not going there.

It had been easier—not *easy*, but *easier*—to inform his cock they were ignoring how goddamn attractive Elliott was when he was driving Mal nuts. When he was an insolent puppy, practically begging to be collared.

Now, *well.*

He was having a little more trouble.

Even right now, in the middle of a practice, on the ice, a place where Mal's focus was usually tight, his cock was half-hard, throbbing as Elliott glanced at him, his bright green eyes skimming over his figure. That look was usually an annoyance. Now it was just arousing.

"Yeah, you can't stand him *at all*," Ivan muttered dryly and patted him on the shoulder pad before skating away.

"Everything all good?" Zach skated in and stopped, leaning over the boards.

"Yeah," Malcolm said. Because what else was he supposed to say? *Elliott's driving me crazy. And not in the usual way.*

"You wanna run some more shot drills?" Zach asked. "Or will that just—"

He knew what Zach was going to say. *Will that just put Elliott and you at each other's throats again?*

"No, we're good," Mal said before Zach could ask the question.

"You know, I kinda think you are," Zach said, a thread of disbelief in his voice. "The tutoring must be going well, then."

"Ah, yeah."

"Well, I'm happy to be wrong."

Mal looked over at the assistant coach, who just shrugged with a wry smile on his face. "I told Coach you two weren't going to be able to work it out. That putting you together more was only a recipe for disaster."

"It's not—" Mal paused. "We're *not* that bad."

"Of course not." Zach clapped his hands and called out, organizing the next set of drills.

Over in the goal, Finn made a face, obvious even behind his helmet.

"I'm assuming you don't want me to take it easy on him," Mal said under his breath referring to their starting goalie and his occasional crises of confidence.

Mal understood better than anyone how much impact a father could have on a son. But then Finn's dad wasn't inflexible and cold like Malcolm's was. He was just famous. More than famous, really. Every time he showed up on campus, he was surrounded by kids, excited to see one of the most famous hockey players of the twentieth century on their campus. And every time he showed up, it felt like Finn shrank more into himself.

"No," Zach said.

Mal nodded once. Set down his Gatorade and picked up his stick. "Alright, then."

Ivan passed him the puck, and he skated down to the other end of the ice.

Mal felt the world around him fold inward as he pulled his focus even tighter.

He could feel Brody next to him, his stick flicking out, trying to steal the puck, but Mal had the best technique on the team—earned through hours of hard practice—and Brody almost never managed to grab it from him.

He didn't now, either.

Down the ice, Mal eyed Finn, who was stock-still, waiting on how Mal might give his next move away so he could adjust accordingly.

He'd practiced these moves a hundred times. A thousand, probably. Even with Finn seeing them a lot over the last year, he could probably still fool him. But instead of pulling out one of them, Mal loosened his focus and let instinct take him.

Took a hard right instead, looping around and then behind the goal, wind whistling past his ears as he picked up speed, Brody behind him swearing as he tried to keep up.

Finn was half a second late, and Mal flicked the puck into the corner right before Finn's stick came down, blocking the way in.

"Goddamn it," Finn cried out, whacking his stick on the ice in frustration.

Mal skated over to the boards and watched as Elliott took the next run. He was sharp, maybe sharper than he ever was at practice—but then Mal knew how good his moves had been, and Elliott never met a challenge he didn't want to exceed.

Ramsey was fast on the ice—but Elliott was faster. He was the fastest, quickest skater on the team, a few inches shorter than Mal himself, a lean machine of efficiency.

He shot across the rink with a determined effort, nearly leaving Ramsey in the dust, and then changed direction twice, effortlessly, when Ramsey actually managed to catch up to him.

"Fuck you!" Ramsey yelled as Elliott pulled a flashy little backwards move, flicking the puck between Ramsey's legs.

He was a great defender. Mal had honed his skills on Ramsey's own, but Elliott had a new speed, a new inventiveness today, and then to Mal's surprise, he approached the goal much as Mal often did. Mal recognized that pattern and was almost pissed that Elliott was skating it better than he did.

But he didn't take the shot when Mal usually did, waiting a second, then another, longer, stretching it out until almost the last moment, before flicking the puck up and in, just above Finn's right shoulder.

A second later, Elliott skated to a stop right next to Mal. He was breathing hard, and Mal wanted to pretend he wasn't affected by the warm body next to him.

But he was.

"Great shot," he said, before Elliott could ruin the moment.

Because he would. Right?

"Really was," Elliott said. "You should try that next time."

"Holding a second longer? It's not my norm—"

"God forbid," Elliott said, but he was chuckling.

"But it's a good idea."

Elliott flashed him a grin, full of heat, and it blasted right through Mal.

Shit.

Patting him on the arm, Elliott gave him one last lingering look and took off.

They went through the drill two more times. Once more with Finn. Then with the backup goalie, Nick.

Mal was feeling good, focused tight, right in the zone, as they walked off the ice. Didn't realize anything was really wrong, until he'd nearly got his gear stripped off.

Then he realized one of his straps had twisted when he'd put it on earlier and the hard knot had rubbed him, leaving a bright red mark.

Or he *assumed* it was bright red, because it was just out of sight, between his hip and his torso, nearly on the top curve of his ass.

He rubbed it absently as he showered and realized he must still be rubbing it when he tugged his underwear on after.

It was annoyingly right on the line, and as he sat down, pulling his socks on, the elastic waistband rubbed it wrong.

He must've made a face, and well, he wasn't all that surprised that Elliott was watching, because he asked in a low voice, "You alright there, man?"

"Uh, yeah. Just a spot that chafed, that's all."

But before he could stop him—tell him again it was nothing—Elliott was skirting around Brody, who was very clearly trying to look elsewhere, and he was kneeling down close. Checking it out. If he shifted his gaze, he'd get an eyeful of Mal's cock. Covered, yes, but perking up, thinking that maybe this might *finally* be the time that someone other than Mal touched it.

No. No. No.

Then Elliott's fingertips grazed the spot. Mal nearly gasped, and not because it hurt. "You nearly broke the skin," Elliott said softly. "You should get it patched up."

"I . . .uh . . .it's no big deal," he said.

"But it could be," Elliott said. There was his touch again, soft and careful, right along the waistband of his briefs.

Mal couldn't help his sharp intake of breath.

"Could be a real problem, since it's right here. Could irritate it all the time. Could get infected, even," Elliott said.

It would be so easy to just tell him, *yeah, I'll go see the trainers. Get it taken care of.*

But he didn't.

Later, he wouldn't know if he'd said otherwise on purpose, because if he did, he *knew* what would happen. But if he didn't know for sure, it was only because he wouldn't let himself ponder the question.

"It's fine. No big deal," he repeated.

And on cue, Elliott reached out and took his arm and tugged him towards the training rooms. Didn't call for one of the guys who took such good care of them. Instead, he gestured towards an empty bench and went over to one of the sets of drawers, full of medical supplies.

He hadn't had time to put more than underwear on, either, and his boxer briefs were tight, a bright green, and hugged his hips and his ass like . . .

Mal swallowed hard.

Always, before this, he'd look away. Not let himself look his fill.

Because it felt wrong, but also because it felt like playing with fire.

If you're not going to touch, you shouldn't look.

And he'd never had any intention of touching.

That certainty was fading by the second.

Not when Elliott raised up on his toes, stretching out that long, lean form as he searched for one last thing. His skin was milky white and strong, muscle bunching underneath it. It looked soft. *You want to touch it. Touch him. All over.*

A creaking noise surprised Mal, and he realized he'd fisted the edge of the bench and it was protesting at the strength of his grip.

"Here we go," Elliott said, turning around finally. His gaze was full of concern. Soft with it, but there was that same challenging spark of heat, too.

The one that Mal always saw when he looked at him.

He'd always told himself he didn't like it. That he didn't want to be challenged.

But maybe he did.

"Turn a bit," Elliott said, and just as Mal complied, he reached out and tugged down the waistband of Mal's underwear.

Not all the way. But nearly enough.

Mal yelped in surprise.

"Sorry," Elliott said, but the corner of his mouth was upturned, and he didn't look sorry at all.

Then he was crowding in close, ointment on his fingers that he soothed over the spot in question. He was practically between Mal's legs, Mal's gaze glued to the top of his head.

His hair was brown. Or else Mal had always thought it was. But it was more than brown too, with hints of red and blond running through it. Elliott kept it cropped pretty close, but there was enough of it that he could easily reach out and tangle his fingers in it . . .

No. No. No, you won't.

The bench creaked again.

"Sorry," Elliott repeated. "Trying to be gentle."

Like Mal was actually losing his mind over *pain*.

Well, it did fucking hurt. If Elliott looked down, he'd get a full view of how much unrequited pain Malcolm was in. All that arousal, going nowhere.

Elliott was actually pretty good at this. Finished putting on the ointment and then stuck a thin pad against it. Expertly tore off a piece of tape with his teeth and then secured the bandage with it.

"There," Elliott said, taking a step back, "that's better." He reached down and tugged the waistband carefully over the spot, eyes never leaving Mal's.

And they twinkled, practically, with mischief and care and something else.

Mal knew he was trembling. So horny that if Elliott touched him one more time, he might not be responsible for what happened next.

Elliott's gaze finally drifted down, not to his cock but to his lips.

It would be easy, Mal told himself. *You could just give in. Lean in. Find out why all these boys pant after him.*

Except that Malcolm had never, ever wanted to be one in a long line of suckers.

He'd pathetically hoped, a very long time ago, that he might be special. He hadn't been. Learned the hard way that maybe he wouldn't be.

But then, if he really believed that was true, why hadn't he ever broken this standoff with his body?

Mal didn't know.

"You good?" Elliott asked, tongue flicking out and wetting his lips. They were moist, now. They looked as soft as the rest of him.

"Uh . . ." Mal didn't know how to speak. Heard the roughness in his throat. Tried to clear it. Once. Twice. "I'm good."

The moment dragged on. Mal wondered why Elliott didn't just lean in and take. He wanted to. At least Mal *wanted* him to want to, and he never really had before.

That's a lie. Lie to him, but not to yourself.

But Elliott didn't. He was still right in Mal's space, definitely in his bubble, but he didn't move a fraction of an inch closer.

"Thanks," Mal finally got out. Knowing he should be appreciative. But not sure for what anymore.

"'Course," Elliott said. "Anytime."

There was a knowing edge to the word, *anytime*.

Like all Mal would have to do was say the word, and Elliott would do something—hopefully a *lot* of things—about that heat between them.

Mal would just have to be the one to say.

And he couldn't say.

The words felt trapped inside him, under too many layers of ice, painstakingly and achingly created over the years.

At first the wall had been on purpose. Now it didn't feel purposeful so much as a force of habit that he didn't know how to break.

"I . . .uh . . .better get going," Mal said, even though deep down, he didn't want to go *anywhere*. Maybe he and Elliott could exist just like this, their skin not touching but close enough that it *could*. Elliott swaying closer, his hair damp and curling at the temples, his green eyes bright and knowing when they gazed up into his own.

Maybe Elliott felt the same, because he didn't move. Not right away.

He'd fought the compulsion for what felt like forever, and he gave up when Elliott finally took a single step back.

Let his gaze sweep down Elliott's torso. The lightly muscled shoulders, his pecs with their pale pink nipples, and then lower, appreciating the taut stomach and abs and finally following the trail of light brown hair down to his waistband.

His skin didn't just feel warm now, but burning.

Then his gaze snagged on the bloom of a dark gray and purple bruise curving around towards his back.

Without thinking, Mal touched it gently, four fingertips pressing against his skin. And it was soft. His cock throbbed with that knowledge.

"Are *you* okay?" he asked softly. "This looks rough."

"It's . . ." Elliott's voice was rough and hushed. "It's fine. Really. Uh . . .from a few days ago."

Mal forced himself to stop touching him. Especially when he was determined not to do anything about it—there was that long-standing habit he didn't know how to break.

But even if he didn't intend to break it, he *could* help Elliott the same way he'd helped him. The bruise was in a weird spot. It must hurt. Mal knew, because Mal had had plenty of bruises in that vicinity over the years.

"I can help," Mal said, and only then did Elliott take another few steps back, allowing Mal to slide off the bench. He knew what he wanted, rummaging through the drawers of supplies until he found what he was looking for.

"This'll help with some of the pain."

Elliott gave a short incredulous bark of laughter. "That's not . . .uh . . .well, not what hurts."

Mal didn't ask what hurt. Didn't need to look down again, either, to know that Elliott was probably sporting a hard-on in his briefs. Same as Mal's.

You know what that means. What it should mean.

But Mal pushed the voice aside, and squeezing numbing ointment onto his fingers, reached over and began to carefully massage it into Elliott's multi-colored skin.

"That should feel better," Mal said with an approving nod.

He grabbed an antiseptic wipe and made sure to clean off his fingertips. He didn't want them going numb, too. He wanted to feel that satin smooth brush of Elliott's skin under them forever.

"Yeah." Elliott nodded.

"You know Brody's thinking about going to med school?" Mal said, because he needed to say *something* to break this nearly unbearable tension and maybe a mention of their teammate might distract him enough that he'd go soft-ish before they headed back into the locker room.

They'd been here long enough the locker room had likely emptied out by now.

"Yeah," Elliott said.

"Guess we're gonna give him a run for his money."

Elliott chuckled under his breath. "Guess so."

Mal tossed the wipe in the trash. Had felt his blood clear enough now that he could look at Elliott without being certain he was about point two seconds away from losing all semblance of control.

Elliott trailed him out of the treatment room. "We still on for tomorrow?"

"Yeah," Mal said, nodding. "You want the library or Sammy's again?"

"I really love those smoothies," Elliott joked.

"Sammy's it is." Normally, Mal would never study so casually but last time had gone so well maybe there was something to be said for it.

Or maybe it had nothing to do with Sammy's at all.

Mal told himself he was *not* looking, but he couldn't help it when the first thing Elliott did when he got back was to his locker was pull his phone out.

"What are you doing?"

"Oh, just forgot to send a text before practice. So sending it now," Elliott said, flashing him a bright smile.

"Oh." Mal wanted to ask who it was to, but that was absolutely none of his business and it would've been completely out of character for him to wonder—and to *care.*

Elliott looked up from the screen. He looked regretful. About the text he was sending? God, Mal hoped so. "Does it ever suck being so honest?"

Mal didn't know how completely honest he was being.

After all, he'd been pretending, nearly from the beginning, that Elliott didn't entice him.

"Yeah, sometimes," Malcolm admitted.

"Ugh," Elliott said, letting out a groan as he finished dressing. He glanced over at the phone again, like he was worried about the response he was going to get.

"But," Mal added, "I've never regretted it, in the end."

"Right. *Right.*" Elliott gave him another one of those smiles that lit him up inside.

Malcolm grabbed his bag. "See you tomorrow," he said. He could wait another minute for Elliott. He could tell he was nearly ready to go, and then they could walk out together and. . .well, and do *what?*

Malcolm didn't know.

Which was why he escaped.

Or at least, as he walked home, that was what he told himself he'd done.

Escaped with his mind and body completely intact.

CHAPTER 7

ELLIOTT MOSTLY LIKED SCHOOL. That was a fact that would probably shock the hell out of Mal if he ever admitted to it, but once he'd started to get the required classes out of the way, the subjects he wasn't personally interested in, he'd really started to enjoy it. Especially his literature classes.

Unfortunately this class was not his literature class.

It was statistics, which, even with Mal's tutoring, was something he was never going to be good at and definitely never going to like.

Dr. Prosser went on to the next slide, explaining in detail how to solve the problem in a slow monotone that more often than not made Elliott want to fall asleep.

Still, he'd been astonished, that first test, at the F scrawled across the top.

Math wasn't his strong suit, but he'd also never sucked at it. And despite the fact that nobody assumed student-athletes would carry their weight in class, Elliott *mostly* tried to stay up on his homework and reading.

Sure, he prioritized the stuff he enjoyed, like reading for one of his lit classes, but he did keep up with stats—and hadn't understood how he could be flunking.

He wasn't the best at math, but Elliott had still expected better.

The two times he'd shown up for Dr. Prosser's office hours, to ask how he could improve his grades before Coach B had intervened, she'd been unavailable and the second time she'd claimed she had to step out for a last-minute errand. She'd promised to email him, but hadn't.

Elliott was pretty sure she just had a problem with athletes. But then, if that was why, shouldn't Malcolm have done worse in her class?

Of course, Malcolm was Malcolm.

Elliott shifted in his seat and tried to pay attention.

AKA tried not to think about Mal.

But it was harder even than normal because Malcolm and statistics had gotten tangled together in his head, and it felt like he couldn't untangle them even if he'd wanted to.

Dr. Prosser continued droning about standard deviation and the more complicated forms of calculating it, and what different real-world applications they could have.

The only real-world applications Elliott had for statistics were for how they were calculated when he was in the pros, hockey becoming his primary career. But then, he hedged, that was probably why so many professors hated athletes. They weren't even willing to pretend interest. Or that this wasn't a massive waste of their time.

Elliott surreptitiously pulled his phone out of his pocket. Typed out a quick message.

This class would be a lot more fun if we could calculate everything with hockey stats.

Elliott didn't expect Mal to respond right away—or frankly, at all.

Unlike the rest of the guys on the team, Mal took school incredibly seriously. Probably because he'd long declared that instead of pro hockey being the end result, it was only a stepping stone for him. Mal wanted to end up managing an NHL team. Making all the personnel and player decisions.

Making his club—and himself—a hell of a lot of money, probably.

Did Elliott think it was a fucking waste, with how well Mal played?

Hell yes.

But that decision wasn't up to him.

To Elliott's surprise, his phone buzzed.

Are you texting? During class?

Elliott rolled his eyes.

Yes, Dad. You caught me.

He was sure that would be it—Mal was painfully uptight about this kind of thing. Frankly, about a *lot* of things.

But, a response appeared on his screen a moment later.

If I was your father, I'd definitely let you know how inappropriate I found it.

Of course he would. This was standard Malcolm McCoy behavior. But there was something more to it, too. Almost a hint of flirtation, buried underneath all that proper, icy behavior. And Elliott had never been good at leaving well enough alone.

You gonna spank me, then?

Elliott entertained himself by imagining the disgusted and pissed off expression on Mal's face as he read it. Because there was no way Mal would reply to that. As soon as Elliott got flirty, he always disengaged, growing even chillier than normal.

But shocking him again, another text came in.

No, Mal texted, **you'd probably enjoy that too much.**

And well, *sue him*, he probably would.

I like you thinking about my kinks, Elliott texted back.

And even though Mal didn't reply to *that* text, Elliott was still grinning as he slipped the phone back into his pocket and tried to drag his attention to what mattered right now: Dr. Prosser's slides, and *not* Mal's assessment of his sexual preferences.

Twenty minutes later, Dr. Prosser distributed their graded quizzes as class drew to an end, and Elliott stared down at the paper on the desk with incredulity.

A C? He'd missed four questions?

That couldn't possibly be. He'd understood the material. Been *doubly* sure that he'd understood the material since he and Mal had gone over it carefully. Had he miscalculated something? He didn't think so. But nothing else made sense.

He flipped the test to the back but there were no comments, even though by glancing around him, he could see that she'd scribbled plenty of notes on his classmates' quizzes.

Elliott rose slowly and made his way over to where Dr. Prosser was packing up her laptop.

"Hey, Dr. Prosser?" Elliott asked, as politely as he could, even with the panic streaking through him. He couldn't keep getting C's. He needed B's—preferably A's, in fact—if he wanted to stay on the hockey team.

She glanced up at him, looking even more frazzled than usual. It was funny, her lecture-mode was so different than non-lecture mode.

"Oh yes, hello," she said.

"I was wondering about my quiz," Elliott said, extending it in her direction. "I was pretty sure I got all of these right."

"Well, obviously not?" She shoved her unruly hair behind her ears and looked everywhere but at him. "I'm not sure how much more help I can be."

That was ridiculous, because she'd been no help at all. Brushing him off every time he tried to talk to her before or after class, and then there were the two times he'd attempted to go to her office hours.

Including the email she'd promised that she'd never sent.

"Do you have any suggestions?"

"Read through the material carefully. Study." She shrugged helplessly.

"I have been, though," Elliott said, trying to keep his frustration tamped down. "I even got a tutor. I tried to go to your office hours, but you weren't there."

"I've been—I have a sick relative," she finally said. But that was all. She seemed uninterested, or actually more like *distracted*, and just brushed him off with a wave of her hand and a, "I'm sorry but I have to go. Email me if you have any more questions."

It seemed transparent what the issue was. She *didn't* like athletes, and she thought he was just blowing this whole class off. But he *wasn't*. He'd studied for this quiz. He and Mal both. Mal had even told him he was ready.

But *ready* was not a C. Elliott didn't need to be Malcolm to know that much.

"Alright," Elliott said, not wanting to push too hard. Frankly, he'd never had to beg a professor like this, and maybe she was right. Maybe he just needed to dedicate himself harder to studying.

Well, next time he and Malcolm met up, he'd insist Mal go over every answer he'd gotten wrong, and they'd figure out how he'd miscalculated so drastically she hadn't been able to give him any points.

He was just walking out of the classroom building when he felt his phone vibrate in his pocket.

It was another message from Mal.

What? Your kinks don't include me kicking your ass on the ice? See you tonight at practice.

Elliott grinned, his mood already better.

Ivan had told him he couldn't die from blue balls, but Elliott was beginning to question that particular proclamation.

He shifted uncomfortably on the weight bench. Telling himself that he was *not* going to look over at where Malcolm was lifting with Ramsey and Ivan.

"If you look over there one more time, you're going to get a freaking neck cramp," Finn said.

"I—" Elliott broke off the claim that he wasn't, because he *clearly* was.

"Exactly. You gettin' anywhere?"

Elliott wasn't about to kiss and tell. Even though there hadn't been *any* kissing, unfortunately. "Don't know what you mean," he said.

"Yeah, you do," Finn said with another knowing glance in Mal's direction. "You two finally stop bickering—and you stop pulling his pigtails, trying to get his attention—something's going down."

"Maybe we decided to be adults," Elliott claimed.

"Maybe you finally figured out why you kept egging each other on," Finn muttered under his breath.

"We give each other an edge."

"Believe me. I'm familiar." Finn's voice was wry. And yeah, he probably hadn't enjoyed yesterday's drill, but Elliott knew it was good for him. It was better to give up goals now, in practice, than it was to do it in a game.

"You're welcome," Elliott said, but he kept his tone kind. Understanding.

He liked Finn and he knew how much the guy struggled.

Every goal an opposing team scored on him churned him up.

"Just don't lose that edge, when you two finally fuck," Finn said and shot Elliott another knowing look as he turned away to head to another machine.

Elliott did another set of reps, his biceps burning.

But not as bad as his balls ached. Elliott didn't know what satisfaction was anymore. He'd texted Austin from Koffee Klatch that he was "involved" with someone else and he was going to see where it went.

Even though "involved" was probably a vast exaggeration.

It felt like he and Mal had barely stopped barking at each other at every available opportunity. But then, there'd been yesterday after practice, when Mal had been hard and ready in his boxer briefs, undeniable heat in his eyes as he'd stared at Elliott.

So he wanted him, too.

It had taken everything inside Elliott to not just lean in and *take*.

But he was beginning to understand what Ramsey had meant about not just telling Mal he wanted him—but making *Mal* want *him*.

If he wanted to melt all the ice around him, he was going to need to find a new reservoir of patience. Wait Mal out, until Mal decided that what he wanted—what he *needed*—was Elliott.

And until then, his balls were going to ache.

Touching himself wasn't going to work.

And he certainly wasn't going to blow it by letting some other guy take the edge off.

No. He was determined now to see this through to the end.

Whatever *the end* turned out to be.

After their workout, he showered and changed and was waiting under the athletic complex overhang, the rain drizzling from the sky in big, slow drops as the sun finished going down.

Well, if he'd been able to see the sun, anyway.

A second later, Malcolm came out.

"Hey," Elliott said, pulling up his hood. Mal did the same, nodding at him, and they headed off in the direction of Sammy's.

"How did the quiz go?" Mal asked as Elliott pulled the door open.

Elliott grimaced. "Not as good as I'd hoped. I got a C."

"But not bad," Mal said, with unexpected diplomacy.

"What?" Elliott joked, as they approached the counter. "Aren't you supposed to pin me to the wall over anything less than an A?"

Mal's gaze swung his way, unexpected heat burning his blue eyes. "What?" he barked.

Elliott's mind rewound and he laughed weakly, even though his double-speak was not very funny. Not funny at all, really, not unless it actually happened for real.

If Mal really pinned him to the wall and kissed him, lips trailing down his neck, hips working hard and relentless against his own . . .

"Uh, joke?" Elliott claimed, shrugging. He'd needed to make the joke to deflect from feeling the way he did about his quiz grade.

Mal rolled his eyes, but when he reached for his wallet in the back pocket of his sweats, Elliott swore his fingers were trembling.

"It's on me," he said, as he paid. "You got it the last time."

"Aw, you're a sweet date," Elliott teased.

And sure enough, he got another one of those looks, full of heat and longing and terror, before something slammed down in Mal's eyes and he went stern, again.

The problem with that was that the sternness, which *had* been a total buzz killer before, was now kind of a turn-on.

When even Mal's annoying habits work you up, you're fucked.

"It's not a date," Mal said, brows drawing together.

Elliott nudged him with his elbow. "Just breathe, Mal. It's not a ring or an invite to my bed."

"It's a study session," Mal said, and yeah, he definitely looked a bit agitated.

"Yep, it sure is," Elliott agreed, nodding. If the word date sent him into a meltdown, then he just wouldn't use it. After all, it really *wasn't* a date, anyway.

"I don't know why you even need to go there," Mal said.

"To *tease* you," Elliott said with exasperation. *To flirt with you.*

Malcolm looked surprised. Astonished, really. "Is that why you do it?"

"*Yes.*" Elliott nudged him again. Before a few weeks ago, he'd gone out of his way to avoid touching Malcolm off the ice. Now, he felt like an addict who couldn't wait to get another hit.

"Well. That . . ." Mal cleared his throat. "That explains some things."

"It's just fun, though I know how you feel about that particular three letter word."

As they settled down in the same booth they'd occupied a few nights ago, the corner of Mal's mouth tilted up, almost into a smile. "That's the same thing, yeah? You're teasing me."

"Finally, you're catching on," Elliott said, pulling out the quiz, sliding it across the tabletop. "You wanna nail me against the wall now or later?"

Malcolm rolled his eyes. "You're ridiculous. But. . .yeah, let's go over this."

Elliott was beginning to learn that when Mal wanted to focus—or when he felt like he *should* focus—there was no dissuading him. No distracting him.

Now was one of those times. Elliott could tell now when that switch flipped. He watched as Mal impatiently pushed his hair back as he leaned over the table, eyes skimming over the paper.

Honestly, he was glad for it. With Dr. Prosser apparently abandoning him because she just didn't expect any better from a hockey player, he only had Mal left to save him from this particular disaster.

"Do you see here?" Mal said, pulling a pencil out of his backpack and pointing to the paper. Elliott craned his neck to read partially upside down.

"No?"

"Ugh, just a sec," Mal said, and then suddenly he was sliding out of the booth, one big hip pushing Elliott over on his side.

It was a lot to suddenly have *his* bubble invaded by Malcolm McCoy.

He'd done it *to* him, sure. But he'd anticipated doing it. Braced for it.

This time, he hadn't been ready.

Mal was big and warm and so fucking close, gazing over at him with those soulful blue eyes. "Do you see it now?"

Ugh, no. But you sure fucking feel *it.*

Elliott forced himself to look down on the paper and focus on something else besides his dick throbbing in his pants. "I . . .uh . . ."

"Ell," Mal said, and he actually sounded amused now. "Are you even trying?"

Normally that question might feel like an accusation falling from Mal's mouth, but now when Elliott looked up, he realized that Malcolm was actually fucking *smiling*.

"That's not fair," Elliott muttered.

"Was it fair when *you* did it to *me*?"

"No. Yes. Maybe." Elliott laughed then.

"Okay, seriously. Focus. At least look at the paper."

But Elliott didn't want to. He wanted to stay pressed up against Mal. Wanted to keep basking in the banked fire in his eyes.

Still, he made himself focus. If he didn't, he was afraid that all this might end, abruptly, and he wouldn't know what to do with himself. Looked at the quiz, and as Mal explained, Elliott began to think something wasn't quite right.

Was it easy with no blood in his brain? No, it was not. But he did it anyway.

"That's how I did it," he said.

"What do you mean?" Mal looked as confused as Elliott felt.

"I mean . . . I *did* it that way. Exactly the way you explained."

Mal pursed his lips. "Then how do you explain this?" He tapped his pencil where Elliott's answer was listed there, in typed black and white.

"I don't know," Elliott admitted.

"Well . . . let's go over the rest of these," Mal said.

They did, and out of the three questions he'd missed, only one of them felt legitimate.

"I can't explain this." Mal hesitated. "Is there any chance you have dyslexia?"

Elliott shook his head.

"I didn't think so," Mal said. "You're such a big reader. I would say there's something weird going on, but Dr. Prosser seemed fair enough when I took the class two years ago."

"Well, I guess I'll just have to do better next time." It was hard not to feel frustrated. Frankly, a little desperate—and not just to get into Mal's pants.

"It seems like you did just fine this time," Mal said, to Elliott's surprise. And then even more, he was rewarded with grudging admiration blooming across Mal's face.

"But I got these wrong—"

"You won't. Not again," Mal said firmly. "You actually did a pretty good job."

"High praise coming from you." Elliott took a risk and teased. Not just to get a rise out of Mal, but to make himself feel better. And he was rewarded again, this time with an actual goddamn smile.

"This is a tough section."

"I can't let it get the best of me," Elliott said with determination.

Mal actually reached out and touched him, patting him encouragingly on the back. "You're doing good, Ell."

"Ell, huh?" He risked another little flirtation.

Kept waiting for Malcolm to freeze up again, but he wasn't.

If Ramsey in fact ended up being right about this whole goddamn thing, then he was never going to let Elliott live it down.

Elliott was never going to let *himself* live it down. Imagine if he'd used this approach from day one? He and Mal could've been hot and heavy *this whole fucking time.*

Because he already knew when he got Malcolm in his bed, he wasn't going to be quick to let him back out again.

"It's your name, isn't it?" Mal slid out of the booth and returned to his side.

Elliott didn't bother to hide his disappointment.

"But you never call me that. I'm surprised you didn't use my full name, all those times you yelled at me."

"You mean all the times you deserved me yelling at you?" Mal raised an eyebrow.

"Well, maybe a little."

"I might've. If I'd known your full name."

Elliott leaned over the table. "Elliott Archer Jones." Then he flashed his best smile. A year ago, six months ago, even a few weeks ago, it hadn't worked. It had only ever put Mal's back up. But today, it felt like Malcolm just *melted* with it.

Well. Goddamn.

"Archer, huh?"

"It's an old family name, and since I was the only boy, I ended up with it. Mom likes to joke that they kept going until they got one. Good thing I wasn't a girl, huh?" Elliott fluttered his eyelashes in a purposefully exaggerated movement.

Stuff like this used to only piss Malcolm off. But today, he seemed softer. More reachable.

Mal chuckled dryly. "Why is that?"

"Well, *duh*, 'cause then you wouldn't be attracted to me."

That got him another eye roll, but Elliott was pleased that Mal didn't immediately protest or deny it completely.

Instead, he changed the subject.

"Well, next time I'll be sure to deploy the *whole name*," Mal said. "Do you want to start the session now or wait for food?" He paused. "Or you could start my paper?"

"You finished it?" Elliott couldn't deny he was eager to cross the seduction finish line, which was looking more and more probable—but he was also excited to read Mal's essay. Something that might give him more than the stingy little bits of himself that Mal was willing to dole out.

Mal nodded. "This draft anyway. I'm sure you'll have a lot to say."

"Maybe."

"I emailed it to you right before our afternoon workout," Mal said.

Pulling out his laptop from his bag, Elliott found it in his email and with his heart beating a little faster in anticipation, began to read.

Was aware that with each paragraph he consumed, the more agitated Mal seemed to become.

Not to anyone else, probably.

But Elliott had made a study of Malcolm's behavior over the years. Even though he'd pulled out that same workbook he'd been scribbling in the other night, he wasn't writing quickly, decisively. And every few seconds, he shifted uncomfortably on the seat, changing positions half a dozen times in only the time it took Elliott to read a few sentences.

"You alright over there?" Elliott didn't look up from the screen. "That chafed spot still bugging you?"

"That—" Mal stopped. "No. No. It's fine. The . . .uh . . .nursing you did with it was satisfactory."

"That's me, Nurse Ell. Happy to tend to whatever ails you," he said lightly.

Finally let his eyes drift up, meet Mal's. Watched as his eyes darkened. Like he was thinking of Elliott tending to a *very specific* ailment.

He was thinking it. Elliott *knew* he was thinking it. That they were both freaking thinking it. But why didn't he give in? Why didn't he say, *screw this study session, let's just screw?* Or whatever that was in Malcolm McCoy language.

But Mal didn't say anything. Instead, he looked back down, at his workbook.

Well.

Elliott's cock throbbed and he had a feeling his balls were about to do the impossible and grow even *bluer.*

CHAPTER 8

MALCOLM TOLD HIMSELF IT was that they were studying at
Sammy's.

That he was distracted, and in unusual-to-him circumstances.

That he was worried about what Elliott really thought of his
essay, though it hadn't seemed like the guy was holding back
when he'd gushed about how improved it was. If Elliott had
only given positive feedback, he'd probably have been even more
suspicious but he'd even given some very reasonable options for
improvement.

Malcolm *should* be feeling good. He was full of his favorite
smoothie—strawberry pineapple—and half an Italian sub, and
Elliott was mostly behaving.

But his focus had seemingly deserted him.

He felt unmoored from the regular concrete reality that he
depended on.

Instead, his mind wandered. And it kept wandering right
into Elliott Archer Jones' pants.

Malcolm didn't know if he could even blame Elliott for it,
either. Sure, he was doing his normal flirtatious routine, with

the little offhand comments and the long, soulful looks, but the truth was, none of that made Mal's heart race the way it was racing now.

It was stupid things that shouldn't matter. Like just now, how Mal's brain had completely deserted its focus on this chapter on negotiation and was instead mesmerized by the way Elliott's hair shone under the fluorescent lights.

The way it stood up, a little, curling at the ends, when he ran his hands through it.

It'd look even better if you ran your *hands through it.*

His brain had apparently completely gone on hiatus, because no matter how many times Mal tried to drag it back to the safe zone, it continued to sneak out. To betray him.

To say nothing of his body.

He still felt the way he'd pressed up against Elliott in the tight booth. How Elliott hadn't tilted himself away, but had leaned in closer.

Come even closer still.

"You're awfully fidgety today," Elliott said, shooting him a knowing look.

They'd finished their statistics tutoring, and after Mal had nearly told him that he had to go. Where? He hadn't had anywhere else to be. But somewhere else had to be better than sitting here and undergoing this minute-by-minute torture.

Maybe he'd thought Elliott was attractive before now. That he could be attracted to him.

Now, it felt like his whole body was attuned to his, vibrating on the same goddamn frequency, and he didn't know how to get it to stop.

Yes, you do.

"I'm . . ." Mal didn't know how to explain without confessing everything. "I'm just . . .uh . . ."

Elliott raised an eyebrow, his stare keen. Mal felt like it saw *everything*. Saw through all his walls. Saw deep down inside where he was a fucking mess.

Deep down inside where he wanted to throw a lifetime of caution to the wind, to ignore everything that had happened in high school, every piece of advice his father had ever given him.

But you won't.

"Just tired," Mal finally finished. "It was a long day. And I . . .uh . . .I should go. Get . . .uh . . .a good night's sleep."

He was so tired of being indecisive. So tired of fighting this. If temptation wasn't currently sitting in front of him, he might be able to focus.

"If you want to, sure," Elliott said, without judgment. But those eyes were still staring at him, like they could interpret every pause, every hesitation. Every stumbled, increasingly inane excuse.

"I . . .yes," Mal said, making himself stick firmly to the last answer. "Yes."

"I'll see you tomorrow, yeah?" Elliott said.

Mal was sure he was going to escape without Elliott's presence pressing itself more indelibly into him, but then he stood just as Mal finished packing up his workbook, and then they were hugging again.

And this time, Mal hugged him back.

Elliott was only an inch or two shorter than him, though he was slighter, and they fit together even better than in those dreams he was still pretending he wasn't having.

Elliott must've agreed, too, because he swayed even closer until they were pressed together and Mal's fingers were cramping from the effort it was taking not to dig in to Elliott's muscles and just *take*.

He was shaking when he pulled away. When he said goodbye.

When he turned away and didn't let himself look back.

It was drizzling and cold outside, but Mal didn't pull his hood up. Instead, hoped the damp chill might extinguish the heat boiling inside him, but it didn't work.

He wanted, with a fierceness he wasn't familiar with and didn't know how to fight, to turn back and tell Elliott, *let's do this. I know you want me, and I. . .I want you too.*

He'd only said that to one other person in his whole life, and it had been an unmitigated disaster. Not through any fault of Mal's, but the ache of it lingered.

Ultimately that wasn't what stopped him though.

It was who had helped bandage over that ache.

He pulled out his phone and dialed his father.

They didn't talk often. Anthony McCoy wasn't one for idle chatter or small talk.

Still, he answered on the third ring.

"Malcolm?"

"Hey, Dad," he said, stopping under a tree, shielding himself from the worst of the drizzle.

"Everything okay?"

His father's concern was not surprising considering that Malcolm didn't call much, especially in the middle of the week, or at night.

"I'm having a problem," Mal said.

"A hockey problem? An injury? Or a school issue? Your grades not up to snuff?"

Like his grades had ever been anything but perfect. Mal had done everything he possibly could to ensure they were.

"No. Nothing like that. An...interpersonal issue," Mal said.

There was silence on the other end of the line. Answering him without saying a word.

Why *had* he called his dad for advice on Elliott? His dad would tell him to just keep white-knuckling it out, but he couldn't. He *couldn't*.

"I...uh...I just can't figure out why someone's acting a certain way towards me." It was not really true. Deep down, Mal knew why. What he didn't understand was why *him*? Why wouldn't Elliott just give up and move on? There was nothing special about Malcolm—or at least, there was nothing special about him that he believed Elliott might actually value.

"Have you asked them?"

Mal nearly laughed. Muffled it just in time. Began to pace back and forth under the tree. "That's a thought."

"If you want to know something, Malcolm, you know you need to ask. To use your words to communicate."

What if I used something else to communicate?

"I know." He paced some more. "But—"

"There are no *buts*. No exceptions. Man up and talk to them."

But Mal didn't want to. He didn't want to address it. He didn't want to shine a spotlight on the elephant in the room. Because if he did, Elliott would invariably want them to do something about it, and *God*, Malcolm didn't know how they could.

Correction. How *he* could.

If he'd called Jane, she'd have told him to man the fuck up, tell Elliott, and let themselves get carried away.

Ironically, even though his father had no idea he was a virgin, his advice was similar.

"Malcolm," his father added sternly, "you don't usually have an issue with shirking away from what needs to be done. Remember you're the man I raised."

Oh, he remembered alright. He couldn't fucking forget, ever.

If he'd ever had a pipe dream of being different, he didn't know *how*.

"So just...just go and ask him."

"Malcolm," his father chided, "that's what I just said. If he's not willing to answer, then he's not worth your time or your energy."

Something in his tone reminded Mal too much of that night.

The night he'd discovered that the guy he'd crushed on so fucking hard, that he'd thought *might* return his feelings, had only been leading him on for a joke.

His father had let him cry for five minutes. No more and no less. And then had set him down and reminded him of the difference between men and boys.

Reminded him of what he was working so hard for. Hockey. A career. Building something he could be proud of.

"People like that aren't anything to be proud of," Anthony had finished dismissively. And maybe he hadn't said *men who like other men aren't anything to be proud of*, but the thought had resonated in Mal's brain anyway.

By the time he'd broken down that assumption, the walls he'd erected were too hard, too impenetrable. And nobody tried.

Nobody until Elliott.

"I can do that," Mal said, even though he didn't know if he could. Not when he wasn't sure what Elliott might say. He might just brush it off, claim that this was just what he did with everyone.

That Mal wasn't special at all.

That the whole thing was one big cosmic joke, yet again.

Oh whoops, didn't mean to lead you on. It's like this with half a dozen guys.

"There you go," his father said. Like they'd solved the whole thing.

After thanking him and saying goodbye, Mal hung up a moment later. Not feeling better about anything. Feeling an inescapable pit of dread. He didn't want to talk about this—and definitely not with Elliott.

But who else could he discuss it with? There was nobody else.

Mal texted him. **You still at Sammy's?**

Elliott responded almost instantly. **No. Why would I stay there without you?**

Mal felt a surge of . . .well, he didn't know *what* it was. Frustration? Anger? Unresolved, boiling hot lust?

Where did you go?

Back at my place. Lewis 468.

Mal was about to put the phone back in his pocket, and despite his anxiety, head right over to Lewis, when a second text from Elliott came through. **You okay?**

Was he okay? He was not fucking okay.

He wanted *answers.*

You want more than answers.

But he tromped over to Lewis anyway, giving himself a pep talk the whole time. At first it had sounded exactly like his father talking to him, but that felt worse, somehow, so he shifted to something like, *He's not going to humiliate you. He's not going to laugh at you. You're going to clear up this misunderstanding and he'll keep his distance from now on, and this . . . weird burning need will eventually fade.*

Mal didn't know if he really believed it was true, but it helped to think it.

He took the stairs instead of the elevator, and when he came to a halt in front of 468, he knocked, feeling breathless.

Elliott opened the door.

He was not wearing a shirt, only the same pair of low-slung forest green sweatpants he'd been in earlier. Gesturing Mal in, Elliott swung the door closed and then leaned against it, arms crossed over his chest.

His muscles were . . . *God,* they were perfect. Slim but chiseled. Perfectly proportionate. He was perfect and gorgeous all over, and Mal swallowed hard.

Objectively, he'd known this was true. Known it was true for awhile.

Now, the truth felt anything but objective. It felt like a hard, hot, inescapable knot in the base of his stomach. Pushing him. Prodding him.

"What's this about?" Elliott asked.

Mal laughed, unamused. "I need to know," he said, dropping his bag on the floor. Shoving his hood back. "I need to know what the fuck you're about."

Elliott didn't react. "What I'm about?" he asked slowly.

"Why you're doing this? Why you're . . .you're in my space and in my mind and making it fucking impossible for me to focus. Why you're . . .stuck in here and I can't get you out? *Why.*"

Mal was pacing again, but he couldn't help it.

Standing still was impossible.

"And," he continued, because he couldn't seem to stop his mouth from moving either, "couldn't you put a goddamn shirt on to answer the door?"

Elliott didn't answer. He just lowered his arms. Stood there, without an ounce of shame and let Mal look, and Mal goddamn *looked.*

"Is this bothering you, Mal?" he asked. It was practically a taunt.

"You *know* it is," Malcolm growled.

"Why is that, do you think?"

"I don't know. That's why I'm asking you," Mal retorted.

Elliott rolled his eyes, but his expression was full of affection. "Mal, you're really a trip."

"I just want to know why. Tell me why. Then it'll stop and we'll just . . ." Mal trailed away, because it hit him just then, sudden and with a nauseating swirl of panic, that he didn't want it to end. He hated feeling this way. But he knew, already, that he'd hate not feeling it more.

"Fuck," Mal swore.

Elliott pushed himself off the door, took a step closer and then another. Mal moved back, trying to avoid Elliott invading his personal space again, but Elliott caught his arm, gently. Gently enough that Mal could've shaken him loose at any point, if he'd wanted to.

And he didn't want that either, it turned out.

"How about this?" Elliott asked intently, his eyes never leaving Mal's. "I'm going to try something and if you hate it, I won't ever do it again, okay?"

Nerves surged inside Mal, and he licked his suddenly dry lips. Nodded.

Elliott tilted his head up and kissed him.

It had been a long time since Mal had kissed anyone. So long. Immediately, he knew, *this is what you wanted.*

This is what you came for.

It was impossible not to be greedy about it, and before Mal knew it, his hands were framing Elliott's face and he was kissing him over and over again, in deep, desperate bites, like he could eat him up.

It didn't matter if he was just a temporary amusement.

It didn't matter if Elliott didn't even mean it. Because *Mal* meant it.

Someone groaned and Mal thought it might've been him—but he wasn't thinking at all. Not anymore. He'd wanted this so desperately, and now that he had it, he only needed more.

More, more, more.

They stumbled backwards, Elliott's back thumping loudly against the door, and then Elliott's leg was wrapping around his, and *oh God*, that was his cock, inescapably hard, against his thigh.

Elliott panted into his mouth, and a hand coasted down his back, the touch practically a caress, and then squeezed his ass, *hard*.

Panic streaked through him and Mal jumped back, breath and hands shaky.

"What are you doing?" he demanded, even though he knew. Even though he didn't want Elliott to say it out loud.

If he did, Mal might lose himself in the desire for it, again.

"You don't know?" Elliott asked slowly. He looked as blown apart as Mal felt. Lips red and wet, hair mussed from Mal's hands, chest heaving.

He looked fucking delectable, and Mal wanted to eat him up.

Even if he didn't know how.

Mal began to pace again. Fear insidiously worming its way through the need pulsing inside him. "I don't do this, I don't know how to do this," he said, not even to Elliott, more to himself.

And then he froze. Realized what he'd said.

Looked up, only to see Elliott frozen, just the same as him.

Shit, shit, *shit*.

"What do you mean by *you don't know how to do this*?" Elliott asked carefully. Mal could hear the complete lack of judgment in his tone, like he'd gone out of his way to filter it out.

"I . . ." Mal didn't think he could say it out loud. If he said it, all that interest and arousal in Elliott would fade, instantly.

He'd sort of intended to *not* tell him, if he was going to do this at all. Muddle through, he supposed. Surely he knew enough to get by.

"Malcolm, you need to tell me."

"I don't do this . . .very often." It wasn't technically a lie.

Elliott frowned. "Not very often or not at all?"

Trust Elliott to cut right through to the right question.

He looked away at the last second. "Not at all," he said quietly. Sure, now, that this whole thing would end before it even started.

There'd been a part of him that thought they could stop at a kiss and that would sate the beast inside him, the beast that Elliott had seemingly woken up, but Malcolm already knew that had been an easy lie he'd told himself to paper over a difficult conundrum.

You're done lying to yourself.

He still couldn't look at Elliott, even as he walked up to him. Put a hand on his chest. Right where his heart was beating too fast. "You're a virgin," Elliott said.

Mal laughed, bitterly. "I'm trying not to say it out loud. Make it worse."

"Worse?" Elliott's hand slid up, and he was holding Mal's chin now, turning it so he couldn't avoid looking him in the eyes anymore. "Why is that worse?"

"It's . . ." God, it was so many things. Embarrassing. Difficult. Too much a part of who he was now to dream about changing it.

"Admittedly I'm trying to figure out how the hell you ended up a virgin at twenty-two, when you look like *this*, when you kiss like *that*, but it's not worse, Mal. It's not a problem."

"It's not?"

"It actually answers some questions I didn't understand that I needed to ask." Elliott chuckled wryly. "Though it does open up a few others, too."

"If this is about your ego again," Mal warned.

"It's not *not* about my ego?" Elliott joked, shooting him one of those smirking smiles that shouldn't have turned him on, but did, anyway.

Malcolm was beginning to figure out why he'd kept his distance from the guy from day one. Had he really been worried about this? Had he, deep down, been afraid that this might happen if he let Elliott get too close?

"What I mean," Elliott continued, "is that *yes*, it makes my ego feel better to think all your rejections were because of this. But it also makes my ego feel better to think you came to *me*."

"I don't know if I came to you," Mal said, trying for bluster.

He didn't know if he was too caught up to do it properly, or if finding out his secret had been the last piece Elliott needed to put together.

Elliott just laughed again and then called his bluff. "Sure then, that kiss meant nothing."

Mal cleared his throat. "Okay, no, it didn't mean *nothing.*"

"So I guess the question is . . .do you *want* to be a virgin? If you do—"

"I don't," Mal said, the words coming out of his mouth before he could consider the implications.

Elliott let out a breath. "Okay. Okay. So we should . . .uh .
. ." Suddenly, he looked as nervous as Mal felt.

Of course Elliott didn't have much experience with virgins. He was *Elliott.*

"We don't have to do this," Malcolm said and leaned down
and picked up his bag. "I just . . .I wanted to know why. And
I guess I've not been struggling on my own. It helps to know
that—"

Elliott leaned in and kissed him again. Kissed the words
right out of his mouth. His lips were lush and determined on
his, and any lust that had been extinguished by the humiliation of admitting the truth to Elliott returned tenfold.

Mal dropped the bag and this time let his hands actually
touch. Let his fingertips drift across all that bare, exposed
skin. As soft as he'd imagined it looked. But tough too, and
strong, and desire roared through him, out of control—if
he'd ever wanted to control it to begin with.

Elliott broke the kiss, breathing hard again. "Jesus, if I'd
known you could kiss like that . . ."

"What do I kiss like?" Malcolm wasn't sure. It had been
so long. Only once since Aubrey. When he'd needed to make
sure, for himself, that Aubrey hadn't been turned off or disgusted by the way they'd kissed.

But once that question had been answered, he'd been done.

Hadn't been tempted, even a little, to do more with the
guy.

"Like you've been thinking about this as much as I have,"
Elliott said. Took a step back. "So are you gonna tell me why?
I feel like before we do this, I should know."

"Why I haven't had sex?" Malcolm hesitated. If confessing the truth had been embarrassing, this was even worse. "There was a guy in high school. I thought he liked me. He said he liked me. We kissed a few times." He rubbed his neck, forcing himself to keep looking into Elliott's green eyes, alive with interest and arousal. "We were going to do more. I agreed to meet him one night, and then I overheard him in the locker room. He was going to stand me up. It was all a big joke."

"Was it?"

It had been almost impossible to confess this thing. The bedrock of so many of Malcolm's best and worst habits. And here Ell was, questioning it.

"Of course it fucking was. He said it was," Mal snapped.

Elliott smiled. "Or else he was just saying that to his friends. High school boys are idiots."

"You're barely *not* a high school boy," Mal said.

"And I can be an idiot, but I'm not going to be an idiot about this. I promise." Elliott reached out, took his hand, uncurled each finger, one at a time, until he released his book bag. It fell to the floor, and Elliott pulled him towards the bed in the corner.

The bed that Mal had known was there, of course, but had refused to acknowledge until this moment.

Elliott gently pushed him against it, the backs of his knees hitting the edge of the mattress, and he went down.

He didn't know whether the heat was lust or embarrassment or anger. Or an intoxicating swirl of all three.

Elliott made him feel all of it. Every single thing, sometimes at the very same time.

"Don't worry," Elliott said. "We'll go slow."

He didn't know what *slow* meant. He half expected Elliott to go to his knees and coax his pants off and then coax his cock into his mouth or his hand, and it would be over very, very quickly after that.

But instead, Elliott slotted himself between Mal's legs and leaned in, kissing him again. His hands curled around Mal's shoulders, digging into the thick cotton of his sweatshirt.

Mal didn't have any of that in the way of touching Elliott. He could explore every inch of his shoulders, every muscle that bunched and then released under all that smooth skin. The way his breath caught when Malcolm's hands curled around his waist, thumbs digging into his abs.

Mal knew he could lose himself in this. It felt so goddamn good to touch someone and let them touch him in return. But at the same time, he knew it wouldn't have been this good with anyone else. Only someone he'd really, really wanted.

Only Elliott.

Elliott wouldn't let him get carried away though. Their kisses were hot, insistent, but they weren't wild like their first one.

He could feel Elliott's cock, hard against him, so he definitely wanted him too, but he was exercising some kind of discipline to not let either of them spiral out of control.

Mal almost wanted to tear his mouth from Elliott's slow, deliberate onslaught, and demand that he *get on with it*. He didn't need romance or nice words or care. He just needed fucking relief.

But when he tried to lean back and pull Elliott with him, Elliott resisted. And he was strong enough to resist.

Another turn-on that Mal hadn't expected.

"Just let me," Elliott murmured into his mouth. "I'm gonna make it good for you."

"Soon maybe?" Mal said, and Elliott chuckled.

"Just enjoy this, alright?"

It *was* hot to sit here and exchange one kiss after another, until their mouths were red and wet and Mal felt like he was drowning in the sensation of Elliott's lips against his, firm and sure.

And increasingly needy.

Because Elliott was still nineteen, and Mal could begin to feel his control slipping. He pulled Mal's sweatshirt off, then his T-shirt and then their skin was touching and Elliott groaned, deep in his throat. His hands digging deep into Mal's hair, tilting his mouth as they devoured each other.

Mal decided enough was enough.

He was a virgin. Not clueless.

And while Elliott was strong, he was *also* strong. Stronger, if he had to guess.

Time to put that to the test.

He gripped Elliott and flipped them, tucking Elliott right underneath him.

Elliott's mouth fell open and Mal was really tempted to just kiss him again.

But he was glad he didn't.

"God, you're so fucking hot," Elliott said, his voice of full of rough awe. His fingers tangled in Mal's hair again, and this time he tugged him down by it.

Mal lost his mind a little after that. His mind and what felt like a lifetime of control. Desperate for pressure and friction against his aching cock, he thrust experimentally against Elliott's, and Elliott gasped into his mouth.

A second later, the kiss went wild and they were moving together like they'd been born to do it. Mal's orgasm was like a freight train, out of control and bearing down. Then Elliott's hands drifted down his back and dug right into his ass, ten specific pressure points pulling him in, and Mal lost it.

He shuddered over and over, his body lost to the pleasure surging through him.

A second later, he could hear Elliott following him. His cry was loud and sharp and disbelieving.

Like he hadn't expected that Mal's orgasm would drag him over his own edge.

But it had.

Mal dropped his head to Elliott's shoulder. Tried to catch his breath.

"That was great," Elliott said, his voice full of sleepy satisfaction. "I think I needed that for about a year."

Mal rolled his eyes and considered rolling onto his back. But he didn't. It felt too good to be lying with Elliott this way. He *liked* touching him, one body stretched out across the other.

"I don't want to think of how long I needed that," Mal said. Then froze. "But—"

Elliott frowned. "Don't tell me you're having second thoughts."

"Not second thoughts. Just . . ." Ugh this was embarrassing too. But he'd just come in his sweatpants, so how could anything really be awkward after that? "Just, does that even count?"

Elliott's laugh was long and lazy. Even a little sweet. He cupped Mal's cheek. "Oh honey, it counts. Congrats, Malcolm McCoy, you're no longer a virgin."

"But I didn't—but *you* didn't—"

"Oh, we can arrange all of those things. Don't you worry about that."

Mal tried to breathe. Tried to ignore that his cock was already twitching again, valiantly trying to get ready to go again at just the thought of *all those things*. "You'd want to?"

Elliott laughed again. "I wanted to the *first time I saw you*. And that never stopped."

"I know you . . .uh . . .well, I didn't think it meant anything. And I was . . ."

"Twisted up? Yeah, I figured that out." Elliott tapped on his back. "Come on, let's get cleaned up."

Mal moved very reluctantly. Sat upright, while Elliott slid out of bed and dropped his sweatpants right there.

"Fuck," Malcolm said, not even bothering to try to hide his reaction to Elliott's sweet bare ass.

Elliott glanced behind him. "Oh, honey, I don't think we're going to get sick of each other anytime soon."

"Don't call me that—I'm not sweet—I'm not—"

"Oh, *honey*, you fucking are," Elliott teased. He tossed his dirty sweatpants into the hamper in the corner and ducked into the attached bathroom, coming back with a damp washcloth. He'd cleaned himself first, semi-soft cock bobbing in a neatly trimmed nest of golden brown hair. Mal looked because Mal was completely incapable of not looking at this point.

And if the guy was going to walk around brazenly naked, then it was almost like he *wanted* Mal to look.

Instead of handing Mal the washcloth, though, Elliott sank to his knees, and *oh*.

He was all business though, tugging down Mal's sweatpants and then his boxer briefs, cleaning him as best he could.

Then he sank back on his heels, totally naked, and gazed up at Mal.

And well, Mal had been horny and unsatisfied for a long, long time. Having the guy he really wanted on his knees, in front of him, was guaranteed to give him a brilliant recovery period.

Could it even be called a recovery period if it felt like he'd never really gotten soft?

He was definitely not soft right now.

"You want some more?" Elliott murmured and leaned in. His fingers were still damp, and so was the sensitive skin of Mal's inner thighs. His touch skimmed up and down them, not minding the dark hair, or the way Mal swore as Elliott's hand wrapped around his cock.

Mal groaned in response.

"You gotta use your words," Elliott reminded him.

"Yes," Mal ground out.

Elliott shot him one of those smirks again. "Good. 'Cause I think you're going to *really* like this."

The moment Elliott's mouth closed around him, Mal nearly shouted, his fingertips digging hard into the mattress.

He'd tried hard not to fantasize about anyone in particular when he got himself off. But this vision in particular felt familiar. New and exhilarating and also exactly what he'd been wanting.

But his brain hadn't been able to even remotely predict how fucking amazing Elliott's mouth felt around his cock.

It was like he knew exactly how to touch him and suck him to maximize it, to make Mal want to scream with how good it was.

And just when it became too much, too intense, he'd tease just a little, backing off until Mal was begging him for more.

"Shit, God, I'm gonna come," Mal cried out. He didn't know what Elliott was even doing, exactly, and that would be a problem he'd deal with in a minute, but right now, it was all heat and pressure, and the pleasure surged through him in a blinding wave.

Elliott didn't pull off, and a moment later, he was coming again, down Elliott's throat, and *God*, that was even hotter.

Elliott kept going until he was almost too sensitive to stand it. Yet, he didn't want to push him off, and he didn't, not until he couldn't take it a moment longer.

"You were right," Mal said, stupidly.

Elliott grinned. "Yeah?"

"I really liked that," Mal said. He was not the kind of guy who used a lot of *reallys* in his speech, but he could add about a hundred more to that sentence and it still wouldn't come close to illustrating just how much he'd enjoyed it.

"Congrats on losing your cherry, again," Elliott said sweetly.

Mal's gaze swept down, and he realized that Elliott had his own hard cock in his hand, stroking himself lightly.

"I want to do that," Mal said. Swallowed hard. "I want to be the one to do that."

"You sure?" Elliott's voice was relaxed, despite the rough edge of desire. Mal knew what he was doing. He was making it easy on him, he could *tell*, but Mal didn't want him to do that. Didn't *need* him to do that.

"Yes," Mal said firmly and reached out, tugging Elliott up.

Elliott straddled him, and Mal put his hand on the first dick of his life that didn't belong to him.

Elliott was smooth and hard, twitching underneath his fingertips.

"You want me to tell you what I like?" Elliott asked, voice hushed. He didn't sound so goddamn calm now, and Mal found that a whole lot more satisfying.

"No," Mal said.

Maybe he'd never done this before. But he was beginning to learn who Elliott was. More than just the front of carefree, fun-loving playboy.

Elliott was a hedonist. He wanted to let the pleasure overwhelm him. Consume him. He threw himself into every single thing he did, sometimes without looking, and often annoying Mal in the process, but Mal couldn't find a single shred of annoyance in himself now.

He moved his fist carefully, deliberately. Squeezing just the way *he* liked. Maximizing the pleasure the best ways he knew how.

Elliott gasped and leaned in, brushing his lips over Mal's, barely touching at first.

Mal took his other hand and shoved it into Elliott's hair, pulling his mouth to his.

Their kiss deepened, tongues stroking together, and Mal—that intense need momentarily assuaged, *finally*—could turn his legendary focus on making this as good as he could for Elliott.

Elliott gasped into his mouth, and Mal lengthened his strokes, slowed down just a fraction, dragging it out of him one heart-stopping moment at a time.

And Malcolm had wanted this. No question of that. He'd had this need stuck under his skin forever, like a splinter he couldn't dig out, but he'd wanted *this* too. To touch someone, to feel their skin and their mouth and to let them close. To *want* them to be close.

He'd hoped it would feel like this, two people folding in together like they fit. Like Elliott had been waiting like this, just for him.

Of course that wasn't even remotely true, and Mal didn't believe in lying to himself, but for this moment, it *felt* that way and he couldn't get enough.

Same as Elliott kept leaning into his touch, gasping as Mal drove him over the edge, come splashing up his chest.

"Fuck," Elliott groaned. "That was so . . ." His eyes, sleepy and satisfied, fluttered open, and Mal realized there was also something to seeing him like this. Something he really liked.

"Yeah?"

"Are you *sure* you were a virgin?" Elliott teased.

"Very sure," Mal said.

He was also very sure that Elliott would slide off his lap, and in that easy, friendly nature of his, ensure that Mal went on his way, no awkwardness whatsoever.

But he didn't. Instead, he leaned in and kissed him again.

Like he couldn't get enough, either.

Mal wasn't going to push him away. He'd done that enough and it hadn't worked any of the times, and besides, he *liked* it.

Wrapping a clean hand around Elliott's back, he tugged him in closer, and they kissed and kissed, like they hadn't just gotten off twice each. Elliott's fingers twisted in his hair, and it was easy and hushed and intimate. The kind of intimate Mal didn't recognize, but enjoyed anyway.

Elliott was the one who finally broke the kiss, pulling back an inch.

But he still didn't act like he wanted to move. A hand slid down to Mal's shoulder. Squeezed. "So much makes sense, now," he murmured.

"Don't say I was uptight because I wasn't getting any," Mal said.

Elliott chuckled. "I wouldn't, ever."

"Of course you wouldn't."

Elliott's smile widened. "I *do* have a question."

Mal had a feeling he knew what was coming.

"Why didn't you just let us do this last year?"

Mal wet his lips. There it was. Maybe after this conversation, Elliott kicking him out of the room would be pretty damn awkward after all. "I didn't know you were serious. We didn't even know each other. I thought...I thought you might be just like Aubrey."

"His name was Aubrey?" Elliott rolled his eyes. "He even sounds like a pretentious dickwad."

Malcolm considered this. Did he even know what a pretentious dickwad was? He supposed that Aubrey would fit the description, based on what he remembered of the guy.

Then he realized that he didn't even really remember the guy. Not details, anyway. Could barely dredge up a vision of him. Instead, his memory felt general, like a black hole of humiliation and rage and rejection. The aftermath—the things his dad had said that he'd taken to heart—those felt specific. Emblazoned on his memory.

Mal could only imagine what Anthony McCoy would say about this thing with Elliott. But he pushed that thought away.

"Yeah, he must have been," Malcolm agreed.

"So you thought I was going to just lead you on? Fuck you and leave you?"

"I didn't even think we'd make it to the fucking."

Elliott's jaw dropped. "Seriously?"

"I was sure once you found out . . .you wouldn't want to anymore."

"Huh. Did I redeem myself in your head, finally?" Elliott was smirking now. It was a little bit *I told you so*, but Mal could tolerate that, especially after the two orgasms Elliott had given him.

Mal nodded.

"Good." Elliott paused, and then to Mal's surprise, that was when he slid off his lap, grabbing the washcloth and cleaning off again, before tossing it to Mal. "Then hopefully we won't have to argue about this."

"Argue about what?" Mal found the one clean corner left and used it to wipe the rest of Elliott's come off him.

"About us doing this again."

Mal swallowed hard. Figured this would be a very good time to start finding his clothes.

Pulled his boxer briefs up. Then his sweatpants.

Reached for his T-shirt, but suddenly Elliott was right there, fingers closing over his wrist. "I mean it," Elliott said.

"You certainly seem to," Mal agreed.

But will you next week when the next cute boy at the Gamma Sigma house propositions you?

Mal had known that if he took this road, it might mean less than he'd hoped it would. That it might only be scratching an itch. But the itch had intensified so much, he hadn't cared.

Then, anyway.

He cared now.

No doubt Elliott would think that the caring was sweet and nice, but in the long run, it wouldn't matter. Not when that cute boy batted his eyelashes.

"Wait a second," Elliott said, frowning. "I *mean* it."

"I know," Malcolm said. Then sighed. "I don't . . ." *I don't want to share.*

"You think I'm going to keep fucking around, on the side."

"It's your right," Malcolm said.

But before he could shuck Elliott's grip and finish getting dressed—finish his escape from this awkwardness—Elliott's mouth was hot and lush against his.

Kissing him hard.

When Elliott pulled back, his eyes were gleaming like hard emeralds, full of determination. "I know my history makes it hard to be convincing," Elliott said, "but I swear, I promise . . ." He broke off, making a frustrated noise. "Here. I've even got proof." He grabbed his phone from the table next to the bed and scrolled through it and finally turned it towards Mal.

"What's this?"

"It's a text. I sent it days ago. To the guy at Koffee Klatch."

And sure enough, there was a message from Elliott to "Cute Coffee Guy" that was nice, undeniably, but blunt, too. **Sorry, it read, but I'm involved with someone else right now and I gotta figure out if it's going anywhere.**

Cute Coffee Guy hadn't replied.

"He left you on read?"

Elliott laughed. "You know what that is?"

"I'm twenty-two, not a hundred and two," Mal said dryly. "And you forget, I've spent four years playing with Ramsey. I was bound to pick up some things by osmosis."

"Fair. And yeah, he did. Can't say I blame him for being annoyed, but it's true." Elliott tossed his phone to the bed. "I'm *very* into someone else right now."

"Me?" Mal could barely get the single word out without stuttering.

Elliott rolled his eyes but he was laughing, too. "Welcome to the party, Malcolm. You were late, but you got here eventually."

It felt too good to be true. But Elliott gave him another one of those lush, wet kisses right before he left, winding his arms around Mal's neck and not letting him go until he'd taken his fill.

Mal nearly took his shoes off and pushed him back onto the bed.

But he didn't.

"Uh, we *should* . . .uh . . ." Mal hesitated.

"Keep this between us? Yeah. Agreed." Elliott shrugged. "I don't think anyone would probably understand. And it's not any of their business, anyway."

Mal nodded once in agreement. And then realized he had no reasons left not to walk out the door.

Truthfully, he wanted to stay. But instead, he left and felt as he walked home that he was floating, feet barely touching the pavement.

CHAPTER 9

ELLIOTT WAS A FREAKING pro.

He could do this.

He could walk into the locker room and get ready for tonight's game without his whole body turning into mush the moment he spotted Malcolm.

You got what you wanted.

Yeah. He had.

But unlike every other time he'd hooked up, it hadn't felt like the end, but instead like the beginning.

Usually when he scratched an itch, it was scratched, and he didn't need to do it again.

But all Elliott had freaking thought about today was doing it again, over and over again, Mal's eyes going blurry and soft as he sent him over the edge.

It was becoming a litany in his mind, an obsession that he wasn't sure how to handle.

Thus, why he was loitering outside the rink, half-hidden as he pretended to be fascinated by something on his phone.

Was it because Malcolm had been, unbelievably, a virgin?

Elliott had had sex with virgins before, but it had never felt like this before. Like the guy had sunk his hooks into him, and Elliott was perfectly, wonderfully happy with that situation.

He'd meant what he'd told Mal in the aftermath, last night. He didn't want anyone else. He couldn't even imagine flirting uselessly with the guy at Koffee Klatch or any one of the many cute boys at the Gamma Sigma house.

But would this fuck with his mind? His focus? His play?

He remembered, too well, what had happened the last time he'd decided to change something between them.

His edge had fucking vanished.

"You okay, Ell?"

He looked up and Ramsey was walking towards him, a frown on his face.

"I . . .uh . . .yeah."

Ramsey didn't look convinced. "Brody mentioned seeing you out here, dawdling. You aren't trying to avoid Mal, are you?"

Elliott winced, internally. "No. No. Not at all." Then winced, in full view of Ramsey, who had a brain like a freaking trap.

Ramsey's gaze narrowed. "That's not convincing, Ell."

"It's fine. It's really fine." *We fucked, and it was glorious. I'm never getting over it. I'm gonna walk into the locker room and he's going to be there, all stern and hot and I'm gonna melt like ice cream on a hot summer day.*

Ramsey shook his head. "I still can't fucking believe you wouldn't take my advice."

Elliott managed to hide his surprise, *barely*. Ramsey hadn't guessed why he was out here. He thought he really *was* avoiding Mal because they were fighting. Not because they were fucking.

"You're not always right about everything."

But, Ramsey *had* been right about this. The high that he'd convinced Malcolm McCoy to come to him, and to *come*—not just once, but *twice*—was never gonna fade. And, unlike what Elliott had always imagined, it wasn't really about ego at all.

It wasn't even about accomplishing something that nobody ever had done before.

It was so much more personal than that.

It was Mal himself. Elliott was beginning to believe *he* was the prize.

Ramsey cackled. "Oh, sweetheart, I'm fucking right about everything."

"Sure," Elliott retorted.

"Well, are you coming or not?"

Elliott nodded. Maybe if he walked in with Ramsey distracting him, he wouldn't look over at Mal and give the whole game away.

He hadn't minded that Mal had wanted to keep this between them. He wasn't even sure what *this* was, anyway. The problem with that hadn't occurred to him until ten minutes ago, when he'd realized the first time he saw Mal, everything he'd thought about all fucking day was going to show, plainly, on his face.

Not just on his face, but on the ice, too.

"You didn't stop by the house yesterday," Ramsey observed as they walked down the corridor towards the locker room.

Elliott shrugged. "Mal wanted to do another tutoring session. I'm not gonna argue with him. The guy is gonna single-handedly make sure I don't fail stats."

"You didn't even want to swing by after?" Ramsey was looking at him closely now—while pretending he wasn't. Elliott had begun to learn some of Ramsey's tricks. Not all of them, but enough to recognize when he was working an angle.

"I was tired." Elliott knew he was a shitty liar. "Mal wore me out." *True in all versions.*

"Ah." There seemed to be a wealth of meaning in that single word, but as Elliott pushed the door to the locker room open, Ramsey didn't say anything else.

And there was Malcolm.

His bare back was to Elliott, that big, broad gorgeous back. He'd touched it all over yesterday. Felt how strong it was. Had discovered how vulnerable Mal was, really.

Then he turned, and Elliott was very proud that he didn't stumble, not once, when their gazes met.

Mal's poker face was brilliant, but then that didn't surprise Elliott particularly. He was beginning to realize just how much of a front Mal showed to the world. And how good he was at getting behind it.

Elliott walked over to his locker and began the long process that he always did before every single game.

Brody wasn't here yet, so there was no obstacle to looking his fill of Mal.

"Hey," Elliott said. Was proud of how steady his voice seemed.

"Cutting it close again?" Mal shot him a look, quick and efficient, but ultimately revealing, as Elliott pulled off his jacket, then his shirt.

"You're not on Ivan's ass, and he's not even here yet," Elliott grumbled. *This is good. Bicker the way you normally do.*

"You don't know that I *won't* be," Mal said self-righteously. Yeah, he'd probably already texted Ivan. Like the overprotective big brother that he was.

How had that energy somehow become really, incredibly hot?

Elliott didn't know. He prayed he'd stay soft and pushed down his pants.

"Had a big win yesterday," Ramsey announced to the locker room at large. "Rented out the arcade tonight."

"First, it's a school night," Mal said. "And second off—"

"Don't say I shouldn't be gambling," Ramsey teased Mal.

"You know you shouldn't be." Mal was so righteous. He practically burned with it. And so did Elliott, for a host of other, far less upstanding, reasons.

"Well, then you're not invited," Ramsey joked, but then his expression softened and he slung an arm around Mal's shoulders. "Come on, McCoy. It'll be fun."

"Fun," Mal grumbled.

"Fun," Ramsey repeated. He exchanged a glance with Elliott. Like he expected him to chime in. And on any other day, he would've.

"I'm busy," Brody said, "but I can stop by for a few."

Elliott was pretty sure Brody was fucking his gargantuan football player roommate, but Brody hadn't told him yet, and he'd been so preoccupied he hadn't been bothering to try to get him to tell him.

But maybe he should, tonight.

"I'm in," Finn said.

"I'd have rented out Darcelle's, if only to see McCoy squirm more, but the kids wouldn't be able to come." Ramsey winked at Elliott and Finn.

Elliott rolled his eyes.

"Like both of them don't drink at Gamma Sigma house," Brody said.

Malcolm made a face.

Elliott decided right now would be a great time to change the subject. "Darcelle's has a drag brunch that's all ages on Sundays."

"Right. We'll have to do that sometime," Ramsey said. "But tonight, we're going to Star Signs."

"I guess I could eke out a few minutes," Mal said, begrudgingly. "If we're all going."

"Such a team player," Ramsey said, smacking him on the shoulder.

When Ramsey finally wandered away, Mal turned to him. "I was uh . . .hoping we might do a tutoring session tonight," he said, rubbing his neck and actually looking ashamed at asking for sex.

Because that was what he was doing. Elliott was certain of it.

"We can still do that. After Star Signs," Elliott said, playing along with Mal's excuse. "You want to come over to mine again?"

"Uh, probably for the best. Jane might be home. She'd be a study distraction."

Elliott chuckled. "Right. We can't have that."

"Then it's settled." Mal nodded once, like he could schedule sex just that easy and Elliott would go along with it.

And you will. You sure as hell will.

Elliott took the ice for the first period determined that he wouldn't let the situation with Mal derail him again. Ruin his edge.

He was going to attack the Cyclones' goal with as much intensity as he would've if he and Mal hadn't had sex last night.

If he still wanted him as bad as he had, pre-sex.

You do. Maybe even more.

"Shit, what's crawled up your ass?" Ivan grumbled midway through the first period as they flopped down to the bench. "Did someone light a fire underneath you?"

"Maybe I want to just put this game away," Elliott said. "We're only up one. Gotta keep getting our shots in."

Mal rolled his eyes. "What, are you trying to set some personal shots on goal record?"

"Yeah," Ivan joked, "'cause it's not like you scored that goal."

Elliott didn't need the reminder that when the Evergreens had scored, it was because Ivan had flipped in the puck in a gorgeous little maneuver, right over the left shoulder of the goalie.

"I'm taking advantage of our opportunities."

The Evergreens were normally a fairly aggressive offensive team, but Elliott had learned how *they* set the tone for the rest of the lines, and as he looked out onto the ice, he was glad to see their second line swarming over the Cyclones' side of the ice, giving their goalie all he could handle.

"Just don't get too aggressive," Mal warned.

"Got it," Elliott retorted, annoyed that Mal was still in warning mode when the whole team was doing a great job keeping the puck on the opposite side of the ice.

It was funny how he'd worried about keeping his edge out here, when Mal's natural state seemed to keep him there, anyway.

The first period continued, then the second, until it was nearly over, Elliott's breaths coming in short, heavy pants as their line came back to the bench, letting the next men up finish the remaining time on the clock.

They hadn't scored again, but the Cyclones' defense felt off and so they'd hassled the Cyclones' goalie the whole period, their shots nearly double that of the other team.

"Keep it up," Zach said, leaning in, as Elliott squirted Gatorade into his mouth.

Mal said nothing next to him, a hot hard pressure against his side, even through all the layers of their equipment.

But even though he was silent, he'd played his ass off out there, keeping up with Elliott, even through some of his crazier play—even going as far as being open when Elliott had inevitably stolen a puck right off a cross-ice pass, and trying to sneak it in behind the goalie's stick.

It hadn't worked but it had given Elliott a little extra boost.

Whistles sounded and Elliott jumped and stared at the ice.

The second line was on the ground—well, two out of the three. The third had his hands in the air, and he was motioning to the ref.

"Shit," Malcolm said, doom in his voice.

The ref called one penalty. High sticking. Okay. That sucked. Not great news. Especially because they'd just gotten off the ice and he and Mal were both on the kill team. But then the ref held up *another* hand.

Another penalty, this time for tripping.

"Fuck," Zach said behind them.

And suddenly, they weren't even on the kill team.

"Andresen. Faulkner. Greene," Coach B barked out. "Get out there."

And Elliott could only sit and watch as the Evergreens were forced to go three on five. A recipe for disaster if there ever was one.

"They're second to last in the league on the power play," Ivan announced. Elliott reached over Mal, ignoring how he stiffened, ever so slightly, as their bodies collided together even more intently, and whacked him on the knee.

"Fuck your superstitious shit," Ivan said.

"You're Russian. You're supposed to be as superstitious as they come," Mal said dryly.

"Fuck that noise," Ivan said.

Most power plays felt like they lasted forever—at least when it was the Evergreens down a man. But this one seemed to practically fly by. Elliott watched, crouched forward on the bench, eyes flicking between the players and the puck and Finn, standing in the goal, every line of his body tense as he anticipated the puck coming his direction.

For five on three, the Evergreens skated well. Ramsey and Brody were dynamite defenders, but the truth was inevitable. Just as it was inevitable with only one forty-seven on the clock, one of the Cyclones' forwards slipped past Nate Greene's defense and flicked the puck right past Finn's shoulder, into the net.

"Fuck," Mal growled.

It shouldn't have been hot. Elliott was mad, too. Mad that it had happened. Mad that possibly his aggression had caused the other line to do more than they should. The line changed, the Evergreens gaining another player, and then thirty seconds later, they gained the fifth back.

Elliott wasn't surprised when Coach B motioned their line back on the ice. He skated hard, looking for an opportunity to grab the puck and take it back down to the other side, to finish off the period on a high note, even after the Cyclones had tied it, but before he could, while the Evergreens were still trying to get their shit together, their center slipped the puck right between Finn's legs.

This time it was Elliott swearing.

They'd dominated the whole period. They'd had two to one shots on goal.

And somehow, they were down. They were *losing*.

It was worse because when they got into the locker room, Mal didn't say anything. Didn't even look at him. Elliott tried to stay focused. On task. Listening to Coach B map out some new formations they could try for the third period.

Tried to quiet his mind. Not let panic get the best of him.

They were a good third period team.

They could score again. Tie it up. Even find a third goal, so they'd win.

Elliott told himself he relished the challenge.

That he wanted it.

That he *craved* it.

And as they took the ice again, for the last period, he believed it.

Evergreens hockey wasn't about giving up when the situation was shit. It was about digging down, deep, and finding a new well of determination.

"We got this," Elliott said to Mal as they got ready for the first faceoff.

Mal gave him a sharp nod, and Elliott took that to mean it was *game on.* Which he was one hundred and ten percent behind.

Mal didn't usually let his emotions get the better of him. Even during a game, he tried to stay calm, methodical. Rely on all the preparation he'd done to be as ready for this challenge as possible.

But he was pissed.

Pissed that they kept pushing the Cyclones and pissed that it kept not working out.

He wanted this one—more than he usually did—and he *liked* winning. Scratch that. He *loved* winning.

Not for any of those crazed, chest-thumping toxic masculinity reasons, but because it was the best way he could prove to himself—and to others—that he'd done what he'd set out to do, which was be the best and to live up to every bit of the potential he knew was inside of him.

The goals they'd given up at the end of the second pissed him off.

Made him emotional.

And when Elliott said, "We got this," Mal felt the determination coalesce inside him.

This time when they took the ice, it wasn't just Elliott pushing, but Mal, too. Harder than he normally did. Getting rougher. Skating faster. Playing fast and easy in a way that anyone with half a brain would tell him was a little too like Elliott Jones for his comfort.

But right now Mal didn't give a fuck.

He took the puck around the back of the goal, one of the Cyclones' defenders breathing down his fucking neck, his blades slicing through the ice as he made the turn.

A second before it happened, he got slammed into the boards, the defender trying to steal the puck, but he blocked him with his stick, once and then twice. Then a third time. They were battling it out now, and Mal was big, but this guy seemed even bigger. Out of the corner of his eye he saw a flash of something, trusted that he understood what—*who*—it was, and he flicked the puck out.

He'd been right.

Elliott grabbed it, and before anyone could react, sent it flying towards the goal. A great shot. A *perfect* shot.

He couldn't have timed it better, or shot it better, but the puck didn't go in. It glanced off the very edge of someone's skate. Mal didn't even know, couldn't get a clear glimpse of whose it was. It might have even been Ivan's.

But it didn't matter, because they missed the rebound and had to fight for control of the puck again.

Rinse and repeat. No time to cry over spilled milk—or missed shots, no matter how goddamn gorgeous they were.

Twenty minutes later, the game was over, and no matter how hard they'd fought, no matter how many shots they'd taken—none as good as that one, but they'd certainly not stopped making the attempt—they'd still lost.

"Hard game. Hard fought game," Coach Blackburn said as they filed into the locker room.

Mal slumped onto the bench in front of his locker. He could feel Elliott's eyes on him, but he didn't want to look up.

He was afraid he'd see an apology—or even worse, *guilt*—in Elliott's face, and he didn't know how to deal with that, on top of his own frustration.

"Yeah," Zach added. Mal saw him exchange a glance, heavy with meaning, with Coach B. "You guys are four and two. *And* you played your asses off tonight. Really great shots on goal. And that one shot? Mal to Ell? That was a thing of fucking beauty."

"How'd you even know he was there?" Ivan asked, stripping off his gloves and tossing them into the equipment bin.

He'd just known. Well, not for sure. Not one hundred percent. But he'd taken a very Elliott-like risk, hoping—*believing*—that he would be there. And he had been.

Malcolm shrugged. "We've been playing together for awhile now."

Ivan made a scoffing noise, and okay, yes, that was fair, though they'd certainly never bickered on the ice the way they had off it. But they'd still not gelled to that extent. Their playing styles were too different. Zach kept telling him it was going to take time, and Mal had been willing to be patient, let the on-ice chemistry develop.

"Well, I'm glad to see it," Coach B said. "More of that trust. That's what I want you to take from this game. Not the loss. But how hard you fought. How you swarmed them, and you pushed every step of the way. And how you trusted each other to get the job done."

But the job hadn't gotten done.

Mal knew that not every game was winnable. They were in a tough conference, and even though the Evergreens were a damn good hockey team, they weren't that much better than a lot of other teams.

Still, it sucked. He finished shucking his gear, and grabbing a towel, headed towards the showers.

He'd half expected Elliott to follow, and sure enough, he did.

"Hey," Elliott murmured, "I want to say—"

"It's alright," Mal said. He actually wasn't mad at Elliott. He'd gone out there, like Coach B said, wanting and willing to do what it took to win. He'd pushed too hard, sure, but it wasn't like *he'd* been the penalized player—either of them, in fact.

Was it still frustrating? Oh, it sure as hell was. But it wasn't Elliott's fault.

"No, it's not alright," Elliott retorted in a voice filled to the brim with guilt and self-recrimination.

Before last night, Mal might have snapped that of course Elliott was going to make this loss all about him, because he always wanted to center every single fucking thing on himself. The good *and* the bad.

But tonight, he kept his mouth shut. Not just because of the sex. Though that was probably part of it. It was impossible to unwind the sex from the rest of it, because it was tangled up inside him, now. It was there and there was no taking it out. No taking it back.

Even if Mal wanted to. Which he didn't.

"I told you—it's fine," Mal said, stepping into the shower cubicle. Flipping on the water hot and letting it cascade down his head, washing away the sweat of the game.

Elliott took the one next to him, and any other time, Mal might've thought that he was doing it to get an extra peek.

But Ell had already seen everything he had on offer. Had tasted and touched almost every part of him, last night. Malcolm felt his blood heat, with remembered pleasure and shock, at the memory.

When he looked over, Elliott had his eyes closed. He wasn't even paying attention to Mal.

That's better. For everyone. No apologies. No guilt. He'll move on; he always does.

Nobody was more resilient than Elliott Jones. Losses slid off him, and he was always ready with a smile after or a snarky joke to defuse the locker room tension.

Mal had kind of hated that, before. But now he wanted it back.

Wanted Elliott to bat those ridiculous eyelashes at him and rattle off a come-on.

But he didn't.

In fact, he didn't say anything else, not until Mal was done showering and was heading back to finish changing. Ramsey had announced they were still on for the arcade, and that would be good for everyone. A nice, healthy distraction to get their heads out of their asses.

But as Mal was about to head out, towel firmly around his waist, Elliott stopped him, wet fingers wrapping around his arm.

"What?" Mal asked. Glancing down at the end of the room, where a few of the very last stalls were taken by a few guys. Brody and Greene. Everyone else had finished.

He half expected Elliott to suggest they take advantage of the nearly empty showers to break a whole bunch of team rules—spoken and *unspoken*.

But Elliott was still looking at him with those puppy dog eyes, sad and depressed and guilt-stricken.

"I really meant it, I didn't mean to—"

"You didn't," Mal huffed in frustration. Acutely aware of how ironic this was. He'd have given just about anything only a few weeks ago for Elliott to be sorry. To apologize. To see the error in his ways. But now, it just pissed him off. He didn't want Elliott to be sorry. Not for something that wasn't his fault.

"You're mad. I know you're mad," Elliott said. "You said it yourself. *Don't push. Don't get too aggressive.* And I did. I kept pushing. I pushed them right into where they wanted us to be."

"Don't give them too much fucking credit. They only took advantage of a lull, a hard moment. They didn't *plan* it," Mal said, chuckling without humor.

"Does it matter if it was premeditated or not?" Elliott's voice was bitter.

"Stop beating yourself up. It happens. Shit happens."

"I can't believe you're not pissed about this," Elliott said. And now he just sounded self-righteous.

Malcolm rolled his eyes. "Get over yourself," he retorted.

"See, I *told* you that you were pissed," Elliott reiterated.

Well, he hadn't been, not before, but now Elliott kept pushing, kept *wanting* him to be mad. Like he was Mal's whipping boy, and that wasn't going to work for him at all.

"I'm not," Mal said, but even he could hear the annoyance in his voice.

"You *are*. You always are, aren't you?"

Mal stared at him.

He'd told himself for ages that he'd been raised by his father, but he didn't have to *be* his father, but maybe he was. Maybe that cold had sunk so far in he didn't know how to be warm again.

Except—that wasn't true, was it? Because Elliott made him red-hot. Burned him so insistently, filling him with the heat of a hundred different emotions. Just like he was doing now.

"That's bullshit," Mal said, his tone blunt.

"Not as much as you'd like it to be," Elliott said darkly.

Mal nearly stormed off. But he paused, just for a second, long enough to decide that he wasn't going alone. He grabbed Elliott's arm and dragged him right out of the showers, down the hall, back to an empty treatment room.

Elliott's hair was dripping in his eyes as Mal pulled him in.

"What the fuck," Mal spit out of him.

He pushed it back. "I just . . . *you're mad*. I know you're mad. And you won't even admit it, which makes me even crazier. Don't take it easy on me? Okay? Sure, we had sex—"

"Is that what you think?" Mal knew he should be incredulous, but this was just like Elliott fucking Jones. To decide what he was thinking. What he was *feeling*. "That we fucked so I'm gonna take it easy on you now? Not be pissed if you deserve it?"

Elliott nodded.

"Fuck that," Mal said and kissed him, hard and insistent.

He'd *been* mad, because Elliott had kept pushing him to be, but the moment their lips touched, Elliott's damp and cool, he wasn't at all, not anymore.

He burned with something else.

Elliott groaned, fingertips digging into his shoulder, hips pressing into Mal's own.

Mal could feel his erection, through two sets of towels, and he didn't know whether to lean in, or to push the guy away.

To laugh or to cry with how good this was.

Elliott's mouth lush and perfect against his, kissing him like he'd *known* all Mal wanted was this, and he was right there, too.

Mal broke off as the anger melted right into lust.

"I'm not mad," Mal said firmly.

Elliott was smiling again. It was like seeing the sun rise again, after a particularly dark night. "You're not," he agreed.

"You . . ." Mal huffed out a frustrated laugh. "I *wasn't*. And then you kept insisting I was, that I had to be annoyed at what happened, and sure I was. But not *at* you. You didn't cause this, Elliott. Shit happens, sometimes. Maybe we did get a little aggressive. But you don't lead this entire team around by their dicks."

Those gorgeous green eyes were glowing now. "Just you, huh?"

Mal wanted to protest and say no. But could he really when his dick was still hard just from kissing him?

He changed the subject, instead. "Don't do that shit, okay?"

"You really weren't mad?"

"I'm not *that* much of an asshole." At least he tried not to be. Maybe they pushed each other, sometimes in good ways, sometimes in bad ways, but he wasn't stone-cold.

Not cold at all, when it came to Elliott.

"No," Elliott agreed. He sighed. "I don't know why I got so worked up. Sure you were mad and that you wouldn't tell me."

It felt safe—relatively so, anyway—to pat Elliott on the shoulder reassuringly. "Trust me, if I'm pissed at you, you're gonna know it."

"Okay." Elliott smiled. Leaned in. Mal's heartbeat felt like it doubled. Then tripled. God, he wanted to kiss him again. Press him back against this door, strip his towel off, and make him feel as good as he'd made Malcolm feel only last night.

But this was *school property.* Maybe Mal wanted this, and he wanted it badly, but he wasn't about to break a lifetime of ingrained respect for the rules.

"We should . . .uh . . ." Mal trailed off. "Uh, go?"

"No," Elliott said, grinned. Then kissed him again. Soft and lush, his tongue nimbly brushing against Mal's.

He felt Elliott's fingers trail up his bare thigh, underneath the towel, and he managed to pull away just in time.

"Oh, come on," Elliott teased. "I know you want it."

It would be stupid to claim he didn't. Not when his cock was only a few inches away, pulsing and erect, from Elliott's magic fingers.

"Yeah, we're not going to do this here. *Ever.*" Mal took a very necessary step back. And then another.

It was still somehow not quite far enough.

"I actually don't think it's against any actual policies, Mr. Rule Stickler. Ramsey told me he looked it up once."

"Of course he did."

"Hey, there's nothing wrong with being informed." Elliott shot him a grin that nearly weakened his resolve. It would be so good. It would be so quick, too. And then maybe they could make it through the team outing to the arcade without feeling like his body was too big suddenly for his skin.

"We're still not doing this here. Not ever," Mal said with as much certainty as he could muster.

"Aw, okay, fine, send me off with blue balls." Elliott batted his eyelashes. "You still gonna tutor me tonight?"

"Actually," Mal said, smiling now, "I think you're gonna tutor *me.*"

CHAPTER 10

"I SHOULD'VE SEEN THAT coming, right after that power play," Finn said morosely as he sipped his Coke.

"You shouldn't have even been in that position," Brody reassured him.

"It was a bullshit call," Nate Greene agreed. "I didn't trip anyone. He tripped sure, but if the refs think I did it, they need fucking glasses."

"Listen, shit happens," Elliott said. "We gotta listen to Coach B. We fought hard. We nearly came back."

"Yeah, that was a fucking sick shot you almost made. The way Mal flicked the puck back to you? How'd he even know you were there?"

"Mal knows more than you think he does," Elliott said.

"I didn't bring you guys here so you could agonize," Ramsey said firmly. "Who's gonna play me in foosball? Oh, yeah, it's gonna be you, Reynolds."

Finn shot him a dark look. "No. No way."

"You're the best, though. If I wanna be the best, I gotta cut my teeth on the best," Ramsey said, shooting Finn his most charming smile. "Come on."

Brody turned to Elliott after the pair of them had wandered towards an empty table. "He's gonna crack up," Brody said under his breath.

"No, he's not." Elliott more wanted to believe it was true than he *actually* believed it was true.

His phone buzzed in his pocket. Pulling it out, he glanced at the screen. It was the sister chat.

Tough loss, baby bro, Nina texted.

That shot tho! How did Mal know you were even there? That was from Connie.

PFM, Macey responded.

AKA, Elliott translated, *pure fucking magic.*

We've been working on some things.

Technically, that was not a lie. They had been working on their on-ice chemistry, sure, but they'd been doing it all year, and despite their success as the top line on the team, it wasn't like it *had* gotten magically better.

No, Mal had trusted him in that moment and he'd taken the shot, and if not for bad luck, they'd be talking about it in hushed tones now.

"Your sisters?" Brody asked, glancing down at Elliott's phone.

"Yeah," Elliott said. "They're something else."

Brody had met them last year when they'd arrived *en masse* for one of the last games of the season.

"Entertaining at best, annoying at worst?" Brody wondered.

Elliott nodded.

"Sometimes I'd like to have a brother or a sister." Brody sighed.

"You got a roommate, though," Elliott teased, remembering what he'd initially hoped to wiggle out of the guy.

"Yeah, what about Dean?" Brody's expression was carefully neutral. So neutral Elliott was convinced he was right.

"I'm just saying. He's probably *very* entertaining. Maybe not so much annoying, though," Elliott pointed out.

Brody rolled his eyes. "What is Ramsey telling you these days? Dean's just a friend. A roommate and a friend."

"Sure, he is," Elliott said knowingly.

"He *is*," Brody said, laughing now.

But Elliott was still not convinced. "Well, I'm your first call when you decide to come clean about how you're climbing his hotness like a tree."

Brody shot him a knowing look. "And here I thought you were only into Malcolm."

"I'm . . ." They'd agreed not to tell anyone. "I don't know what you're talking about. I'm not *into* Mal. He's an annoyance, *at best.*"

"Uh-huh. You're a terrible fucking liar, Ell." Brody's eyes twinkled. "But, I get it."

Elliott wanted to do a fist pump and yell, *I knew it*, but Brody hadn't *exactly* admitted it yet. But he would. Someday.

"Speaking of Dean, I actually gotta go. I said I'd study with him tonight," Brody said.

And just like that, Elliott was ditched, and he couldn't even say he was mad, because he got it. He would love to saunter over to where Mal was talking to Ivan and convince him, without worrying who saw or what they thought, to come back to his place again for some more hands-on tutoring.

But he didn't. Instead, he stopped and got a refill on his drink and headed over to one of the pinball machines. This one was Star Wars themed, but the *new* Star Wars, with Kylo Ren glowering out from its upper artwork and Rey next to him, lightsaber alight and a fierce expression on her face.

He was halfway through his second round, enjoying the challenge of finding the exact right spots to hit when he heard steps behind him.

It was stupid, but he hoped it was Mal.

It wasn't.

It was Zach.

"You're pretty good at that," Zach observed.

"Sometimes," Elliott agreed.

"Good instincts and good reflexes," Zach added.

Elliott knew he was going to ask about the shot before he even did. It was funny, he'd been questioned more about that shot—that *hadn't* actually gone into the net—than some goals he'd actually scored.

"It's why I'm good on the ice, too," Elliott said.

Zach nodded. "Still doesn't explain that shot."

"My sister Macey called it pure fucking magic," Elliott said. He almost asked Zach why he wasn't over by Mal, interrogating *him* about it. But Mal wouldn't have answered, they all knew that. "Would've been quite the goal if it had gone in."

"I just wanna know how Mal knew you were there. I was only watching and I barely knew you were there."

Elliott shrugged and flicked one of the levers on the machine. "We've been playing together awhile now."

"And I want to know how Mal's suddenly out there skating like that." He paused. Waiting, Elliott assumed, until he'd lost his ball. Which he did a second later. "Why he's skating like you."

"He's not. He's . . .he just wanted to win, that was all. Frustrated that we gave up those two goals so quick."

"Right." Zach didn't seem convinced.

"Did Ramsey invite Coach, too?" Elliott asked.

Zach laughed. "Yeah, he sure did. Some pair on that guy. But Coach sent me instead. Wanted me to make sure nobody gets up to any trouble."

"Would we?" Elliott shot their assistant coach his most innocent look, fluttering eyelashes and all.

"You absolutely fucking would. But I'm sure I'll have nothing to report later."

Elliott was so surprised, he straight-up missed his last ball, and it clanged down into the bowels of the pinball machine with a rhythmic *clank*.

"You *report* to him?"

"Oh, well, it's not so formal." Zach chuckled self-consciously. "But yeah, we do check in with each other. At first I—" He stopped abruptly. Like he realized he was saying too much. Sharing more than he should.

Maybe Elliott couldn't get Brody to share, but he couldn't deny he was curious what was going on with Zach and Coach. They seemed awfully close. "'Cause you were worried about him because of his wife?"

Zach didn't agree—but he didn't disagree, either. He just stuck his hands in his pockets and didn't say anything.

195

But Elliott had never known when to stop pushing. At least that was probably what Malcolm might have told him. "I know she died, unexpectedly, and what, he buried himself out in the middle of nowhere, in some remote cabin?"

"He didn't bury himself. He was mourning. We all do it in different ways. And now he's back—and you'd better believe he's back," Zach said, fiercely. Like he felt the need to defend Coach Blackburn, even though Elliott had hardly been accusing him of anything.

"I know he is," Elliott said steadily.

"Good."

He wandered off then, and Elliott went back to Kylo Ren and Rey.

He was half a dozen games in, and was *this close* to setting the high score, when Mal did finally come over.

"One sec," Elliott told him. Maybe if he wasn't so goddamn close to really nailing this machine, he'd have enjoyed Malcolm finally heading his direction more.

"Oh sure, I'm here just waiting on you," Malcolm retorted sarcastically.

A few moments later, Elliott hit the perfect combination of bells and the machine rang out with the sound of lightsabers clashing, followed by a triumphant noise signaling the end of the game.

"I'll take it," Elliott said, entering his info for the top score. "But I'd rather have won the game, earlier."

"Hey, we win some, we lose some. You should come over and see how Finn and Ramsey are going at each other on foosball. I've never seen such a competitive game in my whole life." Mal was trying to be friendly. Elliott could practically see the wheels in his head turning. The effort he was making. It was surprisingly sweet.

"He's trying to get Finn out of his head," Elliott said.

"Well, *yeah*," Mal said. "And I think it's working?"

Sure enough, when they headed over to the loose group gathered around Finn and Ramsey and the foosball table, Finn was grinning and Ramsey looked stressed as Finn expertly flicked the ball towards Ramsey's side.

"Goddamn," Ramsey muttered as he twisted the knob a second too late and the ball sank into the goal.

"You'd think you'd be better at defense," Finn joked.

"You'd think," Ramsey said, wiping his damp forehead with the back of his hand.

Mal leaned in, his shoulder brushing Elliott's, and Elliott was suddenly reminded of the last time they'd been this close. Back when they'd still been in the locker room.

When they'd been kissing. Angrily at first, and then the way they'd come together had been anything but angry.

"You think he's playing Finn?" Mal murmured under his breath.

Elliott wasn't sure. But *he* wanted to be playing. And not foosball.

He shrugged. "Maybe. It *is* Ramsey."

Finn shrieked as Ramsey turned on the jets, moving the foosball players around with a surprising speed.

"You got this," Ivan crowed. "On your right! No! On your left!"

Finn growled, but he barely managed to move his goalie into place just in time to deflect Ramsey's last shot.

His expression was a mask of determination, and he pushed back immediately, and before Ramsey could get into position, he was sinking another goal.

"Goal!" Ivan cried, patting Finn on the back excitedly. "See!"

Ramsey shot Finn a rueful glance across the table. "Told you that you had it."

Finn rolled his eyes, clearly downplaying how much winning had meant.

But Elliott could see it; he'd doubted his instincts, after those two goals today. And now, he didn't have to anymore.

He'd just proven they were solid and strong.

Elliott looked over at Ramsey, and his face was full of exaggerated disappointment, but underneath? That was all opaque. Elliott couldn't read it.

"We're going to take off. Got to get Elliott prepped for this big test, in two weeks," Mal said.

His excuse was a little overdone—if Elliott hadn't been participating, he might've guessed what was *really* happening—but none of the guys seemed particularly interested in what they were going to do.

Even Ramsey was still carefully watching Finn.

"Good game," Elliott said to Finn, patting him on the shoulder and then tugging him into a quick hug. "Both of them."

A few minutes later they were out on the sidewalk, heading towards Elliott's dorm in silence. There was only the pitter patter of the leftover raindrops, from the still-wet leaves, hitting the ground, but it had actually stopped raining while they were in the arcade.

"I'm pretty sure Ramsey threw that game," Mal finally said, breaking the quiet, "but damned if I know how he did it. It seemed really legit, all the way up til—"

"Til it was obvious just how much Finn needed that reminder that he was fine?" Elliott nodded.

"Yeah," Mal agreed.

"Ramsey's a great guy. And he did Finn a solid there." Elliott bumped Mal's arm. Ignored the itch he felt to reach down and just take it, grasp it. He'd feel Mal's callouses. He was almost as familiar with them as he was with his own, at this point. It had been too goddamn long since they'd touched, and it was maybe an hour and a half, at *best.*

You are so done for.

"Finn needs to learn how to do himself a solid," Mal said.

Elliott didn't disagree, but then nobody knew how tough it was being in Finn's skates, except for Finn.

"He's getting there," Elliott reminded Mal. This time Mal bumped *him* back, and okay, maybe they were both in this same situation.

They turned the corner towards Lewis, Elliott's dorm, and went up the stairs, finally hitting the foyer. They could either take the stairs or the elevator.

It was an easy decision. He was tired. They were probably *both* tired, and if he had to wait one more freaking minute to get Mal alone? Well, he didn't know if he could.

The moment they were in the elevator, Elliott wasted not a second more of time.

He pushed right into Mal's space, nudging him against the back wall, pressing his palms against his chest.

After the game, Mal had put on a thick plaid flannel shirt, and from the wedge of skin Elliott could see at the neck, he was pretty damn sure he wasn't wearing anything underneath it.

Elliott was also pretty damn sure he was going to undo every single one of those taunting, tantalizing buttons with his teeth.

"What are you doing?" Mal asked, having the nerve to look surprised.

"What do you think I'm doing?" Elliott retorted, amused.

Mal sighed. Sounding resigned more than annoyed. "Driving me crazy? How do you *do* that, by the way? I don't *want* to be thinking about this, not all the time. It's . . . it's . . ."

"Awesome?"

Mal shot him another one of those hot looks, and Elliott's heart beat a little faster. How could he have ever thought he could have a little taste of Malcolm McCoy and not want a *lot* more?

"Annoying."

"I'm happy to annoy you some more," Elliott said slyly and then finally leaned in and took his mouth, pouring all his frustration at having to wait into it.

The elevator came to a jerking halt and Mal broke the kiss with a gasp.

Luckily for them, it was deserted in the fourth floor hallway, and Elliott's room was only a few steps away—because it was *really* obvious what they'd just been doing. Mal's cock was hard in his jeans, and Elliott had a feeling his hair was already messed up from Mal's hands.

He unlocked the door, fully expecting that they'd be on each other the moment it closed behind them. He was already fantasizing how they'd do it tonight. Maybe he could get his mouth on Mal's cock again. Maybe Mal would even be interested in returning the favor. And then maybe . . . Elliott reached for him, but *no*, because Malcolm, the idiot, actually took a step *back*.

"What are you doing?" Elliott figured it was his turn to ask.

"I thought we were studying. I asked if you wanted to study and you said *yes*."

"Specifically you said a *tutoring session*," Elliott said, emphasizing the words.

"Right." Mal was frowning now. "How is that an invitation to have sex?"

"You might be tutoring me in statistics," Elliott said resolutely, "but I'm sure as hell tutoring *you* in sex."

Mal's jaw dropped. "That's not what we—I never said—I certainly didn't *ask*—"

"Did you even have to?" Elliott challenged.

Mal was quiet for a long moment. Thinking. Elliott knew that he could push him—it would not be *that* hard—but he wanted Mal to want him. He wanted Mal to consider the pros and the cons, and damn any of the latter, side with the former.

"No," Mal said, finally, and there was undeniable surrender on his face as he reached for Elliott this time.

Elliott didn't mind doing the reaching. He enjoyed it. But it was so sweet to have Mal give in to what they both wanted.

To let himself take this, without arguments.

"I mean it," Mal groaned between kisses as they stumbled towards the bed, again. "How do you *do* this? What kind of magical spell have you put on me?"

Whatever it was, it had ensnared them both.

Mal had to know that, with how hard Elliott was breathing and the way his cock twitched, hard and desperate, as Mal slid a hand down the front of his pants.

"All I can think about—when I should be thinking about *plenty* of other things—is getting you naked again," Mal said.

"Well, get me naked again," Elliott said, and this time, after toeing his shoes off, lay down on the bed, shooting Mal his best come-hither look.

Mal rolled his eyes, but he was leaning over him a second later, kissing him hard, tongue deep in his mouth, fingers in his hair, hips stuttering against Elliott's own.

He pulled back a second later. "Promise me we'll study after this," Mal said, and it was annoying how one-track-minded he was. And not even the track Elliott wanted him focused on.

"After, after, *yes*," Elliott agreed impatiently. He'd told Mal to get *him* naked, but he was already reaching up, thumbing those buttons apart, one at a time, exposing the glorious expanse of Malcolm's chest. The ripped ridges of his abs. The firm muscles of his shoulders.

He could write a goddamn essay about the beauty of Mal's shoulders. How he put everything on them, because they could bear that weight.

"I thought I was supposed to be getting *you* naked," Mal teased. And he could tease like this, it turned out. Warm and affectionate, the corner of his mouth quirking up. That icy wall, the one that Elliott had always hated, coming down when it was just the two of them.

"You were too slow," Elliott admitted.

Mal's fingers found the zipper of his sweatshirt and tugged it down, then pulled up on his T-shirt. "If you think I was too slow then, you're definitely going to hate what I'm about to do," Mal murmured.

But Elliott didn't think that was true, at all.

He was going to *love* whatever Mal did.

Especially if he kept going in this poised methodical manner, his gaze a hot counterpoint to how deliberately he kept stripping Elliott down. Once his chest was bare, he moved onto his sweatpants, tugging them down carefully, and then his socks. Leaving him only clad in his tight briefs, cock straining against the fabric.

Mal rocked back on his heels and just looked.

Elliott refused to let himself squirm or feel shame as Mal's eyes took in every single inch of him. He knew he looked good. Had plenty of guys say so. But none of them had ever mattered like Malcolm had.

"Yeah," Mal said, voice gravelly. "I was right."

"About?"

"That I was going to want to take my time and enjoy every single bit of you," Mal said. "I don't know what I'm doing—"

"You know I don't give a shit about that," Elliott reminded him. Didn't think Mal was quite ready to hear that it was already better with Mal than it had been with other guys, most of whom had way more experience. Maybe it wasn't *only* that Mal wasn't ready to hear it. Maybe he wasn't ready to *say* it, either.

Mal didn't answer, just leaned in, hands impossibly warm against his skin, making him shiver as he explored. As he finally tugged his briefs off.

Then his head dipped, capturing Elliott's mouth all too briefly before his lips moved, coasting down his neck, finding every single spot that made Elliott gasp. Nobody had ever taken their time like this on just the apparently sensitive column of his neck.

His cock, rock-hard, twitched against Mal's bare stomach, and he barely resisted the urge to thrust up, to chase the pleasure and his orgasm.

Hadn't he wanted this *forever*? And now that it was finally happening, Mal looking right at him, like he couldn't look anywhere else, he wasn't going to rush it.

If he did, it would be over and Elliott wasn't naive enough to think he'd get everything he wanted from Mal. It would end, and Elliott would wish that it hadn't.

Mal's lips moved lower, across his collarbone, then across his pecs, and down his stomach, nibbling with just the right amount of teeth along his abs.

His cock twitched, desperation rising inside him. Then Mal finally did it, tongue brushing up the length of it, humming in the back of his mouth, like this was a taste he'd been searching for.

Elliott's fingers dug into the bedding, and he tried to hang on—because it was very clear Malcolm was going to take his sweet ass time. First there was just his tongue, slicking up his length, then sucking on the head, and then *finally*, more and more of his dick disappeared into that white-hot heat.

Just when the pressure became unbearable and Elliott thought he was going to explode or die, Mal backed off.

Elliott groaned as he took him deep again. Maybe it wasn't the most expert blowjob in the world—it was maybe slower than he'd have normally liked—but Mal's intense focus meant that the pleasure had never resonated as deeply as it did right now.

He could feel every bit of it. Enjoyed every single incredible moment of it.

Mal's fingers drifted down, releasing from the base of his cock to cup his balls, and Elliott moaned loudly, encouraging more of that, *please God.*

Chuckling, Mal murmured, "Like that, do you?"

"Lower, *lower,*" Elliott begged, squirming as Mal found exactly what he'd wanted, his touch brief and hesitant against his hole.

"You want this?" Mal didn't sound disgusted. He sounded enthralled. Awestruck.

"For you to fuck me with your fingers? Your cock?" Elliott gasped as Mal slipped just a bit of his thumb inside. "Hell yes. There's uh . . .lube in the drawer there . . ." He motioned towards the little set of drawers next to his bed.

"You're sure?" But Mal was already rummaging in the drawer.

"Oh yeah," Elliott said. He didn't warn Mal to go slow, because Mal seemed to have one speed tonight, and it was not fast.

No doubt he'd drive him half crazy with it before he finally got to it.

Mal rocked back on his heels and with a gentle but insistent touch, spread Elliott's legs.

Mal had thought about this a lot—even when he knew he shouldn't be—but he'd hoped, if he'd gotten the chance to have Elliott again, that he could take his time. Really explore the intricacies of his body.

He'd still never imagined that he might be doing it tonight, or that he'd be two fingers deep into the incredible heat of Elliott's ass. Watching as he squirmed against them, mouth slack, his beautiful eyes unfocused, groans falling from his lips.

It was incredible. *He* was incredible.

He leaned forward, wanting more of Elliott's taste, *needing* it, and let his cock slip farther into his mouth. Mal was under no delusions that he was actually good at this, but Elliott certainly didn't seem to be complaining.

As for him? Well, his dick was a wet, twitching mess inside his boxer briefs. It was entirely possible that the moment Elliott came, Mal was going to follow right along with him, whether he was touching himself or not.

"I'm not above begging," Elliott groaned as Mal did his best to find that spot he'd done plenty of research on. "I'm really fucking not."

"What do you want?"

Elliott reached for him, and with a surprising amount of strength, pulled him in. "You," he said and kissed him, wild and hot. "There's a condom in the drawer."

"Are you—"

"If you ask me again if I'm fucking sure, I'm going to pin you down on this bed and ride you until you cry," Elliott said.

Mal's fingers shook as he grabbed the condom. Because this was happening? Or because that vision had made his brain nearly short-circuit? It was hard to say.

He'd just gotten it out of the package when Elliott's hand closed over his. "I got this," he said, and even though he'd been a shaking mess only a few moments earlier, now he pushed Mal back on the bed. Tugged down his boxer briefs, letting out a low whistle.

"Oh baby, you're hot for me," Elliott said, leaning over his cock, his breath searing against the sensitive skin.

"If you touch me, I'm gonna—" Mal ground out. He didn't *want* to. He wanted this to go on forever. Because he'd already figured out that it *couldn't* go on forever. Whenever Elliott called it off, he was going to still want more.

He'd come to terms with that fact. But it seemed like a fucking crime to not enjoy every ecstatic second while he still could.

"Just . . .let me do this," Elliott said and gripped him, Mal groaning before he could swallow the sound back. He slipped on the condom with a few expert movements, and *God*, that shouldn't have been as hot as it was, that he knew what he was doing.

But it was.

Then Elliott was straddling him and the hot heat of his mouth had nothing on the incendiary pressure of his ass swallowing him up as he sank down.

"Fuck," Elliott said, throwing his head back, hands braced on Mal's chest. His fingertips curled, nails biting into his skin, but the pain was good. Reminded him he was here, that he could hang on. That he could be everything Elliott needed.

For so long he'd told himself sex was overrated. Unnecessary. A waste of time.

But he got it now, because it wasn't just the pleasure cascading through him. It was the closeness. The touching. The hushed intimacy of it, Elliott leaning in and kissing him, both of them breathing hard as they broke apart.

"I'm not gonna—" Mal gasped as Elliott moved faster. Thrusting downwards with force. Of course he was good at this. Wrapping a hand around his dick, he fucked Mal like he meant it.

Like he'd been thinking about this, too, for a long time.

Maybe even as long as Malcolm had.

Mal reached a tentative hand out and touched him too, hand moving alongside Elliott's, and Elliott swore.

That was the only warning Mal got before Elliott was clamping down around his dick, pulsing in hot stripes up his chest.

Before, he'd been right. Because that was all it took for Mal to be *gone*. It was supposed to be an orgasm, but it felt like so much more than that. Like he'd been turned inside out, like he'd been reborn.

Elliott slumped down on his chest, clearly uninterested in the mess, and Mal pulled him in closer, wrapping his arms around his back, damp with sweat.

"That was . . ."

Incredible. Amazing. Life-changing?

Mal considered saying all those things. Maybe it would make him look like an idiot, if he did. Maybe sex was always like this, and he'd just been cluelessly missing out all this time.

But then Elliott finished his sentence. "Ugh, that was so goddamn good. I don't think it's ever felt like that before."

Mal froze. "But—"

"I know," Elliott said wryly. He pressed a wet kiss to Mal's collarbone. "I know."

"So it's not always like this?"

Elliott chuckled. "No. Not in my experience, anyway." He paused. "And don't say anything about how extensive my experience probably is."

"Would I do that?" Mal could probably concede that a few weeks ago, when he had been determined not to let anyone—especially Elliott Jones—burn down all his well-constructed walls, he might have said something like that. "Actually, don't answer that. I probably would've."

"You didn't now, that's what matters," Elliott said, a surprisingly earnest look in his eyes.

Mal wasn't sure that was true, but if Elliott was going to give it to him, he didn't want to argue with it. "If you say so."

"I do." Elliott grinned. "I also say we'd better get cleaned up."

It was much the same as it had been the night before. Elliott grabbed a washcloth and came back, helping Mal dispose of the condom.

"I'm on PrEP," Elliott said, explaining, as he tied it off and tossed it in the trash. "And you're a virgin—*were* a virgin—but we still have to worry about other STDs. But I'll get tested in the next few days and then we don't have to use those anymore."

"Is that—is that . . ." Mal stuttered. He couldn't imagine being wrapped up in all that heat without anything in between him and Elliott. He'd come the moment he slid inside him.

"Oh, it's good," Elliott said. "And we don't have to do it again, if you don't want to, but I thought—"

"I want to," Mal said firmly. He would take anything Elliott gave him. "And we could always uh . . .do it the other way, too, if you wanted?"

Elliott had the nerve to look surprised. "Really?"

"Just because I don't know what I'm doing doesn't mean I don't want things, too." Mal's hands fisted in the mussed sheets. "Maybe I want them even more."

Elliott's face softened. "I'm sorry. You're right. I didn't mean to make assumptions. You want me to fuck you? It'd be a privilege."

"Okay." Mal swallowed hard. "I noticed . . .uh . . .some other things in the drawer . . ."

"Aw, you snoop," Elliott teased.

Mal nearly apologized, but then Elliott continued. "Yeah, we'll try those first. It's not . . .it's not easy, the first time. But I'll do what I can to make it easy on you."

"We don't . . .you don't . . ." Mal stuttered.

"Yes, I do, yes, we do." Elliott slung an arm around his shoulders, pressing his mouth to his shoulder. "I'm gonna take good care of you."

Mal squeezed his eyes shut over the sudden onslaught of emotion washing through him. His throat felt tight and thick, his tongue too big for his mouth.

How had he ever believed that Ell was a careless playboy who only cared about fun and the next one-night stand he could notch on his bed frame?

Maybe he'd believed it because it was easier to believe that was true than it was to look right at the guy and see behind the easy, uncomplicated exterior. Easier to avoid it and continue his delusion that Mal didn't want him.

"Hey, hey, it's alright, that was a big thing," Elliott murmured. This time he wrapped his arms around him more fully, and Mal practically fell into his embrace.

Surely this would be the moment when Elliott decided this was too much, too fast, that he'd never signed up for all this baggage. But he didn't let go, and so neither did Mal.

"It's a big thing," Elliott repeated softly. "And it was good, yeah?"

Mal swallowed the lump in his throat. "Better than I imagined. 'Cause of you."

He finally let go.

Elliott rose to his feet, grabbed his briefs, and pulled them on. Then his sweatpants. "Anyone worth it would've done the same. Taken their time with you. Made sure you were enjoying it the way you should." Elliott's voice was self-deprecating, but Mal didn't believe it.

He had too many walls and layers to be fooled when he saw Elliott erecting his own.

"No," Mal said firmly. "No, they wouldn't have. It was you, because it had to be you."

Elliott stopped getting dressed. Turned. "Did you talk to Ramsey?"

"No? Why?" Mal couldn't understand what on earth *Ramsey* had to do with this.

"Uh, no reason. Just . . ." Elliott gestured again. "Just wondering. You know how he likes to interfere."

Mal nodded. "Look at Finn tonight. I'm pretty sure he orchestrated that whole thing, but it was so good, so *seamless*, I couldn't pick out how."

"I know," Elliott said. He shot Mal a look. "Did you still want to study?"

What Mal wanted was to peel Elliott back out of those clothes and tuck him back into bed, their bodies pressed together again. But he didn't.

Instead, he nodded and reached for his clothes. Elliott was too good of a hockey player to not play just because he wasn't very good at math. Mal was going to make sure he made it. No matter what.

CHAPTER 11

"I DIDN'T HEAR YOU come in last night." Jane leaned forward and pouted into the mirror she'd hung right next to the door, putting the finishing touches on her makeup. Bright red lips, dark smoky eyes, all appropriate considering her costume as the devil.

"I was out late, studying," Mal said, willing himself not to flush.

But his friend knew him better than that.

"You? Malcolm McCoy was out late studying? With who?" She paused. "Not Elliott. Oh my God, it *was* Elliott. You're going all red!"

"I am not," Mal said, even though the sliver of himself he could see in the mirror proved him a liar.

Jane whirled around. "You did it, didn't you?"

It had been a few days now since it had actually happened, and Mal had intended to tell Jane, but she'd been so busy with this new choreographer, and he'd been in the thick of the hockey season *plus* classes. Plus, well, he couldn't deny it, plenty of tutoring and also "tutoring" with Ell.

He'd barely seen her. And when they did pass each other, he hadn't known how to come out with it and say, *by the way I had sex and it was great. Better than I'd ever dreamt of. But I think it's not just the sex. I think it's Elliott. He's funny and sweet and thoughtful and even though we're totally different people, I think we're more alike than I ever thought.*

"Yes," Mal admitted.

"Oh my God," she shrieked again, throwing her arms around him and hugging him hard. Her devil horn headband, perched perkily on the top of her blond hair, lurched and nearly fell right off. "Why didn't you tell me?"

"Because of this, right here," Mal said. "You'd make a big deal out of it." *And I'd want to make a big deal out of it, even as I'm trying to stay chill.*

"It *is* a big deal," Jane said reproachfully.

"Only because I waited all this time," Mal said.

"And was it great? Elliott treated you good, right? He was gentle and careful and—"

"How do you know who it even was?"

Jane rolled her eyes. "Like it was ever going to be anyone else. You wanted Elliott, and he sure wanted you. Got you too, I think."

Mal didn't know what to say. He *felt* got, but he also wasn't sure if that was the orgasms talking. Orgasms like the ones he and Elliott were sharing would make anyone feel special.

"Yes," he finally said.

Jane snorted. "I see you really want to share this."

He knew he should say more, but the *saying* was never his strong suit, and it was especially not now.

"I . . .it's really great. It's perfect, actually, he's kind of perfect." Mal stopped abruptly before he could rhapsodize even further.

"I thought he drove you crazy," Jane joked, nudging him.

Mal sighed. "He does. And somehow *that's* even perfect now. I know it isn't real. It's just the closeness. The intimacy." *The orgasms.* "It's all lying to me."

"Is it though?"

Mal shrugged. "I don't know." That was the kicker, wasn't it? He didn't know. And he *always* knew.

"You must really hate that," Jane said. She turned back to the mirror, fluffing her hair, but her eyes were intent on his in the reflection.

"It's different," Mal allowed begrudgingly. "Are you ready to go yet? I thought we were done getting ready."

Jane stuck one of those sharp elbows into his side. "I said *you* were done getting ready." She fluffed her hair again and leaned in, checking her face more carefully.

"I still can't believe you talked me into this," Mal muttered.

"A Halloween party or the costume?"

Mal snorted. "Either one."

The costume was barely a costume—Jane had found a plain white T-shirt in one of his drawers and had thrown it at him, even though it was probably at least a size too small. When Mal had complained about this, Jane had told him it was okay, he looked really, *really* hot.

After she'd affixed the glittery halo to his head and insisted on smearing more glitter across his cheekbones and above his eyes, he'd asked if that was still true, and from her eye roll, Mal supposed the opposite was probably true.

"I guess it's not really so appropriate now," Jane said, grinning at him in the mirror. "But it's still hot. I suppose he'll be there, tonight, right? Elliott?"

"At the party?" Mal shrugged. "If there's a party, especially one as big as the big Gamma Sigma Halloween party? I'm sure he'll be there."

"You didn't ask? He didn't tell you?" Jane finally turned away from the mirror. Pulled on a bright red peacoat that covered her short, tight red dress.

Mal breathed out a silent sigh of relief. They were finally leaving. Which meant he was one step closer to being able to leave the party and come back here. And even better, one step closer to being able to wash all this shit off his face. It itched, kind of, but when he'd pointed this out, Jane had only gone into a long litany of all the crap she was wearing on *her* face.

Mal knew better than to ask why.

"No?" Why would Elliott have shared his no-doubt-very-full party schedule? That had nothing to do with Malcolm.

"Huh. I thought—"

"We're not dating. We're just . . ." What *were* they doing? Studying and "studying" together nearly every night? "I'm helping him out. And he's…uh…helping me out, too. I guess."

Jane snorted as they climbed down the stairs to the street, slowly in deference to her sky-high shiny black boots. "Yeah, that's it. Just a couple of mutual orgasms between bros. You're delusional if you don't think he's crazy about you, Mal. Scratch that—you're both delusional. But probably just you."

"Thanks," Mal said dryly. "Your faith in me is heartening."

"You're welcome," Jane said with her typical brightness. "Well, thank God it stopped raining."

"I said I'd drive us."

"And then you couldn't have anything to drink," Jane retorted. "It's a party, Mal. Try to unclench a fraction."

"I'm plenty unclenched," Mal ground out, fully aware of just how fucking clenched he sounded.

"I really thought when Elliott finally got into your pants, you'd be a bit more relaxed," Jane said in a teasing voice. "Besides, that's not the only reason I'm happy it's not raining. It gets so packed in the house, it's easier when the party can spill outside, too."

"Like a little rain ever stopped the idiots of this school from drinking too much and grinding up on each other," Mal muttered.

"You are really no fun tonight, and that's too bad. I'm sure Elliott will be pretty disappointed."

"Ell's not going to be anything." Elliott knew what he was like. There was a reason Elliott hadn't invited him to this party. First, because they weren't doing that kind of thing. Parties had nothing to do with tutoring *or* hockey. And second, because he had to know Mal wouldn't be into it. Frankly, he wouldn't be going at all, if Jane hadn't guilted him into it.

He definitely wouldn't be wearing all this fucking glitter.

"Sure," Jane said knowingly.

They turned down Clackamas Street. Gamma Sigma house was in the middle of frat row, and even though none of the houses were particularly dark or quiet, that one was bright with flashing lights, Michael Jackson's "Thriller" spilling out of every open window and door. Nearly everyone they passed on their way through the yard and up the stairs to the front door was in costume.

"See, it looks fun, right?" Jane coaxed.

Mal didn't say anything, just shot his best friend a glower.

"Come on," she said, "let's get a drink."

"One drink," Mal said. He didn't normally drink, but if he was going to survive this hellhole, he was going to need *something*.

They wove their way through all the dancing bodies in the packed living room and headed towards the kitchen where the bar was usually set up.

Ramsey was there, leaning against the counter. It took a second for Mal to take in his costume, and when he did, he laughed in spite of what he told himself was disgust. "Are you a *sperm*?" Mal asked, in disbelief.

Ramsey laughed and shook the stiffened tentacles that towered over his blond hair.

"Appropriate," Jane said wryly.

"If you wanted, I'd share some with you, my little she-devil," Ramsey crooned.

Jane rolled her eyes. "Fuck no."

"And you're painfully appropriate," Ramsey said, eyeing Mal's form from his halo to his tight white T-shirt.

"Yeah, he is."

Mal turned and nearly swallowed his tongue.

Elliott was shirtless, a pair of bright red suspenders holding up a pair of far too big jeans, the open waistband flirting with the very bottom of his abs, all that skin making it clear that he wasn't wearing a stitch underneath them. A bright plastic firefighter hat was perched rakishly on one side of his head, and he was grinning, like he knew exactly how much of a wet dream he looked.

Mal swallowed hard.

"I think you just rendered Mal speechless," Jane pointed out. "Might have to put out that fire later."

If Jane was talking about the fire currently raging in his underwear, then he sure as fuck hoped she was right.

"Oh I intend to," Elliott said, sidling closer. He put a hand on Mal's chest, eyes so bright that Mal felt hypnotized by them—and a little by all that gorgeously muscled flesh on display. He'd just seen Elliott naked less than twenty-four hours before this, but somehow this was different.

"I—"

"And I can promise you," Elliott interrupted him, which was probably for the better because God knew what undignified sound was going to come out of his mouth next, "that Mal's not nearly the angel he's pretending to be."

"I believe that," Ramsey said, patting him on the back. "Our Mal's a dark horse."

He was not. He was just a guy in front of another guy . . .

Well, *fuck.*

"Come on," Elliott said persuasively, "let's get you two some punch."

"Punch?" Mal asked, eyeing suspiciously the big bowl full of smoking dry ice and colored an unnatural shade of green.

"You'll like it," Ramsey said.

Elliott put a hand on his arm. "It's safe, I promise. I oversaw its creation with Ramsey, here."

"If you're sure . . ." Mal trailed off.

"I appreciate how much you worry about me," Jane said, "but I trust Elliott. And Ramsey. Nobody's gonna roofie me, I promise."

"If you're sure it's safe," Mal said.

"Promise," Ramsey said.

Elliott picked up two red plastic cups and poured punch into both of them. Handed one to Jane and then passed the second one to Mal.

Their fingers brushed as Mal took the cup.

Mal shivered, and he swore Elliott swayed closer. "Seriously, though," Elliott murmured, "I didn't know you'd be here—"

"And you still wore that?"

Elliott chuckled. "I'm not hooking up with anyone else. You know that. Maybe I just like showing them all what they're missing."

"Is that what you're doing?" Mal couldn't help the frown he knew he was making.

"Making you jealous?" Elliott grinned. "I hadn't meant to, but I think I'm enjoying it."

"I'm not—"

"It's alright," Elliott cajoled. "Trust me, you're not gonna be alone. This angel thing—I didn't think it would be so hot, but holy hell, Mal, did you *paint* this shirt on? And is this glitter?"

"Don't ask," Mal said.

"I *wanna* though," Elliott said, the corner of his mouth tilting up into one of those irresistible Elliott smiles.

"It was all Jane's idea and a bad one to boot, but she insisted and well . . ."

"And you're surprisingly sweet and easy under all that difficult exterior?" Elliott teased. "Even *angelic*?"

"Listen," Mal retorted, "I'll show you how sweet I am."

"Ooooh." Elliott grinned. "*Please.*"

Jane tapped him on the shoulder and he was forced to look away from Elliott for a second, which actually *hurt*.

"You good here? I'm going to go play beer pong with Ramsey," Jane said.

"Wait—"

"Malcolm, I'm not gonna fuck with her," Ramsey said seriously.

"Even if I wanted him to, which I do *not*," Jane said firmly.

"Remind me to tell you why that would be."

"Oh honey, don't tell him, tell *me*," Ramsey said persuasively, wrapping an arm around her shoulders. Jane glared and he just laughed.

"You two have fun," Jane said, shooting him a meaningful look, and then they were walking off.

"You told Jane, didn't you?"

Mal winced. "I know we said we wouldn't, but . . . she kind of guessed?"

"It's alright." Elliott didn't seem particularly concerned. "I'm sure Ramsey's about to figure it out, too. If Jane doesn't tell him outright."

"She wouldn't," Mal insisted.

"He's *Ramsey*."

"Point taken," Mal said. Tried not to worry if Ramsey would spill the beans. Sipped his punch and nearly spit it out. "What's *in* this?"

"A little of this, a little of that."

"It tastes like apple-flavored lighter fluid." Mal made a face. He took another drink.

"Careful, it's strong," Elliott said, slipping a hand down to his hip. Cupping it before letting it go. Parties at Gamma Sigma were notorious and nobody would probably notice who Elliott was with or what he was doing with them—but Mal was another story. He *never* hooked up at a Gamma Sigma party.

At least he hadn't before this.

"You wanna go outside? Sneak off to a dark corner and make out?"

Mal supposed he shouldn't have been so surprised. "You want to do that?"

Elliott's expression was full of disbelief. "Are you kidding me? Please tell me I don't have to convince you that I'm into it again."

Mal noted that he'd said *into it* and not *into you*. Told himself that he wasn't disappointed by Elliott's word choice. He knew what Elliott was. How he behaved, long before they'd ever gotten involved.

You went into this with your eyes wide open. You can't even be mad.

And he wasn't. Not really. Didn't understand what he *was* feeling. But it was some kind of way.

The kind of way that made him want to latch his mouth onto Elliott's neck right here, damn who could see, and leave a mark that said bluntly, *Elliott is Mal's.*

But he's not. He's his own person. He's not available to own, even if I wanted that.

Which I don't.

"No," Mal said. "No, you don't have to. I know you want me."

Elliott laughed. "Oh, I do, baby. Believe me, I do." He took his hand and Mal let himself be dragged out the back door and down the stairs. There were a few knots of costumed partiers around the backyard, but Elliott bypassed all those, pulling him along around the side of the house.

There was a straggly bush, and behind it was an old, worn wooden bench. Elliott sat on it and pulled Mal to him.

Mal went easily, groaning in the back of his throat as Elliott kissed him hard, tongue slipping into his mouth.

For a second, he wondered if Elliott brought all his hookups to this bench—and then he realized he didn't give a shit. Elliott wasn't with them now. He was with *Mal*, fingers digging into Mal's shoulders, tugging down his tight T-shirt, stroking his collarbones.

Elliott sighed into his mouth, and Mal gave up resisting the urge to do some exploring of his own. After all, those pants were *so* goddamn loose and it would be so easy for Mal to just . . .

"Fuck," Elliott moaned. "I hoped you'd come tonight."

"Is that why you wore this? To torture me? So I'd think about sliding my hand in?" Mal did it as he said it, fingers grazing the tense muscles of Elliott's lower abs and then dipping under the waistband, gaping just enough it was so easy to slip beneath it.

Elliott was hard, already. He could feel the heat of him, and it would be incredibly easy for Mal to wrap his hand around his cock and get him off.

They'd have a damn good time. But then Elliott would have no reason to stay out here, and Mal wanted more. Mal wanted it to never end.

So he kept his touch light and teasing, loving the way Elliott's kiss grew more heated by the second.

"God, you're so hot in this I'm surprised I didn't spontaneously come on the spot. You, a fucking angel with a halo and *glitter*."

"You really like it?"

Elliott laughed. His mouth had slipped to Mal's neck, and he was nibbling up and down it with an expert motion that would've turned his knees to jelly if he wasn't already sitting down.

"I love it," Elliott murmured. "It's hot as fuck. You're hot as fuck—"

"We've established that you believe that," Mal joked tightly.

"It's a solid fact. You're a solid ten out of ten. The first time I saw you . . . God, I wanted you so fucking bad. Then and every goddamn time since."

Mal pulled back, taking in Elliott's red, wet lips, the dilated pupils, and the glitter that had somehow smeared across his cheeks. "The first time we met?"

Elliott suddenly looked worried. Guilty. Concerned. "Well, *yeah*."

"The time you hit on me at the party? Last year?"

"Uh, *yeah*."

But Mal had developed an expertly honed Elliott bullshit detector out of sheer necessity, and he knew he wasn't being honest. "I don't believe you." A horrible thought hit him. "Was it a joke?" he demanded. "Did you hit on me that night as a fucking joke?"

Elliott hadn't known then about Aubrey from high school, who'd fucked Mal up for years and years. But he knew *now*, and he'd still not said anything?

"Hold up," Elliott said, gripping his shoulder, fingers still stroking his neck. Gently, persuasively. "I did not *ever* hit on you as a fucking joke. You're thinking of a different time than I am. That's not the first time we met."

Mal was confused, even as his heartbeat returned to normal. He ignored how sweet the relief coursing through him felt. "When, then?"

Elliott's chuckle was wry. "I came to Portland the winter before my freshman year. For a recruiting trip. I went to a game. You were in the locker room after, and you pulled off your helmet, and your hair was longer, then, even longer than it is now." Elliott reached up with his other hand and twisted one of his short curls around his finger. Kind of the way he'd twisted Mal around his whole self. "I saw you and I wanted you more than I'd ever wanted another guy before. I thought I was probably fucked, because you were straight, but then Ramsey made some joke about getting on your knees and you flushed. That's when it started for me."

"*Then?*"

Mal couldn't believe it. He barely even remembered that. He had only the briefest impression of Elliott, then. If he'd thought about him at all, he'd probably decided that Elliott was a good player and they needed good players.

"Then," Elliott confirmed. He tugged Mal closer again, kissed him, and it was sweet *and* hot. Then he broke the kiss and his gaze was so unbearably serious Mal wanted to look away, but he couldn't. "I came here, because of that. Because of you."

"You did not." Mal shook his head, not wanting to believe it. Because if he did, then the first time Elliott had walked across a room to talk to him, at that Gamma Sigma party he hadn't wanted to go to, that meant Elliott had *meant it*. Malcolm hadn't been just any other guy. If Elliott was telling the truth—and Mal had no reason to *not* believe it, not with how earnestly he was looking at him now—then Mal *had* been his destination. His *only* destination.

And, afraid and cold, terrified of letting anyone in and sure that this young, gorgeous guy couldn't mean everything he was saying, Mal had pushed him away. Had been maybe not a complete asshole about it, but at least partially an asshole.

"My sisters made fun of me for ages. Picking a school because I wanted some guy's dick. Joke's on them, I guess, because I got it in the end." He paused, his fingers still stroking Mal's neck, like he had some clue of how this was breaking Mal's mind apart. "Got *you* in the end."

"I don't know what to say," Mal said. And that was the goddamn truth.

Elliott laughed. "I figured you wouldn't, which is why I never told you."

"And all the . . .all the bullshit? All the picking on me? All the shit you pulled, again and again?"

"Got your attention, didn't I?" There was resigned bitterness in Elliott's face now, like he knew how this was going to end, now that Mal knew how *not* casual this was.

But Mal had never wanted it to be that way. Surely Elliott knew that? Or maybe not. After all, what kind of idiot thought it was better to have some attention, *any* attention, than none? Even if it was negative?

"You should have told me."

"Yeah, tried that once. More than once." Elliott rolled his eyes. Tried to move back, like he'd gotten the memo that with the turn this conversation had taken, Mal wouldn't want him anymore.

He really *was* an idiot if he thought that was true.

Except you're doing a shitty job of reassuring him.

"Yeah, I . . .that's on me," Mal admitted. "I was fucked up. I can't say I'm not still fucked up, in some way, but . . .if I'd known you were *serious*. If I had been able to get out of my own way, back then . . ."

Elliott's jaw dropped. And that felt even worse. "You're not fucking with me?"

"Ell, I'd kissed *one* guy since high school, and it was only to prove I wasn't a bad kisser and that's why Aubrey rejected me. It had been . . ." *A really fucking long time.* "A while, for me. I was a *virgin*. Out of habit, sure. And fear. And well . . .a whole host of other reasons. But I chose *you*. I wanted *you*. So much I threw away all that history, decided it didn't matter."

Elliott didn't say anything for so long Malcolm was terrified that he'd said too much. Or maybe he hadn't said *enough*.

"You mean that."

"You *knew* that," Mal retorted.

"Well, yeah, but . . . I thought maybe I just wore you down, or something . . ."

"Or something," Mal said dryly.

"Or something," Elliott agreed. He smiled again, and Mal let out the breath he'd been holding. He hadn't fucked this up. Not irreparably, anyway.

Sometimes it felt like it was always Elliott reaching over their divide. Mal decided that couldn't stand. So he reached out, tugging Elliott back closer to him, kissing him.

Elliott groaned in the back of his throat, cupping Mal's face with his hands.

One minute Elliott was leaning over him, and the next, he had his arms full of him as Elliott straddled him on the bench. His eyes were glowing, pinning Mal to the spot. Even if there was a chance in hell of him wanting to move, he couldn't have. "You *like* me," Elliott murmured.

"You just now figured that out?" Mal asked, unable to help the smile that was blooming across his face.

"Well, *yeah*." Elliott was laughing now, fingers curled into Mal's shoulders like they belonged there. "We're both kind of idiots. I just . . . you seemed like you never wanted to want me."

"I didn't. I thought I was just a passing thing. That you'd have me and then move on to one of your many, many admirers."

"You wanna know a secret?" Elliott leaned in. Lips brushing against his neck. Then his ear. Mal shivered and nodded. "None of them mattered. I was just passing the time."

He didn't say *until you*, but maybe he didn't need to.

Elliott kissed him again, and it grew hot and frantic fast. Mal could completely discard—okay, *almost* completely discard—the fear that this would be the last time. Could just enjoy the feel of Elliott, hard against his thigh.

Enjoy the way he tensed and relaxed as Mal slid a hand down his abs and gripped his cock. Gave him an experimental stroke.

"Yes, *yes*." Elliott gasped.

"You want this?" Mal murmured against his mouth. "Right here? When anyone could walk by and see you?"

Elliott groaned. And okay, he *liked* that. Mal, who before this moment had considered himself a private person, even liked it. He *loved* it, in fact.

This was just another way of marking Elliott as *his*.

"I bet," he continued, "you even picked out this costume, hoping that someone would corner you and slide their hand down your pants. Make you come in them, with everyone watching."

Elliott tensed, and then he was coming into Mal's grip. Then his mouth was lush and insistent against Mal's, and that, with the pressure of Elliott against his cock, was all it took to send him over the edge, too.

"God," Elliott said, as he tried to catch his breath, "if I'd known you were this dirty hot, I'd have seduced you ages ago."

"I think you tried," Mal teased.

"I was shit at it," Elliott admitted with a chuckle. His head dropped down to Mal's shoulder. "Maybe I should have failed a class before this."

"That's not funny," Mal said sternly. Or as sternly as he could, with the pleasurable lassitude of an orgasm still lingering.

"You like it."

And okay, maybe he did. A little.

"I think more glitter ended up on Ell than on you," Jane joked, after they'd cleaned up in the tiny first floor bathroom and rejoined her. She was perched on the kitchen counter, chatting with Wes—the quarterback of the football team—and his boyfriend, Marcus.

"Does Ramsey know about this?" Wes wanted to know.

Mal looked over at Elliott, who only smiled and shrugged. Maybe they weren't going to be keeping this under wraps for much longer.

"Maybe," Mal said. "But I'm not worried about it. He'll keep his mouth shut."

"Well, you certainly don't seem to be," Jane retorted lightly. She jumped down from the counter. "You ready to head out, Mal? I have an early rehearsal tomorrow."

"Yeah, we can go," Mal said. He couldn't stop looking at Elliott who did, actually, have glitter smeared across his cheeks and down lower, even.

"Say goodbye to your . . .uh . . .*friend*," Jane told him. "I'll be outside."

Hugging Elliott didn't seem like enough. After what Elliott told him earlier, they were obviously more than just hooking up, but what had felt right—and *hot*—in the moment, made him nervous now.

"Come 'ere," Elliott said, grinning, and pulled him into a tight hug. "Tomorrow?" he murmured into Malcolm's hair.

Mal nodded, even though he had a full schedule of homework and a game that night.

Elliott let him go. "Be safe," he said. "Text me when you guys get home safe."

"How about you text *me*?" Mal asked.

"Fair," Elliott said, smiling.

When he emerged from the house, walking over to where Jane was waiting for him on the front walk, she shot him a very knowing look.

"You're not being very subtle," Jane pointed out. "If you're trying to keep it under wraps, it's not going to stay that way for very long."

"Probably," Mal said matter-of-factly. Shoving his hands in his pockets as they walked down the street, away from the noisiness of frat row on Halloween.

He was less worried about that now than he had been. Now that he understood that Elliott wasn't just scratching an itch. That he *meant* it.

That he'd been meaning it for a long time.

"You're very calm about this. What happened?"

For a moment, Mal considered changing the subject. Not lying, because he'd never once lied to Jane, and he wasn't about to start now. But she already suspected and if he was being honest with himself, he *wanted* to tell her.

"He told me tonight he liked me from the beginning. That he came here because . . ." Mal hesitated. Elliott hadn't said it exactly this way, but this was what he'd said, meant, didn't it? "That he had a crush on me. For a long time."

"Oh, you just now figured that out, did you?" Jane laughed. "Welcome to the place we've all been forever."

Mal winced. "Was it *that* obvious?"

"That you two were very into each other, and masking it by driving each other nuts? A little, yeah. But it's alright. I understood."

"Because I didn't have a lot of experience." Mal tried not to sound too judgmental about himself, but mostly failed. He *was* judgmental about himself. Why hadn't he realized what Elliott was doing? Deep down, he'd known Elliott wasn't that kind of idiot. That he wasn't stupid and callous and surface-level.

But he'd still put him in that box and kept him there forever.

"Admittedly, what he was doing to get your attention wasn't really changing your mind about him," she said mildly. She wrapped a hand around his arm and tugged him closer. "I'm happy for you."

It was clear from the sweetness in her tone that she was. "Thanks."

"And for me, too."

Mal glanced over at her. "Did something happen?"

"I met . . ." And suddenly that sweetness was suffusing Jane's whole face, and it was lit up, under that mask of heavy makeup. "I met someone."

"Who is it?"

"You're not going to like it."

"I don't know if that's true. Though if it's Ramsey, I'm gonna hate it."

"It's not Ramsey." Jane chuckled. "He's a good guy, but not my type. Besides, I'm not sure he's done sowing his wild oats yet."

"How much wild oats can one person have?" Mal muttered.

"It's . . .it's Ben."

"Ben?"

Jane whacked him on the arm. "*Ben*. The guest choreographer from Oregon."

Malcolm realized immediately why she'd told him he'd hate it. "He's—"

"He's older than me? Technically in a position of authority over me? Lives two hundred and fifty miles away? I know." The happiness in her voice didn't fade, but it did dim.

"Does he feel the same?"

"I don't know. Maybe. It's . . .it's very intense," Jane admitted. He looked over at her, suddenly worried about the concern he heard.

"What kind of intense? Are you okay?"

She laughed. "I'm fine, but it's . . .you know when you're deep in it, and you know it? And it's terrifying? That kind of intense." She paused. "What am I saying? Of course you know.

You're right there with Elliott. You can barely take your eyes off him when you're in the same room."

Mal wanted to deny that, but it was probably true. How had he *ever* looked away from Elliott? Now that he thought about it, it was a fucking miracle he'd managed to keep his wits about him for this long.

"Yeah," Mal agreed. "But you're okay?"

"I'm fine. Scared. Exhilarated. Terrified. Ecstatic," Jane said honestly.

He nodded, because he understood that all too well. He'd been pinging back and forth between those two wildly different states ever since he'd started getting closer to Elliott.

"The first time we slept together, it happened because I went over to his dorm room and demanded he explain to me what he'd done to me," Mal admitted.

"What he'd done?"

"Like he'd put a fucking spell on me. I was going out of my mind, and I didn't understand it. Didn't want to. I just wanted to be put out of my misery."

"And did he?" Jane asked, but the sweet tilt of her mouth made it clear she understood. Yes and no.

Yes, he *had* been temporarily relieved.

But no, because he was in deeper now than he'd ever been before.

"Kinda."

"I get that. We kissed at rehearsal yesterday. And now . . .tomorrow . . .I don't know what's going to happen. Nothing *should* happen, but—"

"But it feels inevitable?" Mal understood that all too well.

"Yeah. He said we shouldn't, but it feels so right." Jane sighed. "I needed to get out. Stop obsessing."

"Thus the Halloween party," Mal said, suddenly understanding his friend's sudden and vehement insistence they take Ramsey up on his invite.

Jane nodded. "I don't want him to think I'm just sitting around, waiting on him. I have a life. A *good* life. A future. I don't *need* him, but I . . ." She sighed again.

"You want him," Mal said. And *God*, didn't that ring true for him, too.

In some ways, Elliott was a fucking terrible idea. He was a teammate. A line mate. They depended on each other on the ice. And then next year, Mal would be in Toronto, and Elliott would probably be back here, though it was certainly only a matter of time before whoever drafted him in the spring brought him to their developmental camp.

He was too good to stay in college for the full four years.

"I do want him." Jane laughed, self-deprecatingly. "I can't believe I told you that Ben was probably gay. Good thing I wasn't planning on hooking you two up."

"Good thing," Mal said wryly.

"Not that it would've worked. You've only had eyes for Elliott forever." Jane patted him on the shoulder as they climbed up the stairs to their apartment.

Maybe that was true. Maybe it was also true that he'd been in such deep denial that it had taken getting closer to realize that the guy was ultimately irresistible.

· Mal unlocked the door and as soon as they were inside, Jane was flopping down on the couch, leaning over to unzip her stiletto-heeled boots. "Ugh, my feet are killing me."

He knew what she wanted, and he joined her, pulling her small but impossibly strong foot into his lap, massaging it gently but firmly the way she always needed.

Jane sighed happily. "Thanks. What am I gonna do without your foot rubs next year?"

"Fly to Toronto?"

"Not an option. Speaking of that, what are *you* going to do?"

Mal tensed. Knowing what she was asking, but barely ready to think about it yet, nevermind discuss it with Jane.

"You know what I'm talking about," Jane said. Pressing the way she always did. "What are you going to do with Elliott? He's being drafted in the spring, right?"

"Yes," Mal said.

"Well, if anyone's built for the long-distance thing, it's probably you." Jane waved her hand. "You'd be stoic and loyal in the face of anything, forever."

But Mal didn't *want* to be stoic and loyal in the face of anything, *forever*. That sounded like it would really freaking suck.

"Or," she said softly, leaning back against the couch cushions, "he could end up close. Even really close. Like Toronto-close."

That was a pipe dream.

Still, for a second, Mal let himself imagine it. Let himself really believe it could happen.

Playing together on the ice with Elliott during the day. And sharing his nights, wrapped up with him in bed.

Enjoying his bright smile in person, not just over a phone screen.

"Maybe," Mal said and was relieved that Jane decided to leave it at that.

CHAPTER 12

THE GAME WAS WELL into the second period when Elliott lost it.

There'd been a defender riding their asses the whole fucking game. He'd annoyed Elliott plenty, but Elliott was quicker and could dart out of his reach, but Malcolm, while being a fast skater, a *strong* skater, didn't have the elusiveness of someone with a slighter, shorter build. Elliott knew he'd been taking the brunt of it most of the night.

Ivan had spent the whole game complaining about it, but Mal's pissed-off face made Ivan look downright happy about the situation.

"Goddamn." Mal exhaled sharply as they returned to the bench, his body thumping down onto it next to Elliott. "Are the refs fucking blind out there?"

"That bad?" Elliott tried to commiserate.

"He was up my fucking ass, which you know, 'cause you saw it." Mal thumped his stick against the rubber padding.

"Yeah."

He had been, and it had annoyed Elliott plenty, but nowhere near how much it was annoying Malcolm now.

"You're gonna get more attention," Zach soothed, from behind them. "You're one of the best scoring lines in the conference. It's gonna happen."

"He plays *dirty*." And yeah, he had been dealing Elliott some of that shit, little surreptitious punches and elbows and jabs with his stick. But clearly, he'd been giving Mal more. Or maybe Mal, with his rigid sense of honor, would hate it even more.

"Everyone plays dirty," Ivan said under his breath, and Mal shot him a glare.

"Not like this," Mal said. He sighed. "Maybe if I can monopolize his attention, one of you can slip a shot in."

"Believe me, we're trying," Elliott said, grinding his teeth together.

He hadn't been exactly happy about the situation before this, but Mal's burning righteousness was infecting him. How had *that* happened?

The next time their line stepped on the ice and Elliott took the puck, that guy was *right fucking there*, slamming Elliott into the boards, elbow practically in his throat, the refs apparently looking every direction other than where Elliott was currently being attacked.

Frustration boiled over.

Elliott pushed back with all his strength and took off like a shot, around the goal, skating fast and watching out of the corner of his eye as Mal flipped himself around, getting positioned.

He was fucking done being acted *on*. He was ready to do some acting of his own.

Mal seemed to get that he was riding right on the edge there, because he wove between Brody and Ramsey, getting even closer.

Elliott passed him the puck, and he grabbed it, before the defender could change direction. And then instead of taking the shot himself, he flicked it right over to Ramsey, who shot it in.

"Fuck yes!" Elliott shouted, pumping his fist as the team closed around Ramsey, congratulating him.

"That was fucking unreal," Ivan said, as they worked their way back towards the bench. "I'm not even gonna ask if you practiced that, 'cause I know you didn't. But *Mal*—"

"Mal is right here," Mal said bluntly as he settled down next to Elliott.

"I just . . ." Ivan trailed off, shaking his head.

He didn't need to say he'd played with Malcolm for years now, and he'd never seen Mal do that kind of thing. They were all thinking it.

"PFM," Elliott said, exchanging a glance with Mal.

He'd calmed down some, but his blue eyes were still blazing with emotion.

Elliott couldn't remember a time when he'd thought this man was frigid.

"Well, break me off some of that," Ivan muttered.

"It's yours, next time," Elliott said, patting their line mate on his helmet.

"Decided to go after them, huh?" Mal said, as the game restarted.

"I was tired of it."

Mal shot him a look.

"Okay. I *was* tired of it. And also tired of you bitching about it."

Mal didn't say anything else, but Elliott didn't miss his sharp grin.

And the next time they took the ice, there was an aggression in Mal's play too. Like he didn't give a flying fuck anymore, and Elliott couldn't deny he loved watching him like this.

Like he was in the middle of breaking all those walls that kept the real Mal battened down and suddenly he just said *fuck it* and kicked the remainder out.

It was an uncharacteristic emotion from him, and Elliott *loved* it.

After the game, which they'd won 1-0 on that sweet goal of Ramsey's, Elliott checked his phone before he headed to the shower and wasn't surprised to see a bunch of messages on the screen from the sister chat.

From Macey: **more PFM!!!!!**

Then Nina responded: **does it count as PFM if Mal didn't score?**

Connie chimed in next. **It sure does, more so because Mal knew he couldn't take the shot himself, before that asshole got to him, so he shot it to Ramsey. A+ choice of a selfless boytoy, bro.**

Elliott chuckled under his breath. Typed out his response. **He's not my boytoy.**

Connie's text back was nearly instantaneous. **But he SHOULD be.**

Nina: **I'm with Ell on this one. He's not a boy. He's ALL MAN. Congrats, baby bro.**

Elliott hadn't told them anything had happened yet. He hadn't known *how*. Or what to even say. He was so afraid to spook Mal, only for him to raise all those walls again, that he was just trying to live in the moment.

Macey responded last. **Speaking of all man, when are you going to give Ramsey my number?**

Elliott chuckled. **Never, that's when.**

I don't need a commitment. I just want to tackle all that for at least one night.

Ew gross, Nina texted. **Save your weird football flavored fantasies for your other group chats.**

"What's so funny?"

Elliott glanced up and Mal was there, hair slicked back, towel around his waist. He'd already finished showering. Elliott felt his heart stutter.

"I was just talking to the sister chat." Elliott glanced over at where Ramsey was re-enacting the goal with Brody cheering him on. "My sister wants me to give Ramsey her number."

Mal looked unimpressed. "Does she know what he's like?"

"Oh, yeah. Doesn't care. She's . . .uh . . .well, she's a bit like me, I guess." Mal frowned, then, and Elliott quickly regrouped. "Like I *was*."

"Oh."

"What I mean is that she wouldn't give a shit if it was . . .uh . . .temporary."

Mal's frown deepened. "I don't understand that."

Mal wouldn't.

"Well, I understand both points of view. If you get my drift."
Elliott really hoped that he did. Because he did not want to fuck
this up, and all because Macey wanted to bed Ramsey.

Mal gave a single nod. "You gonna go get cleaned up?" he
asked.

"I was planning on it, just got derailed by the sister chat,"
Elliott said.

"Good." Mal paused. Lowered his voice. "I was thinking we
could . . ." Cleared his throat.

Elliott took pity on the guy. Though it was hardly pity when
he was going to get at least one—and more like two—spec-
tacular orgasms out of the situation. "We could go back to my
place?" he suggested.

"Actually, I was thinking we could go out first." Mal rubbed
the back of his neck, and Elliott realized his skin wasn't just
flushed pink from the heat of the shower. "Maybe to Jimmy's?
Or the arcade, again? You seemed to like going there."

Elliott was amused. And touched. "Are you asking me on a
date?"

"Yes."

Trust Malcolm to be direct when it mattered.

"Yeah, we can do that," Elliott said, shooting Mal the brightest smile he could. "You'd want to go back to the arcade?"

"Like I said, you seemed to enjoy that a lot. And it'll be quiet.
Ramsey was talking about some big party."

On a Friday night, students would have a lot of other things
to do. Like visit Ramsey's Gamma Sigma party. Or study for the
upcoming midterms.

"Alright then. Let me go get showered."

"Don't take too long," Mal said seriously, and then he turned away to get dressed.

Elliott picked up his phone.

Actually—I think Nina might be right. Mal just asked me on a date.

Macey sent a whole row of exclamation points.

Connie texted: **You get it, baby bro.**

And Nina finished with: **Be safe. Wear a condom.**

Elliott flushed and set his phone in his locker, going off to get showered and then dressed.

God, a *date*. With *Malcolm*.

Malcolm had never been on a real date before, but he knew if he liked Elliott more than just in bed—which he *did*, to his shock and astonishment—he needed to show him.

On Halloween, Elliott had confessed that he'd liked him from the very beginning, and Mal knew it was time for him to do some reciprocating. And not just orgasms stolen away from time studying.

He didn't know where this was going—or if it could go anywhere, with his impending graduation and Elliott's upcoming draft—but he'd lectured himself firmly on enjoying the moment. That was not his normal kind of thing, at all, but he *could* still do it, if it was important.

And Mal knew this was important.

That *Elliott* was important.

He lingered in the locker room as the rest of the team slowly filed out, looking for Friday night amusements. Zach approached him. "Good game," he said.

"Thanks," Mal said.

"You and Elliott are playing a whole other game out there," Zach said.

For a second, Mal froze. Worried that he knew exactly what Zach was saying, and the game he was referring to had nothing to do with hockey.

"Yeah," Mal said, because that wasn't really an admission of anything. Would Coach Blackburn and Zach be upset if they knew what was happening? Probably, but then Coach B was a bit of a different breed than all the other coaches he'd had in his years playing.

"Keep up the good work," Zach said, patting him on the back. "Coach B and I are impressed. You two keep getting even better."

"Ah yeah. Well. He's good. Makes it easy out there."

Zach laughed. "That's not what you said only a few months ago."

It was true. At the beginning of the season, Mal had registered a hopeless complaint that he didn't want to be on the same line as him. Even though Elliott was by and away the best offensive player on the team.

Mal tried to retreat. "He's great on the ice. You were right about that."

Zach shot him a knowing glance. "That all it is?"

"What else could it be?"

Zach shrugged and then changed the subject. "You know, there was some scouts in the crowd tonight."

That wasn't entirely unexpected. There were rumors Elliott was going to be taken in the first round of the draft, if he kept playing like this. Malcolm couldn't deny he deserved it, but if he was being really honest, he tried *not* to think about how many teams were going to want Elliott.

How they were on very different trajectories.

"Yeah, not surprising," Mal said.

"No," Zach said, "but it's good for you guys—and for this team."

"Agreed," Mal said, nodding.

"Did you know Toronto's been at every single game we've played this year?"

Mal's jaw dropped. "No. No. They didn't tell me." The scouts rarely discussed anything with him though. He was always talking to the developmental guys, who he assumed were watching tape of the games. Not getting direct reports from scouts who were here, in freaking person.

"And they're not here for you. I gotta tell you, there's a lot of talk about Elliott."

Mal felt his jaw drop *again*. Or maybe it just dropped even farther?

"*They're* talking about Elliott? *Toronto* is talking about Elliott?"

Zach nodded. "Yep. And this is still developing, so don't mention it to him." He grinned. "Not that I think you would. But I did want to mention . . .this could be a great opportunity for both of you."

It was. Of course, Zach had no idea why that was. He didn't know that they had moved from actively disliking each other to sleeping together to liking each other and maybe even more.

And if Elliott actually ended up in Toronto . . .

Mal tried to tamp down his excitement.

"Yeah, it could be," he agreed. Trying to stay casual about it.

"I mean, you guys are freaking dynamite on the ice. Imagine not having to learn how to play with all new guys? It could be something."

"Something, yeah," Mal said.

"But . . ." Zach patted him on the shoulder. "You gotta tone down the bickering, yeah? Show you're good teammates."

"Teammates," Mal echoed.

Zach had no idea they were way more than teammates, but the reminder hit hard. Would Toronto want to draft Elliott and pair him with Mal again if they knew the truth?

He hadn't been particularly worried about people finding out about them, once he and Elliott figured out what it was, exactly, that they were doing, but suddenly he understood the need for caution.

Out of the corner of his eye, he saw Coach B disappear down the hallway towards his office and he'd known Zach saw it too, because his gaze followed him.

"Hey—I gotta go, but great talk," Zach said, shooting him a smile.

As he walked away, Mal was acutely aware that while he hadn't exactly lied to his friend and the assistant coach of the team, he hadn't been honest, either.

As the guy walked away, Mal considered the conundrum.

Coach Blackburn was unpredictable in a way that Mal wasn't sure he really liked, but appreciated nonetheless. Especially if his unorthodox style meant that he wouldn't get pissed when he found out two of his best scoring players, the foundation of his starting line, were fucking.

No, Mal corrected, *we're not just fucking. We're involved.*

How would Toronto react?

And on top of that, he didn't even know what Elliott wanted. Would he even want a boyfriend? If he could even have him that way, would Elliott be okay with it?

Elliott hadn't had a boyfriend, not since he'd come to Portland U.

Maybe he didn't even want one.

Maybe for Ell, *like* meant the easy way they kept falling into bed and enjoying each other's company.

Don't be ridiculous. That's a boyfriend.

Well, he didn't need to convince *himself*, Mal supposed. He just needed to convince Elliott.

No big deal, Mal thought sarcastically.

When had anyone—even *him*—been able to convince Elliott to do something he didn't want to?

"You're frowning."

Mal looked up and Elliott was standing there. He was in jeans and an Evergreens hooded sweatshirt that brought out that sharp green of his eyes, and he'd done something with his hair that made Mal want to touch it. Mal's heart beat a little faster.

"Everything alright?" Elliott walked closer, but didn't touch him. Even though Mal thought he could see the desire in his expression to reach out.

"Yeah. Just . . . uh . . . thinking."

Elliott grinned. "Don't hurt yourself."

"You're an ass," Mal retorted, but he could hear the fondness, the undeniable affection in his own voice. Like he *enjoyed* that Elliott was an ass, sometimes.

That was something Mal was still getting used to. That Elliott could drive him crazy and also *drive him crazy.*

"Yeah, but you love it," Elliott teased, and this time Malcolm couldn't even deny it.

"Yeah, I kinda do," Mal admitted.

Mal was rewarded with one of Elliott's brightest smiles. A smile that he seemed to save just for him—at least in the last month.

"Well, should we go?" Elliott asked, gesturing towards the door.

They left out the front of the athletic complex, and to Mal's relief, the courtyard around it seemed nearly empty of students and there were no other players to be seen.

As they headed towards the arcade, Mal wondered if he should reach out and take Elliott's hand. It was right there, swinging at his side. That felt like it might be a date thing to do—but would it *also* be a boyfriend thing to do? Mal was suddenly horribly sure that he didn't understand the difference between the two.

It had been Mal's idea that they should go out and do something—something that had nothing to do with sex *or* statistics, but now that it was happening, he felt incredibly out of his depth.

He didn't know how to date.

He had no fucking clue how to convince Elliott to be his boyfriend—or if he even *wanted* Elliott to be his boyfriend? Mal glanced over at him. And okay, *yes*, he did. He wanted Elliott for his own. Even if he couldn't keep him forever.

But how to go about it?

He wished he'd asked Jane some advice about what he should be doing on this date. But she'd been busy and distant, wrapped up in her feelings—and not wanting to feel them—for the guest choreographer, Ben.

The idea had been to not be so insensitive by shoving his burgeoning relationship into her face, but now he realized just how dumb that was. Especially when he thought about how completely out of his fucking depth he was.

"I hear you thinking *very* hard over there," Elliott said in a teasing voice. "Are you sure you're okay?"

He hadn't asked if Mal still wanted to do this, but Mal heard it anyway, even though it was unsaid.

The last thing he wanted Elliott to think was that he didn't want this. Because he did, *badly*.

"I'm not going to be very good at this, so . . .uh . . .temper your expectations. Kind of like the sex," Mal said under his breath.

Elliott's smile softened, and it was he who reached for Mal's hand, squeezing it firmly. "I told you, you don't have to worry about that. Plus, we've been on dates, before, haven't we?"

"Have we?"

"All those study sessions? Even a few at Sammy's. Once you bought my dinner and then I bought yours."

"Those were *study sessions*," Mal emphasized.

"If you want to think so?" Elliott shrugged. "I like to think of them as *study dates*."

Mal had not considered them that way. Or when Elliott had brought it up, during one of them, he'd deliberately shoved that thought away. He'd still been living under extreme denial then, perpetrating the delusion that he didn't really like Elliott at all.

"Of course, that doesn't mean you can whip out a textbook tonight and deflect," Elliott joked, nudging him.

"I...I wouldn't. I don't want to." Mal took a deep breath. "I want to do this right."

"We having fun?"

"Well—"

Elliott laughed. "Wrong question. Are you enjoying yourself?"

"I *can* have fun," Mal insisted, not just for Elliott's benefit, but maybe for his own, too.

"Alright, you can. Question's still on the floor, though."

That was another reason he liked Elliott so much. He wasn't a pushover. He had a strong spine and he didn't break, only occasionally bent. And even more, he'd never let that strength control him. Change him.

"Are you there? Then, yeah. I'm having a good time." It was hard to be so honest. To bare his truths like this, but how could he do anything else when Elliott had already done it on Halloween?

"Good." Elliott pulled the door to Star Signs open and ushered him inside. "What do you want to do?"

"Food, and then we can uh . . .play some games?"

Mal had never really played games. Anthony McCoy hadn't thought they were a good use of time, and even the hockey Mal loved had been turned into something more. A college scholarship. Then even more—a stepping stone to an even more prestigious future.

"Sounds good."

They ordered nachos and hot dogs from the little snack stand, and as Mal helped to carry their food to one of the tables, Elliott joked, "Now I know why you wanted to come here. You couldn't wait to see me put some sausage in my mouth."

"Why would I, when I could have the real thing?" Mal knew he was a shitty flirt, but he *could* be honest.

"Now, that wasn't too hard, was it?" Elliott sat down and fluttered his eyelashes. Now *he* was a fantastic flirt. Mal had hated it, at first.

No, you just hated it when it wasn't directed solely at you.

It was annoying how his subconscious wouldn't even let him lie to himself.

"Harder than you'd think," Mal admitted.

"Well, don't sprain anything." Elliott dipped a tortilla chip into the bright yellow fake cheese. "Now what's your game? You like the video games? The car ones? Foosball, like Ramsey and Finn? Pinball, maybe?"

"I . . .uh . . .don't know," Mal admitted.

Elliott raised an eyebrow.

"I didn't play a lot of games, growing up. Didn't have video games or anything like that. Dad thought it was a waste of my time." It was more than he'd probably have told anyone else. Anyone else, he'd have changed the subject.

Maybe Mal was clueless about dating, but he did know he couldn't possibly expect Elliott to want to be with him, for real, if he couldn't say at least some of his truths.

"Are you serious?" Elliott stared at him. "Nothing? No games at all?"

"Well, obviously I played hockey." Mal finished his hot dog in three bites, and moved on to the next one, squirting mustard from the little packet along its length.

"But nothing else? No Xbox? No PlayStation? No arcades? Not even a little Monopoly?"

"No," Mal said.

Elliott flopped back in his chair. "Fuck, no wonder you don't know how to have fun."

"I know how to have fun." But *did* he? Mal suddenly wondered if that was just another of his delusions that Elliott was slowly breaking down.

Elliott shot him a look full of skepticism. "Do you though?"

"Well—maybe not. But I have a feeling you're going to do your part to correct that," Mal said.

"Oh, you know it, honey," Elliott joked. He leaned forward. "Eat up. I'm gonna challenge you to a pinball battle. Anyone can play pinball."

Mal didn't know if that was true. But he finished his second hot dog, split the nachos with Elliott, and ten minutes later, he was being led to the bank of machines along one side of the arcade.

"Here, this is a good one," Elliott said, gesturing towards one with a Star Wars theme. "I don't know if you're into—" He stopped abruptly, then flushed.

"I'm into what?"

"Uh, Kylo Ren? Adam Driver? But then you wouldn't be—not like me." Elliott chuckled self-consciously.

"Why wouldn't I be?" Mal knew there was something he was supposed to be picking up on, but he couldn't find it.

Elliott rubbed his neck. Looked everywhere but at Mal, which made Mal pretty sure that somehow, tangentially, this Adam Driver guy, wearing a ridiculous mask on the pinball machine, had *something* to do with it. "Well, uh. The truth is, he reminds me a bit of you."

Mal leaned in, looking more intently at the artwork. "I wear a silly looking mask and run around in a black cloak?"

Elliott laughed. "No, no, just . . .your hair is a bit longer and dark. And you're tall. Like him. It's very stupid."

"You're not the only one with a celebrity crush," Mal admitted. "Do you want to know how many times I've watched *Barbie*, only for Ryan Gosling?"

"You? Watched *Barbie*?"

"It's not that surprising." It was Mal's turn to be self-conscious. But Elliott had made a confession, so he'd felt obligated to reciprocate.

"It's really, really surprising, but that only makes it seem legit." Elliott grinned. "Who would've thought you'd be a Ken fan?"

"Who isn't a Ken fan?" Mal retorted.

"Fair point. Sorry, I don't think there's a *Barbie* themed pinball machine here. Sorry. But I think we can find one . . ." Elliott trailed off, glancing around.

"It's alright. I'll try this one if you think it'll be good," Mal said.

"I'll be just over here," Elliott said, shooting him a soft smile.

Mal popped his quarter in and familiarized himself with the controls before he started the game. How hard could this be? He had good instincts and even better aim. He was one of the most accurate passers and players in the Evergreens' conference, instincts he'd honed over the last four years. Maybe he hadn't started out as one of the best, but he'd made himself into that through determination and a hell of a lot of hard work.

But it turned out that pinball was *very* different and harder than he'd imagined.

He flicked the bottom paddle a second too late and his first ball went right down into the bowels of the machine.

"Just your first try, that's all," Mal told himself under his breath. He looked over, watched as Elliott seemingly controlled his play effortlessly.

But he does this all the time.

Mal shot the second ball. This one lasted even less time than the first one.

"Damn it," Mal ground out. Didn't bother getting himself prepped for the third shot, just hit the button and hoped that maybe instinct would take over, and he'd miraculously be good.

But just like when he'd been fifteen and trying to adjust to his new taller frame, figuring out how to put the puck in the net again, instinct wasn't as helpful as it should have been. Back then, he'd ended up doing constant drills, on and off the ice. Re-honing his skills.

Mal reminded himself that if he took his time, he'd figure this out. He was smart. He was good at these kind of things. He'd get there if he approached with a deliberate, cautious attitude.

Three quarters and nine balls later, Mal muttered an oath and pushed away from the machine.

Even masked, Kylo Ren felt like he was laughing at his complete ineptitude.

"What's wrong?" Elliott asked as he sauntered over.

"This machine sucks," Mal said. *I suck.*

"Aw," Elliott said, patting him on the arm. "Is it that bad?"

"It's that bad," Mal said, ignoring the voice in his head that insisted that you didn't show your insecurities or your total fucking incompetence during a date. During a date, you were supposed to be impressive.

"Here, let me help you," Elliott cajoled. "Come on. Try it again."

Mal shot him a dubious look but slid in another quarter, and when he took his spot in front of the machine, Elliott moved right behind him, his touch light on Mal's hands.

"Pinball's a little like hockey, but also not," Elliott murmured.

He was at least a few inches shorter than Mal, but he felt huge behind him. Hot and firm. Mal's brain scrambled, and he struggled to flick the ball with his paddles, even with Elliott's touch reminding him to move them.

"Mostly not," Mal said wryly as he missed the ball and the game made a *sorry, better luck next time* noise.

Mal kind of hated that noise, at this point.

"You've got this," Elliott said encouragingly. "Here . . .let me." Now his touch wasn't quite as gentle, fingers closing over Mal's fingers and moving them when they needed to be moved.

"There, yeah, that's better," Elliott said.

Mal realized that Ell was moving faster than he'd thought he needed to. "You gotta realize," he added, "that you've got another layer in between you and the stick. It's not as quick as you are."

"So I've got to be quicker," Mal realized.

Elliott hummed his agreement under his breath. "You got it."

Mal played two more balls with Elliott pressed up behind him, and it took all his self-control to stay focused on the play in front of him, but focus was something he'd always been good at.

The only one who'd ever frayed it was Elliott. And they'd spent enough time on the ice together that he was *mostly* good at tuning him out now.

Of course, when he tuned him out usually, Elliott's body wasn't plastered against Mal's own, his breath warm on Mal's neck, murmuring encouragements and praise in that sexy-soft voice of his.

"There. You got it. Not a high score, but still really re-spectable," Elliott said as Mal finally missed a last ditch shot to save his final ball.

"Yeah?" Mal turned around and Elliott was grinning at him. He hadn't moved away and it was really easy to just lean down and press their lips together.

Elliott swayed closer and for a second, his tongue was licking into Mal's mouth, making his whole body shudder with repressed desire.

"See?" Elliott said impudently. "That was fun, right?"

"It was something," Mal said.

"Couple more games and we'll go back to my place," Elliott promised.

"I . . .uh . . .it's . . .how did you know?" Mal finally confessed the truth.

"How did I know? You mean . . .how did *you* not know I'm going out of my mind? That I'm dying to get you into bed?" Elliott grinned. "That's a great fucking question."

Mal didn't care who was watching. He snagged Elliott's hip and dragged him up against him. Kissed him again. Deep and long, until his head swam.

"Yeah, it is," Mal said, voice rough when he finally let Elliott go.

"We could . . .uh . . .get out of here *now?*"

Mal just laughed. There was no question he wanted to. Knew that Elliott could feel that desire, pressing into his hip. But he'd wanted to give him a good time. To have *fun*, Elliott would've said, if he was thinking straight.

But he's not. All because of you.

And that was an intoxicating realization. So intoxicating, that Mal nearly said, *fuck it*, and dragged Elliott out of the arcade.

He didn't. "Let's play a little longer," he said, instead, pressing one last kiss to Elliott's mouth. "Show me how it's done, okay?"

He'd worried for a stupid moment that Elliott might be disappointed, but if anything, his smile brightened even more. Like he knew what Mal was picking—for now, anyway—and he was on the exact same page.

"Well, I'll be honest. I'm kind of killing it on this one," Elliott said, gesturing to one of the machines, the one he'd gravitated towards after suggesting the Star Wars machine for Mal.

"Show me?"

Elliott flushed, clearly even more pleased. "Of course."

CHAPTER 13

It was completely possible they weren't even going to make it out of the elevator this time.

Unlike last time they'd been in this elevator together, when Elliott had kissed Mal and he'd been shocked, this time, to Elliott's surprise, Mal had him against the wall the moment the doors clanged shut.

"You're a quick learner," Elliott groaned as Mal's mouth slid down his neck to just the spot that made him full body shiver.

"Am I?" Mal murmured into his neck.

"You know you are."

To Elliott's disappointment, Mal lifted his head. The look in his blue eyes was smoky and intimate. Elliott had known for awhile this was way more than sex, but that look? If he hadn't been sure before, he'd be sure now. "Guess I don't need to keep setting your expectations low, then."

"You never had to do that," Elliott said.

Mal shrugged and the elevator dinged, indicating their floor. He gestured towards the door and Elliott exited, still feeling the warmth as Mal followed close behind, palm flat against his back.

He fumbled with the keys, and when he finally got the door open, Mal practically dragged him to the bed.

It was really fucking cute how he'd been trying to rely on his thinly stretched self-control at the arcade, but it was even cuter that it was snapping now.

Mal pressed him to the bed, kissing him hard and then soft, but every single meeting of their mouths was deep and intense.

Elliott had always enjoyed kissing, but he'd never kissed anyone like Malcolm before. Mal made even the kissing a full fucking meal, and Elliott could barely get enough, greedily stealing every single bit that he could.

He ran his fingers down Mal's shirt and plucked the buttons open one by one, enjoying the way Mal inhaled sharply as his fingers, probably cold, found a wedge of warm, bare skin.

Mal broke the kisses only to pull Elliott's sweatshirt over his head, then his T-shirt. His fingers were cold too—thank you, Portland in November—but they only felt good against Elliott's overheated skin.

His hands drifted lower, pressing against his cock, hard and aching and confined in his jeans.

"Yeah, yeah," Elliott begged mindlessly.

He wanted it to be good, of course, but they'd both learned that they were so wild for each other—especially Mal, who had spent way too many years in painful self-denial—that they almost needed an orgasm each when they first got going, just to take the edge of desperation off.

"You want this?" Mal cupped his dick more firmly, making him groan.

"*Yes.*"

"How 'bout more?" Mal asked as he unbuttoned and unzipped his jeans, then slid off his briefs.

"More?"

Elliott would definitely not mind getting fucked again. Just the thought of it made his cock twitch against his abs. But the truth was, some of the best orgasms he'd ever experienced Mal had given him with his hands. Or even his big, muscular thigh. Elliott was definitely not above just riding the big man under him to oblivion.

But to his surprise, Mal leaned in and Elliott gasped as he slipped the head of his cock into his mouth.

"I wanna try this," Mal said, and Elliott could only nod like an idiot as more of his cock was enveloped in the sweet heat of Mal's mouth.

Part of Elliott wanted to just shut his eyes and enjoy the pleasure. But another part of him wanted to make sure Mal was okay. Was he handling this okay? Was he overthinking? Was he biting off more than he could chew, *metaphorically*?

But Elliott was sure that looking at him was going to feel like staring into the sun, and if he *did* look, it was going to exponentially increase his need to thrust into Mal's mouth until he lost himself in the ecstasy of finally seeing a long-fantasized desire come to life.

He took a chance, glancing down, and groaned again. Because Mal was as gorgeous with his mouth full of his cock as he'd imagined he would be.

Elliott couldn't resist the urge to reach out and touch him.

"Is it okay—"

But Elliott interrupted him before Mal offered another apology for his lack of experience. "Yes. *God*, yes. You're freaking brilliant."

Mal flushed. Curled his tongue around Elliott's cockhead in an expert move that had Elliott swearing.

"No lessons required," Elliott added. "Though if you wanted to spend more time practicing, I'm not gonna complain."

Mal's gaze was hot on him as he sucked Elliott's cock with the perfect pressure.

It was so goddamn good he wasn't going to last. Between the act itself and the way Mal fucking looked, sucking his cock, he was going to come his brains out in a minute.

He tried to pull back as he grew closer to the edge, but Mal put a firm hand on his hip, which, frankly, sent him over before he'd even been able to hold off.

He was coming, long, sweet pulses down Mal's throat, and when it finally ended, Mal crowded him against the headboard and kissed him.

When it finally ended, Elliott was still panting. Whether from the incredible orgasm or the kiss, it was hard to say. Maybe they could try that experiment again. Very soon.

"That was hot when you did it to me, and I hoped you'd like it too," Mal said, licking his red, wet lips.

If Elliott could've gotten hard again, less than five minutes after his last orgasm, he'd have done it.

"Getting a blowjob? Listen, I'm never—"

"Tasting my come on your tongue," Mal said, shaking his head, and *ugh*, Elliott's cock gave a feeble attempt at finding another erection.

"God, why do you have to be this way?" Elliott complained.

"Clueless?"

"Completely fucking hot, in every single goddamn way," Elliott said firmly.

"Oh. *Oh.*"

"*Oh.*" He shook his head, affectionate and in awe of how much he really liked this guy. Even more than he'd ever imagined he would—and he had a fucking fantastic imagination. Elliott regained the last of his energy and found it was actually easy to muscle Malcolm into the spot he'd just occupied.

"Aw, baby," Elliott cooed as he leaned in, finally relieving Mal of his jeans and boxer briefs, "that looks like it's painful."

His cock was hard and twitching, flushed red and drooling onto Mal's abs.

Elliott couldn't help but lean in and clean that up a little. Mal gasped as he slid his tongue around the head.

But he had another goal in mind. A plan he hoped Mal would be down with.

With one hand he reached into his drawer, grabbing what he needed, and the other, he trailed down Mal's thigh, enjoying the way the muscle tensed under his touch.

He slid his thumb against Mal's hole, and Mal stiffened again—not in a good way.

"We don't have to, if you don't want to," Elliott promised.

"I want to." Mal hesitated. "I'm not sure I'm—I *want* to."

"Do you trust me?" Elliott asked, before he could psych himself out, thinking of the possible answers Mal could give to that question.

But Mal nodded, expression solemn and serious. "I do," he said. "I trust you."

Elliott knew what that meant—to him, and to Mal.

"I got you," he said.

He took his time, warming the lube between his fingers then carefully spreading it around Mal's hole, only breaching him a little at a time. First a single finger, then two.

Not everyone liked this, and Elliott wouldn't have minded if Mal didn't. But he did. Liked probably was an understatement. He was biting his lips, face and chest flushed red, and his cock was twitching with arousal against his stomach, not flagging in the least as Elliott fucked him with his fingers.

When he finally slipped them out of the white-hot tightness of Mal's body, Mal groaned in disappointment.

"Trust me some more, okay?" Elliott asked. "You're gonna like this even more."

He had a vibrating plug, but he thought that was going to be a step too far for Mal today, so he took his simpler one, lubed it up, and then slid it carefully inside him, slow and deliberate.

Mal tensed and groaned low in his throat. "I'm so fucking close," he begged. "God, let me come."

If this worked the way Elliott hoped, the plug would rest right against his prostate, driving him crazy with pleasure, when Elliott returned his attention to his cock.

Sure enough—Mal gave a shout when the plug came to rest and practically every muscle in his body vibrated.

"Yeah, that's good, right?" Elliott teased, tapping the base of the plug, enjoying the intensity of Mal's reaction. He loved how responsive he was, how incredibly into this he was. Not just the ass play, but every single minute of their time together.

From the moment they started to kiss, Malcolm was always all-in, intently focused on Elliott, like he couldn't even think about anyone else.

"God, yes," Mal said with a rough groan. "Please let me come."

"Oh, honey, I've got you," Elliott said, and he'd barely gotten his mouth around Mal's cock when he lost it, rope after rope of come falling across his tongue and down his throat.

Mal's cry sounded like it came from deep inside him, and it went on longer than Elliott had hoped, even.

When it finally ended, he slumped back on the bed, the widest smile Elliott had ever seen breaking his face practically in two.

"Fuck," Mal said. "How did you—how did *I*—"

"Good, right?" Elliott reached down and carefully worked the plug out, trying to ignore how his own fingers were trembling. Watching Mal fall apart like that had been so hot he'd definitely found his second wind and he wanted nothing more than to slide right in. But Mal was brand-new at this, and he didn't want to push him, or rush him.

You're playing the long game, Elliott reminded himself.

"Unbelievable." Mal pinned him with those blue eyes. "Fuck me."

Elliott's fingers slipped on the plug as he tossed it onto his shirt to clean later.

"You don't need—"

"I want to. I want to feel you inside me. It'll still feel good, right? Even if I'm soft . . ." Mal trailed off and glanced down at his cock, which was really not all that soft.

"It might, I enjoy it no matter what but—"

"Stop worrying and just do it," Mal begged. "Come on."

And how was Elliott supposed to resist that?

He was just a guy—a guy with plenty of inconvenient feelings, who *really* wanted the man lying down in front of him.

Elliott let out a gust of air. Maybe this was inevitable. Grabbing for a condom, he ripped open the package and rolled it on—resolving that he'd fit in some blood tests this week so they could dispense with the extra protection—and slicked himself up.

"Just breathe," Elliott told Mal as he positioned himself and began to slide his cock in.

"Shouldn't you be telling yourself that?" Mal had reached down and was slowly jacking off his half-hard cock, which was extra hot, frankly. Next time, he was going to need to sit there and watch as Mal got himself off, maybe with that vibrating plug in his ass.

"Uh, probably," Elliott said, panting as he slid home. Mal was tight and hot, and even though he'd come plenty hard earlier, his self-control was already slipping. Mal felt so goddamn good, and it was *Mal.* He was fucking Malcolm McCoy, and *God,* that was almost enough to make him lose it right now.

He gave a short, gentle thrust and Mal moaned underneath him.

"Fuck, this shouldn't be so . . ."

"Shouldn't it though?" Mal wondered. He was fully hard now, and that pushed Elliott in even deeper. He was barely holding himself back from just thrusting mindlessly into Mal.

Enjoying every goddamn second of his glorious body.

"Come on," Mal murmured. "Fuck me like you mean it."

Elliott's control broke and he couldn't say later if he did Mal justice on his first penetrative fuck but it was wildly good for him—and maybe it hadn't been so bad for Mal, either, because less than thirty seconds later, he was coming again, groaning as come splattered up his chest.

Elliott's rhythm broke and he ground in, coming hard.

His knees gave out and he collapsed between Mal's legs, groaning.

"Goddamn," Mal murmured, one of his hands carding through Elliott's hair. "That was—"

"Yeah," Elliott agreed.

Afraid that if he said more, he'd say every single word on his mind.

Which was that he'd never been in so deep before. He'd never felt this way about anyone—wasn't sure that he could fall any harder or deeper.

I love you.

But Elliott pushed the words away. There'd been a time, not that long ago, when Mal could barely stand him. Nevermind *like* him.

This would need to be enough.

For now, anyway.

CHAPTER 14

ELLIOTT HAD BEEN WAITING for this day for weeks now. At first he'd dreaded it, but ever since Mal had started tutoring him, he'd started to find some optimism. He *wouldn't* fail this test or get kicked off the team. Not now that he had Mal in his life.

Maybe he'd been a little over cocky when he'd taken that quiz. A little too certain that he knew what he was doing. But on the midterm, he wasn't going to make that mistake. He'd taken his time. Made *sure* he wrote the right answers down and made sure he showed every single bit of his work getting to that right answer.

Even Mal had seemed confident.

They'd gone to the fundraiser, and when Mal had asked him how it went, Elliott had said, feeling completely confident that he wasn't fooling himself, that there was no way he hadn't passed with flying colors.

Mal had nodded and that was that. They'd skated around the rink a few times, even, not holding hands like Brody and Dean, but Elliott had felt Mal's warm body next to his own and knew that the rest of the team finding out about them was only a matter of time.

He'd shown up today in Dr. Prosser's class, almost *excited* to get their tests back.

The fucking joke was on him, though.

Elliott stared, in complete disbelief, at the bright red D scrawled across the top of the paper.

It didn't even make sense, but it had to be true, because what else could he believe?

Dread pooled at the base of his stomach, and his throat grew tight.

He'd get kicked off the team. This would guarantee it.

He'd let his team down. He'd let *himself* down.

And oh *God*, Mal.

He wouldn't understand. He'd think Elliott was a fuckboy who hadn't taken it seriously. Maybe he'd even think he was stupid.

Frankly, maybe he was.

Elliott knew he should stand up and file out of the classroom with the rest of the students, but he couldn't make his legs work.

If he got up and left, he'd have to tell Mal, who'd texted right before class that he was excited to hear how well he'd scored.

Well, joke was on Mal.

Or on Elliott.

Hard to say which was truer. Or which was worse.

In his pocket, his phone buzzed. It was almost definitely Mal, wanting to know how he'd done.

Elliott swallowed his panic and his grief, but somehow that didn't help.

His whole life, his whole *future*, was suddenly in shambles.

Off the hockey team, and frankly, probably dumped, because Mal would never understand. Mal would blame him, because who else could he blame?

It was his fucking fault.

At the front of the room, Dr. Prosser was looking anywhere but at him.

He couldn't even blame her, even though there was part of him that was desperate to.

Finally, he made his legs move and thankfully made it to the door.

Dr. Prosser still wasn't looking at him. She had to know what this would mean. How this would kill his chances on the hockey team. In the NHL draft.

He wondered if she'd even considered that, or if she'd decided that he'd earned it, just being a stupid athlete who didn't take her class seriously enough.

But you did.

He sure thought he had.

It was drizzling outside, cold and gray which seemed to fit his mood, as Elliott pushed the main door of the Hood classroom building open.

Then it got worse.

Mal was standing there, hood up in deference to the rain and hands shoved in his pockets, and *goddamn*, he was smiling.

Like he was so proud of Elliott, even though there was nothing to be proud of.

Elliott's stomach soured even further.

Nina had told him once that he'd lived a charmed life, easy and carefree. He'd been good at hockey and it had been easy enough to get better. He was good-looking. He was charming without really trying; people generally liked him—of course, not Mal at first, but he'd won him over in the end, hadn't he?

She'd warned him that at some point, he'd struggle with something.

It wasn't that he hadn't believed her. She was smart and perceptive, but Elliott had never imagined that karma would come for him now, or in this particularly fucked up way.

"Hey," Mal said, approaching him.

Elliott didn't know what he looked like, but he must've somehow hidden the guilt and terror raging through him, because Mal didn't seem worried.

He should be.

"Hey," Elliott said.

Mal didn't lean in and kiss him, but the hand on his arm, squeezing him gently, said it all. He wanted to.

And Elliott kind of wanted to let him, because he wasn't going to get many more kisses from the guy he was crazy about. Not once he found out the truth.

"So?" Mal asked. "How did you do? A, right? B plus?"

Elliott felt his mask of numb indifference slip. "No," he said.

"B, then? That should be enough—"

But Elliott couldn't let him get the rest out. The truth had to be easier than this jovial sweetness that he'd believed for so long wasn't in Mal's wheelhouse, but now knew was how he was deep down, underneath. In a place he'd let nobody else see. Just Elliott. "No. I got a D."

Mal's jaw dropped. "No. *No.* You didn't." He snatched the paper out of Elliott's hand. Stared at the scrawled letter for what felt like a hundred minutes, even though it was probably only a single moment.

Elliott turned. He didn't want to see Mal's face when he realized how epically he'd fucked this all up.

But Mal's voice stopped him in his tracks. "There's no fucking way you got a D," Mal said, voice hard. "It's just not possible. You *knew* the material. You did it right a hundred times."

"Guess not on attempt hundred and one," Elliott said, trying for a joke, but feeling it sink hard into the gray drizzle.

"Fuck," Mal said. "No way. *No fucking way.*" He reached out and tugged Elliott along, and a minute later, they were ducking under Koffee Klatch's awning.

Somehow they'd crossed the whole quad, and Elliott had barely realized it was happening.

"No, you didn't do this, Ell." Mal's expression was almost unbearably earnest. "You aced the test. You told me you did."

"I know," Elliott said. God, why was Mal making this worse? He needed him to just cut bait now, before Elliott's heart broke even further.

He didn't know which was worse, that he wouldn't have Mal in his bed anymore, or that he'd lose his chance at skating with him.

Mal pulled the door open to the coffee shop and practically dragged him along until they reached an empty table.

"What about your class?" Elliott knew he had a class right now. Mal had probably never even dreamt of ditching, and now he was doing it, without a second thought, for *him*.

Somehow that felt even worse.

But Mal was dismissive. "Don't worry about it. Sit. Actually—go get us some coffee, okay? I want to go over this test."

"I—"

"No," Mal said inexorably. "Get us some coffee. This doesn't make sense. It needs to make sense."

Of course Mal would feel that way.

"It makes sense," Elliott said, fighting through the lump in his throat. "I didn't do it. I fucked up. I *failed*."

But Mal grabbed his arm and squeezed it, hard. "No, you didn't. I don't believe that. I won't believe that."

"Don't make this worse," Elliott begged.

"I'm going to fix it," Mal said.

Elliott wanted to tell him it was in shambles, broken beyond repair, and even Malcolm McCoy with all his intense certainty couldn't right it, but the words wouldn't come.

Instead, he found himself walking over to the front counter and actually ordering fucking coffee.

Of course the guy at the register was *the* guy. The one who'd gotten his number and Elliott had ignored and then subsequently shut down.

Maybe he should make nice, as the guy looked at him with an assessing expression, because this thing with Mal was going to end. Probably sooner rather than later. But the idea of dating anyone—even *touching* someone—who wasn't Mal made him feel even more like puking.

He couldn't do it.

It was Mal or no one.

"Hey," Elliott said, coming to a stop in front of the register. "Cold brew—"

"Large, with room?" the guy finished. "And what does your boyfriend want?"

The *b* word sounded more than a little bitter, and Elliott supposed he couldn't blame him for that. "He's not my boyfriend," Elliott said.

Cute Coffee Guy shot him a look full of incredulity. "Someone didn't tell either of you that, then," he said. "The way you two look at each other—" He shook his head, looking unexpectedly full of regret.

But Elliott couldn't touch that with a ten-foot pole. Not today.

"Large black coffee, two sugars," Elliott said instead.

He and Mal had never come to Koffee Klatch together, but somehow he still knew his coffee order. Didn't even remember when he'd learned it, only that he'd found out one day and his mind had hoarded that knowledge, like it had collected every other little tidbit of Mal he'd discovered.

It's all you're gonna have now.

Elliott paid and dutifully picked up their coffee and brought it back to the table.

Damp curly hair fell across Mal's forehead as he stared at the test and scribbled something down on another piece of paper next to it.

Mal glanced up when Elliott put his coffee cup down.

"This isn't right," he said.

"Yes, it is. Black. Two sugars," Elliott said dully. He wanted to scream. To yell. To tell Mal that he'd ruined him for every other guy—for every other teammate—forever.

But what was the point of saying it now?

"I'm not talking about the coffee," Mal said. He leaned in as Elliott sat down across from him. "I'm talking about this test. I don't know what's going on. Your work's all right. But the answer's wrong. Just like your quiz, a few weeks back, but worse. I don't know what the fuck is going on, but this isn't right, Ell."

Elliott swallowed his shame and said, not even trying to hide the plea in his voice, "Don't make it worse, okay? Just . . .just let it go, Mal."

Mal stared at him with shocked blue eyes. "What? *No.* This is wrong, Ell. I don't know what the fuck is going on, but somehow Dr. Prosser is trying to fail you."

"Why would she do that?"

Mal shook his head. "I've got no fucking clue, but somehow I think she changed your answers."

"That's ridiculous," Elliott said. "Just face it—I fucked it up."

"No. Never. I'm never going to believe that."

Another Elliott—the Elliott of only a few days ago—would have been thrilled at how hard Mal was fighting for him. Would've been over the moon at his uncompromising loyalty and his incredible belief in Elliott.

But this Elliott didn't know how to react to this Mal. Angry and vengeful and full of righteous frustration—and all of it for Elliott.

"I wish you would," Elliott said morosely.

"Why? God, why are you being this way? You'd fight for me, every day of your life—just for me to fucking pay attention to you, and now, when it really matters, you're gonna just give up? Roll over and play dead?"

"I . . ." Elliott stared at the tabletop. "I guess so."

"Fuck that." Mal reached over and his fingers were firm on his chin as he lifted it. "*Fuck that.* You won't. I won't let you."

"It's not your decision."

"Did you *ever* let me wallow in my own shit?" Mal demanded.

No, he had not.

He'd harassed and poked and teased Mal until he smiled or snapped. But either way, he'd gotten out of his own ass, every single goddamn time.

Elliott took a long drink of his coffee. He wasn't sure what to say.

"No, you fucking didn't." Mal answered his question with a resolute expression that told Elliott that he wouldn't give up. Even if he pushed him away. No matter what he said.

And suddenly it occurred to Elliott that maybe Malcolm felt the same way about him that he felt about Mal.

Because why else would he believe in him this way?

"What do you even want me to do?"

"Just sit there while I look through this test," Mal said.

Elliott made a face. "What if I don't?"

"Elliott Archer Jones," Mal said firmly.

"Fine, fine, *fine*," Elliott retorted.

He pulled out his phone. Found himself navigating to the sister chat without really intending to.

What does it mean when the guy you like wants to fight for you more than you want to fight for yourself? he asked.

Macey was the first to answer. **It means you're crazy about each other, you idiot.**

Connie was next. **Is this about Mal?**

Nina brought in the rear with the question probably all of them were thinking: **how did the test go? Is that what this is about?**

Come on Nina, Connie texted, with a whole string of concerned emojis behind.

Elliott was pretty sure he was turning into that emoji so he couldn't really blame her.

Not great. And yes. He doesn't believe it. Elliott texted back.

Of course he doesn't. I only met the guy once for like a millisecond, but he doesn't strike me as the type to let injustice go, Nina responded.

Not you too, Elliott sent.

All of us, Connie said loyally. **We got your back, baby bro. And we're glad someone else does too.**

Elliott made a face. Then glanced up from his phone to see Mal staring at him intently.

"What?" he said.

"I was right—but no. Who were you talking to?"

"The sister chat," Elliott said, groaning. "They approve of you, by the way."

"Do they?"

Mal didn't ask why they knew—or if they *should* know. He just took it matter-of-factly that they did and that it was alright in his book. Of course, his sisters weren't here. His sisters weren't Coach Blackburn.

"They like that you're fighting for me."

"Did you ask them why *you* won't?" Mal questioned, raising an eyebrow.

"No." Elliott hesitated. "Do you really think that the grade is wrong?"

"Yes," Malcolm said, all the certainty in the world coalesced into one single word.

Elliott wished he could borrow a little of that.

"But," Mal continued, "I don't know how to prove it. We need to get some people on our side. I don't know if my word is going to count for anything, because we're—"

"Friends?" Elliott asked, actually finding himself close to smiling.

Mal shot him a look. "We're not just friends, Ell."

"No," Elliott finally had to agree.

"And really, I'm just a student. Your tutor. And your uh . . ." Mal trailed off, apparently *now* at a loss for words now that he was being forced to actually put a label on it.

"My boyfriend?" Elliott teased gently.

Mal nodded once, with all that ironclad assurance. "Yes. Exactly."

It was impossible *not* to smile now, even with all the dread and uncertainty swirling through him. And impossible not to *keep* smiling when Mal grinned back. Like they were sharing a precious secret, and *God*, it felt like they were. He knew why it had to be a secret, at least for now, but he hoped it wouldn't have to stay like this for much longer.

And frankly, considering the way they apparently looked at each other, maybe they *couldn't* keep it a secret for much longer.

"I just don't know how we're supposed to argue this," Elliott said, gesturing towards the test.

"I'm going to figure something out. But first, we need to tell Coach Blackburn. Well, *you* need to tell Coach Blackburn about the test."

"I'm sure he already knows." Another sweep of nearly nauseating guilt banished his smile. God, Coach was going to be so fucking disappointed in him.

"No, about the fact that this is *bullshit*. And I'm sure you're not going to be the first student who claimed they didn't fail something a prof says they did. So I'm going with you."

"Just for that?"

Mal's expression was soft. Earnest. Supportive. Everything Elliott had never imagined he'd be, especially towards *him*, two months ago.

"No, not just for that," he said simply.

Elliott took a deep breath. "Thank you."

"Do you believe me, yet?"

"I *want* to. I want to believe I didn't fuck all this up. The team and you and *us*. But it's hard. We're . . ." Elliott took a deep breath. "We're conditioned to believe that our professors wouldn't do anything shady. And why would Dr. Prosser even do this to me? 'Cause I'm an athlete? I can't believe that. Because she didn't pull this shit with you."

"No. I don't know why she would. It seems impossible, I know. But I fucking believe in you, Ell. This work is all right. It can't lie. And the same thing happened on that quiz you took before. You knew the right answers. You did all the work to prove your answer, and then it was wrong? That didn't make sense, then, but I chalked it up to you doubting yourself. But this time? You knew that could happen going in and this time you were going to be careful. There's no way you screwed this up."

"I . . ." Elliott found himself getting choked up again, and not because of fear or shame or guilt or sadness. But because he hadn't known he'd needed Mal to believe in him like this, to *trust* him like this, until he did.

"It's just logic," Mal said. But it was clear from the glow in his eyes as he stared at Elliott that it wasn't only that.

And that made Elliott's heart unexpectedly full, even as he knew that the convo they were about to have with Coach B was going to really fucking suck.

❧

Elliott perched in the chair opposite Coach B's desk and tried to keep his breathing steady.

Coach tapped his fingers on the desk.

"I got the report, from your professor, of course," Coach said. "But I was hoping you'd come see me."

"That's what I'm here about," Elliott said, attempting not to squirm too much.

"What *we're* here about," Mal added.

Coach's gaze swung towards Malcolm. "I know I asked you to tutor Elliott, but I'm not sure why you're here now?"

Elliott saw Mal stiffen. "I'm here because it's not right."

"I don't have a lot of choices about this," Coach said apologetically. "If the grade stands, Elliott cannot continue to play college athletics."

Mal frowned now. "I know. But it's not going to stand. When I say it's not right, I mean *it's not right*. Dr. Prosser . . ." He paused, and Elliott *knew* because he was beginning to know Mal, nearly as well as he knew himself, that he was searching for a way to present the information that Coach wouldn't just dismiss out of hand as frustration. "Dr. Prosser didn't grade the test properly."

Coach tilted his head. "What exactly are you implying?"

Mal turned towards Elliott and gave him an encouraging nod.

And yes, he should be the one speaking up in this meeting. Defending himself. Not just letting Malcolm do it for him.

"I don't understand what happened," Elliott said. "I was prepared for the test. Mal and I both made sure of that. I knew how to answer all the questions. Mal's looked over the work I provided and he says it's all right. But for some reason my answers are wrong."

Coach looked astonished. "You're saying the test results are wrong?"

"I'm saying that somehow . . ." *Ugh*, Elliott knew exactly how this sounded but they couldn't beat around the bush with it any longer. "That somehow Dr. Prosser changed my answers. She'd done it once before, we think, on a prior quiz. I had gotten some wrong that I was sure I'd gotten right."

"Huh." Coach looked incredulous. "And you believe this, too, Mal?"

"That's why I'm here."

That wasn't the only reason he'd come. Just earlier today he'd told Elliott it was more. But Elliott wasn't surprised Mal kept his mouth shut about that now. Finding out they were together wasn't going to improve Coach's chances of believing they were right about this.

"This is . . .this is a lot," Coach said, sighing and running his hand through his hair. He stood then and walked over to the door. Poked his head out of it, gesturing to someone out of Elliott's line of vision.

But Elliott wasn't surprised at all to see Zach come in, trailing after Coach B.

"Tell him what you just told me," Coach said, exchanging a look with him as he came to rest against the corner of Coach's desk.

"Tell me what," Zach said.

Elliott went over it again, internally wincing at how truly ludicrous it sounded. Why the fuck would Dr. Prosser give enough of a shit about *him* that she'd be willing to sacrifice her career if this came out?

He supposed maybe she was assuming that it wouldn't ever. That he'd take the D and accept he was off the team, without fighting back.

That he wouldn't have a Mal on his side.

"Wow," Zach said, when he finished.

"It sounds crazy," Coach B agreed. "But Mal swears that the work is right. That Elliott should have had the right answers. Did you ever have Dr. Prosser?"

"No," Zach said, shaking his head. "Never."

"But you did," Coach said, turning to Mal.

Mal nodded. "It was two years ago, though."

"But you didn't observe, back then, any bias against athletes?"

"No," Mal said reluctantly.

"Mal's a different creature though," Zach said with a ghost of a smile.

"He is, but still. I'd have expected some hint of it," Coach B said. "If it was bias, that is. It could be something else."

"But what?" Elliott said, more than a little bitterly.

"Coach, under these circumstances isn't there something you can do about keeping Elliott on the team?" Mal asked.

Coach looked conflicted. Which Elliott supposed was a good thing. Of course this wasn't going to be easy. They had no proof. Partially why he hadn't wanted to fight this at all.

"No," he said slowly. "I can't flout the rules that say he needs to be removed from official practices and games, once that grade goes final, which is in . . .a few weeks? I think?"

"So he has a few weeks. A few weeks where we can prove Dr. Prosser did this to him," Mal said staunchly.

"Theoretically, yes. I'll give you all the time I can. All the help I can," Coach said, but grimaced apologetically. "Not sure what that is, though."

"Support," Mal said firmly. "And not letting Ell beat himself up more than he already is."

Coach looked surprised. Elliott could see worry flash across Mal's face, and then he regrouped. "He's a vital member of this team, sir."

"That he is," Coach said, nodding.

"I have some thoughts, on where we can go next," Mal said.

This was news to Elliott but he didn't say so. After all, he hadn't had time to think through what all this could entail. He hadn't really believed that walking in and telling Coach would fix everything—only that it was the first step.

But trust Mal to already be thinking of the next ones.

"I thought you might," Coach said, with a glimmer of a smile. He shot Elliott a supportive look. "Anything I can do, just let me know."

"We will. Thanks for understanding," Elliott said. Paused. And added, through the lump in his throat. "And I'm sorry, sir, for letting you down. For not passing the class."

Coach shocked the hell out of him by getting up and intercepting Elliott before he could follow Mal out of the room. "No," he said firmly, putting his hands on both of Elliott's shoulders and then pulling him in for a tight, quick hug. "No, it sounds like the school's failed *you.*"

Elliott let out a gust of breath as Coach let go. "Thank you," he said.

Coach patted him on the shoulder, again. "Of course. I mean it. Now go out there and figure out how we're gonna keep you on this team."

It hadn't been *that* bad, Mal decided as he sat on the bench in front of his locker and got ready for practice.

Ramsey was whining about being out for a game or two, due to the concussion he'd sustained right after the fundraiser. Some asshole driving one of those obnoxious pedicabs had nearly run him over, and he'd only just managed to dodge it—just to end up falling off his bike and hitting his head on the sidewalk.

Mal understood his frustration. He always wanted to be on the ice, too. But he also wanted to yell at how insensitive Ramsey was, because soon, Elliott might not be able to be on the ice *at all*. And not just for a game or a practice or two, but *permanently*.

He might lose his chance at that incredibly bright future just because nobody could prove that Elliott hadn't failed that goddamned test after all.

"Ugh. Fucking protocols," Ramsey muttered.

"They're for our own safety," Malcolm said, agreeing with Brody, who'd just finished telling him the exact same thing.

Mal just hoped he'd stop, before he couldn't stop himself from snapping. Or before Elliott put two and two together and lashed out.

"Ugh," Ramsey repeated. "Did you hear that? A fucking parrot in this fucking room."

"Ramsey," Brody warned.

Brody couldn't know about Ell's situation, but Mal wanted to agree.

"If you want to play, they should just let you play," Elliott said. Because of course he would think that.

Especially now.

"No way," Brody said. "If you're not passing, you need to stay on the bench. Coach wouldn't put you in, anyway."

"Believe me, I know that. I practically fucking begged him earlier today."

Mal tried to tune out Ramsey and Brody bickering. Normally that wasn't their way. Normally it wasn't even Brody's way, but he seemed testy at how insistent Ramsey was that he get back on the ice immediately. If Mal had to guess, Brody was actually worried about the guy.

"Think Brody's man might have something to say about that," Elliott chimed in.

Mal glanced over to where Elliott was lounging on the bench, feet stretched out in front of him. He'd said it so casually.

Yeah, they *all* suspected that Brody was seeing his football playing roommate, Dean, but Brody hadn't told them yet. Hadn't even told them that he liked guys.

But Elliott had said it anyway. Thoughtlessly. Without considering the implications or the consequences.

What if he did that with *them*? What if he just blurted out that they were together, and the Toronto scouts found out? What if that ruined their chances of playing together? Of being in the same city?

Fear made him snappish in a way that he hadn't been with Elliott in a long time now.

"Ell, you can't fucking say that shit," Mal hissed. Hoping he would shut the fuck up *now*, before he ruined something before it even began. Now, belatedly, *stupidly*, he realized he should have told Elliott about the scouts, because he might be more aware of how this could get monumentally fucked—but it was too late for that now.

"Why not?" Elliott shot him a glance full of confusion and with an extra fillip of *what the fuck crawled into your ass suddenly?* "Aren't they together? But at the fundraiser—"

Mal tensed and was about five seconds from grabbing his arm and dragging him off. Reminding him that even locker room bullshit could have real life consequences, when Brody said, "Yeah, you're right. Dean's my man."

"I thought so," Elliott said, shooting Mal a triumphant look that promised his own brand of kind of sexy retribution later.

And maybe under other circumstances, Mal could've focused on that. Enjoyed it, for sure. But right now?

With Elliott's future under fire? With what was looking like his own fucking happiness possibly up in the air?

It glanced right off Mal.

"I didn't say they *weren't*. I only said you couldn't go around outing people without their permission." He hoped the look *he* shot *Ell* would make it clear that this was a really, really bad time for Elliott to decide he *also* wanted to be honest.

"Does he look bothered?" Elliott demanded.

"Children," Brody intervened, sounding over the whole conversation.

"Oh, so you're finally going to say something to these two, huh? Where you been all year?" Ivan said, rolling his eyes.

"I've been here," Brody muttered, "but I thought they might work it out on their own without interference."

"We're not fighting," Mal said. Which was true. They weren't. Not anymore. "We're fine." They'd be fine, anyway, the moment Mal could find a second to drag Elliott off and tell him to not give away the whole game.

"Uh-huh," Brody said.

"Maybe you should fuck it out," Ramsey said.

Fear coalesced into a tight, hard, nauseating ball in Mal's chest.

He had a feeling Ramsey knew the truth. And Ramsey was Ramsey, so he would *not* be above letting that truth slip out. Especially right now.

"They should not," Brody said under his breath.

Well, Brody was wrong, but then, that wouldn't be the first time that was true, either.

"Agreed," Zach added.

Mal looked up, deer in the headlights. He hadn't even realized their assistant coach had just walked in. Players gossiping, that was bad enough. But a coach?

Elliott looked amused and sly, like he was about to blow their minds apart by saying they already had, too late, everyone would just have to deal with it, and Mal panicked.

He straight-up, one hundred and ten percent, lost his goddamn mind and panicked.

"Don't worry, I have good taste. I wouldn't ever," Mal said.

He regretted the words the moment they came out of his mouth. He'd fucked it up. What he'd really meant to say was—*well*, he didn't even know what he'd meant to say. But not that.

To Mal's utter shock, though, Elliott didn't look offended or hurt or even fucking bothered. Here he was, eating his heart out because he'd announced to this whole goddamn team that he wouldn't touch Elliott because he had good taste, when he fucking *loved* him.

And Elliott was apparently unbothered by this fact.

Mal didn't know who he was more frustrated with: himself, for saying it, or Elliott, for not giving a shit.

"I think you've got more like *non* taste, myself," Elliott said.

If you knew that Mal was a virgin—at least before he'd practically begged Elliott to touch him—that comment made even more sense.

Elliott's eyes met Mal's and they were dancing with amusement and mischief. He was actually fucking *enjoying* this.

Mal wanted to scream.

Cry.

Fall to his knees and beg his forgiveness.

Maybe fall to his knees and do a few other things, too.

He finished dressing for practice, and thank *God*, Elliott did too, and by another goddamn miracle, by the time they made it to the ice, the opposite end was empty and nobody—hopefully—would notice if Mal lost what was rest of his mind and dragged Elliott over to the boards.

Under what pretext?

Mal didn't even fucking care anymore about pretext.

"That was fun," Elliott said, eyes dancing with amusement.

Mal wanted to throttle him. "*I love you*," he ground out, "and yet I just told our teammates, our *friends*, that I'd have to have shitty taste to touch you. Why does that not bother you?"

Elliott's smile was luminous and that was the moment Mal realized what he'd said.

Damn it. He'd meant to be smoother about this. Sweet. Romantic, maybe.

Not with chocolates or roses or a metric ton of candy hearts, but he'd meant to make his confession heartfelt. Maybe when they were lying together in bed, and Mal could feel their hearts beating with the same goddamn rhythm. He'd tell Elliott, *I've never been so happy in my whole life. You make me the happiest. Nobody's ever done that for me before—and I don't want anyone else to do it. Just you. Only you.*

But instead, they were on the ice, in their practice gear that still carried a whiff of locker room, and Mal couldn't even touch him. Make sure Ell knew he was serious.

"It doesn't bother me *because* you love me," Elliott said. "And it didn't bother me before this, because I could practically see you melting down over the whole thing. You thought after I said something about Brody's guy, I was going to announce to the whole locker room that we were together."

Mal wanted to deny it but he didn't.

"Yes," he agreed. "I was definitely worried you were going to tell everyone."

"We said we weren't going to tell anyone, and that hasn't changed, though I will admit, I was thinking I did want to proclaim, *at some point*, that you're mine and I love you, too. But...I get it. Not great timing."

Mal had *hoped* that was true. That Elliott wanted to tell people *because* he loved him. Not because he wanted to brag. That didn't sound anything like the Elliott he'd discovered underneath his party-hard, fun-loving persona.

"No," Mal agreed. Hesitated. "You really—"

"I love you, you big dumb lunk," Elliott said, smiling. He reached up and patted him on the cheek. "After practice, I'll be *very* happy to show you just how much."

"Yeah?"

"Or maybe you could even make it up to me," Elliott teased. "Prove just how unbelievably exceptional your taste *actually* is."

And that, Mal thought, was absolutely something he could do.

CHAPTER 15

"Well, that was a start anyway," Elliott murmured as he lay on Mal's chest, listening to his heartbeat.

"Just a start, huh?" Mal asked drowsily, underneath him.

"A *good* start."

They'd barely made it to Elliott's room before falling into each other. It was always so white-hot between them—at least the first time around—and tonight had been no exception. Mal had gone to his knees, giving Elliott a blowjob he'd remember for a long, long time.

But even though it had been just as intense as it always was, it had felt like *more* this time. Maybe because with every kiss, every touch, every lick, he'd felt Mal's love. Given him his own in return.

"Well, if it was just good . . ." Mal paused.

"Hold your horses, turbo. We'll get there. Let's just enjoy the afterglow for a minute."

Elliott felt Mal chuckle underneath him.

"Can you blame me for wanting as much of you as I can get?" Mal murmured. "And uh . . .speaking of that."

"No, don't," Elliott said. He'd deliberately been not thinking of how much it was going to suck once this school year ended. Mal would graduate. Elliott would get drafted. And then maybe, they'd be lucky to see each other occasionally. Maybe they'd at least end up on the same coast.

It would be hard, no question, but it wouldn't be forever and Elliott, flush with love, was pretty sure that was what he wanted.

Forever.

They'd figure out a way to make it work.

All he knew was that now he'd gotten Malcolm, he wasn't letting him go.

Maybe they'd always been heading this direction, from the first moment Elliott had seen Mal.

"Listen, I need to say this, because you need to know," Mal said, and Elliott resigned himself to the conversation—because of course, Mal couldn't leave well enough alone. He'd want to have a plan, probably color-coded and sprawled across some spreadsheet. Or *several* spreadsheets.

"What is it?"

"You know there's been scouts at our games."

"Yeah. It's kind of hard to pretend they're not there," Elliott said wryly. He *had* been sort of pretending that they weren't there, almost exclusively, for him. That made approaching every game easier, lessening the pressure so it wasn't an unbearable force pressing down on his shoulders.

"Toronto's been at every single game. Ell—" Mal broke off. "I shouldn't even tell you this, but I don't know how to *not* tell you this. But Zach told me they'd been talking about drafting you. Putting us back together on the ice."

Joy ricocheted through him. "Really? Seriously?" He scrambled up, off Mal's chest, so he could look him straight in the eyes. Make sure he *was* serious, but this was also Malcolm, and there was no way he'd say this if he *wasn't* serious.

Mal nodded, and even though he did look serious, he was earnest too. Hopeful.

"Of course, there's hardly any guarantees, but they like us together on the ice. And we *are* playing together better than we ever have."

It was only a sliver of hope, but it was enough to fill him with light. Elliott smacked Mal in the arm, unable to contain his smile any longer. "It's 'cause you finally started leading more with your instinct. You could be just as good as me—"

Mal frowned. "What do you mean, *just as good as you?* I'm better than you, you young cocky—"

Elliott leaned in and kissed him, swallowing the rest of what might have actually been an entertaining insult.

Mal groaned into his mouth and a second later, Elliott had swung a leg over Mal's body, and it was no big surprise as their kiss heated up that he was getting hard again.

"God," Mal gasped as Elliott broke the kiss, mouth working downwards, meandering around his pecs and down his abs. "Every time you're an egotistical little shit, I wanna fuck you into the mattress."

"And shockingly, that makes you believe I'm gonna stop?" Elliott smirked. His mouth toyed with Mal's cock, which was growing harder by the moment.

Clearly, he wasn't interested in Elliott stopping any time soon.

"Never," Mal said, and when he flipped them over, caging Elliott with his body, Elliott's cock twitched at just the thought that they could be like this *all the freaking time.*

"Yes. Please," Elliott begged, his gaze following Mal as he reached into the drawer for the lube.

"Yeah? You want this?" Mal, murmured, fingers barely pressing in where Elliott wanted them, desperately.

"*Yes,*" Elliott pled and groaned loudly, not even bothering to hold back his approval as Mal finally slid a finger inside him.

"How do you always feel so goddamned good?" Mal muttered, thrusting deep, carefully stretching him out.

But Elliott could feel that he was in more of a hurry than normal, because before he could even plead for a second finger, Mal was giving it to him.

It was just barely enough prep for Mal's cock, but Elliott didn't care. He wanted to feel that stretch, to feel every inch.

"Now," Elliott demanded. "Take me *now.*"

"God, I love you," Mal said, slicking up his cock and beginning to push it in. "Even when you're bossy like this. Maybe *especially* when you're bossy like this."

Elliott gasped. Mal leaned over and kissed him hard as he slid home.

Mal did exactly what he'd promised—he fucked him into the mattress with long, hard, slow strokes that felt shockingly, surprisingly tender.

Maybe it was the way Mal kept kissing him, one hand cradled under Elliott's head, like he was precious.

Like he couldn't get enough.

And Elliott couldn't either. He needed this man the way he'd never needed anyone else before. The thought that he'd let him down? Had been nearly unbearable.

"Stay with me," Mal murmured into his mouth, and Elliott could only nod helplessly as Mal reached down and gave him one stroke and then another before he tumbled into the longest, easiest orgasm he'd ever had.

After they cleaned up, Elliott returned to that same position, cheek resting against Mal's bicep.

"You really meant that, didn't you?"

He could feel, versus actually *see*, Mal smile.

"Yeah, I sure did," Mal said. "We're good for each other. I used to think we weren't. That you brought out the worst in me, on purpose, which actually felt even more aggravating. But—"

"But we're good together. On the ice. Off it, too," Elliott said. "Guess I'm not the only one who thinks so."

"I should have told you about the scouts. Even if Zach told me to keep it under wraps." Mal sounded like he blamed himself, which was ridiculous, because if *Elliott* didn't blame him, how dare he shoulder even a fraction of that blame?

Well, he was Malcolm. *That's* how he dared.

"Why did Zach even tell you?"

Mal chuckled. His hand, making long sweeping strokes up and down Elliott's back, paused for a split second, then resumed. "He wanted me to stop arguing with you so hard. Look at what we were doing on the ice. See what was possible. That I might not have to acclimate to another forward. Give me an opportunity. Give us *both* an opportunity."

BETH BOLDEN

"And he had no idea why you might have another vested interest in keeping me around?" Elliott asked archly.

"Nope."

"Huh. Well. Kudos to you for keeping *that* particular fact under your hat."

"It wasn't easy," Malcolm claimed but Elliott only laughed.

"No, apparently all of us are on a hair trigger of making sudden confessions all the goddamn time," he joked, poking Mal in the ribs.

Mal squawked. "I just . . .it was . . .you *know* why I was worried!"

Elliott did, sure, but that didn't mean he wasn't going to give Mal shit for it. "Uh-huh."

"Well, we should be worried about more than that. If you're off the team, you're not getting drafted."

"You're the one with the plan," Elliott said, trying to banish the sudden flare of anxiety.

"I emailed the vice chair of the department. I took calculus last year for fun—"

Elliott squawked again and smacked Mal on the arm. "You did *what*?"

"I enjoy math, okay? It was fun." At least Mal had the sense to sound defensive about this.

"Jesus fucking Christ, I'm going to end up with a nerd for the rest of my life aren't I?" Elliott shook his head. "When I think of what *could* have been . . ."

Mal's arm tightened around him, and Elliott was ninety-nine point-nine percent sure he was grinning.

"You cry into your coffee every morning?" Mal teased.

"Anyway, as I was saying, I emailed Dr. Bricker, he's the vice chair of the department. We struck up a sort of a friendship last year. If anyone can help us, it's probably him."

"Calculus, *for fun*," Elliott muttered.

"You should be glad I did, otherwise you wouldn't have an in," Mal pointed out.

"Believe me, I *am*, just . . .I can't wait to tell the sisters about this. They always think I go for the pretty face. Not that yours isn't very, very pretty. Guess I hit the lottery, 'cause it turns out you're not *just* a pretty face."

"When I do stupid shit like today, before practice, remember this moment," Mal said dryly.

"Not sure I'll be able to help myself," Elliott said.

For a minute, Mal was quiet.

Elliott liked that too, about him. They didn't always have to talk. He didn't have to always be *on*. Mal was perfectly happy just lying like this, together, listening to each other's quiet breath. Mal's touch warm and reassuring on his back, his shoulders.

"Do you want me to come with you, to meet the vice chair?" Elliott wondered drowsily.

"How did you know I was just thinking that?"

"Sex," Elliott said with certainty.

Mal chuckled. "Even great sex doesn't give you the power to read my mind."

"How would you know? You were a virgin before me," Elliott joked.

Mal made a disgruntled noise that he'd used to pretend pissed him off, but now he realized he'd *always* found endearing and adorable.

"On one hand," Mal said, changing the subject, "it makes sense for you to be there. On the other . . ."

"You're worried he's going to figure out why you're begging for my life?"

Mal made that noise again. "Something like that."

"I don't want him to think I don't have skin in this," Elliott said. "I want to be there. We'll just . . .not look at each other, or something."

"Or something," Mal said wryly.

"It'll be fine," Elliott said, hoping that it would be.

Surely, they could pretend not to be in love for twenty minutes? They did it all the time.

❧❧❧ ❧❧❧

"So, Malcolm, this is your . . .teammate . . . you told me about?" Dr. Bricker shot a fairly incredulous look over the rims of his glasses.

Ugh. Less than two minutes, and he's already suspicious.

And what had they even done? Walked in together and Mal and then Elliott had shaken the guy's hand. They'd sat down. That was *all*.

Weren't math professors supposed to have their heads stuck in theoretical problems? Not the real world?

"Yes, sir," Mal said. "Elliott's who I emailed you about. He's taking Dr. Prosser's statistics class."

"Dr. Prosser?" Dr. Bricker sounded mildly intrigued, leaning back in his rickety chair, putting his hands behind his head.

"That's right," Elliott said, picking up the thread of the conversation. He'd come in here today determined to advocate for himself. Mal had been right; this was his *future*. He couldn't just take this sitting down. If he wanted it—*and he goddamn wanted it*—he was going to need to fight for it.

"There are some . . .inconsistencies in the grading that I don't think are necessarily fair—"

"Or right," Mal added.

Elliott smacked his foot against Mal's. He didn't need to jump in like this. All righteous, like he was a knight on his steed, riding in to save Elliott's life—or his long-gone chastity.

"I took this meeting as a favor to Malcolm," Dr. Bricker said bluntly, "but I'll be honest. If I had a dollar for every student who thought they were graded unfairly, I'd be a much richer man."

"Understood. But it's not just about being graded unfairly. I don't think those are the answers I wrote," Elliott said. He'd known it was entirely possible that his complaints would get dismissed like he was every other disgruntled student. But he *knew* his situation was different.

Dr. Bricker looked surprised. "You're saying that Dr. Prosser changed your answers?"

"I can't think of any other explanation," Elliott said. "And this has happened multiple times. I know exactly how crazy it sounds. Why would Dr. Prosser do that? I thought maybe she wasn't a fan of student athletes, but she loved Malcolm two years ago. He passed her class with flying colors."

"Well, Malcolm *is* Malcolm," Dr. Bricker said with an indulgent glance in the man's direction. "But these are serious accusations, Elliott."

"I know, sir, but with the test results as they stand, I'm off the hockey team."

"Understandably concerning."

Elliott could feel Mal next to him, practically vibrating with the urge to break in. To say he wasn't crazy—that what he was saying *had* actually happened, even though they had no concrete proof of it.

Mal gave up the fight. "What Elliott is too bashful to say is that if he keeps playing the way he is now, he'll easily be drafted in the first round in the spring. He's the leading scorer on our team, and second in the entire conference."

Dr. Bricker sighed and pulled his glasses off, cleaning them on his shirt sleeve. "I understand that, Malcolm, and it's incredibly unfortunate."

"I've been tutoring him for weeks. He knows the material. I made sure of it. The work is all correct. It's just the answer that's wrong."

Mal pushed the test across the desk.

Dr. Bricker's gaze pinned Elliott to his chair. "This is true?"

"According to Mal, yeah. The work's right. The answer's wrong. I could tell you I wrote the right answer down, but I've got no proof that I did."

Picking up the test, Dr. Bricker perused it.

"This wasn't the first time, either. This happened on an earlier quiz, that we know of, but I've wondered if it's been going on all semester, which is why I ended up in this situation in the first place," Elliott added, hoping that some of this, *any of this*, might convince Dr. Bricker that this was worth looking into.

Because he still might not. He still might dismiss them with a wave of a hand and an assumption that Elliott was just like so many other athletes, who didn't bother going to class, who didn't actually *try* to get decent grades, and hoped that their status would help them skate by.

"Hm," Dr. Bricker said. "Well, I can see what you mean about the work being right. I'm going to keep this if that's okay with you, Elliott?"

Elliott nodded.

"And," he continued, "I'm going to do a bit of digging on my own, if that's also okay with you?"

"Of course," Elliott said. "Anything you can do is greatly appreciated."

"I'll be in touch," Dr. Bricker said. Elliott nodded and shook his hand and a minute later, he and Mal were outside again.

"I've got a class," Mal said.

"And I'm meeting Ramsey and Ivan for lunch." Elliott already had a feeling he knew why Ramsey had texted him, wanting to meet up.

"Well . . ." Mal trailed off, looking awkward.

"Don't be ridiculous, we can hug now. Dr. Bricker isn't staring at us, wondering if I'm your teammate or something more," Elliott said, putting his arms around him and pulling him in tightly. He even pressed a surreptitious kiss to his shoulder, in a spot where hopefully Mal would feel it.

When Mal let him go, he cleared his throat. "Speaking of that," he said. "My dad is coming into town at the end of the week."

"For Thanksgiving?"

"Something like that," Mal said. "Did you want to . . .uh . . .well, I thought you should meet him. Or he should meet you. Um. Either one."

Elliott didn't know if he really *wanted* to meet Mal's father. From what he'd heard of the man, he didn't sound particularly pleasant. But even though he'd never had a real relationship before—at least one that entailed meeting the parents—he knew that sometimes you did things because the man you loved wanted you to.

"Of course," Elliott said. "Count me in."

"He'll be in for a day or two. Maybe he'll catch a game and then we'll go to dinner. All three of us." Mal's smile looked more like a baring of teeth, a begrudging acceptance of reality, than any kind of anticipation.

"Sounds like a great time," Elliott said, trying to genuinely mean it.

Mal sighed. Pushed his hair back. "No, it doesn't, but I know you'll do a good job pretending."

"I'll be on my best behavior," Elliott promised. "And after? You can reward me, *thoroughly*, for it."

Mal's smile was a ghost of his normal, but Elliott would take it. "You got it," he said.

Elliott supposed he should just let him go, now, but instead, he pulled him into another hug. Made it longer this time, and Mal didn't protest and didn't try to pull away.

"I love you," Elliott murmured into his shoulder, hoping he heard and also hoping he didn't. Was this the kind of thing they said all the time now or was it only to be pulled out for special occasions? Still, if there *was* a special occasion, Elliott was pretty damn sure anytime Mal's dad came up counted.

"Love you too," Mal said. Gave him one last squeeze, then he was letting go, turning and walking away.

Elliott knew if he didn't want to be late, he needed to get his ass across the quad to the dining hall, but he decided he'd earned watching Mal walk away, broad shoulders and slim hips and an ass that he'd never get tired of ogling.

When he finally made his way over to Beard, Ivan and Ramsey were already at a table, Ivan plowing through a sandwich and Ramsey shoveling rice and chicken into his mouth.

Elliott waved at them and went to get soup—and a big sandwich, too. He was starving. Starving and suddenly anxious.

It was easy to be lackadaisical about Mal's dad and his stats grade when Mal was right there, being delightful and delectable, but when he disappeared, out of sight, it all came roaring back.

On his way to the checkout, he added two big chocolate chip cookies the size of his head. He *deserved* this chocolate.

"What took you so long?" Ramsey wanted to know as he sat down with his tray.

"And chocolate chip cookies, *two* of them," Ivan pointed out.

Elliott made a face. Wishing that he'd smuggled them to the table in his sweatshirt pockets.

"My chocolate consumption is none of your business," Elliott said with a prim, annoyed tone. Annoyed that he was even annoyed.

"What *is* our business is what the fuck is going on with you," Ramsey said bluntly.

"Nothing," Elliott said, but he wasn't sure how convincing it was. Not with the chocolate chip cookies staring at Ramsey from his tray.

"Don't give us that shit," Ivan said. "You and Mal are fucking, and you didn't even tell us."

"To be fair, I didn't need to be *told*," Ramsey said.

Ivan smacked him on the thigh. "Not all of us have this supernatural shit for a brain."

"And that must be a real bummer," Ramsey said, grinning.

"Surprisingly no," Ivan said. He rolled his eyes. Then turned to Elliott. "So, you weren't going to tell us?"

"It's . . .it's delicate," Elliott said.

Ramsey leaned in. "This isn't a fucking Taylor Swift song, Jones. Spill."

But Elliott just sipped at his chicken noodle soup. He didn't have to say a goddamned thing. And if he *did*, then he might not be rewarded by Malcolm for his very good behavior.

That was a fucking easy choice to make.

No choice at all, really.

"Must be serious," Ivan said. "If he's not wanting to spout off about it. Considering I had to hear every single dirty detail of his past hookups."

"*Hear*? I was practically in the same room as him and this kid, once," Ramsey said, though he didn't sound particularly upset by this fact.

"I'm *right* here," Elliott complained.

"Oh, so you *are* alive."

"Mal's tutoring me," Elliott said. Because that was the safest interpretation of what was happening.

"If it happens in bed, it doesn't count," Ramsey said with a dirty chuckle.

Technically, Elliott didn't need the tutoring in bed. That was Mal—or *had* been Mal. He was doing pretty damn good on his own these days.

Elliott shrugged.

"You're really not going to tell us?" Ivan feigned disappointment.

"What is there to tell?"

"There's *something* to tell," Ramsey said. "You two barely look at each other these days and when you do?" He fanned himself.

"Yeah, it's hot, even for me," Ivan said.

"You're a perennial disappointment, Mr. Zero on the Kinsey Scale," Ramsey said fondly, patting Ivan on the shoulder.

Ivan smiled, looking like he wasn't disappointed in the least.

God, Elliott loved his friends. He'd miss both of them when they graduated. And Mal . . .well, *missing him* felt like an understatement when he considered what it might be like if he kept going to school and didn't end up playing hockey.

Or if he ended up playing for a different organization.

"Yeah," Elliott said, "if I tell you, it *has* to stay under wraps. There's things—well, I can't go into the details. But it has to stay between us, okay?"

"Is Mal going to punish you later for saying something?" Ivan wondered.

"If he does, can I watch?" Ramsey added, his light blue eyes gleaming with mischief.

"No, and no," Elliott said. He paused. Once he told them, he couldn't take it back—but he was sure he wouldn't want to. "Yeah, we're . . .well, *yes,* we are fucking. But Ivan's right. It's more than that."

"I knew it," Ramsey crowed. "That whole bullshit yesterday about having better taste than that! That was a prime overcompensation for the truth. I wasn't sure until Mal blustered in, all fervent denial that he wasn't even interested."

"When he *clearly* was," Ivan said.

"It's good?" Ramsey wanted to know. Because of course he wanted to know.

Elliott nodded. "Worth waiting for," he said. "*He* was worth waiting for."

"Aw, Ivan, our baby bro is in love," Ramsey cooed, wrapping an arm around Elliott's shoulders and squeezing him way too hard.

"I'm not your baby bro," Elliott muttered, though he was secretly pleased by both their reaction and the nickname. "I already have three older sisters. I don't need brothers too."

"Yeah, you do," Ivan said, grinning. "Nobody gives you shit like a big brother."

"Clearly, you've never met my sisters."

"*Only* because you keep putting me off," Ramsey teased.

"And that is *not* happening," Elliott announced. "Ever. Ever, ever, ever."

"Hey, if you could fall in love, and with *Malcolm* to boot, then there's hope even for Ramsey," Ivan pointed out.

CHAPTER 16

Malcolm wasn't nervous. Not exactly.

There wasn't anything to get nervous about. His father was his father—there was no point in hoping he'd be different, because if anything Anthony McCoy was as steady as they came—but what Mal didn't know was how he'd react to Elliott.

Specifically, how his father would react to Elliott as his boyfriend.

He'd never had a boyfriend before, so he'd never had to do this.

And while his father had been understanding in that completely unemotional way of his when Mal had told him the truth about his sexuality, he still didn't know what would happen when Anthony McCoy came face-to-face with the obvious evidence that Mal wasn't ever going to fit into the mold he'd designed for his only son.

First, he hadn't gone into the military.

Second, he wanted to play hockey.

Third, he was gay.

Mal finished dressing, pulling on a plaid shirt and buttoning it up.

"You're quiet," Elliott said, coming to a stop in front of him. He was already dressed—in a nice pair of jeans and a dark green button-up. He looked as nervous as Mal was trying not to feel.

"Yeah. Good game, though." It had been. They'd won four to two, the third line scoring and then Ivan flicking a goal in. Elliott had added a pair of his own, both with assists from Mal.

Their numbers would look even better after this, and no doubt the scouts were already sending emails about how potentially valuable the pair of them could be, if they ended up on the same team.

He should be happier about this; he *was* happy about this. But he still felt vaguely worried and more nauseous than he really wanted to admit to.

"You still seem distracted," Elliott said. He lowered his voice. "Are you worried about your dad? We don't have to tell him."

Mal shot him a look. "Of course I'm going to tell him. I don't want to keep you a secret—any more than we have to. And it's not like he comes around all that often. This is the time to do it."

Elliott sighed. "Do you *always* do what you're supposed to do, Mal?"

"What do you think?" Mal tried not to snap, but his question came out harsher than he'd intended. "I'm sorry. I—I know we don't *have* to do it, but I want to. I'm just . . ."

Elliott didn't need him to finish his sentence. "I get it. It's a lot. You've never done this before. Me either."

"Not once? You've never met a parent before?"

"Oh, loads of times," Elliott said, "but it was never serious. Not like . . .he's the guy I love, that I want to spend all my time with, that I'm going to make a future with."

Something about what Elliott said—and how he said it—unwound some of those nerves inside Mal. "You're right. You're really right. We're doing this."

"Yeah," Elliott agreed, smiling. "And maybe he's an ass about it. Will that suck? Absolutely. But that doesn't change anything. I'm with you, every step of the way. This isn't just you telling him, Mal, it's *us* telling him."

Mal hadn't thought of it that way, and he was surprised at how reassuring that felt. It wasn't *only* him, when it felt like his whole life, it had only been him and his dad. Only him to please and to placate and to ensure he was proud.

But not anymore.

He'd never put all of that on Elliott, but to know he'd share it, gladly?

"That . . .that means a lot," Mal said.

"Come on, we're meeting him at Jimmy's, right?" Elliott asked.

"Yeah." Mal grabbed his bag and followed Elliott out the door.

He hadn't been able to in the locker room, but now, once they were past the throngs of people leaving after the game, he could reach out for Elliott's hand and squeeze it.

"Thanks for doing this," Mal said softly.

He'd meant to let go, but Elliott hung onto it firmly. Tenaciously. "You're welcome. I'll admit too, I'm curious."

"About my dad?"

Elliott nodded. "You're a unique kind of guy, Mal. And I know he had something to do with that."

"He did push me to be the best. To take whatever I wanted to accomplish seriously."

"Yeah, and *you* did those things," Elliott pointed out. "As long as you remember that's why you're here. *You* did them."

"I will," Mal promised.

And Mal knew that, of course. Did he forget sometimes? Yes, he did. But he was still startled to hear Elliott bring it up with so much vehemence. The nerves, which had finally just quieted, blazed back to life again. What if Elliott—

No. He wouldn't push his father.

But then wasn't pushing a McCoy kind of an Elliott Jones trademark at this point?

Mal pulled open the door to Jimmy's and held it for Elliott.

He wasn't particularly surprised Elliott only had to scan the occupied tables for a second for him to figure out which was Anthony McCoy.

"Your dad looks just like you. Just . . ."

"Sterner?" Mal supplied.

"Yeah," Elliott said, and they headed towards the table occupied by the very upright gentleman, dressed in a perfectly pressed dark green shirt not unlike Elliott's own.

His father stood up as they approached.

"Hi, Dad," Mal said.

"Malcolm," he said, in his usual formal tone as he greeted him. They hugged but it was brief. Cold. Mal hadn't even necessarily expected it.

"And this is Elliott," Mal said, and he was sure he wasn't the only one astonished when Elliott reached over and, ignoring Anthony's outstretched hand, hugged him warmly.

"Hi," Elliott said, shooting his dad the smile that had never, ever failed to melt Malcolm, even a little.

"The game was good," Anthony said, as they settled down in the booth. Elliott's leg pressed against Mal's, not because, Mal assumed, space was tight, but because he wanted to feel him.

The feeling was mutual.

"Thanks," Mal said.

"Mal mentioned you two are on the same line and playing together well."

Elliott grinned with that same bright, dimpled smile. The one no amount of meeting-the-parent awkwardness or Anthony McCoy's sternness could dim, apparently.

"Yeah, no kidding," Elliott said, sharing that smile next with Mal. "He's an amazing guy to play with. Aspirational, for sure. I wouldn't want to be on a line with anyone else. And," Elliott leaned forward, "*hot,* too."

Mal wanted to die. Just sink through the bench seat and never return.

His father looked surprised. Then speculative.

"Is that why he's here at dinner?" Anthony directed this question towards Mal.

Mal nodded. Bracing himself for the worst. Hoping for the best. "Yes. That was one of the things I wanted to talk to you about. Elliott and I are dating now."

Anthony didn't frown. He didn't look particularly happy either. Neutral, at best, Mal decided. Then *also* decided this was okay. It could've been worse.

"But you're still focused on your studies? You're still on track to head to Toronto after graduation?"

"Yes, sir. Everything's going well." *Better than well*, he wanted to yell at him. But yelling was not something they did in the McCoy house. Sometimes his father would bark if he was being difficult or not listening, but yelling was foreign to them.

There'd never been any reason for it.

"Mal's brilliant. On and off the ice," Elliott said staunchly, perhaps, if Mal had to guess, a bit rattled by the matter-of-fact way his father had merely assimilated their relationship and then moved on.

"As he should be. He has untold potential." There was a hint of a frown now, on his father's face.

Their everlasting argument.

Why should Malcolm waste all his "potential" playing what he considered a "children's game" no matter how much fame and fortune and *joy* it brought him?

"Not so much untold now," Elliott said lightly. He picked up his menu.

Mal cleared his throat. "Ell's major is literature. He's got the most amazing analytical mind. Uses it on the ice, too, but I think his biggest advantage is that he knows when to turn it off."

He knew he'd said the wrong thing the moment it came out of his mouth, but it was appallingly obvious when Anthony frowned.

"Turn off his mind?"

"Instinct, you know? It's what makes me such a great player—and your son, too. He's using his instinct more, letting that guide him, and he's gone from great to extraordinary." Elliott was still partially absorbed in the menu—or he wasn't as attuned yet to Anthony's minute facial changes—so he didn't pick up on his disapproval.

"Hmmm." Anthony didn't have to say anything more than that, but Mal felt the full weight of his disagreement.

"We're learning from each other," Mal said.

"Apparently." Anthony had a very dry sense of humor, and this was delivered in a tone so parched it stung.

Elliott glanced up, and Mal realized then that he wasn't unaware. He was simply pretending that anything his dad said that he didn't agree with just didn't exist.

What a typical Elliott strategy.

Mal wasn't annoyed, though. Instead, he was begrudgingly impressed.

"Let's order," Elliott suggested, flagging the waitress down.

Mal ordered his favorite Reuben and tots—allowing himself the fried choice because it was a special occasion. They'd not only won tonight, his father was meeting Ell, and it wasn't a complete fucking disaster. *Yet.*

After ordering the meatloaf and mashed potatoes, his father shot him a narrowed look. "Tater tots, Malcolm?"

"I don't eat them often. I follow the meal plan." *Nearly.* Strawberry pineapple smoothies and Italian subs weren't really on the dietician's meal plan either but he didn't indulge in those *all* the time. Just when Elliott turned those puppy dog eyes on him and begged, silently.

Mal looked over at where he could tell Elliott was barely restraining an eye roll. "Don't worry, he works them off," he said.

"It's still important to pay special attention to your energy intake," his father said righteously. "I don't want you getting lazy and adopting too many bad habits." His quick glance at Elliott made it crystal clear who was to possibly blame for those and that Anthony had yet to decide if Elliott *counted* as a bad habit.

"I do," Mal said.

"I just don't want you taking your eye off the prize. Not this late in your development," his father said. "You've put a lot of hard work in to get to this point. You've prepared well. You know the hockey protocols now. You can play the game as well as any of them. You have the technical background *and* the business foundation. You should be all set. Have you talked more to any of the Toronto front office about also doing an internship while you're playing on the developmental team after graduation?"

"I've made some overtures," Mal said. He really didn't want to talk about this in front of Elliott, who knew he wanted to go into front office work but not how soon he was planning to do it. How would he take it if he knew the truth?

He wouldn't be happy. Especially not if by some miracle, they did end up on the same team.

"What's this?" Elliott asked innocently. "Internship?"

"Just a discussion we had when I was drafted," Mal said, willing him to not ask any more questions.

"Mal is going to be doing something more with his life," Anthony said and the frigid certainty in him—the rigidness that Mal had never known whether he should emulate or avoid, entirely—made it clear that he didn't want to answer any more questions about this.

And maybe, Mal thought, that was a good thing.

The right thing.

Elliott had thought *Mal* was a tough nut to crack, an impenetrable block of ice.

But his *father*?

He was so much colder.

He tried not to stare at Anthony McCoy as he neatly cut his meatloaf in half, then in quarters and then eighths, then carefully spread the tomato topping evenly across each piece before spearing the first one in his mouth.

Elliott had wondered, of course, even with the offhand comments Mal had made, how Mal had turned into the man he had.

Now, there was no question how that had happened.

Anthony McCoy was unemotional and singularly focused, and Elliott could only imagine how he'd pressed and pushed and maneuvered Malcolm into doing what he wanted him to do.

Speaking of that . . .he was clearly *still* trying to get Mal to conform to *his* expectations.

"How's your sandwich?" Elliott asked, because an uncomfortable silence had fallen over the table after Anthony had brought up all the additional obligations that Mal apparently had to conform to.

"Really good." Even Mal, who'd been more relaxed in his company than he'd been for years, basically, had tensed up.

Elliott could feel it, in every line of Mal's body pressed against his.

"What are you planning to do with your . . .literature degree?" Anthony paused for the briefest second, which made it abundantly clear—though it didn't take a genius to figure out that he didn't approve—that he wasn't a fan of Elliott's choices.

Elliott supposed he could play the nice boyfriend. It wasn't a mantle that fit comfortably on him, but this was Mal's father, after all. And he loved Mal. Wanted to make him happy.

Or he could also give *this* McCoy a taste of his own medicine.

"Oh, I won't have a degree," Elliott said gravely. "I'm sure after I'm drafted I'll head right to the AHL or maybe if I'm really lucky, start in the NHL right away. I just take the lit classes 'cause I enjoy reading so much."

Impossibly, Malcolm tensed up even more next to him, but Elliott decided this was the best time he'd had since sitting down in Jimmy's, so he kept going.

"I'm sure after this, I'll only need to read to review my multi-million dollar contracts," Elliott said breezily.

A vein started pulsing in Anthony's forehead, and he'd gone an unnatural shade of puce.

This was nearly as fun as working up the younger McCoy, except that when he did that, Mal usually tackled him to the bed and ripped all his clothes off.

"You're not going to graduate?" Anthony asked, enunciating every single word like he was now convinced his son's boyfriend was a complete idiot.

"Who needs a piece of paper?" Elliott retorted, keeping his tone cheerful—and okay, maybe a little bit dumb.

Next to him, Mal let out a sigh that even he could hear.

Had he figured him out?

Possibly, yes. But that didn't make this any less enjoyable.

"You don't think you'd like to better prepare yourself for the future? How do your parents feel about that?"

"Oh, they intend to ride my success all the way to the bank. *Sir.*" Elliott added that last bit on with an especially impudent smile.

The noise Mal made in his throat resembled a strangled gasp.

Maybe he could also work *Mal* up enough during this convo to ensure the regular outcome, too. Two birds, one stone, right?

Anthony stared at him, like he was somehow attempting to solve the mysteries of the universe. Or maybe just the mysteries of Elliott's brain.

It was, in his humble opinion, way too easy to convince the McCoy men he was just a pretty face.

"I..." Anthony let out a deep breath. "You're having me on, aren't you?"

"Damnit, how'd you guess?" Elliott shot him another of the smiles that had never failed to loosen up his son.

Mal muttered something under his breath that might've been, *because you're a shitty liar.*

But Anthony actually *goddamned smiled.* It was a small smile, more the upturning of a corner of his mouth, but there it was. And Elliott had done that.

"Because my son would never fall for a complete imbecile," he said, and there was an unmistakable hint of fondness in his voice now and in his eyes, as they looked at Mal.

"That's fair," Elliott said.

"And you said you'd be on your best behavior," Mal said, elbowing him.

Elliott just laughed. "I decided to shake things up a bit."

"It was just the right amount of shaking up. I'm sorry, I do get too serious sometimes. It's hard for me to relax. At work, it feels like every decision is life and death and I carry that with me, too often. I gave that tendency to Malcolm, too, unfortunately and I'm glad to see he's got you, to, as you put it, shake things up for him."

"I'm not," Mal muttered under his breath. And Elliott knew he'd be in for it later—but only in the best, totally sexiest way.

"Yeah, you are," Elliott said happily. "You totally are." He kissed Mal noisily on the cheek and while Elliott couldn't say the rest of the meal was *comfortable,* necessarily, it lacked the awkward chilliness of the first part.

And when the time came to go, Anthony picking up the check, Elliott was happy to see that their hug was a trifle longer than the first, and when Mal pulled away, he was *nearly* smiling.

It wasn't nearly enough, but it was something.

"Before you start in on the inevitable lecture, let's get to your apartment first, so I can at least listen to it while staring at your naked body," Elliott said, the moment they were out of Mal's father's hearing.

Mal sighed. He'd known something like this might happen—but to his astonishment it had actually *helped*.

Maybe Elliott knew him—and therefore his father—a little too well.

"Oh, come on, I *mostly* behaved," Elliott teased.

"Mostly," Mal said darkly, because that was less complicated than confessing the truth.

Thank you for getting both of us out of our own heads—and our own asses. Thank you for being a fucking beacon of sparkling light even when I'm not. I hope you never, ever stop being you.

"You enjoyed it. I saw your smile." Elliott nudged him, and there was more of that undeniable sparkle, dusted over Mal, like he *deserved* it.

"I . . .I did. I . . .I kind of dread him showing up. And you made it better. Easier."

"A *lot* better. A *lot* easier," Elliott retorted fondly.

It was hard to deny. "Yeah," Mal agreed.

Elliott looked even more delighted. "So no lecture? I was looking forward to it."

"You were not. You were looking forward to getting me naked," Mal faux-grumbled—because how could he be annoyed that Elliott continued to want him with the same burning intensity that Mal felt?

"Well, *yeah.*"

"Uh . . .me too," Mal murmured, wrapping an arm around Elliott's waist and pulling him close. It was late on a Friday and there were pockets of students around, but in the darkness, they were just two anonymous guys in love. He pressed a hard kiss to Elliott's mouth and then softened it when Elliott grabbed him and wouldn't let him go.

"You're welcome," Elliott said when Mal finally pulled away.

"Thank you." It was hard saying it, but Elliott deserved him tackling the tough shit.

"Yeah, I know." Elliott's touch was soft, tender as he stroked his back. "It must have sucked, growing up with him."

"Yes and no." Mal sighed. "He wasn't always *this* intense. He just . . .I know he has hopes for me to do things."

"Like not play hockey anymore?" Elliott asked pointedly.

"Ell . . ."

"We don't have to talk about it," Elliott added. "I just . . .I don't get it. You're *good,* Mal. And if you really want to give it up and join the front office, fine. I'll support you every step of the way. But I want to know that it's what *you* want."

"I . . ." Mal cleared his throat. He didn't know. He *didn't know.* And the idea of saying that out loud went so radically against everything he'd been raised to be he didn't know how to do it.

"It's okay," Elliott said. "You don't have to decide—or even *know*—right now. You've got all kinds of time."

Mal hadn't considered that, and to his surprise, that was actually a very reassuring thought. He *didn't* need to know now.

"I bet that's not something you were told very often," Elliott continued dryly.

"No," Mal agreed. "But I like it. I really like it."

He'd thought forever that he had to have all the answers. That if he didn't—well, he'd *need* to find them, ASAP. It was a breath of fresh air to think he could take his time.

Kind of like Elliott.

They approached the apartment, Elliott reaching down and taking his hand, squeezing it.

"I got something you're gonna *really* like even more," Elliott said. "Tell me Jane isn't going to be home."

"I'm sure she's at rehearsal still," Mal said, as he unlocked the door.

Sure enough, the apartment was dark and quiet, and it was too easy to let Elliott keep leading him in his bedroom.

Mal was sure Elliott, with his desk piled with books and papers and overflowing hamper and pictures tacked up all over his walls, would no doubt find his extreme neatness somewhat austere.

But Elliott didn't even look around the room. He was only looking at Mal.

Elliott nudged him back towards the bed.

Mal, now that he had some experience under his belt, didn't always let Elliott take control in the bedroom.

But today, he went easily, the backs of his knees hitting the bed.

BETH BOLDEN

"God, just look at you," Elliott said in a hushed voice. He leaned in and Mal turned his face up, hoping for a kiss, but Elliott only dropped his backpack to the floor, and to Mal's surprise, went rummaging inside it.

"I thought we might need this tonight," Elliott mumbled as he found what he was looking for, "and I was right." He pulled out one of the toys Mal had seen in his bedside drawer, the one that Elliott told him vibrated.

Mal swallowed hard. "You had that in your bag while we were at dinner with my *father*?"

Elliott just laughed. "Hell yes, that's exactly why I had it. I knew you were gonna be all tense and cold after we saw him. And I'd want to melt you right back into my Mal."

"I'm still your Mal," he protested weakly, even though he knew exactly what Elliott was talking about. Every time he saw his dad, he could feel that tenseness creeping in along his neck, until the muscles felt nearly locked with how rigidly he was holding himself.

"You will be," Elliott said, waggling his eyebrows.

Mal wanted to laugh, too, but it was hard when Elliott was gesturing with the toy. His cock was already growing hard, thinking about it, and he shifted on the bed. Already thinking of how good it would feel buzzing away inside him.

Elliott finally kissed him, lush and intense, tongue slipping inside Mal's mouth, even as he felt Elliott begin to pull his clothes off.

First his plaid shirt, unbuttoning it temptingly slow. Then his jeans, Mal gasping as Elliott palmed his hard cock through his boxer briefs.

He only broke the kiss to slip his T-shirt off, fingers trailing down his bare chest. Tickling and tantalizing in equal measure.

Slipping off Mal's underwear, he took a step back, his gaze admiring.

"Now this is the view I like," Elliott mused. Then his tone changed, dropped lower, grittier. "Get back on the bed."

What else could Mal do but follow his orders?

He knew he'd enjoy every moment of letting Elliott take control of his body.

Crawling up towards the pillows, he let his legs fall open and Elliott made a satisfied noise in the back of his throat that got Mal even harder.

"God, how are you so fucking sexy? And all for me," Elliott crooned. Leaning in and kissing Mal again. But not nearly deeply enough. Not nearly long enough.

A minute later, he was pulling away, and Mal could feel the cool touch of lube against his hole.

"Sorry it's cold," Elliott apologized. His other hand stroked Mal's thigh, encouraging him without words to relax into it. To enjoy every moment.

Mal didn't need the encouragement, but he did need the reminder.

"It's okay, I'm . . .uh . . .*hot,*" Mal stuttered as Elliott's thumb circled his opening.

Then it slipped in, and they both groaned.

"Yeah, you fucking are," Elliott said, sounding nearly as wrecked as Mal felt.

He went slowly—too slowly if Mal had anything to say about it. He wasn't a newbie at this anymore. But Elliott was so careful with him, always. Wanting every moment to be extraordinary.

"I can take more," Mal panted. "Give it to me. And *God*, please touch me." His cock felt like an over-sensitized mess, rubbing against his abs, smearing precome all over.

"I *am* touching you," Elliott pointed out, thrusting two fingers deep. Holding them there and letting Mal squirm around them.

He kept tapping that spot that drove him insane, but never letting him have more than a second of it.

"You know what I mean." Mal moaned as he thrust again. And again.

"Oh, we're gonna get to that," Elliott promised, the corner of his mouth turning up into a sly grin. "Don't you worry about that."

"I'm not worried—I'm fucking desperate," Mal begged.

But Elliott didn't move that other hand to his cock, though more than once, he leaned over him, warm breath washing over it.

"That's so good," Mal cried out, as Elliott finally gave him what he needed so bad, the calloused pads of his fingers dragging over where he needed him to be, so deep inside.

"Yeah? This is gonna be even better. Promise." Elliott pulled his fingers out and a moment later, Mal felt the smooth silicone of the toy slipping inside him.

It was all the way in when Mal felt it rest directly against that spot.

"Fuck," Mal cried out.

"Yeah, told you you're really gonna like this." Elliott paused and looked him right in the eye. "Don't touch your cock, okay? Not yet."

"I wanna," Mal said, panting.

"I know, but *trust me*. You're gonna get what you need."

Then Elliott pressed a hidden button and Mal's back nearly jackknifed as the vibrations surged through him.

It was glorious and terrible and so intense he needed to touch his cock more than he'd ever needed to in his whole goddamned life, if only to relieve that nearly unbearable pressure building inside him.

Instead, he dug his fingers hard into the comforter and tried to ride it out.

"Oh, yeah, that's it. Good isn't it?" Elliott crooned. To Mal's surprise he was suddenly straddling him, up near his chest and leaning in, kissing him hard.

Mal groaned.

If he bucked up just a little, his cock would *just* brush Elliott's back, the gorgeous spot right where the muscular slope of his back met the generous curve of his ass.

Mal had never wanted anything more. He knew it would only take a moment, and he'd be coming harder than he ever had in his whole goddamn life.

But Elliott had promised him he'd get what he needed. If all he needed was this incessant pleasure, building and building, and Elliott pressed to his chest, his tongue in Mal's mouth—then he'd accept it.

"Fuck, you're so hot like this." Elliott pulled back, and to Mal's surprise, as he cracked his eyes open, somehow Elliott had taken his clothes off.

"Damn," Mal muttered.

"You went somewhere else for a moment there," Elliott teased. But love was shining in his eyes. Mal didn't need him to say it for him to know, without question, that he loved him just like this.

Put together *and* torn apart.

"Want you," Mal said, panting.

"Gonna give it to you," Elliott said, nudging his body closer, until his hard cock was nearly brushing against Mal's mouth. "But first—"

Mal didn't need any instructions. He reared up, licking the head, licking everywhere he could reach. He couldn't take Elliott very deep, but he could suck the sensitive head of Elliott's dick and make him moan.

It was good too, to do this, and to take a little of his mind off the fact that he was going insane with the overwhelming need to come.

"Yeah, yeah, suck me, baby," Elliott crooned, hand drifting down to cup Mal's face, feeling the slide of his cock into his mouth. "Someday, I'm gonna fuck your face just like this, and you're gonna love every second of it."

Mal made an encouraging noise, best as he could, with his mouth full of cock.

Elliott held back, though. "Someday," he murmured, patting Mal's cheek.

But he did feed him a little more, flexing his hips and ass, and Mal closed his eyes for a moment, imagining how fucking incredible he'd look from the back right now. He felt like he was being driven to a place he didn't understand—but he was along for the ride, anyway.

It wasn't even about wanting to be on it, about liking or disliking it; it was about a deeper, more visceral need.

"That's it, baby," Elliott said with a moan. Thrusting his hips just a little, and everything inside Mal tensed.

And then, he was coming, waves of it washing over him over and over, a silent scream around Elliott's cock.

"Fuck," Elliott said, pulling out and scrambling down Mal's body.

A stripe of come hit his chest, and Mal gasped.

He thought the orgasm was almost over, but then Elliott leaned over and instead of pulling out the toy, or *God,* turning off its insanity-inducing buzzing, he pushed it farther in, and Malcolm honest to God screamed, cock kicking up again, a last dribble of come leaking out of him.

He slumped back and Elliott finally turned the vibrator off, before he turned to him, hand stroking his cock.

"Shit that was hot," Elliott said.

"Come here," Mal begged. It had been beyond words, but the one thing he knew he still needed was to make Elliott feel good too.

"Don't have to beg *me,*" Elliott said softly and slid closer again, smearing the come pooling on Mal's chest. But he didn't give a shit. Fuck messiness. He just wanted Elliott's dick.

And he got it, Elliott feeding it to him, until a minute later he tensed up and he was coming down Mal's throat.

He swallowed, and if he hadn't already been lying down, he'd have collapsed.

"One second," Elliott said, breathless from his orgasm. "I got you, baby."

Gently he pulled out the toy and tossing it down, collapsed onto Mal's chest.

Apparently he didn't give a shit about the mess, either. Of course, this was Elliott, so that was far less surprising.

For a long time, neither of them spoke.

Mal because he wasn't sure he had a single fucking word in his brain and Elliott probably because he knew that.

After all, he'd known to give Mal that experience. Surely he'd had his version of it.

Even though he was spent, Mal's blood rose a little at the idea of getting to do that *to* Elliott. Of watching him unravel that way.

"You okay?" Elliott asked, nuzzling in closer, sliding a leg over Mal's thigh. "Warm enough? Comfortable?"

"I'm . . ." Mal didn't know *what* he was. Only that he'd needed that. And somehow Elliott had known.

"Good, yeah?" Elliott propped an elbow onto Mal's chest and the look in his green eyes was serene and satisfied. "Pretty incredible, isn't it?"

"How did you know?"

Elliott somehow knew that Mal meant the question to mean, *how did you know I needed exactly that?* and not, *how did you know how to do that?*

'Cause frankly he didn't give a shit who'd shared Elliott's bed before this. He was here now, and if he was very, very lucky he wouldn't ever get kicked out of it.

"Every time your dad comes up, your shoulders tense. Even mentioning him makes you tense." Elliott sighed. "I knew seeing him would be worse. I just wanted to melt you down a little, after."

"Thank you," Mal said, pressing a kiss to Elliott's palm. "Fuck. I didn't even know that was what I needed. But I did. Promise me something?"

"Anything." Elliott's tone was deceptively casual, but Malcolm could see how earnest he was. That he *meant* it.

"Melt me every time I need it?"

It was hard to ask, but Mal knew it would've been harder to ask if Elliott wasn't the man he was.

"Always," Elliott said and relaxed back into his chest.

He didn't need to say it was a promise, because Mal felt it in every molecule.

CHAPTER 17

"YOUR PHONE ISN'T MAGICALLY going to show you whatever it is you're looking for," Jane said, amused, as she stirred her coffee, spoon clanking against the side of the cheap ceramic mug.

They were enjoying their standing Tuesday brunch at Jimmy's, but Mal knew he was distracted and that his heart wasn't in it.

Because it was breaking over this whole situation with Elliott.

"I know," Mal said with a sigh, setting his coffee down on the tabletop reluctantly. "I just wish I'd heard from Dr. Bricker by now. Coach keeps making noise that he can't keep Elliott on the team much longer, even with some of the questionable details of the test."

"I need something from the department," Coach had said apologetically just last night. "Or else he's off the team by the end of the week. Before this weekend's games."

Elliott had been quiet all evening, even though they were studying as they usually did, Mal dragging him to Sammy's to try to cheer him up, but a peanut butter banana smoothie didn't do it, and neither did the blowjob that Mal had given him later, back in Elliott's room.

Mal couldn't blame him. The whole situation was unjust, and there wasn't much he could do about it. They'd talked about maybe opening an official case with the provost, but Elliott had seemed reluctant to take on Dr. Prosser without any actual hard evidence.

Mal wasn't sure he blamed him.

"That's awful," Jane said sympathetically. "So unfair."

"It is. I want to break something when I think about it." Elliott was such a good guy—and *smart*, too, and a fucking brilliant hockey player. This shouldn't be happening to him.

"I suppose I shouldn't be surprised you'd change your mind, but seeing you become his number one defender is more than a little surprising. And satisfying, too. Like you're growing into the man I always thought you could be if you could get out of your own ass for a second."

"Thanks," Mal retorted.

"And hearing about him going to toe to toe with your dad? Chef's kiss," Jane said. "Have you thought about contacting Dr. Bricker yourself, again?"

Had he? Only about a million times. But he worried that it would look exactly like what it was: that Malcolm was madly, stupidly in love with the guy.

And while he wasn't really worried that Dr. Bricker would happen to inform the Toronto scouts of this, Mal *did* worry that it made him look even less impartial and it certainly didn't magically improve their case.

"Yeah," Mal said. He pushed his hash around his plate. He'd been hungry when he'd walked into Jimmy's, but now his corned beef was curdling in his stomach.

"I get it. But you've got to fight for him. Fight for a future if you want it."

"Of course I want it," Mal objected.

Jane's gaze softened and she reached across the table, grabbing his hand and squeezing it. "Of course you do."

"You going to take any of your own advice?" Mal wondered. Maybe it was unfair to turn the tables on Jane like this, but frankly he wanted the distraction—and the change of subject.

"Honestly, is it still a bad idea to get involved with Ben? Absolutely. And I'm doing it anyway. Like I said—sometimes you've got to take a risk. Sometimes you've got to fight. Even fight dirty." She paused, shooting Mal a lopsided smile. "Yes. Even you can fight dirty."

"I just choose not to," Mal protested.

"And that means you can choose differently," Jane pointed out. "Play dirty. Fight dirty. If you really want something, you'll find a way to get it."

"It's not—"

"No, it's not your dad's way. But he's not always right, Mal. For him, or for you." She squeezed his hand again and then let go.

"That's kinda what Elliott was trying to say, I think. The other day. He wasn't happy to hear about how my dad's pressured me to do this internship. He thinks I should skate as long as I want to."

Jane made a terrible faux shocked face. "And now you're just seeing this?"

"I thought *I* wanted it, too," Mal said. "But things are different this year . . .it's different playing this year. With Elliott, and Ivan too, of course."

"But you're not in love with Ivan and hoping that he'll be drafted to your future NHL team," Jane said dryly.

"No," Mal agreed.

"I think it's not that your situation is all that different. It's that *you're* different."

Mal could feel it too. He was having more fun on the ice than he ever had before. He'd approached it so doggedly and diligently before. But now, he was leaning into his instincts more, and as Elliott liked to claim, he was, "skating now with his heart, not his head."

Mal pushed his hash around his plate more, forced himself to eat another bite. "Yeah," he agreed, because Jane was not wrong.

Jane was rarely wrong.

Which probably meant Jane was right about this fighting for what he wanted thing, too.

If he wanted to help Elliott, he needed to work for it.

"You're welcome," Jane said, grinning.

"I'd ask how you got so smart, but you've always been so smart."

Her mouth tilted up. "Yes and no. You were good for me, too, Mal. And you know what? I'm glad Elliott has you. And you have Elliott."

"Me too. I . . ." Mal's voice cracked embarrassingly, but there was only Jane here. No need to feel humiliated. "I just want to fix this, for him. Let him fix it himself. *Something.*"

"Well, you know what to do," Jane said. She waved her hand to the door. "I got this. Go play white knight—or maybe in this case, we can call you the morally gray knight."

Mal nodded and stood, pulling on his coat and tossing a few bucks down on the table to cover the tip.

He kind of hated the thought of being 'morally gray' and he couldn't even think of what his father would think about it.

But then he considered how it would feel next year or the year after if he was playing for Toronto and Elliott was doing . . .well, what would Elliott even do without hockey? He was a born hockey player.

And, it wasn't like Dr. Prosser's behavior was all above-board either. Mal *knew* there was something going on, a hidden agenda he couldn't quite discern, but was unbelievably sure existed.

Nothing else made sense.

Mal headed in the direction of Dr. Bricker's office. It wasn't normally his time to be in there, receiving students, but maybe he could persuade him to make another exception for him.

In his pocket, his phone buzzed, and he didn't even have to look at the screen to know who it was. Elliott had just gotten out of his morning class and was no doubt asking if he'd heard anything. He'd told him he'd call, while he walked to his next one.

"Ell, I'm *working* on it, I swear," Mal answered without glancing at the screen.

"Not Ell," a deep voice said with amusement. "It's Dr. Bricker."

"Oh. *Oh*. I'm sorry. I just thought it was going to be—"

"Your boyfriend?" Dr. Bricker was definitely smiling now. Mal could hear it.

"Yeah," Mal admitted.

"I've got good news for both of you. I brought your concerns and a copy of the test to the chair, Dr. Howard. She's agreed that there's something going on. Can you and Elliott come by this afternoon for an hour or two?"

Mal mentally sifted through both of their schedules. "Yes, I think so. An hour or two?"

"Dr. Howard's going to administer another test. One *she* grades."

Oh shit.

It was not what Mal had expected to hear, but it would absolutely be a way for Elliott to prove, once and for all, that he'd been graded unfairly the first time around.

Would Elliott freak out? Absolutely. But Mal was sure that he knew the material. He'd been confident—but not cocky—going into the first test.

"I'll let him know," Mal said, switching directions. If he was quick, he might be able to cross the quad and catch Elliott before he ducked into his next class. Tell him the good news in person. Reassure him if he panicked.

"Three PM sharp," Dr. Bricker said.

"We'll be there and he'll be ready to take whatever test you need to give him."

"Good." Dr. Bricker hesitated. "I'm glad you brought this to our attention, Mal. Dr. Howard's very concerned."

"So are we. Elliott, especially," Mal added. "This could kill his whole future."

"If he genuinely got mis-graded, we'll fix it, I promise," Dr. Bricker said.

Mal hung up the phone and accelerated into a slow jog, getting a few weird looks as he cut across the quad.

But it paid off, because Mal spied Elliott about to walk into Hood, the farthest classroom building.

He caught up to him on the stairs up to the front door and grabbed his arm.

Elliott's whole face bloomed into a pleased but astonished smile.

"Mal, what are you doing here? You have class in—"

"I know," Mal said. He'd be late, for sure. But he'd stored up plenty of goodwill over the years and if he used a little of it now, it wouldn't be the end of the world. "I talked to Dr. Bricker just now. Dr. Howard, the chair of the department, is going to administer a second test and grade it herself. This afternoon."

Elliott's jaw dropped. "Today? This afternoon?" His voice was edging higher, into nervous hysteria.

"Yeah, it's quick, but think about it—you *know* this material. We made sure of it. And tonight, you're never going to have to worry about missing a single practice, at least not because of that bitch Dr. Prosser."

"Mal!" Elliott exclaimed.

"What? She *is*," Mal said. "She fucked you over, and if she gets fucked over because of that, I'm not going to be sorry." Maybe there was something to this morally gray hero business. It felt *good* saying those things. Sure he was really righting an injustice, but it felt like more than that, too.

Sometimes, like Elliott liked to say, you had to color outside the lines to end up with a beautiful picture.

"You really believe I can do this?" Elliott asked.

Mal knew what he was asking—what he was *really* asking, because there was a vulnerability in his eyes now that Elliott didn't show to many people. Or to anybody, really. A vulnerability that Malcolm hadn't been convinced even existed until he'd gotten to know him better.

"I've never believed anything else," Mal said.

The corner of Elliott's mouth tilted up. "You sure about that?"

"Even when I thought you were a careless, thoughtless party boy, I still thought you were good at what you did. It made me a little crazy, but it's true."

"A lot crazy, I'd imagine," Elliott teased, swaying towards him. Mal wanted to touch him, to pull him close, to kiss him. But they were right on the quad, standing at the steps of Hood. Everyone would see, and imagine they understood what was going on.

Well, they'd be right.

"I want to kiss you," Mal said.

Elliott made a face. "I want you to kiss me. We should—"

Mal had a feeling he knew what he was about to say, "No," he said, pressing his fingers lightly to Elliott's mouth and then pulling them away. "Not yet. Let's get through this, first."

Mal's gaze was sober and intense. "Two months ago I'd have told you no. No way. There wouldn't be any circumstances I would tell you picking this over even the *chance* you could play in Toronto was a good idea." He sighed. "But you're right. It would be awful."

He reached down and took Elliott's hand, squeezed it. "I told Dr. Bricker you were my boyfriend. You are. And I don't want to hide that."

"This could really suck, you know," Elliott said wryly.

"Yeah, it could, but we'll deal. It could be worse, you know?"

Mal tugged on his hand and they were walking, hand in hand, towards the rink. And Elliott thought, because he couldn't help himself, *it could be like this all the time. But even if it's not, it's still worth it.*

"How exactly?"

Mal shot him a shit-eating grin. A grin he'd never even imagined, two months ago, that Malcolm McCoy possessed and now here he was, giving it to *him*.

It turned out dreams did come true.

"You could still think I'm an unfunny and way-too intense asshole? And I could think you're a party boy who doesn't take anything seriously?"

"Did I *ever* say that you're funny, McCoy?" Elliott chuckled.

Mal shot him an incredulous look. "Are you fucking kidding me?" Then he hesitated for a second. "You're totally winding me up on purpose, aren't you? God, I hate it when you do that."

"No, you don't," Elliott said, grinning. "Because just think of what you can do to me later, in retribution."

Mal nodded and then suddenly, Elliott was being yanked into a pair of firm arms and he was being kissed.

Here was the thing: Malcolm wasn't ever going to be a comedian. He was always going to take some things a little too much to heart. He could, occasionally, still be a stubborn asshole. But he was also the fiercest, most loyal friend and partner that Elliott had ever dreamt of having.

Actually—scratch that. He'd never dreamt that Malcolm could be that, or that he even *wanted* that. He'd only thought Mal was the hottest guy he'd ever seen in his whole life.

And he was still that, too.

Mal pulled back, patting him on the cheek. "Yeah," he agreed, his gaze full of happiness. "Just think of what I can do."

"Oh my God, what *is* this?"

Elliott looked up and Zach was standing there, a shocked look on his face.

"I thought he knew," Mal said under his breath. "Why else say that thing the other day before practice?"

Elliott nodded.

"Honestly, what the fuck, you're just making out now?" Zach shoved a hand through his hair and there was no denying the complete astonishment on his features.

"You had to know this was an inevitability," Elliott said. "And if you're mad about Coach, we're literally on our way to tell him."

"Yeah, right now." Mal nodded, too.

"Are you fucking kidding me?" Zach nearly shouted.

Elliott had never seen their assistant coach look like this before. He was livid. Really, truly upset.

"I told you to get along with him!" Zach exclaimed, pointing at Elliott.

Mal shrugged. "Admittedly, I took it a step further than that."

"You're going to give him a fucking heart attack. God, can't you just keep it in your pants for ten seconds?" But he didn't seem to be talking to them, anymore, more like exclaiming, pointlessly, to the sky.

"We're young, and we've got needs," Elliott said matter-of-factly.

"Of course you do," Zach said, sarcastically with a tinge of bitterness.

"Are you okay?" Mal asked.

"No! I'm not okay. I'm . . .this is going to fuck it up. Fuck him up. You know that right?"

"I don't think Coach is going to be all that surprised," Elliott ventured.

"Maybe surprised that we're just showing up and telling him bluntly," Mal said.

"He's—" Zach stopped abruptly, like he'd almost revealed too much.

"He got over Brody and his hulking big boyfriend. He even got over Brody not wanting to play pro hockey," Elliott offered.

But Zach didn't look reassured. He was pacing now, back and forth on the concrete courtyard in front of the entrance. "It's just one more thing," he muttered, barely loud enough for them to hear.

"Is he okay?" Elliott asked under his breath.

Mal shrugged.

"I don't think Coach is going to go round the bend over me and Mal falling in love?" Elliott tried next.

Zach just threw his hands up and his look said that he really thought Coach Blackburn might.

"He seems pretty even keeled," Mal agreed.

"Seems. *Seems.* Did you know—" Zach stopped abruptly again. "No, you wouldn't. And he wouldn't want you to."

He and Mal exchanged glances. "Is everything okay?"

"Oh, everything's fucking peachy," Zach muttered.

"Well. . .uh . . .we're gonna go do that thing," Elliott said, gesturing towards the building. "If you're not going to stop us?"

Zach frowned but waved them on.

"What the fuck was that about?" Mal wanted to know as he held the door open for Elliott.

"Hell if I know," Elliott said. "It was weird though. Do you think Coach . . ."

"No, he's alright. I know he hasn't always been." Mal hesitated. "But he seems solid now. This isn't going to send him spiraling or anything. He handled Brody's shit just fine."

"Why do you think Zach is so intense about him, then?" Elliott wondered.

Mal shot him a knowing look, and Elliott gasped.

"*No*, you don't think so? Do you? Oh my God."

"I mean, I don't *know*. But it's a theory. Being so intense over someone usually doesn't mean you're indifferent to them."

Elliott grinned. "Firsthand experience with that?"

"Just a bit," Mal said with an amused chuckle.

The door to Coach B's office was open, and he was sitting on his couch, watching some game film of their upcoming opponent on the big screen TV mounted on one of the walls.

"Hey, you got a minute?" Mal asked him.

"Sure. And I hear congratulations are in order," Coach said, gesturing them in. They took the other couch as Coach paused the game.

"I . . .uh . . ." Mal hesitated, and Elliott realized he thought Coach was talking about their relationship—not his newly passing status in statistics.

"You must have heard pretty quickly from Dr. Howard," Elliott said, shooting Mal a look.

"I think she emailed me right away, knowing how difficult of a situation this was for you," Coach said. "I'm relieved. And you must be, too."

"Definitely," Elliott agreed. "But that's not why we're here."

He could feel Mal shifting around next to him. Was he just trying to get comfortable or was he nervous? He hadn't *seemed* nervous when he'd kissed him in front of anyone who might've been watching, less than ten minutes ago.

Elliott nudged Mal with his knee, and Mal nudged back.

"You've got something else?" Coach asked.

"Zach told me something a few weeks ago, and I wasn't sure if it was true," Mal said, finally speaking up.

"About?"

"How Toronto's interested in Elliott."

Coach laughed. "Just about everyone's interested in Elliott. But yes. I suppose it couldn't stay under wraps forever. They're very interested in reuniting the two of you. Obviously, Ivan's part of your line's success, but he's already been drafted by Boston, and I can't imagine what situation the Toronto GM would have to create to get the Bruins to let him go."

"There's . . .uh . . .something else that can't stay under wraps, not much longer," Mal said.

Coach raised an eyebrow.

"It's partially your fault, you know. I'd imagine you thought asking Mal to tutor me might help us understand each other a little better," Elliott said, suddenly and acutely aware that now that the moment of truth had finally arrived, he wasn't as easy about this as he'd imagined. But it would be worth it. He looked over, met Mal's gaze, and saw the same truth written there.

"I can't deny that was a thought I had," Coach said. He frowned. "What else?"

It was the moment of truth, right now. Elliott swallowed hard. "We understood each other even better than you might've hoped. We . . .uh . . .we fell in love." He reached over and took Mal's hand. His palm was sweaty, despite the chill in the air, but Elliott understood.

If anyone'd told him that at the beginning of the year that not only would Malcolm McCoy be capable of love and affection, but that he'd feel it for him, and rank that love and affection above anything else, Elliott wouldn't have believed it.

But he was doing it. If that wasn't true fucking love, what was it?

"You fell in love," Coach repeated, a bewildered look on his face. "Wait. You mean this? You're together? But you're—"

"I know we haven't always gotten along," Mal said apologetically.

Coach laughed. "Son, that is an understatement. At the beginning of the year, you told me if I put Elliott on the same line as you that you'd transfer."

"You said that?" Elliott wasn't offended, but he was a little surprised. "But you'd never want to transfer. Think of all those partial credits you'd end up with!"

Mal rolled his eyes. Shot Elliott a look that promised some especially sexy retribution later. "I wasn't really serious."

"Serious enough to make the threat," Elliott teased.

Coach cleared his throat. "Okay. Okay. I see it now. Well. Uh."

"We didn't want to hide it," Elliott said.

"Not anymore," Mal agreed.

"I can see that," Coach said dryly. "I'm beginning to be surprised you were hiding it at all."

"We know the risks. We know what could happen. We're hoping for a different result, though," Mal said.

"For Toronto to still want Elliott?" Coach appeared to be seriously considering this. "Well, it's not the problem it used to be, for sure. And they see how well you're skating together, especially recently. Like you each took something from the other . . ." He cleared his throat, awkwardly. "I can see why, now."

"Yep," Elliott said happily. "I removed the stick from Mal's ass."

"Don't talk to Coach about my *ass*," Mal hissed under his breath, and Coach flushed.

"I don't see a huge, insurmountable problem," Coach said. "Keep playing the way you're playing and it won't matter. Teams want results. They want more goals than the other team, and with the pair of you leading in so many statistics, making each other better every week, I can't see that this would be enough to discount that."

"Really?" Mal sounded shocked.

How badly had Mal believed this would torpedo his future? And he'd *still* agreed. Elliott felt a new wave of love for his guy.

He trusted him.

He trusted *them*.

Coach waved a hand. "Maybe they'll even like it? I can't say for sure. But I don't see a huge problem. Could another team take Elliott first? Sure. Still, I appreciate the heads-up. And an effort to keep the PDA to a minimum, at the rink . . ."

"That won't be a problem," Mal said quickly.

"I don't know about—" Elliott started to say.

Mal interrupted him, shooting him a quelling look. "It won't be a problem," he repeated, even firmer this time around.

Elliott grinned. He was going to get exactly what he wanted.

No.

He'd *already* gotten exactly what he wanted.

"Good," Coach said. "See you both at practice."

They got up and were almost to the door when Coach said, "And really, Elliott, *don't* talk to me or anyone else about Malcolm's ass."

Elliott cackled, Mal groaned, and he knew then—it was going to be okay.

Better than okay, actually.

CHAPTER 18

ELLIOTT DIDN'T KNOW HOW he'd feel, going back to statistics class after he'd taken Dr. Howard's test. He hadn't heard anything from either her or Dr. Bricker—or from Dr. Prosser herself, but he was still surprised when he walked into the lecture hall and she wasn't there.

Instead, it was Dr. Bricker setting up his laptop at the front of the room.

"Dr. Bricker, hey," Elliott said, approaching him.

He met his eyes and stood up to his full height. "Oh, Elliott, I'm glad I saw you. I was hoping I would."

"Dr. Prosser's not here," he said. He frowned.

"No. No, and she won't be, again." Dr. Bricker sighed. "Dr. Howard didn't tell you, yet?"

"No," Elliott said uncertainly. He'd told Dr. Howard that he didn't want her overly punished.

"Well, it's complicated, and I probably shouldn't tell you all the details—but frankly, you were the one who lost out here, so I think you deserve to know. Essentially, Dr. Prosser ended up in debt to the wrong kind of people." He pulled his glasses off, cleaning them. Elliott had a feeling he was trying to pick his words carefully. "She thought she could take the house in an illegal gambling ring. She needed money for a sick relative, and it spiraled out of control—and then to settle the debt, they wanted her to take you out of the equation."

"Me?" Elliott couldn't believe this. He was just . . . well, *him*.

"Elliott, you might not realize this, but you're the highest scorer on your team. The second highest scorer in the whole conference. Taking you off the board? That would change everything. And for bookies? That's power."

"So she didn't hate me? Because I was an athlete?" Elliott hadn't realized how much this was bothering him, until he realized that it hadn't mattered. That she hadn't targeted *just* him.

Dr. Bricker's face softened even more. "Not even close, Elliott. In fact, when Dr. Howard and I spoke to her, she cried. She felt terrible about what she did to you, but she felt like she had no other choice. Some bad people were leaning on her very hard."

Elliott felt terrible, too. "She didn't feel like she had a choice, so did you really have to fire her? Even after she told you how much she needed the money?"

"We're working on it, but she is most definitely not teaching this class for the rest of the semester. I can't say anything else, but there *is* a major investigation going on. I don't know if we'll need you to give a statement. But possibly yes. And not only for us, either."

"The cops?"

Dr. Bricker didn't react, but it was clear that the police were now involved.

"Well, I hope you nail those bastards to the wall," Elliott said in a hard voice. "And *not* Dr. Prosser. She got taken advantage of."

Patting him on the arm supportively, Dr. Bricker nodded. "We'll see. But I'm just glad to see you in class so I could tell you that it wasn't you at all."

"Guess I should've been a shittier hockey player," Elliott said, shrugging.

"I know at least *I'm* glad that you aren't, and I'm sure that Malcolm is, too."

Elliott grinned. "Definitely."

"Alright, I've got to get started, but don't think I'll be taking it easy on you, Jones."

"I wouldn't expect any less."

Elliott barely made it to his seat before pulling out his phone.

You're not going to believe what I just heard from Dr. Bricker about why Dr. Prosser targeted me, he texted to Mal.

Are you texting in class again?

You gonna spank me, finally?

Mal didn't answer right away, and Elliott had actually just slipped his phone back in his pocket, when he felt it buzz again.

Trust me, you ask for it, I'm not gonna deny you a single goddamn thing. Lunch? I want to hear what happened with Dr. Prosser.

Lunch? Does that mean I have to wait for my spanking? Elliott sent a pouty face.

You figured it out. Lunch. Now go pay attention.

Dr. Bricker had a different style than Dr. Prosser, and it also helped Elliott to focus—he'd gotten scared enough of what could happen if he *didn't* pay attention to just blow any class off again—and to his surprise he found that he *almost* enjoyed the lecture.

Or maybe it was just the thought of Mal bending him over his knee and spanking him.

Still, he was surprised to hear when Dr. Bricker announced that class was over.

When he exited the building, Mal was standing at the stairs, waiting for him.

"Hey," Elliott said. Looking forward to the weekend, when he and Mal had agreed they'd tell the rest of the team. After that, they could kiss whenever they wanted. Elliott was *really* looking forward to that day.

"Hey, so what's going on?" Mal asked eagerly. Probably, unfortunately *not* eager to go spank Elliott, and instead eager to find out what had happened to Dr. Prosser.

Disappointing.

"Apparently she got into an illegal gambling ring to raise money! For a sick relative!" Elliott whispered-exclaimed.

"*What*? Are you serious? You're actually serious." Mal looked shocked. "I thought she just didn't like athletes." He paused. "Okay, just *you* as an athlete, maybe. But I guess this makes more sense."

"If only we were in an awesome drama movie. If we were, I'd totally be attacked next by the illegal bookies, trying to get me out of the way using any method they could. And then you'd have to protect me." Elliott beamed up at Mal.

Mal just rolled his eyes. "I'm a hockey player, not a body-guard."

"But you could be both! Defend me with your hockey stick and your bulging muscles," Elliott teased. "Sounds like a good time. Almost as good of a time as the spanking."

Mal flushed and then chuckled. "God, you and your one-track mind. Lunch first, *then* we can go back to my place. Alright?"

"Not like I'm twisting your arm, big manly protector," Elliott said, batting his eyelashes.

"Never," Mal said, grinning at him.

⟫⟫⟩ ⟨⟪⟪

"Are you worried at all?" Mal asked as he and Elliott walked down the street towards Darcelle's. It was mid-morning on a Sunday and Elliott had already complained twice that they could have spent a long, lazy morning in bed.

Frankly, Mal felt the same. But they'd promised to attend this unofficial team event that Ramsey had put together, and they'd also agreed that it was high time they told the rest of the team what was really going on.

"Everyone still thinks that your version of good taste is avoiding me," Elliott had reminded Mal, still impossibly sounding delighted by the whole thing. "They need to know what *really* good taste is."

Mal had rolled his eyes, but he couldn't disagree.

They'd told Coach. He knew Elliott had told Ramsey and Ivan.

"No, not worried at all." Elliott wasn't, of course. Elliott had flawless confidence even if Mal was sometimes convinced it was more of the "fake it til you make it" variety.

Elliott turned to him, squeezing his hand reassuringly, and continued, "It's going to be okay, you know?"

"You don't know that." And there was the one thing that worried Mal: the unknown. Everything he could control, everything *Elliott* could control—that would be fine. But their futures weren't necessarily their own.

"Yeah, I do," Elliott said. "I love you. You love me. Nothing else matters."

Mal raised an eyebrow.

"Okay," Elliott conceded with a wry smile, "*almost* nothing. I really wanna play hockey. And I want to play with you."

Mal squeezed his hand back. "I want to play with you, too."

"Do you though?" Elliott asked, grinning impudently.

Mal rolled his eyes.

Elliott kept going, because this was Elliott. Mal reminded himself that this was the man he loved. The man he wanted to love for the rest of his life.

"I don't know, I'm half-expecting you to retire at twenty-three, right when I get to the team."

"I'm not—I *won't*."

"Just because your dad wants you to. Because he'd decided that's the only 'worthwhile' hockey-related occupation he can come up with," Elliott finished.

Mal winced. "I'm considering not doing the internship, okay?"

He was more than considering it. He'd reached out to the team, to his contact at the front office, and expressed some misgivings. He'd said he'd fallen back in love with playing, this season. Slipped in a sentence about how great his line mates were. Didn't mention Elliott by name, because he was afraid if he did, he would start and not stop—and the front office didn't need a rhapsodizing treatise on how fucking unbelievable Elliott was.

On *and* off the ice.

"Good," Elliott said. "I just want you to be happy."

He didn't need to say, *I just want you to find and make your own happiness*, but he didn't have to.

Mal understood, anyway.

He pulled open the door to Darcelle's, set down the street from frat row, and took in the surprisingly light interior.

Ramsey had dragged him here a few times, for a show or a drink, over the years, but he'd never been here during the day, with the heavy candy pink velvet drapes open and the weak sunlight streaming in. The stage was still lit with the strobing stage lights in a rainbow of colors, the gold fringed trim on the black T-shaped stage gleaming.

Their table was obvious, not only because half a dozen guys were sitting there, already, but because it was the biggest one in the small space.

Mal's hand tightened in Elliott's as they approached the table.

"Hey, guys," Ivan said, and a few of their other teammates chimed in.

"Hey, what's this?" Nate Greene asked, gesturing to their intertwined hands. "You slummin' it, Jones?"

Mal hadn't known how this would play out. He had faith that ultimately it would be fine, but he hadn't been exactly sure how they'd get there.

He didn't expect Elliott to pull himself up to his full height, shoot Mal a look full of love and affection and say, proudly, without a single tremor of anxiety, "Actually, the opposite. Turns out Mal is the greatest guy." He grinned. "Joke's on me, guys, because he didn't just become my tutor or my friend, but I fell head over heels for him."

Mal was never going to be one for PDA. He'd spent too many years avoiding it. Avoiding anyone's touch, really. Now in private, he felt like a glutton, getting as much of Elliott as he could.

But today was an exception.

What else was Malcolm supposed to do after his man had said all that but pull Elliott to him? Kiss him with every bit of the love surging through him?

"Wow," Mal thought he heard someone say. "I guess they really are fucking now."

Someone else chimed in that apparently Mal wasn't a robot after all—was it Finn? Mal discovered he didn't even care.

He sure felt flesh and blood enough with Elliott in his arms.

Like he'd never been warmer.

There was a fierce catcall behind him, and it was what finally got his attention enough to lift his mouth from Elliott's. Elliott's green eyes were hot and dreamy, filled with affection.

Filled with lust.

Mal wanted to lose himself in them again.

But he couldn't. Not here.

Later, he promised himself.

"Look at you two," that light, smooth voice cooed, and Mal glanced over Elliott's shoulder to see one of the drag queens, hand on her black tulle tutu, hip popped, and with a delighted expression on her face. Her bright pink bob wig matched her lips. "Aw, and they blush too! I can barely make my man blush like that anymore."

"That's 'cause your man's too used to your saucy ways," an older queen said, sliding in and patting Mal on the shoulder. "Don't you mind Sassy over here. She dropped in from bum-fuck Nebraska to do an extra show or two while her man's on the road, and she always gets extra sassy when she's missing him."

"Sassy Solo at your service," she said, shooting the pair of them another flirtatious smile. "And you two big hunks are?"

Elliott recovered his voice first. "I'm Elliott. This is Mal."

"Well, you make sure you stick around to see the show. Then you might see how sassy I *really* get," she teased, flipping her hair and sauntering off with a graceful sway.

"This is awesome," Elliott said excitedly, sliding into a seat next to Ivan. Mal sat down next to him. "I haven't been to a show here in ages."

"What?" Mal squawked, even though he knew Elliott had a fake ID in his wallet. Knew and pretended it wasn't there, because if he thought about it too hard, he'd probably slip back into old habits. Into old, cold, unforgiving habits. And he didn't want to be that man anymore.

Upright, honorable, loyal, yes.

But the rest, no.

Not now that he'd seen a new way, not since Elliott had shown him that he could be the best parts of himself, without the rest.

Elliott grinned. "You *know* I've been here. I know *you've* been here. And don't say you were twenty-one when you were."

He put a pair of fingers over Mal's mouth, and he tried desperately not to think of when Elliott had done that before. Just last night. Elliott had been riding him slow and relentless, dragging out both their orgasms after forbidding Mal to touch his cock. So Mal had grabbed his hand and sucked his fingers down, pretending they were his cock.

Tried and *failed*.

Mal shifted uncomfortably in the chair, hoping the table would hide the worst of his erection.

"So, you finally decided to tell everyone, huh?" Ramsey said, sliding into the chair at the head of the table. Like he was their benevolent ruler—or their father.

"Can't keep a secret as good as this one," Mal said. Maybe it wasn't the speech Elliott had given, but Elliott leaned in and pressed a kiss to his cheek like it was actually *even* better.

Ramsey nodded his approval. "It's about time."

"Agreed," Ivan said.

"You two are gonna tear up the NHL," Brody said, leaning in.

"That's the plan." Elliott still sounded so confident. Mal loved that about him. That his confidence seemed to permeate Mal's own brain, like he was sharing half his hope.

Ivan raised his glass. "To the two best line mates a guy could hope for. Glad you two finally got your heads out of your asses."

"I don't know about that," Ramsey said slyly and the whole table erupted in laughter. "Now who wants a mimosa?"

Their breakfast demolished, two rounds of mimosas and the first half of the show later, Elliott watched as during the intermission, Finn ducked outside.

He didn't want to leave the warm camaraderie of the table—or the warm circle of Mal's arm, wrapped around his shoulder—but he'd been noticing how Finn's smile didn't reach his eyes.

He could tell Brody or Ramsey—or he could intervene himself.

The answer ended up being a fairly easy one. He gently shrugged off Mal's arm, gave a slight nod towards the door when Mal gave him a questioning look, and took off to follow Finn.

He was standing right outside the door, prowling back and forth.

"Hey, what's going on?" Elliott asked, as the door swung shut behind him. "Everything okay?"

Finn's gaze was bleak, his gray eyes full of a worry that Elliott couldn't say he'd ever personally experienced. But even if he hadn't, maybe he could sympathize. After all, he'd been a good shoulder for Mal to lean on, hadn't he?

"No," Finn said shortly.

"What happened?" Elliott took a step closer. Put a hand on Finn's shoulder. He hated how discouraged he looked. Finn was a great goalie and would be even better if he could stop worrying about—and stop comparing himself to—his famous father.

"Dad saw the score from last night and just texted."

Elliott had seen a few of Morgan Reynolds' texts over the last few months. They weren't terrible, honestly. Morgan didn't expect Finn to be a replica. Always told him to be his own man. To make his own success.

But Morgan didn't seem to understand how every supportive comment he made still managed to poke and prod at his son in a sensitive spot he apparently didn't even know existed.

How he could be so completely fucking unaware, Elliott didn't know, but he'd decided Morgan's obliviousness made him partially complicit in Finn's insecurities.

"What did he say?" Elliott asked.

"Oh, just a comment about how lucky I am that I have such a great offense behind me, ready to bail me out every time," Finn said morosely, staring at his sneakers.

"Is that really what he said?" Elliott would be surprised if that was the case. Morgan wasn't typically *that* direct.

Finn pulled his phone out of his pocket, unlocked it, and handed it over.

Sure enough. Finn had repeated the text nearly word for word. Which Elliott knew was bad. Finn didn't need to be memorizing his father's passive-aggressive bullshit.

Of course, he hadn't said "bail" but it didn't matter if he'd said "support" instead, because the meaning was clear enough and Finn had taken it to heart.

"Finn," Elliott said as kindly as he could, "you gotta stop letting him matter."

"Oh? That's all I should do? Just tell myself he doesn't matter? That *Morgan Reynolds* doesn't matter? And I'll be alright? God, why didn't I think of that before?"

Elliott winced. "I know it's not easy."

"Damn straight it's not easy," Finn retorted. "What if someone had told you to just leave Mal alone? Would you have? Oh wait, I know you wouldn't have, because we *all* said it. We all told you to stop harassing him, but you didn't. You kept at him. Because you wanted him and you weren't willing to settle for less."

"I might've," Elliott protested, but he knew his position wasn't exactly strong if Finn actually wanted to debate this concept.

Because he had persisted and he *had* gotten everything he'd wanted.

The guy, and very possibly the hopeful future together, too.

"You did what it took to get his attention. It was a little insane, and we all knew it. *You* even knew it, but you did it anyway. And it fucking worked." Finn was back to pacing, and he seemed to be saying this more to himself than to Elliott.

Elliott tried to tamp down the worry spiking, but it didn't really work. "What are you thinking of doing, Finn?"

Finn's gaze swung his direction, and it was impossible to read. "Nothing," he said, but Elliott wasn't sure he believed him.

"Don't do something stupid or insane because I did, and it worked," Elliott said.

"You still don't have a fucking leg to stand on here," Finn retorted.

"I know," Elliott said persuasively. "But there was every chance it *wouldn't* work. It still might not. We might end up on separate coasts, doing this whole long-distance thing."

"And you'll still be in love," Finn said.

"Well, yeah," Elliott said. He wasn't ever going to be *not* in love with Malcolm.

"Exactly." Finn's voice was resolute. "Are you really going to stand here and tell me not to fight like hell for what I want? What I *deserve?*"

What Elliott wanted to tell him was that his relationship with Mal wasn't the same as a future in professional hockey.

But he didn't, because he could see the pain in Finn's eyes. So he just nodded. "Yeah. I mean . . .*yeah*. You want something? Don't let anything stop you."

"Or anybody," Finn said, shoving his hands into his pockets. "I'm glad for you and Mal, I am. But I gotta go, okay? Tell Ramsey I'll see him tomorrow, at practice."

"Are you sure—"

But Finn waved off his attempt to stop him. "Seriously. I'll be fine. Go inside. Enjoy your boyfriend."

Elliott didn't. He watched Finn walk away, and he was almost out of view when the door opened behind him.

"Everything alright?" Mal wondered. "You didn't come back." Mal didn't touch him, but he didn't need to. His gaze was as good as a touch, concern written clearly in his blue eyes.

"Now, yeah," Elliott said. He sighed. "Finn's just going through a tough time, but I think he'll get through it."

"With you as a friend? It's guaranteed," Mal said firmly. "We'll make sure he's taken care of."

"Yeah," Elliott said, agreeing. "We take care of our own here."

"You wanna go back in?" Mal said.

What Elliott really wanted to do was curl up in bed with Mal wrapped around him, but he nodded. "Yeah," he said.

It was easy—too easy, maybe—to hide away from the world with the man he loved. Facing reality and its sometimes harsh turns was part of life. It gave and it took away, but either way, he'd always have Malcolm by his side. That was the one thing Elliott knew he could always rely on.

Mal reached down and took his hand, squeezing it firmly, and Elliott knew he was thinking the exact same thing.

They'd have each other. Always.

EPILOGUE

Five months later...

"How're you doing, honorary brother?" Nina nudged Mal with her shoulder. Mal knew he'd been staring, eyes glued to where Elliott was giving an interview to one of the media outlets.

It was an absolute circus, which made sense, since this year's draft was being held in Vegas. So many people, and a lot of them wanted to talk to Elliott. And surprisingly, a lot of them wanted to talk to Mal, too. But right now he was hiding by Elliott's table, using his sisters as human shields.

Elliott, on the other hand, looked calm and relaxed, laughing at a question that the reporter had asked.

"Honorary brother implies that your brother and I are related, not dating, and that's illegal," Mal said.

Nina just cackled though. "I can't call you my brother-in-law, *yet.*"

Mal let himself crack a smile. More like forced himself to crack a smile. Not like Toronto's front office was going to divulge who they were picking in the first round, especially to a player currently working their way through their developmental system. But they hadn't explicitly told either of them that they *wouldn't* be drafting him, either, and from what Mal heard—and so many analysts had predicted—chances were better than ever that by the end of the night, Elliott Jones would be a Toronto Maple Leaf.

Did that mean Mal was resting easy?

Hardly.

Still, he was here, plastering a supportive smile on his face, after reassuring Elliott—and himself—a million times that it didn't matter what team drafted him. They were going to stick together, even if he was three thousand miles away.

But Mal didn't *want* him to be three thousand miles away.

He wanted Elliott in his bed, every night. He wanted him on the ice, right across from him.

He'd take him however he could get him, but Mal knew exactly what he wanted.

"We've only been dating a few months," Mal reminded Nina.

"Eight," Macey chimed in, sticking her head into the conversation. "Nine if you count the time before you and Ell actually discussed dating and were just fucking."

Mal flushed. Every time he told himself he was going to get used to Elliott's sisters, they slyly threw something in that made him sure that he wouldn't.

"Mace, you can't say that shit to Mal. Makes him uncomfortable," Connie reminded Macey.

But Macey just shrugged. "He did it, he can at least own up to it."

"Nine months then," Mal said hurriedly, hoping that by acquiescing to Macey's timeline that this whole conversation might change to a new subject. He could always tell Macey that Ramsey was going to be here after all, and he'd introduce them, even though Elliott had made him swear that he wouldn't.

But literally anything had to be better than enduring the three of them interrogating him about his and Elliott's sex life.

"Hey, if Ell was a girl, he could be pregnant right now, just about to give birth," Connie said. "*Or* he wouldn't even have to be a girl."

"Don't be ridiculous," Nina said.

"It's in those books she reads," Macey chimed in.

"Well, he's not going to get pregnant, which is a good thing, if he's about to become a professional hockey player," Mal said, straight-up desperate at this point.

"And how do you know that it wouldn't be *Mal* who'd be impregnated?" Macey asked archly.

Oh, God.

"True," Nina said seriously, like she was actually considering this suggestion.

"They do switch, you know," Connie said.

Mal wanted to drop through the floor and die.

"See, now you're not worrying about how far away Elliott's going to end up, you're worried about what Macey or Connie are going to say next about your sex life," Nina said with a chuckle.

"Is that better? I'm not sure it's better," Mal said bluntly.

"It's better," Connie said with certainty.

"Oh, is that Ramsey over there?" Macey asked, brightening.

"Macey—" But before Malcolm could stop her, she was heading in his direction.

A few minutes later, Elliott returned, glancing over at where his sister was talking animatedly with Ramsey.

"You didn't stop her," Elliott said, but he was smiling.

"A natural disaster couldn't have stopped her," Mal grumbled. "And on top of that, I wasn't particularly inclined, because she wouldn't stop speculating about which of us would end up pregnant."

Elliott grinned. "Twins!"

Mal shook his head. "I don't want to know."

But Elliott leaned in, and he looked and smelled and *was* so good, Mal felt a little lightheaded. Even nine months in, he was still figuring out how deep in love he was. How lucky he truly was. How lucky he hoped he'd be for the rest of his goddamn life. "Hey," he murmured, "I bet you that you'd want to know, later tonight, after we get back to the room . . ."

Mal swallowed hard. "Don't do it, Ell," he warned, under his breath.

"Aw, but it's so fun to work you up," Elliott teased.

"Yeah, but not when I'm probably going to have to talk to someone who has a camera trained on us."

Elliott shrugged. Like he'd done worse, like *they'd* done worse, and that was probably true.

He'd never tell Coach Blackburn the truth about what they'd done in one of the empty treatment rooms after their last game.

Even after the draft, there was a chance that Elliott would don an Evergreens jersey again, next season, but it was Mal's last game.

They'd celebrated, in what Elliott claimed was an appropriate way, but Mal knew, without question, that if Coach ever found out about it—and God, Mal hoped he wouldn't ever—he'd have a *very* different opinion.

"You guys ready?" Nina asked, arriving back at the table, her hand wrapped around Macey's arm. Macey was pouting, probably because she'd been forcibly dragged away from Ramsey.

"You two are a *bad* idea," Connie said to Macey. "You're too much alike."

"No?" Macey said and huffed. "Okay. Well, maybe. A little."

"A lot too much alike," Elliott said. "And yeah, we're set. We're good." He looked over at Mal. "Right?"

Mal nodded.

"The parents are about to come over," Nina said. She nudged Elliott. "If there's anything you want to say out of their earshot."

Elliott turned to Mal. He looked so fucking gorgeous like this, dressed up in the slate gray suit that fit him like a glove, green shirt that brought out the color of his eyes, hair styled like he'd just rolled out of Mal's bed.

He was flawless, just fucking perfect, and he was all Mal's.

"Listen," Mal said, because even though he'd said this probably a thousand times since they'd gotten together last November, he *needed* Elliott to understand it. To believe it. "Listen, it doesn't matter what happens in the next hour. I love you, no matter what. You've got me, no matter what."

"No matter what," Elliott repeated, eyes glowing as he reached up, linking his hands behind Mal's neck, stroking the exposed skin there. "You're not getting rid of me, even if we have to fuck over FaceTime every day."

"Aaaaand this is exactly why I warned you the parentals were on their way over," Nina said dryly.

"I love you," Mal said and deciding he didn't give a fuck, leaned down and kissed Elliott.

"Love you, too," Elliott murmured. Then he let go and Mal had to shove his hands into his pockets so he wouldn't grab him back again.

Sure enough, five minutes later, the Jones parents arrived, hugging both Elliott and Malcolm.

He liked Elliott's parents, but it was going to take a long time to feel comfortable with them—not because they weren't welcoming or kind or thoughtful. In fact, they were all three of those things. It wasn't hard to see how they'd raised a man like Elliott. Or the sisters for that matter.

But their open warmness was a hard thing for Malcolm to trust. To even understand. He was working his way around to it. Frankly, the load of bullshit that the sisters liked to give him put him more at ease.

Except when Connie and Macey tried to decide which of them was going to end up pregnant.

They all took their seats, and under the table, Elliott reached for his hand. Squeezing it. Mal could feel the dampness of it, and he *knew* without being told, that despite Elliott's breezy, confident exterior, he was nervous, deep down.

How could he not be?

This was the first day of the rest of his life.

With every name that was called from the stage, Malcolm held his breath. Would they be okay? They would. He'd stake his whole life on it. On their love making it, in the face of any adversity.

But he didn't goddamn *want* the adversity.

He wanted happiness and ease and light. Elliott in the mornings, pillow crease on his cheek, stealing all the covers.

He'd get it eventually, no matter what, but he wanted it now. He craved it *now*.

When the team before Toronto picked, and Elliott's name wasn't called, his fingers crushed Mal's.

"Hey, hey, it doesn't matter. Whatever happens, it doesn't matter," Mal said, leaning close. Aware that probably every goddamn camera in the place was probably panning to their table now. They weren't super open about their relationship, but it wasn't a secret, either.

Elliott was tense, now. Malcolm could feel it. Not just in the iron grip of his hand, but the plastered-on quality of his smile.

"Yeah?" Elliott asked.

"You know it doesn't matter. I love you. No matter what."

But please, don't make this no matter what.

The contingent announcing the Toronto pick walked onto the stage. Mal recognized everyone—from the general manager about to announce their first round pick, to the current and past players surrounding him.

They'd asked him if he wanted to be up there, but Mal had shaken his head. He knew they'd only asked him because there was a good chance they'd be drafting Elliott, but Mal needed to be with him, whether he was drafted by Toronto or another team.

The GM stepped up to the microphone.

"With the tenth pick in the NHL draft," he said, "the Toronto Maple Leafs are extremely proud to select . . ." He paused, and Mal had to clench down, wishing there was something to hold on to, to let out some of that unbelievable pressure. "From Portland University, Elliott Jones."

The whole table erupted.

Mal could count on one hand the number of times he'd ever lost control.

He lost control today.

He lost his whole goddamn mind.

Jumping up together, he and Elliott grabbed each other, and for a second, there was only them as the room erupted in applause around them.

"See you on the ice," Malcolm said.

That had seemed like enough to say, only five seconds earlier, but now it wasn't enough. Couldn't possibly be enough. He leaned in and pressed a quick kiss to Elliott's cheek. Not enough to steal his thunder or his spotlight, but enough to tell him everything Elliott should always know.

You're loved.

You're admired.

You're needed.

You're mine.

"See *you* on the ice," Elliott said impudently, that grin he'd always loved—and hated, too, for a little while—plastered across his handsome face.

Six months after that...

The music was booming, reverberating throughout the rink, lights flashing and strobing with every bass drop.

Elliott gripped his stick tighter with his gloves and tried not to panic-slash-anxiety puke all over the ice.

He knew it wasn't just him feeling this way. "Even *I'm* freaked out," Mal had told him, a few nights ago as they lay in their bed together. Mal had bought a king, to celebrate Elliott being drafted by Toronto, and they'd spent the summer training and getting ready for opening day, hoping they'd both make it on that opening day roster.

And here they were. Together again.

Though, Elliott wondered if you could really say *again* when it felt like they'd never left each other's side.

And now, he was sure that they never would.

"You good?" Mal leaned in and Elliott could still barely hear him over the music and the announcer.

He'd just announced the starting line, which they weren't in—*yet*, Malcolm kept saying, like it was only a matter of time and at this point Elliott had to believe that was true. They were good, individually, but together? They could be great. Toronto knew it too, and that was exactly why they'd drafted Elliott.

The rest of the games they wouldn't get a special intro like this, but because it was opening night, every player got recognized. Especially the two rookies.

Elliott stepped onto the ice, and felt the impact of it resonate through him.

"Introducing number thirty-five, fresh to Toronto ice for the first time, forward Elliott Jones!"

Elliott skated down to the line of players, taking in his teammates' nods and acknowledgements.

He'd worried, the tiniest bit, if he and Mal were going to be a problem, but right before their first official practice, one of the older guys had thrown a towel at him and catcalled, following that up with, "Don't fuck in the showers and we'll be kosher."

They had not fucked in the showers. Honestly, they'd been working so hard on the ice and also off it Elliott hadn't even been tempted, and that was saying something.

"And also introducing number thirty-six, also new to our ice, forward Malcolm McCoy."

Elliott tapped his stick on the ice, welcoming his boyfriend to the ice for the first time.

Malcolm came to a stop next to him. "Hey," he said, grinning through his helmet. "Imagine finding you here."

Elliott grinned, his smile so wide his face practically hurt.

The announcer finished the rest of the team, and final warmups began.

Elliott skated over to the bench, grabbing some extra tape for his stick. Making sure it was good and ready. Mal came over after he'd made a few extra rotations on the ice.

Elliott nudged him with his elbow. "You ready for this?"

Would Malcolm ever be as free and easy as Elliott was? No, he wouldn't. And Elliott was perfectly, one-hundred-percent okay with that. He didn't want a clone of himself. He only wanted his stupidly stalwart, still-too-serious, ride-or-die, loyal and true guy, Mal.

And he'd gotten him.

"Honestly? No. But with you? I'm ready to give it a go."

Elliott laughed. "Oh, baby, we got this in the bag."

Even with the lights and the music still echoing through the arena, it was not hard to see hope blossom on Mal's face. It mattered that Elliott believed in him. In *them*.

"Yeah. We're a team out there, baby, and we're gonna tear it up. Never felt so sure of anything in my whole goddamn life."

"I got just one thing," Mal said, leaning over. "That I love you. Gonna love you today and tomorrow and even when you can't even get a shot off. Even when you can't get it up."

Elliott laughed. "That'll be the day."

"Probably, but it's true." Mal's eyes gleamed, and was he having him on again? Pushing him the way they sometimes liked to push each other? Hot damn, he probably was, and Elliott didn't even give a shit.

"We'll see about that," Elliott said, now more determined than ever to prove to Mal that he was going to make some shit happen tonight.

And sure enough, ten minutes later, knew he'd been proven right when Mal flicked him the puck with prettiest little pass, and he shot it in, right above the goalie's shoulder pad.

Elliott shot him a triumphant look, the one that had used to piss Mal off, and now, he knew, only turned him on.

They both knew what it meant now. And they both knew what it would mean for later.

"Hell yes!" he yelled across the ice, pumping his fist. He and Mal collided in a hug. Mal put a hand on his helmet, patting it. It couldn't have been more perfect.

But later that night, as Mal set him on their bed and proceeded to strip every piece of clothing off, somehow it was.

-

To preorder Finn's book, *On Thin Ice*, click here.

-

To read a sexy short that tells how Mal and Elliott celebrated their last game as Evergreens, click here.

INTERESTED IN READING MORE OF
BETH'S BOOKS?

CHECK OUT A FULL LIST OF TILES
BY SCANNING THE QR CODE
OR VISITING HER WEBSITE

WWW.BETHBOLDEN.COM/BOOKLIST

WANT TO FOLLOW BETH?

MAKE SURE YOU NEVER
MISS A RELEASE?

SCAN THE QR CODE BELOW
OR VISIT HER WEBSITE
FOR A SOCIAL MEDIA LIST,
NEWSLETTER SIGNUP,
AND SO MUCH MORE!

WWW.BETHBOLDEN.COM/ABOUT

Made in United States
Orlando, FL
11 April 2025